Teacher's Pupils

By: Randall Christopher

This book is dedicated to Katalina. *May you forever dream big.*

Table of Contents

Prologue

The television flickered to life as it always did when the Council desired the populace to view something it deemed worthy of their attention. If an individual was watching something else entirely, the screen would automatically change to the Council's intended broadcast. Even if the television was off, as it had been in the home of Jan Sparks, it would simply power up of its own accord, and one was expected to watch. Even tablets, cell phones, or computers were not immune to this invasion of privacy and establishment of control the Council so craved.

Jan Sparks had been running late for work when the television chimed on with its audible ping, indicating the Council's desire to pay very close attention to what appeared next. In some regard, she was relieved. Her tardiness would now be excused. However, part of her psyche felt a general sense of annoyance that she had to disregard her daily routine for the Council's everlasting whims.

Of course, Jan was not the only person who had to give up part of her day for the fancy of the Council. Everywhere, all over the Americas, everyone was doing the very same thing. So Jan, along with millions of other citizens, sat on her couch and awaited the Council's broadcast.

The image of the Pavilion outside of the Elliptical Ward Square suddenly came upon the screen. The Elliptical Ward was where the Council conducted their main business they didn't want the public to see, and the Pavilion was where they allowed the public to view their business being conducted. In fact, the public wasn't merely allowed to see it, they were required to see it for themselves, in order for the Council to usurp the authority over the general public.

President Stuckey stood on the balcony overlooking the crowded Pavilion stage. And a stage it truly was; meant to portray a scripted scene to the citizens of The Americas, in which the Council had written. At least in Jan's mind, that was what it appeared to be. Of course, she couldn't divulge that information to her colleagues, or even to her closest friends. To say such things would most definitely get her a direct invitation to the very stage in which she mocked.

Jan was truly amazed at how quickly the Council could draw a crowd. With little notice, it seemed, they had the Elliptical Square swarming with a writhing throng of individuals, bloodthirsty for whatever game the Council deemed worthy of playing. The crowd, most likely, didn't even possess the knowledge of what sort of pageantry it was about to pay witness to, and that worried Jan the most. The crowd had simply commenced because they were told to, not necessarily because it was what the people in the crowd had desired. It amazed her how powerful President Stuckey and the Council truly were.

President Stuckey slowly raised his hand to silence the crowd and they immediately stopped the cacophony of noise.

"Ladies and gentlemen," President Stuckey spoke with a sardonic tone, though the crowd did not seem to notice. Jan Sparks did, however, and felt she was the only one that did at times. "I am pleased to introduce the new Council Secretary, war hero, Jack Kruger.

Stuckey panned his arms toward the center of the Pavilion and the cameras went from President Stuckey's visage to the familiar face of Jack Kruger.

The Americas were very familiar with Kruger due to his exploits as a pilot in the recent war with most of Asia. It was because of this war that most of the major cities were a pile of rubble or a radiated wasteland. Also because of this war, North and South America were no longer separated by geographical adjectives. Instead, what was left of each simply was referred to as The Americas.

Jack Kruger was not elected Council Secretary, but instead was appointed by Stuckey himself. Stuckey knew The Americas would feel a sense of pride having him as one of their leaders. His confidence and ability to accomplish any task made him the perfect choice as well.

In fact, Stuckey's first assignment to Kruger had already been accomplished, and it was for this reason, not simply an introduction, that Stuckey had brought the media and this crowd to the Pavilion. Stuckey sat in his ornately decorated chair and watched as Kruger took over.

"Thank you, Mr. President," Kruger began. He looked directly into the camera, as if directing each citizen individually. "Citizens of The Americas, as President Stuckey has stated, I am now your Council Secretary. As Secretary, it is my job to help you all feel safe. I intend to do just that, but I need your cooperation to do so."

8

Kruger looked away from the camera and directed his next comment toward someone to his left, out of view.

"You can bring her up, now."

A woman was brought to the Pavilion's center by three men, and directed to stand to Kruger's right on an elevated platform. Her hands were handcuffed in front her. Kruger left the podium at the center and went to a similar platform at the left of the stage. There was a microphone for the woman, as well as Kruger, so the crowd could hear each of them speak. Kruger spoke first.

"Your name is Madeline Gruber is it not?" Kruger asked.

"Yes," the woman answered in a timid voice.

"And what is your profession?" Kruger continued his questioning.

"I am a teacher," Madeline replied. "I teach fourth grade."

"A teacher?" said with mock surprise. "That is a very admirable job. You should feel proud that you possess the important task of providing our kids a chance at a better future. I thank you for all that you do each and every day for our kids."

"I am very proud, yes," Madeline replied. She seemed to gain a bit of confidence from Kruger's words.

"How long have you been teaching fourth grade?" Kruger asked.

"Five years," she replied. "I taught third grade for a year before that."

"Those are some of the most valuable years for a student," Kruger continued. "They are very impressionable at that age aren't they?"

Kruger continued after his rhetorical question expectedly went unanswered.

"Your colleagues inform me that you frequently, and purposefully, refused to follow the standard course of study the Council has designated for your students. Is this true?"

"I do not deny those allegations," Madeline answered proudly. "The students that I teach are given a chance to interpret the world around them for themselves, not simply given a list of chores to accomplish by year's end."

"But those lists are what we deem necessary to encourage future success," Kruger explained. "Your defiance has been detrimental to your students' advancement. The past three years your students have scored the lowest marks on the quarterly and yearly assessments in your region. Your methods do not seem to be working, Ms. Gruber. Do they?"

"I can only work with what has been given to me," Madeline stated. "My students come from a low-income area where most of them live with either one or both of their parents missing from the equation. These kids have very little chance of passing these tests you design for them, and then when you put them all in one place, it becomes even more difficult."

"Instead of answers to my questions, you give me excuses," Kruger declared. "And Poor excuses at that."

With those words, the crowd gave a loud roar of encouragement.

"Those aren't my excuses," Madeline stated. "They are my simple observations."

"Oh, simple *observations*?" Kruger mocked. The crowd roared again. "Here is one of my own *observations*. In the past three years, you have had ten of your fourth graders in which you have requested for retention. It is my obligation to mention also that your total is ten times the number of students your colleagues have requested."

"Yes, but," she started to explain, but was cut off abruptly by Kruger.

"No more excuses," Kruger demanded. "I am through listening to them. Your goal should be to provide students with the given information we have determined necessary. How audacious of you to believe that you can ultimately make that determination yourself. We know what's best for your students, not you."

"But you barely even know their names," Madeline poignantly declared. "You think you know them, because you have a designated number beside their name from a test you created. But do you really know Hector Corales? Do you know that he dislikes reading because it reminds him of his mother? A mother who is no longer alive due to a car accident when he was eight. Or Serenity Phillips, whose father was killed in the very war you, yourself, served. He used to Skype with her and help with her homework each night. I was there to see the confused look on her face the day after he didn't show up on the computer like he always had. I was the one who gave her an extra day to complete it, fearing the worst. And it was I who attended the funeral once she finally found out the truth. *I* was there, not you, or anybody else in the Council."

Kruger gave her a blank stare, and she continued, "You can plug in those scores to predetermine the expectations you have for each of these students before those tests are even administered, but you don't ever consider the fact that they perform up to those standards, simply because they have already learned what is expected of them by the people they know are in charge."

"You are speaking of the self-fulfilling prophecy," Kruger explained. "That is simply a myth with no concrete data to substantiate it. We have looked at each of your students and each of them is performing way below their intended score. You claim to know them by name, but it seems that's not enough to know what they ultimately need to succeed. It is for this reason that you have been brought to this trial."

"Trial?" Madeline gave an incredulous look. "That's what this is? I call it a witch hunt."

"This is most definitely not a witch hunt. You are charged with treason," Kruger explained.

"On what grounds?" Madeline demanded.

"You are holding the minds of our children hostage," Kruger answered. "You have hijacked their brain's functional ability to accept authority by allowing them to disregard the rules we have set out for learning. You have given them the impression that they need not heed the commands of those in charge, and through your treasonous action, your students are hindered with doubt for the very Council that gives them a livelihood when school is no longer required."

Kruger turned to Madeline to speak to her directly.

11

"You admit to allowing this to happen on your watch," Kruger stated. "In fact, you even claim to have encouraged this kind of behavior in your classroom. The Council cannot allow someone to ruin the impressionable minds the future needs to gain a more peaceful existence. Without our children learning from us, we cannot contemplate a world without corruption; the kind of corruption you breed in your classroom each and every day."

"I breed inspiration, not corruption," Madeline vehemently declared. "How dare you manipulate the facts to make me appear to have malicious intent."

"I do not need to manipulate the data," Kruger responded. "It speaks for itself. We cannot deny how ineffective the data portrays you as a teacher, and your total disregard for the teaching practices we have put into place that we know garners results is an embarrassment to your profession. You have even admitted to these allegations."

"I have done no such thing," she replied. "Though life is full of decisions we make on a daily basis, that does not mean it is a multiple choice test. I prepare my students for life, not a single test with four answers to choose from."

"We simply narrow it down for them," Kruger smirked as he said this. "We make life easier by doing that. If there were no choices, then there would be endless possibilities."

"And the council wouldn't want to encourage *that*," Madeline said tritely.

"You had better watch your tone with me," Kruger chided.

He nodded to his left again and the same three men who led the woman to this spectacle made their way back onto the stage. They roughly grabbed her from the pedestal and she fell to the stage, skinning her knee. The men tried to help her up, but she tried to shrug them away. This act of insolence prompted the men to withdraw their pistols. Two of them aimed their pistol, but the closest of the three brought his across Madeline's face. He then did it again. Blood quickly splattered the stage and a bruise materialized on her right cheek as she crumpled to the stage.

"Enough!" Kruger interjected, and the guards stopped. "Madeline Gruber, the Council has no choice but to find you guilty of treason. Take her to the Ward."

The crowd gave a raucous cheer to show their approval of the punishment.

The three guards carried her lifeless form through the crowd, who cursed at her, threw things at her, and even spit on her as she was carried past. The cameras followed her all the way to the heavy Elliptical Ward door, catching every second of her shameful exodus.

When she was finally escorted through the door, the cameras zoomed back toward Kruger, still in his spot on the Pavilion. He looked determinedly into the camera and made his point very clear.

"The Council does not put up with insubordination. We take education very seriously, and testing has proven to show that our youth benefit most by the practices we have in place. It is a proven commodity, and those people who believe otherwise will continue to face the Council's justice. Our future depends on today. Our present can no longer live in the past. And our past can no longer harm our future. I am Council Secretary, Jack Kruger, and I promise to not let a few misguided souls to ruin what the Council has built to keep you safe, and to preserve what The Americas have left."

He stepped down from the platform and walked from the Pavilion into the Elliptical Ward. A loud burst of cheers echoed in his wake, and then the television went back to a black screen.

Jan Sparks sat in stunned silence. She most definitely couldn't tell a soul about her mocking thoughts about the Pavilion, or her true feelings about the Council. Jack Kruger was the new Council Secretary, and he was clearly the one in charge.

I. Lost

Chapter One: The Visitors

Thursday – Day One

It was getting late and Mike Manna kept looking at the digital timepiece hanging on the south wall. All timepieces were digital now, because most people couldn't tell time otherwise. However, Manna still possessed an archaic wristwatch in the old analog style, which he kept in a desk at home. Manna was definitely a lover of antiquities. He even had an original print of *1984,* his favorite book when he was much younger. This sat on the same desk which contained his wristwatch. Printed books were mostly becoming obsolete due to the internet and other technologies that processed materials to read things electronically. Newspapers and magazines were even more obsolete than books these days. He could remember waking up just before his father in order to surprise him with the Sunday paper. His father would then read it at the breakfast table, while Manna ate his breakfast with his mother. Those were some of the fondest memories he still maintained of times before the big war. Now, even the mail had stopped coming in paper form. Bills, letters, even magazine and newspaper subscriptions were sent via email. The thought of his novel at home made him desire to hold it in his hand and read it straight through in one sitting, for the hundredth time it would seem.

He wanted desperately to call it a day. It wasn't because there was anywhere he had to go, he didn't. It was Thursday, the end of the school week, and he was allowed to go home at seven o'clock to start his weekend, instead of the normal nine o'clock on the weekdays. It had been only fifteen years ago, he remembered, when the school days ended on Friday, because the three day weekend gave the students more time to work on their various extracurricular activities, which were becoming ever more important. Manna had seen a drastic shift in the education system since he started working as a custodian at Holly Pines High School twenty-five years ago. Not only did the school week get shorter, but the school day as well. Students were leaving at quarter till two, almost a full hour sooner. Class sizes were bigger, homework was frowned upon, and testing was the end all cure for assessing a student's knowledge. But who was he to say what worked and what didn't? He hadn't even done well in school when he was a student, some thirty-odd years ago.

"Christ, has it been that long already?" Manna spoke aloud as he mopped the floor. He stopped mopping to ponder this question. His voice was gravelly, like he spent his life gargling acid from a car battery. He hadn't been a smoker, but he sounded like he was because he was constantly breathing in fumes of bleach, ammonia, and about forty other cleaners he used on a daily basis. He thought it over again. Sure enough, he would be having his thirty-eighth high school reunion this year. How the time did fly. Was it already ten years ago that Felicia had passed? It seemed like just last spring. An audible click awoke him from his reverie. He peered at the clock.

"Time sure can fly when you're lost in thought. It's already time to go," he said aloud as he put the mop back in the bucket of water and steered it toward the supply closet door. He dumped the water down the drain on the floor and put the mop back in the bucket. Then, he shut the door and locked it behind him.

He made sure to turn on the security cameras, alarm system, and lock the doors before he got into his two-door, navy blue Pontillac Hybrid, which got 62 miles per gallon; burning cost-efficient bio-fuel, which was three dollars cheaper than gasoline these days. He was glad to have been given the car for his twenty-fifth year of employment at HPHS. He was more glad that it wasn't taken away from him after the government demanded each school system pay back funds given to them two years after the car was given to him. Many of his colleagues were not so lucky. He still couldn't believe the government could give away money, but then, just as quickly, demand its immediate return. Never mind the fact that most schools had already spent the money to purchase materials for the school year. The schools could think of only one way to fix this problem, release faculty members to save the money in order to pay it back in time for the deadline set by the Council.

He started the car and heard the familiar dings of the seat belt security system the car employed. The car would not drive until the driver buckled his or her seat belt properly. Since he had already buckled his safety belt, he put the car in reverse and backed out of his parking space. Then, he put the car in drive and went to start his journey home.

He only went a couple feet, when he had to stop the car abruptly. The tires screeched slightly on the pavement and his head whipped forward from the sudden stop. Two figures stood in the shadows just beyond his headlights; facing him. He kept his foot on the brake, but had it in his mind to be ready to make a fast getaway if the need should arise. He rolled down the window and stuck his head out a little ways, but he still could not see the faces of the two shadowy figures.

"Can I help you two?" He asked, trying to keep his voice from shaking. The two figures still stood in silence. Manna was starting to get annoyed. They were probably some high school punks out to cause trouble. "Well, can I?" He asked after the silence finally got to him.

"Teacher," one of the shadows finally replied in an indiscernible voice.

Manna couldn't distinguish from which side the voice had come.

"What?" He asked confused, looking from one shadow to another.

"We're looking for Teacher," this time he could tell it had come from the one on the left. The two figures still hadn't stepped into the light, so Manna tried squinting to get a good look at them.

"We're closed for the weekend," Manna answered, "so you're gonna have to come back Monday."

"We *need* to find Teacher," the one on the left said as he stepped into the light. He was average height, average build, and had a receding hairline of short, black hair. He wore a tight-fitting black shirt with no print on it, a pair of faded blue jeans, and a pair of all-black running shoes. The other figure also stepped in the light. He was dressed similarly, except his shirt and shoes were a creamy white. He was a few inches shorter, but also had a receding hairline of short, black hair. It was difficult for Manna to judge their age. Their ages could have been from anywhere between sixteen and thirty-two.

"He's in trouble," the other one said in a straightforward manner, with no hint of sarcasm. "And so is everyone else."

Chapter Two: Names

Manna wasn't sure what to make of these two strangers. What or who was this *Teacher* they were talking about? The school was filled with them. Which one of them was in trouble? Was this some kind of joke? Curiosity took control of his mind, though he definitely wasn't in the mood for games like this.

It had been a long week; the students were uncharacteristically messy and unruly this past week. He had to clean the bathroom stalls three times in the boys' bathroom because of graffiti. Typical things, about which girls were easy and which wouldn't put out. One even mentioned a male teacher's name and how he liked a certain male appendage. If the teacher mentioned had seen that, he would have seriously flipped his lid, even though it wouldn't have been such a shock if it were true. There were even rumors about it between the other faculty members. He had to clean up vomit, probably from a binge drinking party the night before, as well as a mysterious powder found in the girls' bathroom, most likely some type of new drug the girls were into these days. Whatever happened to just smoking pot and leaving it at that? Hell, even he only did it once just to see what it was like. Nowadays, there was always some new "it" drug that was being passed around, and administration only caught wind of it after it was being overlooked for the newest craze. They never seemed to catch up to what was hip at that time, it seemed like they were just days behind at all times. Manna usually knew before other faculty members what the drug of choice was, because of his line of work. Right now, the two drugs of choice were Snow and Stardust, whatever those were. As long as they didn't do any of that on Test Day, it didn't matter what they did the other one hundred sixty-nine days.

Manna looked at the two gentlemen in front of him and asked very seriously, "Why are you wasting my time?" When they did not give an immediate answer, he said, "It's the start of the weekend. I would like to go home and relax, not to mention I'm starving." It had been nearly six hours since he last ate.

"We need help finding Teacher," the one in black said again. "Can you help us?"

"I have no frickin' clue what you are talking about," Manna replied, even though he did. In the way the two strangers kept saying the word *Teacher*, and not *a* teacher, Manna finally realized the meaning behind the strangers' words. Everyone knew who Teacher was, even though no one really *knew* who he truly was exactly. Teacher was like a myth, or legend. Someone who was always in the news for being the most wanted person in The Americas. Some even said that Teacher was just something created by the government as a common enemy of the people. Manna wasn't sure what to believe.

"We were told we could trust you, that you could keep secrets," the one in white said.

"That was a long time ago," Manna replied. "I don't want to be bothered anymore." He was starting to breathe heavier, and he was starting to sweat, even with the coolness of the night. It was true, though. He could keep a secret. He just didn't bother to tell anyone all that he knew about everything. That was why the administrators didn't know about the newest drugs until after the fact. Manna was the type of person who didn't mind keeping to himself and staying out of other people's business. He observed a great deal, but didn't feel it was his place to go and spread all the gossip, or get into the thick of things.

"The future depends on us finding Teacher and warning him," the one in black stated directly.

"There is a traitor who will give him up," the other one in white stated. His steely gaze was unflinching and bore into the deepest corners of Manna's soul.

"Get in the car," Manna finally said after a brief silence. After the two gentlemen got into the car and they rode in silence for a mile or two, Manna asked them their names.

"I am Giovanni," said the one who wore white.

"And I am Pierre," said the one in black.

They both looked at Manna in the rear-view mirror and nodded their heads in introduction.

"This is not going to be a very relaxing weekend," Manna replied with a deep, regretful sigh. "Not one bit."

Chapter Three: Conspirator

Manna washed his face with cold water in his bathroom sink and hung his wet, bearded face over the white porcelain. He was bent down and had his eyes closed. The fifteen minute drive to his two-story home was made in absolute silence. Pierre and Giovanni each sat straight and unmoving in the back seat; he was unsure if they had even blinked.

Manna stood and dried his face with a pink bath towel, something he could never find the courage to box up in storage after his wife had passed. Now, the two strangers were in his home, in the den, awaiting his return from the bathroom. He had needed a brief reprieve from the two strangers and their strange request. The Teacher was, somehow, in trouble, and, for some reason, he was being asked to aide in helping him. *Why him? Why couldn't someone else?* He thought to himself as he looked in the mirror at his aged face. He still had a strong jaw and penetrating eyes, but the passion and intensity that had inherently won him over with Felicia seemed to have dissipated over the years. His few days' growth of stubble had fully turned gray ten years prior, but the hair on his head still had traces of dark brown left in it. He patted down his hands and face one more time with the towel, this time to relieve himself of the sweat slowly making its mark down his neck onto his shirt. He was now poised to face the proposition and fully understand what he had gotten himself into by giving these gentlemen a ride.

He stepped out of the bathroom, shutting off the light, and gently closing the door behind him. He made his way back to the den where Pierre and Giovanni still sat exactly as he had left them, no curious wanderings of looking at the various pictures scattered throughout the room. They certainly were two of the oddest birds he'd met in recent years.

"Let me formally introduce myself. I'm Mike Manna," Manna said leaning on the doorway leading into the den. He still hadn't made his way fully into the room; he was still skeptical of his odd guests. He held up his hands as if to say, "Welcome to my humble abode."

"We know who you are. We've been told you can be of help to us," Giovanni replied as he slowly stood from the chair he had been sitting in. "It is of great urgency that we make contact with Teacher to warn him of the threat against his life."

"Tell me again of this threat," Manna replied, finally coming into the room and sitting on the small sofa to the right of the doorway.

"We have news from Forest Oak that there is a traitor within the Teacher's inner circle," Pierre said looking gravely into Manna's eyes. He could see the pain in Pierre's eyes as he forwarded the news. "One of the Novice Orderlies is conspiring to do damage from within the circle and bring everything down that has been achieved up to this point toward the cause."

"Teacher is unaware of this threat of conspiracy, so we desperately need to find him," Giovanni stated again. "The reward given by the Council for his arrest has reached one hundred million dollars. This has tempted the defector to greedily turn on him."

"Where does my name come into the mix?" Manna asked.

"Simone Petra sent us to find you. She said you were to be trusted," Pierre answered.

At the mention of the woman's name, Manna tried desperately to hide his shock, and to a less observant individual he would have hidden it well. Giovanni and Pierre, though, saw right through the counterfeit reaction.

"Then you do know this name?" Giovanni asked him, forcing him to give up the charade.

"Yes," Manna said as he admitted to defeat, "she's my daughter."

This time it was the strangers' turn to have a look of bewilderment. Manna took a small amount of solace in being able to return the favor, and smiled with a hint of satisfaction.

Chapter Four: Institute

Simone was his only child. She had changed her last name to her mother's maiden name after Felicia's death. She was flaxen-haired with crystal-blue eyes that never ceased to sparkle. She had been a rebellious young girl, who only seemed to become more rebellious as she grew older, which was typical of the times. She had just graduated from Institute when her mother had died. In his day, it was still called college, or university. After the big war, it was given the name Institute by the Council, and a person's vocation was chosen by the Council, rather than the person himself or herself. She had gone to Institute for accounting; she had always been good with computations or anything dealing with numbers. That is why the Council had chosen this to be her path.

Each year, tenth graders, the modern senior classes, were given tests they were required to pass in a variety of subjects. There were tests for computer skills, Council law, mathematics, sports, and pop culture. The Council took out the writing and reading tests, due to the fact that only thirty-eight percent of the students passed them in their final year of administration. They were deemed too hard, so the tests were simply eradicated. Now, the teachers simply stood in front of the class and gave notes on various things that may appear on the test. The students were given note cards to attempt to memorize these obscure facts and whatnots.

After testing results were in, students who didn't pass were shown the problems they missed and were given another chance to change their incorrect answers. This method was repeated until each student made, or was given, a passing score.

Then, each student was admitted to Institute based on these scores, and these scores alone. So, those students who scored highest on the sports test became the athletes. The ones scoring highest on the mathematics became accountants and treasurers. The highest scorers on the Council law were the politicians. The computer technicians and programmers were the students who scored the highest on the computer skills test. And finally, the celebrities scored the highest on the pop culture test. Each person went to Institute for eight years after their senior year to learn about their chosen profession. That is, except, the students who didn't have a score high enough to be placed in Institute. These people worked at the grocery stores and fast food joints in every city in The Americas, all thirty-two of them. Nearly fifty percent of The Americas were in this category. It was for this reason the unemployment rate was so high in places such as Holly Pines, which generally didn't do well on these mandated tests. Every so often, a student would score high enough to go to Institute abroad, such as in Japan, England, or France. To these places, education was taken more seriously, and they wanted only the best The Americas had to offer.

There was no choice or thought put into anything. A number was placed next to a name and each person was shipped to the suitable Institute. Manna hadn't been rich enough, or smart enough, to go to college, but he did have some say in what he wanted to do with his life. This new way of doing things just seemed silly to him. Manna felt old and cynical, and maybe it was because of his graying hair, but a person should have the right to become whatever he or she wanted to be, in his opinion anyway. He couldn't disclose this to anyone, however, or he would be just like the Teacher, hunted by the Council as a kind of terrorist type who was a threat to the sanctity of this regime's structured lifestyle.

He believed Simone had felt the same way before she went off to Institute. She was great with calculating with any form of number you would give to her, and she was also good with the written word. Something, with the emergence of computers, which was frowned upon by the Council. Libraries were becoming like museums for antiquities. Poetry was thought to be the work of someone who lacked respect for authority; that form of self-expression was what the Council was seeking to eliminate from society. It thought once one person expressed his or her opinion and stood up to the Council for the sake of virtue or principle, then there would surely be more rebellion.

This was the very reason Teacher was so sought after by the Council. Manna had seen news clippings almost daily of another *Pupil* being brought to justice and being punished for standing up to the Council. Each day he wasn't caught, the reward went up an insurmountable amount, and according to Giovanni it had finally reached a hundred million dollars; an amount most people would be lucky to see in three lifetimes. Manna could remember the day Simone had come to him and told him she was a Pupil. It had been three years after her mother had died.

"What do you mean you're part of this cult?" The venomous tongue in which Manna spoke showed his vehement dislike towards Teacher and his followers. Simone stood adamant in her own virtuous stance toward the cause. They were standing in the kitchen neither side budging.

"It's not a cult," Simone retorted. "It's a group of people who are finally thinking for themselves, without the Council's required involvement. I thought you'd understand. I know you think the same way I do." It was true; he couldn't deny her of this.

"But you're putting your life in danger," he replied.

"I'm a grown woman," she said with her steely gaze, her piercing blue eyes bore into his, and somehow he knew he was fighting a losing battle. There was to be no persuading her; she had already made up her mind.

22

"What would your mother have to say about this matter?" He feebly asked.

"She would have given me her blessing," she stated with conviction. "Don't you see what Teacher is trying to give to his Pupils? He is providing us with the liberation we need to pursue our own ambitions. He is guiding us to fulfill our dreams by convincing us to attempt to be innovative and imaginative. He wants his Pupils to deduce the answers we were too afraid to inquire about as children. We were forced to replicate ideas and unconsciously recall details about what the Council wanted us to understand. Teacher is forcing us to consider new concepts the Council would never let us explore. That's not putting my life in danger; that's putting my life in motion for the first time ever." Simone was laboriously breathing, which Manna could tell by the outward thrust of her chest as her diaphragm expanded and contracted with each new breath. It was evident she believed her passionate words. The two stood unblinking, both being too stubborn to allow the other to see any sign of defeat.

"Have you considered the implications of your actions?" Manna finally said, breaking the eerie silence.

"Teacher does not let us make up our minds without first contemplating all possible outcomes, both desirable and undesirable," Simone answered. "So, yes, I have."

"Then I cannot argue," Manna answered. "You have already made your decision."

"I hope you can accept it as my own to make," she stated.

"Unless I am to lose both you and your mother, I have no other alternative," he said.

"I must go then," she said as she kissed him on his cheek and briskly exited the house through the kitchen door without another word.

"Be safe," Manna whispered as he watched his daughter drive off to pursue this fervor.

Chapter Five: Seeking

Manna looked at the two gentlemen still sitting across from him in his den. Their demeanor hadn't changed since first meeting them in the parking lot of Holly Pines High. The mention of his daughter's name brought back a wide array of emotions, both pleasant and distasteful. It was unrealistic for him not to recall the traitorous moment in his kitchen when he last spoke with her, and it was infeasible to justify his obligation to assist her where he could.

"What does she need of me?" Manna asked Giovanni and Pierre, almost reluctantly.

"She said you could help us find Teacher," Giovanni replied.

"I wouldn't know where to start," Manna stated. "How does she even know of this conspiracy?"

"One of her jobs is to monitor the Council however possible," Pierre declared. "There is a Pupil correspondent within the Council's headquarters, and this person overheard a conversation with President Stuckey and an unknown individual within the Elliptical Ward. The conversation was about a plot to lure Teacher to the Pavilion to be identified. The spy relayed the message to Simone in order to warn Teacher of this traitorous act. It is of utmost importance we locate Teacher and warn him of this before it is too late."

"Why did Simone assume I knew how to find him?" Manna asked, astonished at the task set forth upon him.

"One of the eight Novice Orderlies is secreted within your school, and Simone thinks you can help us pinpoint who that is," Giovanni explained. "This person can then help us locate Teacher and his Cohort's current location, so we can warn of this devious plot against him."

"Who is this Novice Orderly at Holly Pines?" Manna asked, a little taken aback by the news. He was assured he knew most everything that went on within his place of employment, due to his often overlooked job status. Most people at the school didn't even pay him a passing glance as they conducted their questionable, and oftentimes illegal, activities. He could pass through the halls, seemingly unnoticed, and gather intel on any number of things going on around the school.

"We are not entirely sure," Giovanni stated, "that is why we have summoned your help."

"You don't know?" Manna replied incredulously. "Then I can't help you because I haven't a clue either. I'm sorry you wasted your time by coming here.

I really wish I could've helped you in this matter."

"You are not the only one we were sent to seek out," Pierre said. "There is also another we need to find to help in this pursuit."

"Who is this other person whom you seek?" Manna asked, still uncertain he could be of any help.

"A'ron Guidry," Pierre replied. "It was told to us by Simone that you both could help us discover the identity of this Novice Orderly hidden within Holly Pines."

"A'ron Guidry?" Manna asked, perplexed. That was a name Manna hadn't heard in years. It was a name that evoked sour, unpleasant memories from his nostalgic past. "How can he be of any help?" It was true that he and Guidry had been friends at one point in their lives, but that changed after the arrest.

Guidry was a no-nonsense man a year older than Manna. His gut hung out a little more, his hair was a little less gray, but his personality was a lot more overbearing. Guidry was one who usually ruled a conversation; not giving the listener much time to verbalize his own pedantic ponderings or anecdotes, but only listening to what Guidry's confluent musings had to offer.

His face was usually kept in a Van Dyke, with a bit of salt and pepper to flaunt an intelligence of an experienced college professor or neurosurgeon. He was, however, neither of these; his speech, nonetheless, belied this fact. He was one of the most elegant speakers Manna had ever heard. One could be enamored for hours when listening to Guidry's viewpoints on a myriad of topics: politics, history, science, and his favorite technology. One topic he usually stayed away from was ethics, because he had none. This was why he was such a great speaker, and what ended up getting him into trouble with the Council.

Nearly everything that developed in his unethical brain, and traveled the length of his unrelenting vocal chords to his smooth, elegant lips was pure fabrication. He was a habitual liar who created counterfeit stories and plagiarized ideas from experts in a variety of fields. It was one of these fantastical yarns that ended the friendship with Manna.

While at a dinner party for Julian Colander, prospective mayor-to-be, though he ended up losing the election, Guidry told a group of enraptured guests a heroic tale of saving an Egyptian from a crocodile attack on the Nile.

According to this tale, Guidry was on vacation with a tour group boating down the Nile. The Egyptian had fallen overboard during a strong current, and

Guidry, acting on instinct, dove in after him. He surfaced, holding the man, and noticed two crocodiles coming toward them in the water. He tried to swim back to the anchored boat. The other passengers gawked at them and pleaded with them to hurry. Guidry said that he could still remember the hysterical screams of a woman on the boat whose daughter had fainted upon seeing the crocodiles. There were screams from other passengers, but he said that this woman's seemed to stand out above the rest. As they approached the side of the boat, the boat's crew, the tour guide, and passengers frantically tried to pull the Egyptian and his savior closer to the boat with long wooden poles. Finally, they were close enough where the passengers could reach down and pull them up. Guidry was pulled in first, but as the Egyptian was being pulled up a crocodile lunged at him with its bone-crushing jaws.

Here, in the story, Guidry would normally give some fact about how much force is behind the crocodile's attacking jaw. Its intended purpose would usually get the audience to open their eyes a little wider, step a little closer to hear more of the story, and elicit a few gasps from the growing crowd. The story would always end with a gunshot from the boat's driver, wherein the lunging crocodile would be terminated with one skilled shot, and the other would inexplicably swim away in fright. The Egyptian was eternally grateful to his rescuer and the rest of the passengers paid their respects with endless praise, free beers back at the hotel, and even a few free meals.

Manna knew this story and was always amazed at how many people would actually believe such an unbelievable story. He knew, in fact, Guidry had never been to Egypt. The closest Guidry had ever come was the pyramid-shaped sand castles he made on the beach when he was ten years old. Guidry, however, would always have the skeptics, so he would ask Manna for confirmation on the accuracy of this story. Manna would always answer that it was true, so of course on the night of Julian Colander's dinner party, he replied with the rote answer he always had. This time, however, Guidry didn't end the story where he usually did. This audience was more prolific; he needed to add a few more harrowing details to make it even more sensational. So, after Manna confirmed the story as accurate, he continued, much to Manna's chagrin.

In this telling, Guidry told of a late-night meeting with the Egyptian at the hotel where the tour group was staying. The Egyptian told Guidry that he was, in fact, a Pupil of the famous, or infamous, depending on who was asked, Teacher. He was in debt to Guidry for saving his life, because Teacher had always taught him to redeem oneself in the eye of the benevolent Samaritan. He said that this was to be done, so the world would then be more accepting of their ilk.

"I was in total disbelief that I was in the presence of an individual who could lay witness to the true identity of *the* Teacher," Guidry had told the dinner guests still listening to his story. "The Egyptian spoke to me of the philosophies Teacher had spoken to him. He tried to brainwash me and persuade me to go with him to see Teacher in Egypt."

"He was in Egypt at the same time of your trip?" asked one of the guests with a bit of disdain. "And you expect us to believe this?"

"It doesn't bother me one iota if you believe me," Guidry said with an equal amount of scorn in his voice. "As I was saying, this infidel was trying to convince me to follow him to his cult. He tried to manipulate me with a bunch of hullabaloo about being indebted to me for unconsciously jumping in to save his miserable life. If I had known who he associated with, I would have left him in the icy water for croc cuisine. Nevertheless, I took him up on his offer, if only to prove him an imposter. Truth be told, imposter he was not."

"You mean you actually saw the real Teacher?" asked a woman showing a little too much leg, wearing a little too much lipstick, and not showing enough willpower to say no to champagne. She was on her eighth flute of the bubbly drink.

"From what I was told, it was the real one," Guidry confidently replied. "And unless I had as much to drink as you and was seeing things, he was real, too." The woman choked on her gulp of champagne, and this blunt sarcasm gave way to more gasps than the story actually had.

Manna grabbed Guidry by the shoulder, apologized to the shocked guests around him, and pulled him out of harm's way. "What the hell do you think you're doing?" Manna asked him when they were far enough away from everyone where they couldn't be overheard.

"Lighten up," Guidry said. It seemed only around Manna he didn't speak with the embellished tone he spoke with others. "It was totally harmless."

"Harmless?" Manna spoke agitatedly. "You just told a mass of people that you have seen the most hated, and wanted, person on the planet. How is that harmless? And worst of all, it's not even true."

"What if it is true?" Guidry retorted. "So what. What's the big deal? It's not like I *am* him. It's not like I have the same *beliefs*."

"I don't know why you had to change the story like that, especially without telling me," Manna said. "I told everyone that it was true. Now what am I supposed to say?"

Before Guidry could respond, a tall man wearing a blue blazer came up and interrupted the hushed conversation. "Are you A'ron Guidry?" He asked.

"Why, yes, I am," Guidry responded in his fake, intelligent way. "Who, pray tell, are you?"

"I am with the Council," the man replied. "You are under arrest for conspiracy against the Council and withholding evidence in the search for a known fugitive. Please, come with me." The man took Guidry away. Guidry's eyes rose in shock, and he was so perplexed that he didn't even put up a defense.

As they walked away, another man, shorter than the other, came up to where Guidry was just standing. "You need to come as well, for questioning." The man said in Manna's direction.

"Me?" Manna asked incredulously.

"Yes, please follow me," the shorter man said to Manna. Manna was led out of the dinner party in disgrace and embarrassment.

Manna was questioned and released once it was acknowledged that he knew nothing of the incident in Egypt, or the whereabouts of Teacher. Guidry was given three years in prison for falsifying information about Teacher's location. Manna did not once write to or visit Guidry while he was imprisoned, and he had never forgiven him for the humiliating events of that night. The two friends stopped talking, and when Guidry tried to reconcile at Felicia's wake, Manna refused to speak to him ever again.

"Let me ask you again," Manna said to the two gentlemen in his den. "How can A'ron Guidry be of any help to us and our present situation?"

"Because the person's life he once saved is the father of the Novice Orderly we seek within your school," Giovanni replied.

Oh shit, Manna thought to himself. *Guidry's never going to let me forget this one.*

28

Chapter Six: Moon Haven

Friday – Day Two

The next morning, after a quick breakfast of rye toast and eggs that was eaten with none of the usual satisfying chatter between friends or acquaintances, but instead it was rife with the silent hollowness of individuals who knew the extent of their current situation, Manna and his two guests again sat in the den, this time planning their next move.

Giovanni asked Manna if he knew the current whereabouts of A'ron Guidry.

"After his release from the Council's custody, Guidry was placed in a *sanctuary*," Manna informed them, "which was meant for the criminally insane or the emotionally despondent, or it was simply a place the Council could still keep tabs on a *person of interest*. For all I know, Guidry's still a resident there. I think it's called Moon Haven Manor."

"Simone has already hacked into Moon Haven's database and saw the current list of *guests*," Pierre replied. "Your former friend was not on that list." The verbal jab was not unnoticed by Manna.

"Which means he has been moved elsewhere, not included on the official registry, or has been released," Giovanni continued.

"Or worse,' Manna stated with a noticeable shake of his head, which showed a hint of remorse, "he's dead."

"In any case," Pierre interrupted before any of them could get the idea in their head that the one person they needed had perished, "we need to go to Moon Haven to see if we can find anything the computers are lacking."

"But how are we going to get in?" Manna asked. "We can't seriously walk in and ask them to see confidential files on past or current residents."

"No, we can't" Giovanni agreed, and Manna swore he saw a glimmer of a smirk develop at the edge of his visitor's mouth, which would have been the first glimpse of any emotion either man had shared up to that point. "But we can get in by just walking through the door." Manna looked perplexed and glanced over at Pierre, whose infectious grin couldn't be concealed.

"I think one of us is about to get committed," Pierre stated mischievously.

Manna was amazed at the transformation he gazed upon through the rear-view mirror in his car. The two men in drab clothing he'd first set eyes upon in the parking lot of Holly Pines, not twenty-four hours earlier, had altered their appearance so much he couldn't recognize them. Not that they stood out before. In fact, they were so plain and ordinary, Manna felt he couldn't pick them out of a line-up in their original appearance, even after spending half a day with them already.

Giovanni, whom Manna had shortened to Gio, wore long, black dreadlocks, a purple and black tie-dyed skullcap, and a pair of the darkest sunglasses Manna had ever seen. He had traded his blue jeans for a pair of camouflage cargo pants, and his plain t-shirt was now a bright orange long-sleeved shirt, despite the sudden heat wave, that said *I Think, Therefore I Am...Persecuted*, handwritten in black marker on the front.

Pierre wore a pair of black slacks, a crimson hooded sweatshirt with the word *Institute* on it written in black, stenciled letters, and a black collared shirt underneath. The crimson color represented the Law Institute. Each Institute had a different color to represent it, to show which program a student attended. He also had a brown wig of spiky hair with frosted tips to cover up his short black hair. His face now sported a goatee of the same brown hue as the wig. He wore a pair of black-rimmed eyeglasses that made him look ten years older than he looked without them. His previously black eyebrows even had changed to the matching brown of the wig and goatee, which made it appear that his true hair color was brown and not black. Manna had trouble envisioning what the true Pierre and Gio looked like based upon these two new strangers he gazed upon in the mirror. The strangers were no longer Pierre and Gio; they were now Cameron and Dominick.

Manna glanced at himself in the mirror and had to laugh at the site staring back at him. His graying hair was now a full mane of white. He now wore a small pair of eyeglasses that hung daintily on his pointed little nose. He wore a pastel blue button-up shirt with different shades of orange sporadically splashed upon it. His tan khaki pants went down and partially covered his brown loafer which was putting pressure on the accelerator. His two new friends also added some rouge to his cheeks to make him look like a vacationing Santa Claus. They even gave him the name Klaus for his part in the subterfuge.

They could see Moon Haven appear as they approached it from the south entrance. It was recognizable from its ominous appearance atop a lone hill with a fifteen foot tall stretch of obsidian fence along the exterior of the property. An expanse of trees, the start of a woodland grove, covered the rear of the estate. The building was a cross between a mansion and a castle set in a myriad of structural design. There was a hint of Gothic, a trace of Baroque, and a tinge of Contemporary. The ivory exterior of the building was a direct contrast to the darkness of the fence and the shade provided by the overabundant rows of trees.

The Moon Haven estate was first purchased by Victor Luna, who was the owner of a conglomeration of million-dollar companies. He was born into high wealth, but earned his profits the non-nepotistic way, through hard work, perseverance, and a great deal of sweat. It was a guaranteed fortune to anyone who created a testing method that worked, so it was no surprise that his first million-dollar company was the one that developed the Horrisburg Test, which was a widely accepted educational barometer of student progress and future course of study. He then transferred those funds into developing the Halsey Analysis, which was the present testing method used in the school systems across the Americas. This took the better part of fifteen years of research and study to perfect into the current form. He married six times after his recognition as the Most Eligible Bachelor under 30 on the *Now Who?* website.

Now Who? was the most widely used website on the Internet. It was a gossip site that told the people of the Americas, and around the rest of the world, who was worthy of praise or attention at the present moment in time. There were lists about anything related to people anyone could imagine. There was a list for Most Eligible Bachelor, Most Popular Athlete, Most Watchable Actor, and even Most Popular Person in America. The brother site, *Now What?*, listed for the American people what was new and worth buying in terms of technology, transportation, or any other aspect of life the site felt worthwhile. It held the latest fads popular among the youth, and if it was widely known that if a product got its name on this list, it made an easy million in its first week. However, the following week it could lose that million just as quickly as it was earned. Companies had to be careful about how much product to produce or they would lose so much money they couldn't stay in business for too long.

Luna's most recent wife, Claire, was also his longest tenured spouse. Luna always said that she was, "His one truest love; even above money." Together they transformed Luna's assets into a majestic opulence never seen before, or since. Everything they touched seemed to prosper beyond expectation. Like the touch of Midas, they prospered in nearly every endeavor.

Moon Haven Manor was their shared vision of lavish beauty and represented their everlasting love for one another. They furnished it with antiquities from around the world. On the eve of when they were to move into their fairy tale home, they inexplicably vanished. Authorities found no clue as to their whereabouts and found no sign of foul play. The home sat empty of any occupant, excepting the extravagant furnishings.

On the five year anniversary of this mysterious vanishing act, Moon Haven's deed was perplexingly handed over to the Council. They, in turn, made it into its current holding tank for the incapable and mindless refuse of the Council. It was spoken, in whispers, in some circles that the place used unusual methods upon those within its walls. It also took on the moniker of the Lunatic

Lair, which took its roots, understandably, from the Luna name itself. There were many theories of what the true purpose of the place really was, but most people believed the whispered stories to be myth or some sort of urban legend. As Manna peered at the peculiar edifice staring ominously at him through the windshield, those unbelievable fabrications he frequently overheard, definitely seemed plausible to him now.

Chapter Seven: Committed

"You must be Klaus Van Ranken," a man in a tight-fitting blue shirt said to Manna as he stood to shake his hand. The man stood a few inches shorter than Manna, but he conducted himself as if he were the taller man. He looked to be in his late forties, but it was very apparent that he still exercised regularly. "I'm Dr. Fredrickson. We spoke on the phone this morning." Pierre and Gio stood in the doorway as Manna introduced them using a slight German accent.

"This is my eldest son, Cameron," he said as he introduced Pierre. "And this is my son, Dominick, whom we spoke about on the phone. We had Dominick lightly sedated before we came, in order to get through this whole ordeal."

Dr. Fredrickson pushed a hand through his tangle of chestnut brown hair as he took in Dominick's appearance. He read the writing on the shirt, looked at the disheveled attire, and made two conjectures within the first twenty seconds. The first; *this young man can be helped*. The second; *the Council will definitely want to know about this one*. "That was a wise decision. Come on in and sit down," Dr. Fredrickson said, gesturing to Pierre and Gio to sit in the overstuffed leather chairs. They did as requested, and Manna followed suit. Fredrickson sat in his chair across from them at his desk.

"Thank you for meeting with us on such short notice," Manna told him. "On a weekend at that."

"That is not a problem," Fredrickson smiled warmly. His green eyes conveyed the sincerity in his words. "We keep our hours flexible to accommodate our guests, current or prospective. Tell me again about your situation. We only spoke briefly on the phone."

"My son, here, Dominick, had been missing for almost four years," Manna started into the story Pierre and Gio had rehearsed with him. "He was presumed dead by the Council and was even given a funeral, but my wife and I refused to attend. Two weeks ago he showed up at our doorstep in a sort of daze. His hair had grown an immense amount, his weight had dropped quite significantly, and his clothes were mere rags. My wife didn't recognize him and thought him to be a criminal of some sort. She screamed, which made me come to her aide. The scream had no effect on Dominick; he still stood where my wife had spotted him, in the same daze. When I realized who it was, I honestly went into hysterics. Can you imagine, Dr. Fredrickson? The son who someone told me was dead, was now standing in my sights, like a wraith. Do you know what that's like?"

"I can't say that I do," replied Dr. Fredrickson, "but I can imagine the myriad of emotions coursing through you. Shock. Relief. Not to mention the confusion of the whole ordeal. So what made you contact us?" He said this with a hint of skepticism, which almost unhinged Manna's nerves. In all of this, Gio, as Dominick, kept the outwardly appearance of being miles away. His pupils were dilated and he hardly moved a muscle, but when he did it was as if he was in slow motion.

Manna, however, kept his composure and went into the prepared story. "Well, within days of his sudden reappearance, we all noticed Dominick acting strangely. He became angry at any mention on the television of the Council. When the president would address us, he would become agitated and aggressive in a way none of us recalled seeing before the disappearance. He also started growing his hair longer, dressing in a more disheveled manner, and keeping mostly to himself."

"Did he go anywhere on his own or have any visitors during this time?" Dr. Fredrickson asked. He listened with rapt attention, and whenever something piqued his interest, he would quickly jot it down in a small notebook.

"Not that anyone is aware of," Manna answered. "We tried to keep an extra-close eye on him after his long absence from the family. We weren't ready to lose him again."

"That's understandable," Dr. Fredrickson replied looking Manna in the eye, then to the notebook. "Continue."

"He also started to get these strange habits," Manna continued, "like he was paranoid someone was after him. He would spend countless hours locked up in his room, which he kept dark at all times. He even put up shades to make it look even darker. A week after he arrived home, he moved all his stuff to the spare room in the basement and isolated himself from us all. He started wearing homemade shirts like the one he has on today. All the shirts had mention of the Teacher on it. I tried asking him if he is affiliated with that scoundrel, but he's evasive and downright hostile if anyone questions him. Then two days ago, my eldest son found this letter."

Manna gave a folded piece of paper to the doctor who perused it with definite intent.

Dear Teacher,

I relinquish all outwardly knowledge of my existence except to your cause. I pledge my allegiance to the forthright foundation you have established for the common good of mankind. It is with great honor I call myself one of your disciples. I only hope to be recognized as a Pupil soon, by showing my unwavering loyalty to you and your Novice Orderlies. I have been away for nearly four years searching for all possible forms of knowledge I could obtain in that time. I came home to see my family one last time, but I leave soon to commence my quest for the greatest knowledge of all provided by the greatest teacher from whom one can hope to gather that knowledge. That teacher is You. I will not falter in my lessons, as I am incapable of it. May I impress upon you that my words are genuine and hide no ill intent, and may the assurance of your words speak into the hearts of others like me.

Your Humble Disciple
Dominick Van Ranken

After reading the letter, Dr. Fredrickson gave it back to Manna and wrote something down in the notebook. This time he seemed to write for an extraordinarily long period of time, which only made Manna more nervous. The awkwardness of the silence, except the scribbling of the pen in the notebook, seemed too scripted to Manna. It was, as if, Dr. Fredrickson could tell they were lying and was waiting for them to come clean. Manna, however, didn't take the bait and simply waited it out for an excruciating length of time. At last, Dr. Fredrickson stopped writing and slowly looked up.

"This seems very serious, Mr. Van Ranken," he finally said. "It seems your son was about to embark on an unwise journey. One which could have been most damning indeed. I believe you brought him to the right place. It seems he has been brainwashed to some extent by some faction of Teacher's outer order. It says in the letter that he hoped to be 'recognized as a Pupil'. This is good news to you, because it means he hasn't yet been strongly influenced by this faction. He is just in the first stage of corruption. He has the desire to join, but he has yet to be initiated."

"This is good news?" Manna asked incredulously. "How is this good news?"

"Mr. Van Ranken," Dr. Fredrickson began his reply, "we have had a large amount of residents at Moon Haven in this first stage of corruption. The success rate in which we convert them back to their normal selves is very high indeed. In fact, we have a success rate of ninety eight percent. In a few months, you'll have the son that you remember before he went missing. I promise. In fact, I guarantee it."

"So you're willing to help?" Manna asked, ecstatic.

"Mr. Van Ranken, I'd like to officially welcome your son," said Dr. Fredrickson as he shook Manna's hand. "Once we sign the commitment papers, he will be an official guest of Moon Haven Manor."

Chapter Eight: Inside Moon Haven

Manna was even more nervous, even after completing his pseudo-signature and getting past the initial complication of getting Gio committed. Phase one was already complete, which Gio and Pierre predicted to have been the most difficult. In reality, it wasn't difficult at all. Dr. Fredrickson fell for it without a hitch. No, the reason for this nervousness was because Manna was now alone with Dr. Fredrickson. It was up to him to continue the subterfuge by himself. Something he wasn't used to doing. Pierre was with Gio, acting as concerned older brother and helping Gio make the transition easier. Only Manna knew the true reason for this accompaniment. Pierre was attempting to get a 3D mental image of the building, rather than the schematics they had already collected thanks to Simone. He couldn't help but be proud of her; she had always been a stickler for detail. Pierre was also looking for a way to sneak in some necessary tools for Gio to use later that night. The plan was to leave Gio with an earpiece to communicate with them when the rest of the place was asleep. It was also planned to leave him with a miniscule device with the capability to make a copy, much like a Xerox machine, without the bulk of the entire machine. All one had to do was press a button and scan over the desired image for it to save it on the device. Later, they could look at the copy from any computer terminal or print it if they needed a hard copy. The device even worked on computer screens, which was where they thought they would end up finding A'ron's file. The final item Pierre was to leave was a change of clothing, so Gio could escape more easily.

"This is the commune," Dr. Fredrickson said, interrupting Manna's thoughts. "This is where your son will be eating with the other inhabitants."

"You mean *patients*?" Manna asked.

"We prefer the term *residents*," Dr. Fredrickson replied. "But from certain perspective, they are patients as well."

"Doctor," Manna replied a little too scornfully, "we both know what you do here. I just want you to make sure your facility gets me my son back. Whatever methods you see fit are okay with me. You have my permission to use any revolutionary or experimental techniques you deem necessary."

"I thank you for your courage," the doctor replied. "We do have some new experimental treatments. We'll do whatever it takes for you to see your son back to normal. Do you have any questions about his stay with us?"

Manna had already been shown the room where Gio would be staying. It was rather small, but had some nice, comfortable-looking furniture that looked better than his own at home. There was a computer lab where the residents could read leisurely, or even check their personal email accounts. Of course, these were monitored very carefully by a group of people handpicked by the Council. He was even shown the washroom, where the residents did their own personal laundry. Dr. Fredrickson let it be known that the entire place was under surveillance twenty-four hours a day. This fact made Manna rethink their overall plan, but he had faith in Gio and Pierre. They seemed to know what they were doing. The last place that was shown to Manna was the commune, where he now stood. It looked like a typical cafeteria with long tables covering the whole of the commune. They were a pale, pink color that reminded Manna of a hospital bedpan. There currently was nobody in the commune, but a quick look at the digital timepiece, and Manna noted the dinner hour was quickly approaching. As if on cue, Pierre appeared with a Moon Haven employee with a name badge that said Burt.

"We thought we'd find you two here," Burt said with a smile. "This is usually the last place Fredrickson here takes the resident's kinfolk. Name's Burt. Your son, Dominick, is currently in his room. We gave him an early bite to eat and a small dose of medication to help him sleep well tonight. He's in good hands."

"We found that the first night was the most difficult," Dr. Fredrickson stated. "So, we have recently tried to medicate new arrivals on the first night before getting them into our routine on the second day. Especially, arrivals like your son with a history of unpredictability."

"Thank you, Doctor. I think it would be easier for me if I didn't have to see him in that state before leaving," Manna replied. "I can see that he is in good hands. Can you recommend a place nearby for a quick meal before heading back home?"

"Eat here," Dr. Fredrickson replied. "Our head chef, Margie, would be delighted to cook you up a special order of whatever you like. It's on the house. I'm sure your day has been filled with as much stress as is needed for one day. No need to stress over a place to get a hot meal."

"Then, we'll have to accept," Manna replied with a smile and a quick glance at Pierre. "Can you recommend anything in particular, Burt?"

"Oh, Ms. Margie makes a mean chicken pot pie," Burt said rubbing his head sheepishly. "It's even better than ole' Meemaa's, but don't tell my Meemaa I told you that."

"We won't," Pierre stated with a smile. "Your secret's safe with us."

After a second helping and a few more pleasantries, Manna and Pierre left Gio alone in Moon Haven, except with the communication device to keep in contact with them. It was now up to him to get the information, get out, and meet them at a secret rendezvous.

Manna and Pierre were currently set up in the Lunar Hotel a mile and a half away from Moon Haven. It was just about half past midnight, the time Moon Haven was known to officially shut down for the night. Sure, there was still security, but Phase Three was soon to be set into motion. Pierre was sitting at a desk with a small microphone set up in front of him. Speakers were also set up on either side of him, as well as a recorder, which Manna knew was about to record Gio's observations. A small laptop also sat on the desk in front of Pierre. It was obvious to Manna that this was not the first time Pierre had used this surveillance technology.

It made Manna wonder who this stranger truly was. It had been just the night before that he met this man, and now he was in a hotel room waiting for a new clue as to the whereabouts of a former friend. It was all just too surreal. Pierre had set up the surveillance without even a word. He was strictly business. Manna had to wonder what the normal conversations between his two new acquaintances were like. He couldn't imagine many of them being longer than five or ten minutes. The tension in the air was definitely enhanced due to Pierre's silent nature.

"We should hear from Gio soon," Pierre said, finally breaking the eerie silence. "You should sit down; you're starting to make me nervous."

It was obvious from his flat voice that he was only being sarcastic. Manna couldn't think of a single thing that would seem to faze his two companions. Even through the sarcasm, Manna decided to sit at the end of the bed near where Pierre sat at the desk. He felt the need to sit close, but not too close, so as not to get in the way.

"Do you think he'll find anything?" Manna asked awkwardly because he had nothing better to say. It was obvious he was out of his element.

"If there's something there, he'll find it," Pierre said matter-of-factly.

A noise crackled the speaker awake; Manna couldn't discern what was said, but it was obviously Gio. Manna recognized the straight-laced voice.

"Pierre, are you there?" Gio said more clearly.

"We read you," Pierre said into the microphone. Manna felt embarrassed to be included for some reason, like he was somehow an integral part of the mission when he truly didn't feel all that important.

"I got the package you left," Gio stated. "I will be making my way toward the offices. I plan on checking Fredrickson's first. I'll be in contact when I get there."

"We'll be waiting," Pierre said back to him. He looked over at Manna, who had a bead of sweat on his brow.

It seemed like hours, not the mere ten minutes it took for Gio to sneak to Fredrickson's office and report back. Manna couldn't help himself from peaking at the clock. It was as if he saw each of the ten minutes pass by from his constant peaking, which only made it seem all the longer. He also couldn't help from sweating, even though the air conditioning in the room was on, and in fact was just above him blowing a direct current on the top of his sparsely-covered head. Even this couldn't break his sweat, because it was made, not from being overheated, but due to nervousness. His right leg was in a constant state of movement as well, but this was not entirely due to his present situation. It was actually brought on by his hyperactive nature. In his line of work, he was in constant motion which usually controlled his movements and kept his mind focused.

When he was younger, it was usually diagnosed as ADHD, which, to him, made no sense. Just because someone wanted to be active, he or she was considered to have something as stigmatic as a disorder. It was looked down upon and, most often, led to his teachers giving up on him as a lost cause. He could remember his fourth grade teacher, Mrs. Serling, telling him, in a private hallway conversation, to stop purposely acting out in class. All he had been doing was tapping his pen on his desk and tapping his foot, both to a different made-up beat, in order to concentrate on her words. She hadn't even noticed the goody-two-shoes girl next to him drawing cartoonish caricatures of the entire class, including the teacher herself, in order to concentrate herself. Sure, it was less distracting to the rest of the class, but it had been for the same exact reason. Just because she made A's and he got C's, even then he had realized the unfairness of society; the double standard boys and girls were given.

Manna glanced toward Pierre, who seemed to get even calmer as each minute passed. His shallow breathing gave the impression that he had even fallen asleep. If Pierre's eyes weren't open, Manna would have guessed that he had, in fact, taken a nap during one of the most intense moments Manna had ever faced in his life.

This time it was Gio who broke the silence, nearly making Manna slide off the edge of the bed. He caught himself before making a complete fool of himself, but his heart felt like it was about to explode. If he didn't know better, he could almost be certain that a smile had crept across Pierre's face, but only for an instant. By the time Manna situated himself back onto the bed, it was gone.

"I made it to Fredrickson's office," Gio's tinny voice whispered to them. "I'll check the filing cabinet first, then the computer."

Manna could hear small movements through the radio, drawers slowly opening and closing, papers being rustled. He pictured Fredrickson's office in his mind. The filing cabinet was in the right hand corner against the large window. Manna couldn't help but think that a security guard making his rounds could easily hear the movement of the drawers in the hallway. Just as the paranoia started to reach its upper echelon, Gio stopped making any sound.

"There's nothing in the files about Guidry," he replied. "Seems they don't have much use for paper records anymore, not much of anything in the past fifteen to twenty years. Checking computer, now. I searched for any files containing Guidry's name."

Manna got to his feet and walked over to where Pierre sat in front of the equipment. The tension had finally gotten to him. He continued his mental image of the room. The computer was on the other side of the room from the filing cabinet. It sat on the opposite side of the desk where Manna had been sitting just hours earlier. Directly above it hung a painting of Victor Luna shaking hands with the former head of the Council, Walter Hapsburg. Hapsburg had his left arm embracing Luna as the two shook hands. It was a very famous picture. It had been in all the e-magazines and commemorated the ten year anniversary of Luna's Halsey Analysis. It seemed strange that was in the office of one of the doctors and not hanging out in the open for all to see as they walk into the establishment. Manna suddenly had a crazy idea.

He reached for the microphone, "Gio, I know it might be a little far-fetched, but check the painting. I have a feeling there might be something hidden behind it."

"Since I'm having no luck here finding anything on the computer, will do," Gio replied back. A few bumps and curses later, Gio's response made it evident Manna was correct. "I'll be damned. It looks like a safe is in the wall behind the painting."

Pierre looked shocked that Manna had proven helpful to the mission beyond his earlier acting. "Nicely done," he said in his usual stoic manner.

"I'll need time to get into it, but I have a feeling we're going to find what we're looking for inside," Manna sensed a bit more excitement coming from Gio, but he chalked that up to having a little more adrenaline pumping inside him at the moment due to being out in the field.

"I'll search for some clues on the computer for a viable number sequence he might've used," Pierre stated.

A proud smile crossed Manna's face as he went back to the edge of the bed and sat back down.

"It might be awhile," Pierre told him. "Why don't you head down to the lobby and pick us up some coffee. I have a feeling we're going to need something to keep our brains fresh."

Manna exited with the room card and made his way back to the lobby. The lobby was empty at this hour, except for a woman at the front desk reading something from her computer. As Manna walked up to her, he noticed two things. First, her name was Gretchen, and second, she had been reading the latest issue of *Now What?*

"Do you still keep the coffee brewing this late?" Manna asked Gretchen.

She looked disdainfully at Manna like he had just purposely taken away the final ten seconds of her life. "We have a pot around the corner. If it isn't full, there should be a packet of instant coffee in a basket beside it. Is there anything else I can do for you?" She made this last remark with a faux-smile that radiated such contempt that Manna didn't even thank her.

He headed in the direction Gretchen had pointed him and easily found the coffee pot. She had correctly predicted that it would be out of coffee. *It's probably because she's the one who was supposed to fill it*, Manna thought sarcastically, *and she does her job so well.*

"You were right, empty," Manna told her with the same faux-smile and a nod. He even had the insolence to hold up the coffee pot to prove his point. Gretchen gave a little snort and went back to looking at her computer.

Manna saw a small bag of coffee grounds, so started the process by pouring it into the filter. He also saw a small crate of bottled water and picked up one to use for the coffee. The label read Evian, which was fine by him. He poured the Evian water into the machine and waited for the brewing process to reach completion.

He used to find it comical that Evian was *naïve* spelled backwards, and felt paying for something you could get free was definitely, in some sense, showing naivety. That all changed when the tap water started becoming tainted with high levels of lead, mercury, cobalt, and a myriad of other chemicals due to the constant industrialization of the Americas. All the advancement in technology and excessive use of natural and unnatural resources had a dramatic effect on the ability to produce drinkable water locally, and this didn't even include the drastic effects the war had on the environment. These days, drinking water was exclusively produced overseas and bottled up for consumption. Manna wondered what it was like to be able to live in one of those few places where he could still get a cold glass of ice water from the kitchen sink. He would have to move to a place with a natural spring to have that experience again.

As the last drop of brewed coffee fell into the pot, the automatic doors at the lobby entrance opened and three men walked through them. All three wore thick, rain-drenched raincoats, and Manna could see that, indeed, it was raining steadily. The man who stood in the middle wore a black bowler hat pulled down and the raincoat's collar was pulled up, which partially hid his face. All Manna could see was a shaggy, white beard covering most of his face. He also held a cane, which made him look a bit more refined than his two compatriots. The other two men had thick, black goatees, broad shoulders, and no necks. Their heads were completely shaved and the rain seemed to have made them shine more than they normally would. The three raincoats walked up to Gretchen and started talking indistinctly. To Manna, it seemed like just a bunch of mumbles, grunts, and a few groans from Gretchen.

Manna went back to pouring the finished coffee into two Styrofoam cups. He put sugar and cream in his, and debated on what to include in Pierre's. From what he gathered from this strange companion, he would assume he would prefer it a deep, charcoal black, but he grabbed a few sugars and creamers just in case. He put the extra pack of sugars in his pocket and headed for the elevator. He pushed the up button and waited for the elevator car to return him to the long night ahead. He could still hear the raincoats mumbling with Gretchen, but a few words became a little more discernible.

One of the raincoats told Gretchen that something was very urgent.

"I understand," Gretchen replied. "I can get you in."

As the elevator door closed, he heard Gretchen give the raincoats a room number and he tensed. *Did she just tell them 324?* Manna frantically thought. *But that's our room!*

Chapter Nine: Room 324

In Manna's mind, the elevator ride to the third floor could not have gone any slower. He set the two coffee cups on the elevator floor, because he felt he would either drop them or spill the smoldering liquid on himself due to his unsteady hands. A third-degree burn would not make matters any better. He paced the small elevator car and looked up intermittently to check the floor. *Why's it taking so long to go up three floors?* Manna thought to himself. Perspiration dripped off his brow, and he was getting all he could out of his convenience store deodorant he bought on the way to the hotel. Of course, he had forgotten to bring his own in the hurried packing he did before coming on this insane mission. He had also picked up a toothbrush from the convenience store, which he had accidentally left in the car. Finally, he heard the familiar ding, and in his haste on exiting the car, he knocked over one of the cups of coffee.

He made his way to Room 324, and inserted the key. He listened for any unusual noises coming from the room before entering. Pierre was still in front of the equipment and turned to see Manna's empty hands.

"Forget why you were going down there?" He asked with a sly grin.

Manna quickly shut the door and typed in a password on a key pad on the door. The door was now locked from the inside, and not even the maids were able to get into the rooms. This was meant for the hotel guests to feel safer, as well as keep the rooms more private. Manna had always thought it was developed so the copious amounts of adulterous politicos could keep their various "matters of state" all the more private. They could "break in" the new intern and not have to worry about the maid totally ignoring the *Do Not Disturb* sign on the door in order to bring in a fresh batch of clean towels. In fact, the hotels were making it easier for promiscuous trysts by not requiring identification, or even providing a name in order to obtain a room. In essence, it was for this reason Manna was able to get this room so easily under his new guise, which made it all the more shocking to have the men downstairs asking questions about them.

"I think the lady at the front desk just gave somebody our room number," Manna declared. He described the three men in raincoats and the conversation he overheard.

"Are you sure that's what she said?" Pierre asked him.

"I am almost positive that's what she said," Manna replied trying to remember exactly what it was he heard her say.

Pierre picked up the microphone in order to speak to Gio. "Giovanni, we've got trouble here. We're going to skip out of here and come get you. Manna thinks we might have been found out. What's your status on the safe?"

"Not much luck here," Gio replied back in a low voice. "I looked around for any clues as to the number code, and tried some of the more obvious ones, important dates and birthdays you gave me, but nothing worked. I was going to start drilling, but some guard keeps walking by. Didn't want him to hear it."

"We're getting out of here. Meet you at the original rendezvous point," Pierre replied back.

Pierre took the CD from the appropriate drive of the laptop which they had been recording onto and left everything else. He put the CD into a slim casing and turned to see Manna's astonished face staring at him.

"We're just going to leave all this stuff? Won't someone trace it to us?" Manna asked him.

"They'll actually trace it to someone named Sampson Eldridge," he explained, "but don't worry, he's dead."

"What about fingerprints?" Manna asked. In reply, Pierre pulled out a small aerosol bottle and sprayed a fine mist onto the equipment.

"Quick, spray the doorknobs on the room door and bathroom," Pierre told Manna as he tossed the can to him. "It'll remove fingerprints from any type of material, except fabric. The mist simply absorbs into the fabric before it has a chance to take effect."

Manna sprayed the bathroom door handle on the inside and outside doors, and was just about to spray the inside of the room door when he heard an audible click. The raincoats were on the other side of the door trying to get access into the room. They had just slid their authorized key card into the slot and were given clearance by way of the outdoor lock. The only thing keeping them out now was the password Manna had just initiated when he came back from getting the coffees. Manna froze with the aerosol bottle a few inches from the doorknob, and then held his breath as he watched the doorknob start to turn. It turned a few centimeters and then the safety lock caught and held firm. Manna took a deep sigh of relief. He would be certain to vote for the most promiscuous politician in the next election; his promiscuity had just saved his life.

"We know you're in there," a muffled voice stated. "We would simply like to ask you a few questions."

Pierre shook his head and nodded in the direction of the balcony. Manna understood and quickly sprayed the doorknob with the mysterious mist. Then, he followed Pierre to the large, glass balcony doors on the other side of the room. Pierre already had on a pair of gloves and slid open the glass door. Manna could see that the rain had not subsided. The balcony had an attached ladder to a landing on the second floor. This, in turn, had the same type of ladder attached to the landing at ground level. These were put into place in order for those individuals who used the indoor locks to get out in case of fire. Or in Manna and Pierre's case, to escape an unknown assailant.

Both Manna and Pierre made their way down the slick ladder and reached the second floor. They were about to head down the second ladder, but suddenly all the lights inside, and even the streetlights surrounding the hotel went out. Manna and Pierre both understood the purpose of this unexpected power outage. The indoor locks were automatically reset during a loss in electricity. It was a failsafe for the hotel in case someone was injured, or died in the room when the locks were engaged. In fact, most hotel chains set up a time during each day for the power to go out, in order to reset all indoor locks to the rooms. It was usually done in the early hours of the day, so it wouldn't affect the hotel patrons as much.

"This couldn't be one of those scheduled power failures, could it?" Manna asked Pierre.

"Pretty good coincidence if it was," he replied. "Besides, I'm not waiting around to find out." He reached for the first step down the second ladder, and Manna followed.

They heard voices during their descent and Manna looked up. The three raincoats were overlooking them from the balcony they left only minutes before. Manna slipped on the rain-soaked ladder, but caught himself in time to prevent himself from tumbling the rest of the way, and a possible broken bone. He focused on his descent more closely, and finally heard the scuffle of feet on the pavement below. He looked down momentarily to see Pierre had made it down successfully, and he, himself, was only a few steps away. Manna joined Pierre moments later, and the two ran through the rain to their parked car around the back of the establishment.

"Give me the key," Pierre demanded. "I'll drive."

Since his nerves were just about shot, Manna obliged and threw him the keys. Pierre reversed the car out of the spot, and sped toward the exit. The raincoats had just made their way to the second floor landing when they passed, and Manna saw Bowler Hat shaking his cane in their direction. He let out a deep sigh of relief and sat back in the seat as Pierre drove to Jeb's Diner, the rendezvous point.

Jeb's Diner was an innocuous looking place about a half mile from Moon Haven. It sat across from Koko's, a dance club open at all hours. What Koko's possessed in overabundant self-absorption, Jeb's made up for in low-profile normalcy. Koko's had a bright, red and orange Neon sign, which was like a glowing beacon hoping to entice some shameless patron simply driving by on a late night excursion. Even at this hour, thirty or forty people were standing in line waiting to get inside. Manna could see young girls in skimpy skirts, low-cut shorts, and little lacey travesties, he wouldn't even classify as clothing. Since it was officially the weekend, modesty wasn't what was expected or preferred.

Jeb's, however, barely looked to have a functioning light bulb, compared to the extravagance across the street. It looked dark, dreary, and bland. Its modest blue and white sign was barely noticeable in the shadows of the surrounding opulence. However, in Manna's mind, it looked somewhat inviting in its own unique sense. The sign on the door simply stated *Open* in red, block-lettering. No neon lights to force the issue, just a simple offering of warm food for a weary traveler, which is what Manna was. The night had proven exhausting, and they hadn't even accomplished what they set out to achieve. Pierre parked the car so they could see the oncoming traffic, but didn't shut off the engine.

"I don't think they could have followed us," Pierre said a little doubtfully. He kept peaking at the passing cars, but they were at a disadvantage because they hadn't seen the car in which the men had come. "Did you recognize any of the men you saw in the lobby?" He asked Manna without taking his eyes of the road.

"No, I didn't" Manna replied. "However, I really didn't get a good look at one of them, the one in the bowler hat. The other two, I definitely would have recognized if I'd seen them before. I would never forget faces that damn ugly."

"I wonder why they're after us," Pierre stated, more to himself than to Manna.

"Do you think they're from the Council?" Manna asked.

"I wouldn't doubt it," replied Pierre. "Moon Haven probably gives them the names of patients who come in claiming knowledge of Teacher, or claiming to be Pupils. They probably give the names of family members as well. We probably have nothing to fear, but Giovanni might be in trouble."

"What are we going to do if he doesn't show?" asked Manna.

46

"We'll have to complete the mission without him. He's been trained not to speak of our mission to anyone on the outside," Pierre replied back. "Why don't you go get those coffees you seemed to forget back at the hotel? We'll need something to warm us up."

"Sure thing," Manna agreed. "Just make sure no scary guys come in with raincoats. I don't think my heart will be able to take any more excitement tonight."

Manna paid for the coffees and got back into the car without incident. He kept his black this time, because, who was he kidding, sleep was something which would elude him anyhow, and straight black coffee usually did the trick of keeping him up. For some reason, any sort of creamer seemed to dilute it in some psychosomatic way that confused his mind into thinking it wasn't really coffee. Even though he gave the blistering liquid ample time to cool down, when he took a drink it still scalded his tongue and upper lip. He continued to sip at it sparingly as the two men waited for the third member of their party to arrive. Except for the intermittent slurps of the coffee, they waited in silence.

Manna's mind drifted back to the line outside Koko's; something to take his mind off the troublesome night. He was able to see the final dozen or so people still waiting outside, with umbrellas. The distant figures seemed to all mingle into one noiseless blob of overindulgence and sexuality. He was too far to see any facial features, but the glow of people on cell phones was very discernible. It was a cacophony of blues, pinks, yellows, and other assortments of brightness that Manna was too callous to register. Mixed with the Neon, pounding music and the endless stream of various perfumes and colognes made Manna's over-stimulated brain seem to falter. He could also sense the fragrant smell of cigarettes, as well as other alternatives both legal and not. He felt as if he was in a drug-induced haze himself. The world started to sway around him and he experienced tunnel-vision. He glanced into the side mirror to divert his eyes from the intense lighting. He blinked a few times, but the tunnel-vision only became worse.

He could no longer sense Pierre's presence beside him in the car. Instead, the conversation he had with Simone in his kitchen, their last real conversation in years, replayed in his mind. He could hear her pleas to accept her decision, her fate. He could visually see the conviction in which she spoke. She inherently believed each and every word she spoke. She didn't seem to have to think about her words at all. It was, as if, the words had already been formulated in her brain for this exact conversation. Manna realized, in fact, this conversation had already taken place, in Simone's mind. Then, he saw her turn and walk out his door again, as it had happened a million times in his mind. This sight haunted his dreams. This vision was etched in his mind, and he knew it would be this he would see as he took his last breath. None of the grand memories he had made in his years of life would crowd his thoughts at that moment, but this one haunting sight would. His final words to her, to *be safe*, were never heard.

He could feel a tear streaking down his cheek which he reached up to stop before Pierre noticed. In the process, his right elbow accidentally put too much pressure on the button which started to put the window down. This startled him out of his reverie. Pierre looked at him with a bit of confusion, but the look also contained some concern as well.

"Sorry," Manna stammered. "I think I dozed off there for a minute."

"It's okay," Pierre replied with a sort of smirk. "I think I was dozing too."

Manna went to push the button to put the window back up, but a hazy form materialized in the rain-soaked window. Manna jumped and gave a small yelp of surprise. Gio's face appeared more clearly as he tapped on the glass.

"You scared the hell out of me," Manna told Gio as he got out letting him into the back seat.

"Sorry about that," Gio replied once he was seated. Manna could see he was soaked from the rain, though it was beginning to lighten up quite a bit.

"I think I have an emergency blanket in the trunk for you," Manna told him. "Let me check."

Manna took the keys back from Pierre and went to the trunk to see about the blanket. He opened the trunk and found the black and green striped blanket he was expecting would be back there. He heard a small scrape from behind him and turned to see what it was. Before he could, he felt a sharp pain in his back as someone hit him with something that felt like a baseball bat. Manna fell to one knee and felt another pain at the back of his head. He fell in a heap and struggled to make sense of what was happening. *Was he being mugged?* He thought as he lay in a bloody mess. He raised his head slowly and saw two things before he was kicked in his face and blacked out. One: The two no-neck raincoats were wrestling Pierre and Gio out of the car. And Two: The last person in line at Koko's was being ushered in, which meant there were now no witnesses.

Chapter Ten: Wanted

Saturday – Day Three

Simone Petra awoke in her Forest Oak apartment promptly at quarter till seven, which was the time she would have awakened anyway if it hadn't been the weekend. It was a routine she had difficulty breaking. Even though it was a Saturday, she went through her typical morning schedule as well. She got out of bed and right into her pink slippers at the foot of her bed. Next, she went to the bathroom and started her bath water, adding a scented bubble bath to the water, which she liked scalding to rid the water of any foreign contaminants. Then, she went into the kitchen to fix herself a cappuccino, which she decided today would be hazelnut. While the bath water continued to run, she got out a cinnamon bagel and applied a thick layer of cream cheese. She took a bite, placed it on a plate, and went back to the bathroom to check on the bath water. It was at her desired depth and temperature, so she turned off the faucet. She went back into the kitchen, picked up the plate holding the bagel, and also her mug filled with the hazelnut cappuccino. She then returned to the bathroom, setting her bagel and mug on the windowsill beside the tub. She undressed and eased herself slowly into the deep, ivory tub.

A half hour later, Simone, with a towel wrapped around her hair, exited the bathroom with empty plate and mug. She wore a tight-fitting shirt over a pair of Capri pants, and was now ready to face the world. Since it was the weekend, she turned on the news to see what was going on in the world around her.

If it had been a weekday, she would have blow-dried her hair and found a conservative piece of clothing to wear to work. It was usually a Kay Julia skirt of moderate length; long enough to look professional, but short enough to show off a little leg. She was the only woman that worked at C & A Accounting that was not a secretary. C & A was the official accounting firm of the Council and its associates, which was how it got its game. She felt the need to work someplace she could keep her enemy in check. She had been able to get a variety of useful information for her fellow Pupils during her five years at her current position.

In fact, it was only four days ago she had discovered that one of the Novice Orderlies was, in fact, a traitor who was willing to turn over Teacher to the Council. When Griffin Blake, one of her own spies within the Council, told her about the conspiracy, she was not as surprised as she should have been. It didn't strike her as entirely implausible, only because she had, in fact, been doing the same thing for the past nine years when she finally made the decision to join a small faction of Pupils she had met at Institute.

As far as she knew, none of the Pupils she had met over the years had actually met Teacher. There were only a few individuals alive who had been graced with that honor. It was through his Novice Orderlies that his ideals were spread through the masses. Simone hadn't even seen a Novice Orderly in person.

Her first exposure had been from a fellow Pupil, Zachariah Moonstone. Zachariah, whom she called Zeke, or sometimes just Z, was in one of her math classes at Institute. He was a technology major, specializing in computer information. Zeke was a bear of a man, and looked intimidating to those who didn't know he was as soft in demeanor as he was large in body. He wore wire-rimmed classes, though he didn't really need them. He had once told her that the glasses were to make him look more intelligent.

Zeke sat behind her in the class and managed to confiscate a short verse she had been writing while note taking. She had figured it was a safe place to write the couplet, hidden away in her algebra notes, but somehow Zeke found her out. He had been dozing off and missed part of the notes, so he took hers to copy. Before she could protest, he had them in hand and was skimming over them for where his notes had ended during his brief nap. She feebly tried to take back the notes, without bringing any extra attention to their section of the large lecture hall, but to no avail. Then, his eyes got wide and she knew he had read the strange addition she had included. *Beauty beholds much truth, yet it remains in our youth.* She felt her face go flush and started to panic.

"Don't worry," Zeke whispered with a wink. "I won't tell anyone." He then placed the notebook on his desk, wrote something in it, and gave it back to her.

Simone took it and looked at what he wrote. It was an address. She glanced up at Zeke with a confused look. "What's this?"

"*Think* about it," was his reply. He gave her another wink and went back to taking notes as if nothing had happened.

She knew she wasn't really supposed to *think* about much of anything, so this perplexed her. Her own curiosity and understanding of what Zeke was suggesting took hold of her and she went to the address he had written on her paper. While there, she heard people recite poems, sing songs, and delve into philosophies she never knew existed. It was totally exhilarating. Her dormant mind was finally awakened, and she attended on a weekly basis, then almost daily, until even she was reading aloud her poems. Zeke spoke doctrine that he said was told to him by one of the Novice Orderlies. Debates were done regularly and freethinking was encouraged. Simone knew after her first meeting that being a Pupil was what she was meant to do with her life. For the first time, she was allowed to possess thoughts of her own, not those diluted ideas forced upon her by the Council.

The sound of the phone ringing interrupted her reverie. She picked up the special phone Zeke had given to her a few years after that initial meeting. It could not be traced or eavesdropped in any way. All Pupils in Forest Oak owned one, but the only two people who actually called her on it were Zeke and Griffin. This time it was Zeke. He skipped all formalities and got straight to business.

"Any word from our men?" he asked her.

"Not yet, Z. Pierre said they were going to Moon Haven yesterday to see if they could find any information on Guidry," Simone told him. "Haven't heard from them yet today, but it's still early. It may take them a few nights. I sent them the schematics Griffin sent me of the place to familiarize themselves with the grounds, but there could be things such as hidden rooms that aren't on it."

"So they've already made contact with your father?" Zeke asked. "I mean Manna."

"Z, he *is* my father," Simone replied. "I'm not ashamed of it. We just haven't talked as much as we should. It is what it is."

"And Manna's helping?"

"Yes, from what I've gathered from Gio and Pierre, he is on board," Simone answered. "It wasn't him I was worried about. I know my father better than I probably should, given our past. He's more like us than one would think. His thoughts are just as radical, but he's not interested in acting on them. That is where we differ."

"So you're more concerned about Guidry?"

"Guidry is sort of a loose cannon," Simone responded. "He only does the things he thinks up first. He is also very opinionated, which is why he likes the Teacher's ideals so much. I think he'll help out, but he'll be unpredictable."

"That is not a trait I like dealing with on a mission of this importance," Zeke retorted. "Are you sure we can trust him?"

"Oh, I'm sure we *cannot* trust what he says," Simone told him. "He used to tell me so many lies when I was younger. If he would have done a third of the things he told me he did, then everyone would know the name of A'ron Guidry. He'd be the most interesting person on the planet."

51

"Then why do we need him again?" Zeke asked skeptically.

"He's our possible link to one of the Novice Orderlies," she explained. "I have a source that says that he once rescued the father of one of the current Novice Orderlies. Guidry is a consummate liar, but there has to be slivers of truth within those lies. Nobody has the craft to create a lifetime of lies without placing in bits and pieces of truth, right?"

"You'd be surprised," Zeke shot back.

"I think Guidry will come clean to my father, though," Simone stated. "It would be a way to reconcile after what happened between them."

"What *did* happen between them?" Zeke asked her.

"It's what got Guidry put into Moon Haven to begin with," Simone started, but the television suddenly chimed on and caught her attention. "Could you hold on a moment?" She pulled the phone away from her ear to better hear what was being said by the newswoman on the television.

"*....escaped from Moon Haven sometime last night. The man was checked in under the name, Dominick Van Ranken. Authorities have since found that name to be a false identity. The Council was notified this morning of this particular case as the Moon Haven guest was visiting the manor because the man claimed to be in conjunction with a known terrorist organization. This terrorist cell is believed to be headed by the cold-blooded fugitive, Teacher. Though authorities are uncertain of the true identity of Mr. Van Ranken, they do have a photo, which was taken when the guest first was given clearance to visit Moon Haven. Here is that photo.*"

A photograph appeared on the screen. It showed a man with dreadlocks and skullcap. He also wore a bright orange shirt with something written on it. In what appeared to be black magic marker, it read *I Think, Therefore I Am...Persecuted*. The newswoman continued.

"*The man is wanted for questioning, and is considered to be extremely dangerous. The man is suspected to be traveling with two other males, who claimed to be Mr. Van Ranken's father and sibling. These two...*"

Simone pressed the mute button on the television, which still showed the photo of the man who claimed to be Dominick Van Ranken. This man was reported to have escaped Moon Haven last night and was wanted for questioning about his association with Teacher, who according to the newswoman was a known terrorist. The man on the screen looked like no man Simone had ever seen, save for the eyes. She knew those eyes. The passion was unmistakable. They belonged to Giovanni, and now he was wanted by the

Council. Simone pulled the phone back up to her ear.

"Z, turn on the news," she said to him.

"Why? What's wrong?" He asked her.

"Z, just turn on the news," she repeated.

"Oh, shit!" Zeke exclaimed.

Simone couldn't take her eyes off the picture on the screen. It was as if Gio was looking into her eyes, pleading for her help. "Either they found the information."

"Or they're in deep trouble," Zeke finished from the other end of the line.

Chapter Eleven: Meeting

Simone told Zeke to meet at her place in an hour, then called Griffin and told him the same. Then, she picked up the few stray pillows on the floor and cleaned up the few dishes that were left in the sink from dinner the night before. The rest of the hour was spent watching the news for anymore information on Gio, Pierre, and her father.

She felt a pang of guilt for getting her father into this, but she felt things would get done quicker that way, due to his once close friendship with Guidry. Finding Guidry was key, and her father had known the man better than anyone. Even though they hadn't talked for many years, which was eerily similar to her own estranged relationship with her father, she knew Guidry could be coaxed by his former best friend to help.

Her attention went back to the news anchor on the television. He was giving her no new information, so she changed it to another news channel. This had more of the same. She considered it to be good news that Gio's true identity could not be ascertained at this point, only that Dominick Van Ranken was a pseudonym. Several people from Moon Haven also came forward to describe the other two men that were with the wanted man. All three were said to be of interest to the Council. Several artists' renditions of the descriptions were shown, and there was no doubt the two other men were Pierre and her father.

Simone's eyes couldn't help but linger on the sketch of her father. It was an uncanny resemblance, with a few differences due to the disguise. Like the passion in Gio's eyes, which she first recognized, there was no denying the kindheartedness in the drawing of the man they were calling Klaus Van Ranken. It always amazed her how much the eyes of a person could give away about him.

Simone heard a knock at the door announcing the arrival of one of her visitors. She looked through the peephole and into the anxious eyes of Griffin. She opened allowing her friend to come into the apartment.

"Hi, Griffin," Simone greeted him as she closed the door. "Z should be here in a few minutes." She motioned toward the large, flat-screen television on the wall. "Have you been watching this?

"Yeah," Griffin replied. "I started watching once I got your call. Have you heard from them at all?"

"No, I haven't," she had an apprehensive look on her face, and she wasn't able to look him in the eye. "I could have put my own father in extreme danger." She still glanced at the floor in a daze.

"He agreed to help," Griffin said reassuringly. He put his hands on each of her shoulders trying to give her the strength he possessed. It was not the first time they had had physical contact with one another, but this was by far the most intimate. "Your father knew what he was agreeing to do, and he was still willing to help. He could have told Gio and Pierre to find Guidry on their own, and they probably would have been able to do it themselves, but, if what you say is correct, they need your father to accomplish the mission. For all we know, they found him and are searching for the Novice Orderly right now. It was probably inevitable that Gio, or whoever decided to enter Moon Haven as a patient, would become a person of interest to the Council."

"You're probably right," Simone said as the tension began to subside. "There's just so much at stake right now to have them bring added attention to themselves. I was hoping to avoid the Council's notice at all cost."

"You told me last night of their plan," he stated pulling his hands away from her shoulders. "It seemed the best way for them to get into Moon Haven, but it would bring this kind of attention to them whether they accomplished their mission or not. We'll only have to worry if they get themselves caught."

Simone nodded in agreement. There was another knock on the door and she went to let in Zeke. He was not alone. Vivienne Delacroix was with him. Her lithe form was hidden behind his more ample girth, and Simone didn't see her right away. It wasn't until she was fully in the room Simone noticed her presence.

Vivienne had green, almond-shaped eyes which seemed to draw all the attention to her face. This was, indeed, in her favor, as she had a prosthetic arm from her elbow down. The prosthetic, however, didn't appear as a normal arm. She could easily have made it appear as such, but she, instead, wanted it to exhibit the appearance of her true passion, robotics. She was, in fact, a robotics engineer, and had designed her own prosthetic. The arm was lost in an automobile accident, which also took her husband and young son. The accident also left her with a slight limp, which most people didn't seem to notice, because of her robotic arm, but even more often it was because of those eyes.

Simone could see that she had changed the pink stripe in her hair, to a more eccentric, neon green, which only intensified the dominance of her eyes.

"Vivienne," Simone said with a bit of shock. "Sorry, I wasn't expecting you."

"I was coming to meet Z to discuss an algorithm I came across at work, and he told me about what's been shown on the news," Vivienne replied. "I

55

hope I'm not intruding."

"No, not at all," Simone answered without showing the least bit that she was upset. Vivienne was not someone she was inclined to trust entirely, as she did Zeke and Griffin. "I'm glad you caught him before he left."

"All right," Zeke interrupted. "If you two are done exchanging pleasantries, can we get on with our little meeting here?"

Simone could see Griffin smirk, and she gave him a playful shove.

"What was that for?" he asked playfully. She just gave a little shrug and walked passed him and into the living room.

They kept the television on, but turned the volume low enough for them to hear themselves over it. They wanted to be sure they were able to catch any updates.

Zeke was the first to speak, as usual. "Simone, have you heard from Gio or Pierre since we last talked on the phone?"

"No, the last time I heard from them was yesterday when I sent them the information on Moon Haven through the secure line," was her reply. "That was early yesterday morning."

"How long before the Council pieces things together and can identify them?" Zeke asked Griffin, since Griffin worked most closely with the Council.

"It'll take a few days, I'm sure," Griffin answered confidently. "They'll promise the public that they'll know today, but it's not practical. They need more time to process the pictures through their database. Considering that Gio's the only one they have a true photo of, it'll take even longer."

"That's good news, indeed," Zeke said enthusiastically. "The best we've heard all day."

"So, what do we do next?" Vivienne asked, as if she had been part of it from the beginning.

"We'll have to have some sort of backup plan, in case Gio and the others get caught, or we don't hear from them," Griffin stated.

They all seemed to be looking at Simone for an opinion, since she had been in charge of the mission that possibly went awry.

"We can either search for Guidry ourselves, or the Novice Orderly at Holly Pines," she mused. "It will be more difficult without my father's help, since he was our link to both, but we could attempt it."

"Which would be easier to find on our own?" Zeke asked urgently.

"Maybe we can split up," Griffin suggested. "Two of us can search for one and two seek out the other."

"I think we should all focus on one," Vivienne chimed in. "We all have our talents that could help either task. If we split that up, we might lose some of that edge."

"Good point," Zeke said from beside her. He slunk back on the couch, visibly perplexed. "What do you suggest?"

Again, everyone stared at Simone for advice. She never really relished the idea of being the center of attention. When reading her poetry, she shied away from the spotlight and would blush when the inevitable applause would erupt after her beautiful verse was read. Being a leader, however, came naturally to her, and she never backed away from that kind of attention.

Before she could reply, another knock interrupted her. She gave a bewildered look as she got up to answer the door. She looked through her peephole. It was Nigel Harris, the tenant from across the hall.

"It's the guy from across the hall," she whispered to the group of Pupils.

"What would he want?" Griffin asked, visibly confused.

"I don't know," Simone replied.

The neighbor knocked again, but this time he spoke.

"I'm sorry to bother you," he said politely, "but do you still have that e-mag I let you borrow last week. I believe it was the *Forest Frontier*."

With the new e-mag format, individuals were able to share their subscription for a small fee. All one had to do was bring the two tablets into contact with one another. Once this happened, however, the original subscriber was not able to read the e-mag until the tablets came into contact once again. Nigel Harris was requesting for her to do just that.

Simone gave a sigh of relief. She hadn't realized how on edge she was.

"Yes, I do Mr. Harris," she said as she went into the kitchen where she had left her tablet. She picked it up, headed to the door, and opened it.

"Here, you are," she started, but was interrupted by five men busting

57

through the door. They each had a gun up and one was pointed at her.

"Simone Petra, you are under arrest for suspicion of conspiring against the Council," said the man holding the gun. "Please, come quietly or we'll be required to use force."

Simone instinctively put her hands up, and turned to look at her friends. Her first suspicion was that Vivienne had turned them in, but as she turned, she could see all three of her friends being forced to the ground at gunpoint. She turned back to the gun aimed at her and went down to the floor to join her friends. Another man came over and handcuffed her hands behind her and gagged her mouth with a wash cloth that tasted like it had been soaking in sour milk.

She could see Nigel Harris standing timidly behind the man with the gun pointed at her. His face was white and he was visibly shaken by the presence of the men with guns.

"Ah man," said the man with the gun. He had a look of disappointment on his face. "I was told you were a smart lady. I was hoping we were going to get to use some force."

"You still might get the chance, Mac," said a voice from the hall. Another man came into the room. He came over to Simone and knelt beside her. "We're going to have to see what these *traitors* know."

Simone turned to see the man kneeling beside her. President Stuckey was the figurehead of the Council. The man kneeling beside her held the true power. It was the head of the Council's Elliptical Ward, the Council Secretary, Jack Kruger.

Chapter Twelve: Interrogation 1

Manna awoke in the dark. He could feel the burlap bag over his head, which was the cause of the darkness that consumed him. He tried to move, but his hands were bound to the arms of the chair in which he sat, and his legs were bound to either leg of the same chair. Nothing else was ascertainable. Then, he heard a rustle behind him and the burlap bag was quickly removed. This did little to let him see his surroundings, as the room was sparsely lit. Manna could see boarded up windows, and one plank was loose, giving off the little light in the room. He frantically looked around for any semblance of recognition, but nothing else stood out. The person who had removed the burlap bag was visible briefly before stepping into the shadows. His captor was one of the no-necks from the hotel, so Manna deduced that Bowler Hat was within the shadows somewhere watching as well. A cane knocked on the floorboards to prove Manna's deduction.

"Who are you?" Manna asked into the shadows with a calmness that belied his true nervousness. "What do you want with me?" He then remembered Gio and Pierre. "Where are my friends?"

"You are filled with questions," said a cool, silky voice from the shadows. It was too authoritative not to be Bowler Hat. "Don't you know that questioning is no longer allowed? The Council has prohibited that very aspect of your life. Don't you know the trouble you can get into for those types of *questions*?"

"It looks like I'm already in a great deal of trouble," Manna said with a bit of a smirk. "I doubt my questioning can make it any worse."

"Looks like we got a wise guy on our hands, boys," the smooth voice replied. A few chuckles followed. "You are correct to believe you are in great peril. I cannot deny you of this. I doubt, however, that you know how dire your situation truly is."

"Why don't you tell me how *dire* it is then?" Manna retorted. He was not in the mood to be bullied by these men he couldn't even look in the eye. "Better yet, why don't you come out from behind your own shadow and tell me to my face how grim my situation actually is?"

"I haven't shown you my face, because I'm not sure whether or not I'm going to kill you just yet," the man replied in the same cool manner. "You most definitely *don't* want me to tell you anything to your face, because it will be the last thing you will see on this earth."

Manna stirred a little, losing a bit of his bravado, but quickly recovered.

"What do you want from me then?" he asked into the shadows. He squinted his eyes, trying to pierce through the shadows for a better glimpse of the man. He had already seen the man's face, though from a distance and partially hidden.

"I ask the questions," the man said forcefully, losing some of the smoothness in his voice. "What is your interest in A'ron Guidry?"

Manna decided to fake ignorance.

"I don't know anyone by that name," he lied, but the truth was obvious in the tremble in his voice.

"I suggest you look down at the back of your hand before you give me anymore lies," the voice stated matter-of-factly. "I will now activate a nerve transponder. The blinking that you see is one of many transmitters I had placed inside your body. The transmitters are connected to different locations along your body's one main nerve. With the push of a button, I can change your own feeble definition of pain. Any time I think you are lying to me, I will test your pain tolerance, that threshold you may bear, yet not realize its true minimal capacity. If you cooperate and answer my questions truthfully, I can also push another button to disintegrate these transmitters. So, let's try that first question again. What is your interest in A'ron Guidry?"

Manna looked at his hand. It was, in fact, giving off a dull blue light every couple of seconds. He noticed another on his leg. He could imagine many more like these on his back, neck, and possibly even his brain.

"I'm still waiting," the voice was growing impatient. "We already know you were looking for him. One of your men performed a search for him on one of the computers at Moon Haven. Why is Guidry of interest to you?"

Manna sat dejectedly in the chair; his head slack and shoulders drooped. He didn't want to disclose any information about the Council's traitor and searching for Teacher, but he could talk about Guidry without giving away this information, he'd hope.

"We thought Guidry would be able to give us information on the whereabouts of a specific person," Manna finally confided.

"Who is this person of significance?" the man asked with a curious tone in his voice.

"I am not sure, exactly," Manna replied.

"That is most definitely a lie," the man said with a hint of annoyance.

"No, no, it's not," Manna said in a panic. "The two men I was with were looking for this person. They thought Guidry could help because he had been a close friend of mine in the past."

"So, you were an acquaintance of Guidry in years past?" the melodious voice seemed to consider this. "Interesting. Were you aware that Guidry had escaped Moon Haven?"

This news struck Manna as odd. "Then why hadn't I heard of it on the news? If he had truly escaped, he would be wanted by the Council like all the others they show."

"Guidry was a liar by trade," the voice disclosed. "He was very charismatic and pragmatic, therefore grew friendly with many of the other patients, or inmates as I should say. One patient, however, he did not get along with in the least. His name was Jermain Locklear. The two were in many tussles, and needed to be separated constantly. One night, however, Jermain snuck into Guidry's room and stabbed him to death. Moon Haven did not want this news to leak out, so it never got out to the masses."

"I thought you said he escaped," Manna was visibly hit hard by this news. Though he hadn't been in contact with Manna in years, he still had a past with the man.

"He did," the voice stated with pleasure. "He escaped the deception that Moon Haven was trying to get him to believe. He escaped the world that didn't believe the truths he so passionately tried to convey. You see, the world didn't deserve such a magnanimous man; a man such as Guidry, because it so callously shunned him for his desire to live life on the edge."

What is this nut talking about? Manna thought. This conversation had taken a rather odd turn, and Manna felt even more confused than when it had started.

"What?" Manna voiced his own confusion, because he didn't exactly know what else to say to the strange ramblings of the man in shadows. If this man was the brains of the operation, he'd hate to see the I.Q.'s of the two no-necks.

"What is your true…moniker?" The man slowly asked, taking a pause with the last word of the question. "We know you're not really Klaus Van Ranken. We saw as much from the news. And remember the nerve transponder, so don't attempt to purloin me of the trust that has grown on me."

Manna decided it best to tell the truth.

"My name is Mike Manna."

There was a hushed silence that seemed to grow more unpleasant by the minute. The man in the Bowler Hat stepped out of the shadows holding a remote transmitter in his hand, and the two no-necks behind him on either side.

Manna gasped.

"Interesting," the man replied just before he pushed the button on the transmitter. Manna let out a blood-curdling scream.

Chapter Thirteen: Interrogation 2

Simone awoke in a dimly lit room. It was small, approximately eight feet in length and ten in width. A Formica table took up most of the space in the room, with two metal chairs on either side of it. Simone sat in the one facing the door, and she had dozed off waiting for the questioning to begin. Simone assumed Zeke, Vivienne, and Griffin were in similar rooms. The Council was letting them contemplate the seriousness of their predicament, in order to work on their psyche. This was the very reason Simone decided to let herself doze off, to show the Council her true resolve. She wasn't going to let Kruger and the Council win in the battle of wits. If she was going to let the Council succeed in conquering her logically, she might as well spit on the Teacher's doctrine and forsake the cause altogether. She would never let that happen.

On the wall to her left was a mirror, which she knew without a doubt was a two-way mirror. Kruger was, most likely, watching her right now to see if she would squirm. The satisfaction she felt in knowing he could not break her was almost worth being in her current situation. She always knew the risks she had been taking when she chose a life dedicated to Teacher.

The door opened with a slow, meticulous creep and two men stepped in to join her. The last to enter quickly shut the door once they were both inside. Simone gave each man a look over and a smirk. They both wore expensive suits, one gray, one blue, with ties that matched each respective suit. She also noticed they both wore the same type of black shoes made of Italian leather. Simone glanced at the mirror and gave another smirk with a raise of her eyebrows, as if to say, *That's the best you've got?* The man in gray took a seat across from Simone while the man in blue continued to stand; he held a manila envelope under his arm. Simone leaned toward the man in gray and strained her mind to not lose focus.

"There's no purpose in you being here, Mr. Gray, I'm not telling you anything," Simone told the man sitting in front of her. She leaned back in her seat to show how comfortable and confident she was. "You're wasting your time."

"Confident are we?" said Gray Suit. "Your friends showed the same confidence, but they soon caved. But, let's not get ahead of ourselves."

Simone flinched her eyes for the briefest of moments, but regained her composure. They were surely lying to get her to break.

"It's sad really," Gray Suit continued. "A truly loyal friend is hard to find these days. You've got to be more careful to whom you divulge your secrets. Going against the Council fills so many people with a sense of guilt, they turn in their friends, and even themselves. It's simply best not to get involved in something that goes against the Council, especially when Teacher is involved."

"Teacher allows us to think for ourselves," Simone said back. She figured there was no reason to deny her affiliation with Teacher and his Pupils. They already knew the basics. She did not, however, wish to divulge the fact she knew there was a traitor in Teacher's inner circle. If they knew that she knew about the traitor, it might speed things up on the Council's end.

"Yes, you are permitted to think for yourself when you dedicate your life to his Teachings," Gray Suit replied. "You live a life with no boundaries, no rules, no sense of moral responsibility. Do as you please; what's best for you and no one else. Does that sound about right?"

"That's not how it is at all," Simone replied defiantly. "It's pointless trying to explain it to someone who's not willing to use his mind how it's meant to be used."

"And how *is* it supposed to be used?" Gray Suit asked amusingly.

"It's supposed to be used to think, to create," Simone replied confidently. "It also has the ability to question, debate, and formulate ideas, opinions, and answers. But, it's most powerful asset is the capacity to reason. It can logically put itself into any situation, and, if put to good use, can get itself out."

Blue Suit, who had been leaning against the table listening to the exchange, gave a short snort.

"And how do you plan on getting yourself out of this situation?" Blue Suit asked her.

"Don't underestimate my ability to reason," Simone replied. Then she looked straight into the mirror and said, "And don't underestimate Teacher's ability either."

"We surely won't do that," Gray Suit replied.

"Why am I being held here?" Simone asked. "You obviously want to ask me more than how the brain is used."

"Very perceptive," Blue Suit observed.

"What do you know of the young man who escaped Moon Haven last night?" Gray Suit asked.

"I know as much as what was on the news this morning before your people took me away," Simone replied.

"For some reason, that's a little hard to believe," Gray Suit retorted.

"Well, you better believe it 'cause it's the truth," Simone told him.

"There were three other Pupils meeting at *your* apartment," Blue Suit explained. "It would seem you are a little more important than you're letting us to believe."

Simone glanced at Blue Suit and could see his piercing gray eyes. Two things seemed ironic to her at that moment. The first was that Blue Suit had gray eyes and Gray Suit had blue. The second was that for a group which seemed so against reason and logic, they seemed to use it quite well.

"We switch the meeting place each week," she lied.

"Like my friend said, that's a little hard to believe," Blue Suit replied, and he placed an envelope down in front of her.

Simone glanced at the two men and back toward the envelope. They both stared at her expecting her to open it with curiosity. In fact, she was very curious. What could be inside the envelope? Phone or Email records? Pictures of her attending Pupil meetings? Or worse, pictures of her friends' dead bodies?

"We'll let you look at it in private," Gray Suit said as he stood, methodically pushed the chair in with a wink at her, and exited the room with Blue Suit.

Simone glanced toward the mirror. She could still feel Kruger's eyes watching her, or whoever was on the other side. She had little doubt that it had to be Kruger himself.

She picked up the envelope, unclasped the metal prongs, and opened it. Inside were two photos. She slid them out and brought them to her face for a better look. She gasped audibly and glanced back toward the two-way mirror. She could almost see Kruger's smiling face on the other side.

Chapter Fourteen: Re-Introductions

Manna's scream echoed in the nearly empty room, but it was only brief. He could feel a gentle vibration on the underside of his arm, and nothing else. No painful shock, no nerve-endings firing chaotically. He looked down at the blinking lights to find they were no longer blinking. The transponders must have been disintegrated as promised, for giving the truth. Manna gave a deep sigh of relief and looked quizzically at the man who had, seconds earlier, emerged from the darkness. Something about his demeanor looked familiar; like someone from his past. The way Bowler Hat handled himself, in the mannerisms of how he was standing, slightly putting more weight on his left foot, which seemed peculiar due to the fact he held the cane in his right hand, making it appear as if the cane was simply for show; it reminded him of the very man he was just told was dead. Only a man with a unique mental capacity to excessively lie would create such an elaborate hoax as making one believe a walking cane is needed to walk, when no such thing was necessary.

"You've got to be kidding me," Manna said with a small amount of uncertainty. "Guidry, is that you?"

"Weren't you able to ascertain my previous vocalities?" the man replied. He gave a sharp flick of his left wrist, the opposite of the hand holding the cane, and seemed to be studying the cuff of his shirt, or perhaps his fingernails, as he spoke, as if the nonchalance of the action were to make the fact that Manna was still tied to a chair seem perfectly normal. "I notified you of the premature demise of one, A'ron Guidry." As he said this last statement, he gave a wry smile, making his point quite clear. "My name is Eric Matheson. I was the innocent man across the hall the night Jermain Locklear snuck in and killed A'ron Guidry." He, again, gave Manna that same wry smile.

"Are you saying, what I think you're saying?" Manna asked the man calling himself Matheson. And if Manna was deducing things properly, this too was a lie.

Matheson went back to studying his shirt cuff, this time Manna was certain it was the cuff. "I humbly apologize for my lack of telepathic prowess; I am incapable of discerning the thought processes of another human being without a certain degree of doubt in its accuracy."

"If I am understanding you correctly, I believe you are saying that Eric Matheson, the true Eric Matheson, was killed in A'ron Guidry's room as he was posing as Guidry, and you, whom I believe is Guidry, was in Matheson's room posing as him. But how would Locklear, the guards, and the rest of the Moon Haven staff possibly believe the man killed was Guidry? And how did you really get out of Moon Haven?"

"You always were able to interpret the truth from my lies," Guidry replied, ending the charade. His voice dropped an octave, the smoothness was still there, but it lacked the persuasiveness which was there only seconds earlier, and with a dexterous toss the cane was shifted to his left hand and the lean switched slightly to his right. He bowed his head and the Bowler hat methodically fell onto the handle of the cane with deft precision.

"Holy Christ," Manna exclaimed. "It is you."

"A'ron Guidry, in the flesh." He said as he finished his theatrics with a slight bow. He tossed the hat with his cane and caught it on his head as he stood and leaned on the cane again, in one fluid motion. For a man of his size, he was very nimble. "It's been many a year, dear friend."

"It has been a long time," Manna replied. "But do you think you could untie me, now? Or does the term *friend* mean something else these days?"

"Where are my manners?" Guidry asked aloud shamefully. He skillfully produced a knife, which seemed to come from the sleeve of his shirt. He cut the binds that held Manna in place.

Manna remained seated and turned his head to the side; he gave a soft groan when it cracked. The two no-necks turned and entered the shadows, seemingly to an unseen exit. Guidry stayed and his eyes seemed to sparkle with the common mischievous nature Manna knew all too well. He reached for Manna's hand to help him out of the chair, and the sparkle faded briefly, as if to ask for forgiveness for past indiscretions. Manna hadn't seen this man in years, and hadn't given much thought to ever seeing this former friend again. He decided to take the hand, since he recently had found out, at least one lie had been the truth. This act brought a smile to Guidry's face, and he pulled Manna up effortlessly.

"Thank you," Guidry told his friend. "And my deepest apologies for knocking you unconscious. If I had known it was you, I would have done no such thing."

"Heck, if it was two days ago and I had known it was you," Manna replied, "I would have been the one kicking you, most likely." He smiled and could feel the tenderness on the left side of his face where, no doubt, a bruise had started. Manna also noticed a dried up bloodstain on the front of his shirt.

"With that cleared out of the way," Guidry started as he headed in the direction the no-necks exited. "Why don't you come upstairs and explain why you were in Moon Haven searching for me; using some false identity, no less. A false identity that even sounded like a false identity, by the way." he turned to give Manna a smirk and continued in the direction of the stairs.

Manna complied and began to follow Guidry up a steep set of stone stairs. Concrete walls adorned either side of the steep stairwell. They were colored a drab gray, which bemused Manna. The eccentric nature which Manna knew Guidry to possess was in stark contrast to the dullness in which he was now gazing upon. He would have expected marble, some precious metal, or even quartz, not gray concrete.

He ascended the stairs into a long hallway. Guidry took a right, and then an immediate left after only about five quick steps. Manna followed and entered a room about the size of his school's mid-size classrooms. Instead of the typical desk, he saw a collection of circular tables. He quickly estimated about ten of them, a dozen at most. Upon each table sat four computers with a single person manning each one, not a single computer was empty. The gender and ages varied, as Manna could clearly see a middle-aged woman sitting next to a boy no older than sixteen or seventeen.

"What is this place?" Manna finally asked, trying to take it all in with one slow sweep of his head. He looked at Guidry for an answer.

"This is how we ascertained you were inquiring about my whereabouts," Guidry replied. "We have a cadre of people hacking into a plethora of sites and companies, with the direct task of discovering who is searching for the people in our little clan. You see, we are fugitives, a collection of renegades, and we need to be aware of anyone who is looking to detect our location. Our pack sticks together, like Robin Hood and his merry men."

Manna was shocked at how proudly Guidry spoke of this, as if it was some sort of accomplishment. Something had changed in Guidry, it seemed. Guidry must have noticed his shocked expression.

"Don't look so condescending. Here, we all live life in a constant state of trepidation. We need specific knowledge of our enemy's intentions as it pertains to us, or we may as well submit to the bludgeoning of the Council's everlasting whim."

Manna couldn't question the passion Guidry possessed. It had always been his friend's most endearing quality. The bitterness of Guidry's experience seemed to add a callousness to him that was definitely palpable. "You've got a tap on those searching for each person in this room?"

"Not only each of the people you see in this very room, but there are others as well," Guidry responded. "On our premises, we have nearly seventy, who like me, have fled the persecution we have all been forced to adhere to the Council's every desire. We also have others watching news programs across the Americas, listening for anything about one of our members. We are a very resourceful bunch."

"I'm guessing, then, that you were able to find Gio's search for your file on Moon Haven's database," Manna was starting to see the intelligence behind the paranoia. "Then, how were you able to find us at the hotel? We didn't do any kind of searching for anyone."

"We zoned in on the frequency you used when communicating with your partner at Moon Haven," was Guidry's reply.

That made sense, Manna thought.

"Our technology is quite sophisticated," Guidry said smugly. "Not to mention that the people manning that sophistication are quite good at what they do."

"It seems they are," Manna replied with a wry smile. "With all that skill, do you think they could locate my ill-fated partners you were just speaking about?"

"Again, how uncharacteristically callous of me. They are in the other room, recovering from their unfortunate injuries. Follow me."

Guidry led the way out of the room, down the hall, and only two doors down to a small alcove. Manna saw Gio and Pierre in opposite chairs from each other. Gio had an icepack covering his swollen eye and Pierre had a bloody rag up to his lip. Neither man looked pleased to be there. Before any of the men had a chance to speak, one of the two no-necks entered the room. He looked at Guidry, as if asking permission to speak aloud a message he was asked to relay to him.

"Yes, Vinnie?" Guidry asked giving the man the floor.

"Jamison found something on the news, boss," Vinnie answered. "In fact, it's being broadcast all over the place. You'll want to have a look." He nodded toward Manna, Gio, and Pierre. "They'll want to come take a look as well."

The men exited the tiny alcove and turned left. They passed the stone stairway and entered the first room on the left. Instead of computer screens staring back at him, Manna now saw flat-screen televisions and a person watching each one. Each television was turned to a different channel, which was displayed in large, yellow numbers in the top left hand corner of each screen. Each viewer of the television had on a pair of large headphones in order to listen to each broadcast in private. Several of the televisions, though broadcasting different channels, seemed to be showing the same news story. Manna could tell because the same picture was shown over the right shoulder of the news broadcaster. The only telling difference was that each picture had a different news anchor. Someone turned on the sound of the largest television in the room, the one in the middle of the room, and everyone seemed to gravitate toward it.

The news anchor was explaining about the capture of a group of four Pupils who had been trying to spread the Teacher's philosophy to others. It was a small terrorist plot, but it had been diverted because of the dutiful conduct of Council Secretary Kruger. The smaller pictures behind the anchor's shoulder ballooned on the screen, as the anchor disappeared from sight. Manna gasped as he recognized the picture on the far right. It was his daughter, Simone. She was now in the Council's custody. A prisoner, and terrorist, as a follower of Teacher. Manna knew, as anyone else in the Americas did, what the punishment was for such a crime. His eyes locked with Guidry's.

"I need to go get her out of there," Manna said as he turned toward the exit.

"Wait, Mike," Guidry replied, sounding like the friend he once knew. Manna turned back to look at his friend again. This time he saw his friend of old, and not the liar and faker he thought about for all those years. "You can't just go up to the Council's door and ask for her back. Don't forget, you're a fugitive too."

Manna knew Guidry was right, but now was not the time for thinking logically; it was time for immediate action. His daughter was in the Council's custody and needed his help. He remembered her needing him at night when she thought some hidden boogeyman was out to get her. As she got older she needed him less and less. Now, she needed him again.

"Well, I can't just sit here and do nothing," Manna replied back.

"I didn't say that," Guidry said. "I might know a way to break her out."

"How?" Manna asked skeptically.

"Just remember, I was once in her same predicament," Guidry tried to convince him. "Through deft observation, I was able to pick up on a few secrets, and I was also able to befriend one of their guards. Let me help get your daughter back."

"Okay, then let's go save my daughter," Manna told him.

Chapter Fifteen: Dis-Membering

Simone Petra sat in her jail cell contemplating how the photographs Kruger showed to her made the situation with Teacher even worse. Not only was there a Novice Orderly about to betray Teacher's trust, but someone she thought *she* could trust was also implicated in one of the two images forever etched in her memory. One photo had shown a picture of someone she had never seen before. The person was accepting a briefcase, which she assumed was filled with money, from Kruger himself. This stranger, she assumed, was the Novice Orderly she had sent Gio, Pierre, and her father to seek out. The second photograph showed the same stranger, along with Kruger, but also another person. One she knew quite well. The three individuals were forever locked together in that one jovial pose, as though they had all teamed up to take over the world. It pained her to see that image again. Though the photograph was no longer in her possession, it was still scorched into her retinas, as the first image gazed upon after staring at the sun a little too long. A sound interrupted her thoughts and she turned toward the door opening into her cell.

The Council Secretary entered along with another man, who seemed to be a guard of some sort. Without a word, the guard seized her and took her out of the room. The guard led her down a long corridor to another room. In this room was another man, this one donning a surgeon's mask, hiding any identifying facial traits she would use to know if she had seen him prior to this meeting. A chair sat in the middle of the room, a metal table on wheels beside it. It was of the type used to hold utensils surgeons would use in the hospital. Kruger smiled maliciously and introduced the man accompanying him, and the guard strapped Simone to the chair.

"Let me introduce you to Dr. Cletus Sanford," Kruger told her. "He is the Council's foremost expert on brain activity, more specifically memory. I will let him explain the process to you. I'm sure you will enjoy its purpose, since you do love using your brain to do so much outside-the-box-thinking."

"The brain's mental capacity to remember things is somewhat like a bank vault," he began. "The memory is stored behind the combination lock and needs the right combination in order to open up the locked up memory. Some memory combinations are so overused, that the brain's ability to quickly ascertain the correct combination can be done at incredible speeds. Quick synapses are at the ready to retrieve these locked permutations because of the many times spent thinking of these memories, and the arrangement is ingrained into those nerve fibers making the vaults, in a sense, no longer locked. Other memories are harder to retrieve, as you might expect.

"In either instance, the memory is perceived in the mind's eye, in a matter of microseconds, at times. Other times, it may be longer. Either way, the memory is experienced, sometimes even relived in some individuals. Those with photographic memories can remember esoteric details about the said event, as the vault proves to strongly contain the exact experience of the memory. You may remember every word of a conversation, for example, or what every individual wore to your third birthday party.

"For some people, the memory seems faded or changed in some way. It can be as if someone has *mis-remembered* the event over the years, adding details that didn't exist to make the memory more pleasant, or outstanding."

As he was telling her this, the doctor was hooking up medical equipment, with the help of Kruger, who seemed to also know what he was doing. It seemed this was not the first time they had attempted this procedure. After the equipment was all hooked up, the doctor began to take out of a bag the utensils needed for the particular procedure they were planning. Simone watched with wide eyes, and her body shook with each new instrument that was taken out of the medical bag.

Kruger interrupted Dr. Sanford's explanation, "Aren't you just so fascinated by the brain's ability to not only remember, but also its capability to create new truths through lying to its owner?" He smiled at Simone's refusal to answer. "Ah, the ever-present willingness to hold one's tongue in the face of imminent danger. How noble of you." He turned to Dr. Sanford. "She now knows *mis-remembering*, now explain to her what *dis-membering is.*"

The doctor noticed her squirm as Kruger said *dis-member*. "Have no fear, my dear patient. *Dis-membering* is not what you think. We will not be cutting off any of your lovely body parts." He rubbed a gloved hand on her lower left leg, exposed by the Capris. "Instead, this kind of *dis-memberment* deals with my area of expertise, the brain.

"Like I told you, some people change the facts of their memories, sometimes on purpose, like to make the memory more bearable to deal with, or others times it gets so fractured over time the person doesn't know it is changed. The person may start to believe in the changed memory, because the true memory has been forgotten. That is, in a sense, what I am going to do. I will pinpoint the particular memory I want forgotten, and manipulate it so that you will not know what the true memory is. You will not remember what is real, and what is not about that one particular memory."

"Think of it like this," Kruger interrupted again. "In your true memory, you are wearing a pink dress. You know it is pink, and even still have it hanging in your closet. After we manipulate it, however, the dress is yellow. Then, you think about it again, and it is red, then blue. You see, the memory is constantly changing. The more you think about it to try and get it right, the more the memory changes. It changes so many times, you don't know which is real and which is a dream, and paranoia starts to set in. All the other memories, you start to doubt as well. That is the beauty of *dis-memberment*. It is psychological warfare at its best."

"After a day of it," Dr. Sanford chimed in, "you may be asking us to dismember your body parts, and end the suffering." He smirked as he took a needle from the table. This won't hurt a bit. She felt the sting as he inserted it into her right temple and unloaded the yellowish liquid it contained.

Dr. Sanford took out a laptop, and Simone could see an image of her brain. "Now, let's go searching for that memory," the doctor stated, mostly to himself. He held up a picture of an apple, and Simone watched as a part of her brain turned a bright green. Dr. Sanford zoomed into that portion of her brain. He showed another picture of a triangle. Again, a small portion turned green, and the doctor zoomed in. After six more pictures, the doctor brought out a manila envelope. It looked similar to the one Kruger had given her.

Sure enough, the contents inside were the same pictures Kruger had shown her. The ones she had tried to erase from her memory after viewing. Now, she tried to hang onto the memory. She tried to ignore all other thoughts, but that, if what Dr. Sanford said was true, didn't matter. It was going to be replaced with another, in fact many others.

"I have pinpointed the vault, and combination," Dr. Sanford told Kruger.

"Good. Now, do the rest," Kruger told him. "We don't have much time." He put his mouth by Simone's head so he could whisper into her ear. "Do you, *now*, see the power of the human mind? Not even it can be trusted."

Tears started to stream out of Simone's eyes as she struggled to keep the memory from being taken. She saw Kruger exit the room in a ripple effect, and could hear him laugh down the hall as it echoed back. She knew that laugh was something she wouldn't ever forget.

Chapter Sixteen: Rescue Attempt

Manna sat in the back of a semi-truck's cab with Guidry. Gio, Pierre, and about a dozen other of Guidry's crew, including the two no necks, were in the trailer. They were on route to the Council's de-facto prison, where they kept all suspected traitors before being tried. This was the place Simone should be kept overnight, if Guidry was correct in his assumptions. It was, at least, where Guidry had been taken when he was first accused and interrogated. He had told Manna that he had spent a full week there before being moved to Moon Haven. It was a good a place as any to start their search at least.

Guidry had called the guard he had befriended during his stay. The call was made from an encrypted phone so it couldn't be traced. Gio had even given them a small piece to put on the phone to scramble any bugs either phone may have had from someone trying to listen in on their conversation. Gio had explained that it even replicated a made up conversation in order to not draw attention to the call. It also used a sophisticated voice recognizing system to make the call more authentic by duplicating the voice of the caller on the other end of the line in mere seconds upon hearing the person answer the phone.

Manna overheard Guidry say the name Polchinski several times during the call, so he assumed that was the man's name. The guard did not know for certain if Simone was currently there, but he was trying to get that information to them as soon as he could. He also was making an attempt to pinpoint her location if she was still on the grounds. That was a full three hours ago. Manna was constantly on edge each time Guidry's phone rang. Due to the extent of the materials needed to pull off the plan and the number of people involved, it seemed to go off every ten minutes. Those calls produced confirmations of the men taking part in the mission and acquiring the semi-truck they were currently in, as well as the weapons they needed to force their way in and out if needed.

However, the plan, if implemented properly, wouldn't need the weapons. Manna was no stranger to guns, as most younger men were. Although he didn't go into battle, it had been a requirement of all men before the war with Asia to train for combat. The war had lasted five years and his training hadn't been complete before it had all ended. Though now, he was still not comfortable having to use one again. The targets he had been shooting at during his training were not flesh and blood, but mere cardboard cutouts or paper targets. He wasn't even sure he had it in him to pull the trigger when faced with the decision to use it, though every time he saw his daughter's innocent smile, he could think of nothing he wouldn't do to protect her.

Manna could feel Guidry's eyes on him and looked his way.

"We'll get her back, my friend," Guidry tried his best to reassure him, though his eyes belied his outer confidence. "Getting out is going to be a little harder than sneaking in."

"And you think getting in is going to be easy?" Manna replied.

"I didn't articulate as much, I simply alleged getting out will be harder," Guidry retorted. "We must have reliance on my inside man, my saboteur, being where he says he's going to be."

"And you trust this man?" Manna said doubtfully. "I mean, he still remembers you?"

"You doubt my ability to stay in one's mind?" Guidry said with a smirk. "Don't worry. My man says the Council is expecting a delivery. We'll use that to get us in the building. As long as no one can ascertain that we are not who we say we are, there should not be a problem. Trust me."

"I was afraid you were going to say that," Manna said with a smile.

The phone rang again and Guidry looked at the number projected on the phone's tiny screen. Manna had finally stopped anticipating the call, as the tension was unbearable to his psyche, knowing that each passing minute meant more possible pain and torture for Simone.

"Tell me good news, Polchinski," Guidry said as he answered the phone. At the mention of the caller's name, Manna directed his full attention to Guidry. Guidry nodded. "That's astounding information. Our estimated arrival is thirty minutes. Make sure you are at the predetermined rendezvous. See you soon."

"Polchinski says the captives are definitely still there," Guidry said with a smile.

Manna gave a quick sigh of relief. At least they were headed in the right direction.

"It gets better," Guidry said pointing the phone at Manna. "He also knows the whereabouts of one Simone Petra and her friends."

*****

Simone awoke with an intense pressure from her forehead to her temples. A bandage was wrapped around her head; doing its best to soak the blood created from the incision. She could feel the wetness which proved the blood was still flowing. She could remember that Kruger had taken her from her home and brought her here, but the rest was a complete haze.

A blurry image formed in her mind's eye, but flickered out before she

75

could establish what it was. The searing pain she felt as she awoke waxed and waned as she figured out her location hadn't changed. She was still in the room with the chair and metal table.

She realized she was no longer strapped to the chair, but the pain refused to ebb in order to raise her upper body sufficiently enough to stand. Even the lighting in the room seemed to bring hot flashes of pain. As her pain threshold continued to reach its maximum limit, she felt uncontrollable tears begin to fall. She closed her eyes and let the tears plaster her face with their salty residue.

*****

Manna could see their destination as they made the turn that lead up to the Elliptical Ward. The building was a bit foreboding in the dark. He expected to see a spark of lightning as they made their approach, in order to add to the ominous feeling he felt in the pit of his stomach. Though they had meticulously planned their rescue attempt, in the short time they had to do it, he still felt like something was about to go wrong. Considering nothing had gone right since he left school Thursday, he felt justified in feeling so pessimistic.

"Stick to the plan and we'll be out of there before you can say *Teacher*," Guidry said with a wink. He pointed his cane at Manna. "And don't go all hero on us. Simone needs you to be smart, not heroic."

"Simone needs me to do whatever the hell I need to take her back from these monsters," Manna replied.

"Just stick to the plan, and we'll get her back," Guidry responded. As they approached the gate, Guidry pointed with his cane again. "It's show-time," Guidry said as he ducked down low behind a pile of blankets and old rags. Manna did the same.

The driver brought the semi to a halt in front of the Council gate. Manna heard the guard ask a question, but the words were too muffled to hear the extent of the question. Manna's heart was racing as he felt the plan backfiring.

"Weekly food delivery," the driver responded to the guard's question. "Running a little behind schedule, tonight. With all these recent fugitives on the loose, seemed like we got pulled over once on every road. Can't be too safe, though, with all those maniacs running around out there. Did you see on the news they are looking for three more? I hope those bastards get what's coming to them. We won't be safe until every last one of them is rounded up."

Another muffled response from the guard and the driver produced a clipboard. He proffered it through the window and the guard received it. This was the telling sign to see if Guidry's sources provided accurate information. Manna could feel himself holding his breath, but he dared not exhale as to not give himself and the others away.

With the additional remarks about the wanted individuals, one happening to be Manna himself, Manna almost felt compelled to believe the driver as well. It seemed Guidry thought of everything by hiring this fella.

The guard gave the clipboard back and the driver released the brake. The truck began to move toward the docking bay. Manna could feel himself getting closer to his daughter. He popped his head up out from behind the pile.

Guidry did the same with a huge grin on his face. He looked like he was having the time of his life. It shouldn't have surprised Manna in the least. Here was A'ron Guidry where he was most comfortable, getting others to believe in one of his lies. And there was Manna again, along for the ride.

*****

Simone cleared her eyes as the tears began to subside. She felt foolish, knowing Kruger was most likely watching her through a hidden camera. It was just like Kruger to sit behind the glass, or safe in another room, watching someone else's suffering. Her earlier resolve returned to her. She didn't want to give him any of the pleasure of seeing her in a weakened state. The pain was still at an immeasurable intensity, however, Simone tried her best to ignore it and stand. It took her a full ten minutes to brace herself against the chair and gather her legs underneath her. She felt like a newborn foal, trying to learn to walk for the first time.

When she at last could stand without holding onto the chair, she eased her way to the door. She turned the handle. As she expected, it was locked. She made her way back to the only other thing in the room, the chair, and leaned against it again. The memory of being strapped to it was alive in her mind, so she couldn't bring herself to sit back down into it.

*****

Polchinski was at the door, as promised, to allow them into the building. Manna and Guidry got out with the drivers and Guidry and Polchinski shook hands. Manna and Guidry quickly made their way through the entrance with Polchinski. The two drivers went to the trailer to unload the boxes and crates, which contained the others. It was planned for four men to stay inside the trailer as back up. Gio and Pierre were two of these four, against their wishes however. Manna could imagine what their demeanor must be like, since their argument proved to be the strongest emotion Manna had seen from the two since he met them just two nights ago.

Manna couldn't help but think of the Trojan horse story he read when he was a kid. In fact, he thought, it had been taught to him in school. The students no longer learned such tales as they got in the way of testing, as did a lot of other things. He imagined Guidry as Achilles or Odysseus, a larger than life leader who outwitted the opponent through deceit and trickery.

Polchinski lead them to the security office and produced two security officer uniforms, dingy green buttoned shirts and slacks with black belts. A gun holster was attached to the belt, and a Stun Gun was holstered in it. Guidry removed his and replaced it with his own pistol that he had brought with him. Manna kept his in place and stuffed the Beretta he had brought into his pants at the small of his back. He preferred to reach for the Stun Gun in a knee-jerk reaction rather than the deadly weapon, which would be a bit harder to get to at its present location.

Manna saw a half dozen security monitors assorted on the wall and could see their men bringing in the first load of boxes with more men. He had to admit, it looked no different than men delivering boxes or crates of food. He felt a little more optimistic that Guidry's plan would work.

"You said you knew where my daughter was located," Manna said to Polchinski as he completed the full uniform ensemble by placing the hat on his oversized head. Guidry did the same. "Where is she?"

"The prisoners were brought in late this afternoon and each was interrogated separately, almost immediately upon arrival," Polchinski explained. "They were then taken to separate rooms. There were four prisoners, two male and two female. The men were taken to the fifth floor, rooms 528 and 530. The women are on the sixth, rooms 628 and 630.

"That's where she is, the sixth floor," Manna stated as he rushed for the door.

Guidry stopped him. "We came for all hostages, as that is what they are. Hostages of a war Teacher feels could have been prevented. Your daughter is a priority, but not the only priority. We check the sixth floor, but we need to get to the fifth first. We'll have two of our men meet us on the fifth."

"You're right," Manna said as he stopped before exiting. "Get the men from that first box they brought in to meet us there. The longer we're here the more likely it is that they will find us out."

Guidry brought a small microphone transmitter, which attached to his cane, up to his mouth. "We are necessitating two brave men to meet us on the fifth floor to navigate the hostages back to the rendezvous, preferably the strapping young men contained within the boxes I am perusing at this moment."

"Gio and I are more than willing," Pierre's voice responded back in Manna's earpiece.

Guidry had one as well, so he responded with a confused tone, "I thought you were left back in the trailer with Jonathan and Kyle."

"We traded places," Manna recognized Gio's voice this time. "Sorry, to have to divert the plan, but we couldn't sit back on something as important as this."

"Just meet us on the fifth floor," Guidry replied. "Use force if necessary. But don't get caught." He looked at Manna. "Guess, the plan isn't going to go entirely as planned. Let's just hope this is the only alteration, or we could be in trouble."

*****

Simone was starting to get used to the way the pain seemed to come and go at irregular intervals, as well as disproportionate intensities. She reluctantly sat in the chair that had once prevented her from fighting back her captors. She tried to think of a way to get out, but nothing seemed to be a justifiable plan of escape. She wondered when Kruger would come back to gloat, or when the doctor would come back to see if he accomplished what he wanted. She was starting to remember bits and pieces. She remembered the doctor, Stanford or Samford she thought. No, it was Sanford. She was sure of it. He had planned to do some sort of head surgery on her, though she couldn't remember what it was exactly. She dug deeper and remembered her father was in trouble.

Maybe that was why they took her. They saw through the disguise and discovered the wanted man was her father. No, she could remember Kruger had said she was being arrested for being suspected of being a Pupil herself.

Some Pupil she turned out to be. Not covering her tracks so Kruger could get to her. It was compromising the cause with each person who got caught. Though it put the cause into the light, it made a negative impression.

Teacher needed her, though. Within the week, he was going to be betrayed. At that thought, the image of the manila envelope came into her head. There were two pictures. Yes, she remembered she saw proof of the two traitors. She tried to think of the two images again.

Who was it? She thought to herself. *Who were the two traitors?* She remembered one was someone she had never seen. But she couldn't even envision the face she saw in the picture, nor could she remember if the face had been male or female. The second picture showed another traitor. A traitor she hadn't already known about previously. Again, she couldn't visualize the visage in the portrait.

It had been Kruger in the middle. Yes, it was finally coming to her. The unknown traitor stood to the right. And the traitor on the left was…the image seemed to reveal itself before her very eye, like an old Polaroid picture. As the image materialized, she gasped at the face represented on the left side of the photo as she remembered it.

What have I done? She thought to herself as she understood her mistake. She had sent her father to find the man who would betray them to Kruger.

The man standing on the left in the picture was A'Ron Guidry.

*****

Polchinski had mapped out the fifth floor for Manna and Guidry and directed them to the stairs. Guidry had felt the stairs were easier for concealment purposes. He had explained to Manna he had always felt trapped in an elevator, and the circumstances did not warrant being trapped at any point. It could get in the way of completing the mission.

"Once we salvage the men, and purge them from captivity, we'll let Gio and Pierre take them back to the truck," Guidry explained as they reached the large, black painted three marking the third floor and continued toward the fifth.

The two men kept a quick pace and their boots echoed in the empty stairwell. "I detect you desire to be the one to secure Simone."

"You're damn right I do," Manna replied as he picked up his pace. He kept a few steps ahead of Guidry drawing strength from the knowledge that Simone was getting closer with each step. It tore him apart knowing he would have to stop a floor short, in order to free the two men. He didn't even know who the men were, but they were friends of Simone, and she was unselfish enough to want him to get her friends before her as well.

"We have arrived," Guidry replied as the black five came into view.

Manna reached the door first and drew it open slowly. He peered down the hall, but could see nobody down either side.

"See anything?" Guidry whispered in Manna's ear.

Manna simply shook his head and held the door open for Guidry to enter the fifth floor. Guidry turned right and followed the directions Polchinski gave them. After a left and a second right, they saw the two men standing guard outside the doors. One stood on the right side of the long hallway and the other on the left. They were facing in opposite directions.

"What are you two doing here?" the one on the left, which was facing them, asked suspiciously. The other turned around to face them as well. He also had a suspicious glint in his eye.

"Yeah," the one on the right responded. "We're not supposed to be relieved for another twenty-five minutes."

Right on cue, Guidry began to do what he did best. He told a brazen lie.

"Polchinski told us to come relieve you early," he started. "He wanted to ask you guys something."

The one on the right started to take a step forward to leave, but the one on the left didn't budge.

"Why didn't he just ask over the radio?" The man on the left asked. He seemed to be a more senior-ranking guard in his overall demeanor. The way he could smell out the lie quicker proved his seniority as well. He took a closer look at Guidry and Manna and quickly removed his pistol. "I've not seen you two before. Who the hell are you?"

The man on the right removed his pistol as well, but he looked a little less sure of the situation. His confused eyes and the way he shakily held the gun showed his overall lack of experience with situations he now faced.

For all Manna knew, this was the first time this guard had ever had to pull his gun out for real. He went for his radio, so it proved he did have the ability to remember his training, however. As he brought the radio up to his mouth to speak into it and blow this whole mission, a dull thud emanated from behind him and the man took in a gasping deep breath. A moment later he was on the floor.

The other guard made a slight turn, but before he could complete his full rotation, he too was on the ground. No blood was present on either guard, but a large tranquilizer dart was stuck in each one.

Gio and Pierre appeared in the absence of the two guards, and Pierre was dropping his arm holding the gun. Guidry and Manna both gave a sigh of relief. Guidry wasn't used to having his lies backfire as this one had. Manna had only seen Guidry's bluff called one other time and it had broken their friendship. This one, however, had seemed to do the opposite.

By staring down the barrel of guns together, it proved their friendship was back to flourishing as it once had. Manna couldn't blame Guidry this time for getting him into trouble, for it had been Manna's daughter's imprisonment which had brought them to this point. Not that he blamed Simone either. He now saw who the enemy had always been. The Council had forever been the true entity to cast blame upon. It was they who had taken away his friendship; they who had taken away his daughter. And it was they who had taken away everyone's passion to dream up their own future.

No longer could someone dream of being a doctor, lawyer, or poet. Dreams, ambitions, were no longer options; instead they were forced upon an individual. Like being forced to take a bad-tasting medicine when sick, it left you feeling better, but still left a bad taste in your mouth in the process. For too long, Manna had lived with that bad taste in his mouth, as did the majority of the population.

He was starting to grasp why his daughter did what she did so many years ago. Teacher's lesson was finally reaching him. Now, he would fully devote his efforts to the cause and help find the villainous traitor if it was the last thing he did. At least, he would, after freeing Simone from the Council's clutches.

"You arrived at the proper interval of time," Guidry stated to Gio and Pierre. Manna figured it was Guidry's way of saying *Thank you* or *It's about damn time you got here!* Either way, Gio and Pierre didn't seem to care. Guidry produced a ring with eight keys on it. It took three tries to unlock the first door, 528.

A man sat on a small cot with his hands on his head, as if he were in deep regret, in deep thought, or in great annoyance at the situation - Manna couldn't tell. He raised his head slowly, as if he were annoyed at the interruption.

"What do you want?" he asked.

Definitely annoyed, Manna thought to himself.

"I already told you all I know," the man told them. Then he noticed Gio and Pierre were not dressed as guards. "Who are you?" he directed the question to Gio and Pierre, but he could have been asking any of them.

"We're here to rescue you, Griffin," Manna told him. He recognized the face from the news broadcast earlier.

"How do you know who I am?" Griffin asked, completely baffled by the revelation.

"I am Mike Manna," Manna replied to the confused gentleman. "Simone's my daughter and we're here to take you all out of here."

Griffin stood from the bed and quickly followed the four men out the door.

Guidry moved to the next room to the left, room 530. He unlocked it, using the same key he used for Griffin's door, and the men entered to retrieve the other man they came to rescue. He seemed even more distraught than Griffin. Manna recognized him as Zachariah Moonstone, the other male arrested with Simone. Zachariah quickly noted Griffin's presence and didn't seem to know how to take it.

"What's going on?" he asked no one in particular.

Griffin quickly tried to fill him in on the situation. Manna noticed Griffin referred to Zachariah as Zeke, and sometimes Z, as he was speaking to him. *They must be nicknames*, Manna thought to himself as Griffin continued to explain.

The six men exited the room. The guards were still feeling the effect of the tranquilizer as they lay unconscious on the floor. They made their way to the set of stairs Gio and Pierre had used to sneak from behind, as it was closer than the one Guidry and Manna had used. Gio and Pierre lead Zeke and Griffin down, as Guidry and Manna turned to head up to the sixth floor.

"We'll meet you guys back at the truck. Radio me when you get there," Guidry told them as they headed in their respective directions.

"Will do," was Pierre's reply as they disappeared around the bend in the stairs.

Manna and Guidry could hear the echo of the quick descent from the others, but that dissipated before they took their first steps.

"What's the plan, now?" Manna asked Guidry as they ascended the stairs. "We can't tell them the same thing we told the other guards. We saw how well that worked."

"I'm a man of many lies," Guidry replied. "You should be able to discern that by now. Something will ruminate when the time arises."

"Get that thinker of yours working overdrive, cause the time has officially arrived," Manna demanded as they came to the door for the sixth floor.

Manna slowly opened the door, as he had done before on the fifth floor. Again, no one was on either side of the hall. They made a left, this time as they were coming from a different direction. They walked briskly, yet cautiously, to the location of rooms 628 and 630, but noticed something quite odd. This time, no sentinels were standing guard.

"That's strange," Manna said. "Where are the guards?" He turned to Guidry with a puzzled look.

"That is quite peculiar, no doubt," Guidry replied. "But let us not notice how slovenly the dentures look on our gift horse. Let us, instead, ride that antediluvian steed for all it's worth into oblivion, and see how far we get."

Even through the tension of the moment, Manna couldn't help but laugh at this odd remark. "How long have you wanted to use that one?"

"For quite some time," Guidry responded with a smile. "You like it?"

"Come on, you old codger," Manna stated, still smiling. It sure felt like old times with Guidry, again.

He led the way to room 630. Manna continued to look shiftily down each side of the hall as Guidry tried a key in the door to unlock it.

Where are the guards? Manna thought to himself as Guidry tried the second key on the ring Polchinski gave him. *Did someone figure out what had happened on the fifth floor and disperse the guards to help? Were there no guards here because the prisoners were women, and thought to be less of a threat? If they knew anything about Simone's temper, they would definitely have someone up here.* She was more menacing than any man Manna had ever met. Manna continued to think of possible reasons for the absence of the guards on this floor.

Guidry finally found the right key to unlock the door, and turned the knob to enter. Guidry quickly entered and then gasped. Manna turned to see what had taken his friend by surprise, and the sight stunned him as well.

A woman was sitting on the hard bed. She had a stripe of neon green in her hair, but that wasn't what was so shocking. The woman had one arm of human skin, but the other looked robotic. She looked almost like a cyborg. It took the two men by surprise, and immediately Manna felt a pang of guilt. He hadn't meant to respond in such a disrespectful manner, but the sight was totally unexpected. Manna's only hope was that the woman hadn't noticed the reactions of her two rescuers.

"Here we go again," she said scornfully. She seemed to have the same derisive attitude as the others. "Don't you guys have anything better to do then to relentlessly pursue an entity doing absolutely no harm in the world? Shouldn't you guys be looking for some inconsiderate punk who's trying to steal a woman's purse, instead?" She held up her hand. "Haven't I been through enough?"

"I'm sure you have," Manna answered after a brief silence. "But, we're not here to answer questions. We're here to take you out of this God forsaken place." He spoke with such disdain and conviction; it nearly took him by surprise. Never before had he spoken with such raw emotion. Not since Felicia died, at least.

"You're Simone's father," the young woman stated matter-of-factly. "I saw pictures of you in her home." This knowledge brought great pride in the man, to hear his daughter kept at least a picture of him, her estranged father, somewhere in her home for people to view. "I'm Vivienne."

"I hate to say it," Guidry interrupted, still in the doorway, "but I don't think we have enough time for pleasantries at this juncture. We still need to get Simone, and get the hell out of here."

"He's right," Manna retorted. "Let's go, quickly."

Vivienne quickly followed the two men to the next door, room 628. Guidry paused before placing the key in the keyhole to unlock it.

"You ready to get your daughter back," he asked Manna with dramatic flair. The rhetorical question went unanswered as the key slid in, turned, and released the lock.

*****

Simone was overcome with panic with the realization that Guidry was the betrayer, but the panic escalated when she heard a set of keys jangling on the other side of her locked door. She had anticipated Kruger returning, but not so soon. The angst and frustration she was experiencing wasn't at critical mass, yet. Kruger should have been good for another hour of watching her suffrage. Simone decided to feign being unconscious upon his entrance, in case he hadn't been watching from another room. She let her body go slack and closed her eyes as the doorknob turned for the person to enter.

*****

The shocking cyborg woman in the last room was no comparison for the complete bafflement that faced Manna in the next. As Guidry stepped aside from the opened door and bowed, ever playing the showman, expecting to deliver Manna his daughter, Manna stared aghast in utter disappointment at the empty room.

*****

Simone could hear the door open and quickly shut as an unknown presence entered the room. She heard the trespasser moving in her direction; then almost cringed as she felt a hand rub up and down her leg, down by her calf. Though she didn't move a muscle, she couldn't help but feel the repulsion course through her body. The warm, damp hand was in stark contrast to her cold, exposed skin. Somehow, she knew she had experienced this hand's touch before. Like an intimate lover, she knew the sensation these hands produced. Rather than affection, it provided her with a feeling so revolting that it nearly made her cry out in disgust and weep.

"Let's see how my pet is doing after surgery," a husky voice whispered provocatively in her ear. Simone immediately realized it was not Kruger, though the voice had a familiar tone to it. "Let's see how much she *remembers*."

She felt the speaker's breath on her ear, he was that close. The acrid odor of the person's breath wafted up to her nostrils making the situation all the more revolting. Then she felt the person's tongue flick her earlobe in a disgusting show of dominance. The hand touching her leg began making a path upward to her upper thigh, and that's when Simone tensed up.

"Good, you're awake," the speaker said with satisfaction. "I was worried you wouldn't be able to put up a fight."

Simone did just that, or as best she could with her assailant in such close proximity. She kicked her leg up, releasing his hand, and pushed off his chest with all her might. This did two things. First, it made her accoster fall back and slightly lose his balance. It also made her fall out of the chair with a large thud. Simone figured she bruised her tailbone from the crashing impact she felt upon hitting the floor.

She looked up at her assailant and immediately recognized Dr. Sanford catching himself on the chair, or else he too would've joined her on the floor. He tried reaching for her, but she was just out of her reach. She kicked the metal surgeon's tray toward him, and it rolled right into him. It produced a small gash under his chin, as he was slightly bent over reaching for her over the chair. Rather than slow him down, it only seemed to infuriate and focus him more.

"Don't worry, my pet," he said as he sneered down at her. "I can help you forget the whole ordeal afterwards."

Still on the ground, she scrambled to get as far out of his reach as she could, though it proved difficult in the confined space of the room. Sanford wiped the blood from his face and continued to pursue her to the back corner of the room. She was finally running out of real estate. She was pinned up against the corner. As he got within a few feet, a large bang reverberated in the room. It was loud enough to make Simone jump and reach her hand to her ears. Her scream was drowned out by another loud bang, then another.

It took her a few moments to figure out the sound resonated from behind Sanford. It wasn't until she saw the doctor fall and saw the pool of blood spewing from his lifeless body that she realized he had been shot.

The intensity of the moment, the effects of her head injury, as well as the tears pouring down her ashen cheeks made it hard for her to see the shooter clearly. As the blurry form materialized before her, just as the photograph from her memory had just done minutes before, she stared at the eerie presence of A'ron Guidry.

As quickly as the panic had subsided, it started to begin anew as she realized the true nature of her predicament. She began to cry hysterically and pushed her way into the corner that trapped her from this monster.

"No..Please! No," Simone pleaded in between sobs. "Don't...come..near.. me. GET AWAY! GET AWAY FROM ME ...you....you...TRAITOR!"

Chapter Seventeen: Accusations

Simone's panicked state was yet another surprise in a series of surprises for Manna in the span of a few days. He was dumbfounded at her words. The smoking gun, which he chose over the stun gun at the sight of someone trying to accost his daughter, was still held in his hands from shooting the man who lay dead on the floor. He aimed it toward Guidry in a disposition of confusion upon realizing the extent of Simone's words. It was as non-threatening as one could get pointing a gun at another human being.

Guidry appeared just as shocked and awed by her statements. Guidry's face contorted into a look of consternation, and Manna almost brought the gun down at the absurdity of such an accusation. It was clear this was news to Guidry as well, though Manna knew the culpability of Guidry's lies. It was too engrained into his inner core to cast blame on him at this juncture. In many ways, Manna blamed himself for putting his trust back into a friend who betrayed him so long ago.

"She's lying," Guidry told Manna as he held up his hands, as if they could somehow defend against the bullet if Manna chose to pull the trigger before hearing him out. He took a few steps back as well, pinning him into the opposite corner of the room from Simone.

"Why would she lie about that?" Manna demanded. "What does she have to gain from it?"

"I don't know," was Guidry's weak reply. "The Council obviously has her convinced I am someone she shouldn't trust. Trust me, I am not a traitor."

"Trust you?" Manna asked pointing the gun in a more threatening manner. He couldn't help but to lash out and raise his voice. The passion and adrenaline he felt just moments before, as he stared down the barrel of a gun, had not had time to dissipate. "All you tell are lies. Why should I believe that just this once you are telling the truth?"

"Why would I help the Council?" Guidry demanded. He took a few steps forward to show the true conviction behind his words. "They took away my family and friends. They took away my freedom. They painted me as a traitor to society, because I believed in Teacher's words. I had years taken away from me locked up in Moon Haven like some kind of sociopath who couldn't be trusted to even talk to on the street. I had to fake my own death and go into hiding to escape their ever-seeking eye. So, tell me why I would align myself with them in order to bring down the only person I hold in higher regard than you." His jowls shook as he spoke each word with animated intensity, and his face turned a bright pinkish hue.

Manna could not find any flaw in what he just heard, as he could usually pinpoint it in any of Guidry's lies. It all seemed legit, so he looked to Simone for help in the matter. He kept the gun pointed in Guidry's direction, however.

She was covering her face and weeping uncontrollably, but seemed to sense his want for an explanation. It took her a few seconds to calm herself down enough to clarify her hysterics.

"Kruger showed me a picture of the Novice Orderly who is to betray Teacher," Simone divulged through fits of sniffling and heavy breathing. Manna had never seen his daughter so worked up over something. It scared him more than anything to see his baby girl in such an agitated state. "He also showed me another picture with the Novice Orderly and him," she pointed to Guidry, "shaking hands as if making a pact. I saw it with my own two eyes. A'RON GUIDRY IS A TRAITOR!" She screamed this last statement so hard, Manna could almost see blood spit out of her mouth.

"She is mistaken," Guidry replied, quick to defend himself. "I have never been in such a pose. The only reason I would shake Jack Kruger's hand would be to get close enough to spit in his face. You've got to believe me."

"I don't know what to believe anymore," Manna stated totally dumbfounded.

As Manna contemplated what to do about the situation, the third member of their party crossed the threshold into the room. Vivienne Delacroix cautiously entered the room. Guidry had told her to wait outside as they retrieved Simone and watch for guards. She must have been curious as to why it was taking so long, or overheard the commotion. Upon her entrance, Simone covered her ears as if an intense pain wracked her brain and tightly shut her eyes. All eyes were on her as she screamed in agony. Manna couldn't hold off comforting her any longer and went to her side. He caressed her head and tenderly held her in his arms to try and push away the demons inside her head that were causing her pain.

"I was wrong," she hoarsely whispered to her father. "Guidry is not the traitor. It is Vivienne."

Chapter Eighteen: Shattered Memories

Simone felt a penetrating, searing, throbbing sensation in her temples that reached the inner sanctum of her brain as Vivienne walked through the door. Every neuron and synapse seemed to spark at the same moment as the image of Guidry with Kruger and the Novice Orderly faded and was replaced by the image of Vivienne, Kruger, and the Novice Orderly who now had black hair instead of brown. The only image that stayed the same was Kruger's smug smile captured in the photograph, even his blue suit changed to a charcoal gray before her eyes.

As Vivienne's face replaced Guidry's, she felt her father's presence, gently trying to console her anguish. She didn't know why the photograph changed so quickly, but knew the revelation needed to be heard.

She remembered providing the indictment against Vivienne, but wasn't convinced of its validity. If her memory could change in just a short flash, where moments ago she had been totally convinced it was Guidry and now Vivienne seemed to be the culprit, maybe everything wasn't as it seemed. Perhaps, she was in a purgatory-like hell where all her loved ones were proven enemies.

She could see Guidry and Manna's accusing eyes peering into Vivienne's soul to see if she was capable of such a malicious crime. There was also a glint of palpable uncertainty in their glares as well, as she had just moments earlier falsely accused another.

Guidry was the first to take his condemning gaze off Vivienne, seemingly no longer convinced of its damning nature. Manna did as well, not entirely sure what to think at this sudden change of events.

"What the hell is going on?" Manna seemed as perplexed as ever. "Why did she just vary her story so quickly? She must be in shock or something. What did they do to her? Those bastards!"

"It seems Kruger has done something to plant a seed into Simone's brain of who the traitor is," Guidry offered. "That seems to be the only explanation, unless one of us is a traitor." He glanced in Vivienne's direction offering her a chance to plead her case, since up to that point she offered no denial of the allegation.

"Of course, I'm not a turncoat," Vivienne replied. "I'm just as emblazoned with Teacher's loyal seal as anyone in this room. Or any Pupil out there for that matter." She emphatically swept her arms around in a circle to emphasize she meant every Pupil in the world.

Again, Manna could not deny the passion and conviction in which she spoke. It could not easily be faked, and he was willing to put his faith in her claim as he had Guidry's. He looked at his daughter, and she looked broken to him, as if a part of her was torn from within and flung into the fiery pits of Hell. Manna couldn't think of a way to mend it, and knew she may forever be a shell of her true self, but he vowed to find a way to restore it if possible.

A loud screech from Guidry's cane broke the silence and made three of them jump; Simone seemed lost to her scattered memories. Guidry realized it was the transmitter on his cane and brought it to his mouth.

"Please, repeat," he said into it. "We couldn't read you."

"We made it back to the truck," Gio's voice responded.

"Good," Guidry replied back. "We have attained the other mark and will be joining you shortly. See you in about ten minutes."

"Better make it quicker than that," Gio warned. He seemed very concerned. "Something strange seems to be going on up there. We haven't heard from our men inside in over fifteen minutes. The drivers of the truck haven't returned in what was it…?" He seemed to be conferring with another individual. "Seven minutes; the two drivers went in seven minutes ago and haven't returned. They're not responding on the mikes either. We have lost communication with everyone inside but you. Proceed with caution."

"We copy that, Gio," Guidry replied. His face looked blanched at the news Gio just relayed to them. The plan was definitely not going as expected. "If we aren't out in ten minutes, take the truck back to home base. We'll find our own way home."

Guidry looked around at the other three individuals in the room, and Manna could tell he was calculating their next move.

"We need to get out of here, now," Guidry told everyone, as if they didn't already know. They had all heard what Gio just told him on the transmitter.

First, however, he tried to reach Polchinski on his other radio to see if he could rouse him and see the extent of the situation.

"Polchinski, you there? What's going on, man?" Manna couldn't help but notice Guidry's panicked tone, and its short, clipped words. He was no longer trying to impress, now he had only one thing in mind; survival.

Polchinki's voice seemed just as nervous as he responded.

"I hear, you. Kruger knows you're here. He's assembling some guards about to surround the truck, now. They plan to blow it up. You need to get out of here, quick. Where are you?"

"We're still on the sixth floor," Guidry replied hurriedly. "We won't be able to make it back to the truck in time. Our friends are out in the truck, now. I need to warn them." He gave the cane to Manna to warn the others in the truck, and Manna stepped out into the hall. "Do you have another way for us to escape?" Guidry asked Polchinski.

"I can get you a few bikes maybe, as in motorcycles," Polchinski answered. "That might be it. The others will have to find their own way out."

"Okay, tell us where to meet you," Guidry did not look pleased. His perfect mission was crumbling with each passing minute.

"Meet me in the basement in twenty minutes," Polchinski stated. "That should give me enough time to get the bikes. Whatever you do, don't be seen. Make sure you warn the others. Sorry, this didn't work out as planned."

"Manna's warning the others now," Guidry told him. "We knew this wouldn't be easy, my friend. Don't be sorry. Thanks for the help. See you in twenty."

Guidry clipped the radio back onto his belt buckle and started toward the hall. Manna came into the room with a dire look on his face.

"I wasn't able to contact anybody," he told Guidry. "Nobody is answering the call."

He offered it to Guidry so he could try.

"Can anybody read me," Guidry yelled into the transmitter. His booming voice reverberated around the still room. Each of the inhabitants of the room was on edge, barely breathing. "The mission has been compromised. Anyone in the truck needs to abandon it, now. It is about to blow. I repeat, the truck is about to blow. Get out now. Abort mission and get back to the rendezvous as quick as you can. Does anyone copy?"

They waited what seemed like eons, but was only about two and a half minutes. Then a familiar voice came over the transmitter which drew everyone's attention. Even Simone seemed to snap out of her stupor and held her breath. She seemed as lucid as ever as she stared at the small cane transmitter that filled the room with its disturbing drone.

"I am sorry to not be able to come to the phone right now, but we're all dead" Council Secretary Jack Kruger's voice melodically enunciated each word. "If you leave your name, room number, and present location after the beep, we will be sure to get back to you. Beep!"

As he said the last word, a reverberating concussion of sound resonated through the entire building, like an earthquake or nuclear explosion. The four realized immediately what had just happened. The semi-truck, with Gio and the others in it, had just exploded. Kruger, now, had the upper hand, and their time was officially running out.

Chapter Nineteen: Escaping

Manna still held Simone on the floor of the room. He hoped her current mental state was not going to totally debilitate her ability to get out of there, because they had to get out now. She seemed to have snapped out of her funk once Kruger spoke, but after the explosion she began to hyperventilate, and Manna was trying to calm her. It took the efforts of all three, Guidry, Manna, and Vivienne, to finally get her lucid again. Manna helped her to her feet and Guidry helped Manna walk her to the door. Manna gave one last look at Dr. Sanford's lifeless form and felt no remorse for the man before he turned his back and exited the room.

Guidry led the way to the stairs with Vivienne and Simone close behind. Manna brought up the rear as he ran almost sideways, constantly turning around to glance behind him for any guards following. Kruger had to possess at least some conjecture as to what they were trying to do, so the cavalry should be on their way to recapture the stolen prisoners. Hopefully, they would be out of the area before Kruger's men came. If they were lucky, they wouldn't run into any of them on the stairs, but the way their luck was going this night it would be wise for Manna and the others to assume they would.

Guidry held the door open for Vivienne, Simone, and Manna as they made it to the stairwell. The group of four stopped and listened for the telltale sign of footfalls on the stairs below. They heard nothing. Vivienne decided to take off her shoes, as she said the socks would be less likely to be heard. The rest of them did the same. Guidry started to slowly lead them down the stairs as to not give away their position.

Manna wished they could move faster, but knew it was not wise. They needed to be able to hear any doors open or footsteps below. They made it down to the third floor entrance before they heard their first noise on the stairwell. Luckily, it was above them. Guidry stopped and put a finger to his mouth to warn them against making any noise. However, they all knew that any noise was certain death, so the warning was unneeded.

The strides of an unseen security guard or soldier echoed like a shotgun blast and it was impossible to tell if they were heading toward them or away from where they stood. Another door creaked open and the footsteps disappeared. They all let out a sigh of relief as another door opened and closed. This time it came from below!

Manna reacted quickly and opened the third floor door. Thankfully, this one was not as loud as the one above, and the echoes of the boots on the tiled floor echoed loud enough to drown out the slight clicking noise as Manna shut the door. Vivienne, Simone, and Guidry had moved to the side of the doorway, and each stood as close to the wall as possible. All Manna had time to do before hearing the steps land on the third floor landing was duck down below the small window on the third floor entrance door. He still had his hand on the door's handle as he barely had time to close it. He, too, tried to look as small as possible as he huddled next to the door. No one dared take a breath, as if the sound of it could be heard through the heavy door, or perhaps it could be seen through the glass if the guard decided to take a glimpse.

Which is exactly what he did. Manna heard the guard stop and could feel his presence on the other side of the door. Manna hoped his presence couldn't be felt as well. The guard stuck his face to the window in the door; Manna could see the shadow of it as he looked up above him. The guard was in the stairwell and Manna tried to will him to keep moving from the other side of the door.

Guidry held Simone close to him and covered her mouth. She seemed on the verge of hysterics. Vivienne closed her eyes as if to wish away the guard, but he was not some imagined entity she could just make disappear with a mere thought. He was very much alive. Somehow, though her wish seemed to work. The shadow disappeared as the man turned around to head upstairs. They could hear his retreating footsteps.

Simone gave an audible gasp, sigh, or somewhere in between, as Guidry eased the pressure on her mouth. He immediately brought it back up, and everyone tensely froze.

The footsteps stopped and tentatively came back down. The shadow of the guard's face appeared again in the window. He looked around again and tried the door. Manna still had a grip on it, and decided to hold onto it for dear life. The guard turned it slightly, but with Manna holding on, he couldn't get it to open. He pressed his face fully against the glass to try to see what was obstructing the door. In one fluid motion, Guidry produced his cane from some hidden sleeve, belt, or somewhere else altogether, and struck the guard in the face through the glass. Manna had no idea where he had the cane hidden. All he knew was one moment it was there, and the next a shower of glass was raining down on him. He heard a muffled sound come from the guard through the door and then silence.

Manna opened the door and the glass had exploded on either side of it. He stepped over the glass and saw the guard, unconscious, at the bottom of the next set of stairs. His head was bent at an awkward angle and Manna was almost certain he had a broken neck. Blood covered the downed guard's face, as Manna saw the damage Guidry had caused with his cane.

"Quick," Guidry told him as he started past him down the stairs. He was putting on his shoes again. "That crash is bound to alert someone to our location. We need to get out of here, and fast. No need to worry about making noise after all that ruckus"

Manna, Simone, and Vivienne also slipped on their shoes. Their steady patter echoed down the empty stairs like a klaxon notifying an escape. Anyone listening would know where they were heading, but lucky for them no one alive was currently on the stairs. They reached the basement without running into any other guards.

Guidry looked around for Polchinski.

"He said he'd be here," Guidry said.

"Has it been twenty minutes," Manna asked. He looked around to get a consensus from the others on how long it had taken to get down there. "He said he'd be down here in twenty minutes."

"I don't know how long it has been," Guidry replied.

"It sure felt like twenty minutes," Vivienne said adding her encouragement.

"He just has to be here," Simone was frantic. "He has to be." She was on the verge of another breakdown.

"Did he say where in the basement he'd be?" Vivienne asked, clearly a little more annoyed than frightened.

"He just said the basement," Guidry answered. "How the hell am I supposed to know where in the basement he'd be?"

As he said this, the sound of a motorcycle's engine revving drew their attention to the right. They followed the sound to a vast expanse of pavement that resembled a parking garage.

A sleek motorcycle stood propped up by its kickstand. Polchinski was on another one easing it beside the other. He parked it, got off, and made his way to where Manna stood with the others. He tossed a set of keys to Guidry, and the other to Manna.

"Anybody asks," Polchinski told them. "I was never here."

Simone looked at the man and immediately panicked. As soon as she saw him, she saw his face in the picture with Kruger. He was the Novice

Orderly traitor. He was who she was trying to find. Manna glanced in her direction and knew something was wrong.

"What is it, sweetie?" He asked her.

"He's not someone we can trust," she declared. "He's a traitor. He is the one I saw in the other picture Kruger showed me. At least I think he is."

Manna looked at her, wanting to believe her.

"This man, here?" He asked her pointing at Polchinski. "He's a traitor? He's trying to help us."

"I don't think we can trust her memory," Guidry replied. "At one point, I was the traitor. And then it was the cyborg." He emphasized this notion by pointing at Vivienne. She, in turn, flicked him off with her metal finger for the cyborg remark. "I think we've got to stop believing what she says for now, until we can sort through it all logically."

"But it was him," Simone replied. "I saw the picture. I can still visualize it now. I saw it. It was him."

As Simone became more confident in her belief, the picture changed in her mind. It was no longer Polchinski but another. Someone she remembered from a class in college. That, too, changed to someone totally different. Another unknown stranger replaced her old classmate.

"I thought it was him," Simone replied as the confidence waned. "It's not him. I mean, it might be him. I don't know what to believe anymore." She seemingly gave up trying to convince them of anything.

"You better get going," Polchinski told them after a small moment of silence. "The longer you stay here, the more likely you are to get caught. And if you get caught, they'll know I helped you."

"You're right," Manna said. "We need to get out of here, now. We can't put someone else's life in danger. Not after what already happened to the others. No more blood needs to be spilled."

"You're right," Guidry said. "Let's go. Thanks for the help, Polchinski. We owe you one."

"Don't mention it," Polchinski stated. "Just don't let the Council win."

"Don't worry," Guidry told him as he got on the bike. Vivienne got on behind him.

97

"We won't," Manna finished. Simone rode behind him.

They started the motorcycles, and quickly made their way to the exit. The sound of the bikes died out as they made their escape from Jack Kruger and the Council's headquarters. Polchinski stood and listened to the sound until he knew they had made it far enough to escape.

He turned with a smile to leave and noticed a person had snuck up behind him. He pulled out his gun and aimed it at Council Secretary Kruger. He kept the gun aimed as beads of sweat started to form at his brow. He took deep, shallow breaths to calm his nerves at being surprised.

After a brief standoff, Kruger clapped his hands in applause and Polchinski withdrew the gun.

"Stellar performance, young man," Kruger said still applauding. "You almost had me convinced you hated the Council as well."

"Thank you, sir," Polchinski said as he holstered his gun. "Just trying to do my civic duty."

"To think, Ms. Petra was right about you," Kruger chuckled. "You were a traitor after all. Did you attach the homing device as I asked?"

"Yes, sir," he replied. "On both bikes."

"Good," Kruger had a gleam in his eye. "Now, we can find where A'ron Guidry has been hiding out all these years. Your family will be properly rewarded for your actions today. You are a true patriot."

"Thank you, sir," Polchinski said as he saluted the Council Secretary. "I am just glad I could help."

"You did, indeed, help," Kruger smiled proudly, returning the salute. "You did, indeed."

Chapter Twenty: Rendezvous

Sunday - Day Four

It was past midnight when they finally made it back to Guidry's hideout. The motorcycles proved most helpful in getting them there quickly. Manna could feel Simone trembling behind him. It broke his heart that he couldn't stop in order to provide her the comfort she needed. It had to wait until they reached Guidry's place. Her tension did not die completely on the ride over, so Manna held her when they got a chance to sit down on the couch. She unleashed the tears and cried until she was no longer able to formulate tears. Manna offered consoling words, but felt like he couldn't provide her with the proper encouragement. He wasn't fully aware of what she went through while in Kruger's possession, but had an idea.

He had assumed she was shown some sort of evidence to prove who the traitor was, but he wasn't sure if the evidence was truly authentic. She seemed to have suffered from some sort of memory lapse, as she couldn't quite pinpoint the traitor's true identity. There seemed a bit of confusion in Simone's mind, causing her to become ultra-paranoid. It was taking all their efforts to calm her down enough to explain the situation. It seemed their labors were starting to pay off as she was finally tranquil enough to start talking about it.

"Kruger was watching me," Simone was explaining. Vivienne, Manna, and Guidry were huddled around her listening intently. A few of Guidry's compatriots were also listening, and others only heard brief snippets of it as they passed by. "I just know he was watching me as they asked me all those questions. It was more intuitiveness than anything, like I could sense his presence in the room without him being there. They were trying to convince me to divulge that I was some sort of lead Pupil; that I lead others to follow Teacher's doctrine. They also wanted to tell them where the men who escaped Moon Haven had gone. They seemed to already know I was a major player in the game, but wanted me to confirm their assessment. Finally, they showed me two pictures disclosing the identity of two traitors." She imagined herself holding those pictures, and they seemed to come into focus slowly. The two traitors were clear in her mind. One was an absolute stranger, and the other was someone she thought she could trust. "I didn't know who the one traitor was, and assumed it was the Novice Orderly I sent Gio and Pierre after you to find." She nodded her head at Manna as she stated this fact. "The second person was not a stranger, but someone I knew quite well." She closed her eyes to try to remember. "It was a friend of mine that I trusted full-heartedly. Griffin Blake was the second traitor. He was shaking Kruger's hand, along with the other blond haired man."

"Are you sure it was Griffin?" Vivienne asked. She looked mortified at the implication that he could have been untrustworthy all this time.

"You said there was a blond individual?" Guidry asked as well. "Are you certain he was blond?"

"Yes," Simone replied confidently. "Absolutely sure. He was blond." The picture in her mind changed again, and the blond changed to a woman. "Wait, not a man, but a blond woman." It changed again. "No, black hair and male."

She addressed Vivienne.

"And it wasn't Griffin, but Z," Simone looked wide-eyed at all of them, unsure of what to think about these constant changes. "Now, I see Pierre has replaced Z's place in the picture."

"Are you even sure they showed you an image of the traitor at all?" Manna asked uncertainly. "Maybe, they gave you some false information. Maybe, they showed you a picture with one person, then drugged you enough to forget what you saw, and showed you the same picture with another person added in place of the other."

"That would be brilliant," Guidry thought aloud. "Then she wouldn't know who to trust. That way everyone was a liar in her mind."

"And the true traitor's identity would be safe," Vivienne chimed in.

"Not to mention we would doubt everything Simone says she remembers," Manna stated. "It is true psychological warfare on a massive scale."

"It helps make everyone paranoid, unsure of who to trust," Vivienne declared totally aghast.

"Maybe there is a kernel of truth to what she is saying," a younger woman eavesdropping stated to the group.

"What do you mean?" Manna asked the young woman.

"I mean she remembers being shown two pictures. And that those pictures were of two traitors," the woman explained. "What if that part is true? And she remembers that one of the traitors was someone she considered a close friend, or at least someone she felt she could trust altogether, or someone she knew quite well. Let's say this is true as well."

"Okay," Manna interrupted the woman not seeing her logic. "Still, I don't see where you are going with all of this. If we believe this is true, then we'll have to be at a stalemate and not go any further, as to not tip our hat to the traitor of our next move. We won't know who to take and who to leave behind, as far as the mission goes. We could be taking the traitor, and wouldn't know."

"Actually, it could be to our advantage though," the young woman replied, still believing her own rationale. "If we know a traitor is already amongst us, then we make sure to have multiple eyes on everyone at all times. We disallow anyone to be alone even for a second. That way any knowledge the Council gathers from this informant is stopped altogether."

"Excellent deduction, Gina," Guidry responded, very pleased that one of his disciples had used her brain to deduce something positive from this mess. "We'll have to be ever diligent in using the information to our fullest advantage. No single person can be alone at any given moment. We'll need to split off into groups of no less than three, as we are not certain that there is only one Council traitor who breached our interior."

"We know the traitor is someone close to Simone," Gina explained. "Let's get a list of people who could fit that distinction."

"Vivienne and Guidry have already been accused as such," Manna replied. "And I guess I would be included as well."

"Then there's Gio and…" Guidry stopped as he remembered what had happened to the others. "Oh, never mind."

"What?" The young woman, Gina, seemed confused.

"It could've been one of them, but it wouldn't matter if it was," Simone somberly broke her silence. "Because they're all dead."

"You might have to change that statement," a voice shouted from the doorway..

"Yeah," another voice stated from the same direction. "Kruger's gonna have to do better than an explosion to take us out."

Gio and Griffin came into view followed by Pierre and Zeke.

"He wasn't betting on us getting out of the frying pan before he turned on the heat," Zeke stated. "It sure was cutting it close, though."

The foursome received much adulation from everyone in the room. Four more of Guidry's men came into the room behind them, including the two no necks Manna had seen before. He tried to recall their names, but their presence seemed too stunning for him to remember them.

Simone raced to Zeke and Griffin and gave each of them a hug. Then she did the same with Pierre. Gio, however, got something a little more intimate. Simone hugged him a little tighter than the others, and when she was done gave him a passionate kiss on the lips. When the kiss was done, however, she looked at him a bit skeptically, not wanting to consider that he could betray her love by being aligned with the Council this entire time.

"What?" He asked her, not understanding the reason for her cryptic look. She was still in his embrace, but it didn't seem as tender.

Simone glanced around the room; at Vivienne and Guidry showing their relief on seeing the rest of them alive. Then, she glanced in the direction of Pierre, Griffin, and Zeke. She even looked at her own father. Finally, she looked directly in Gio's eyes.

"The traitor is in this room," she said coldly. "We are all not safe."

Chapter Twenty-One: An Un-Restful Rest

After the events of the night, everyone decided they needed a brief rest. Simone rested her body on the bed, but her mind would not let her sleep. She was lying awake pondering the circumstances behind the forgotten picture in her mind. Every time she closed her eyes, the picture shifted to a different individual. After each individual volleyed around her mental rolodex a half dozen times or so, she tried her best to meditate and focus on something else. It took her full mental capacity to think about her relationship with Gio and where it planted its roots.

He had been in a class of hers, a different class than the one she shared with Zeke. It had been her first year at Institute, during the second semester. She could still recall the large podium the professor stood behind when bleating out information for students to copy.

 He never faced the students, just stood behind the podium reading notes from a screen. That was why she could always remember that podium. She never understood its purpose. It was really the first time she started to search for the reasons of certain behaviors, attitudes, and the like. Before that day when she first asked herself about the cause of the podium's existence, she never recollected ever asking herself the question of why. It simply was not acceptable behavior permitted by the Council. The reasons never had to be given, because the question was never supposed to be asked. Even the mere thought of asking was absurd.

She remembered the first time she ever met Gio, because it had coincided with the day she first came up with the question about the podium. Simone had always been a good student in high school; copying meticulous notes and reading them each night, nearly verbatim, without even a glance at the notes themselves. She was always so attentive during class, and always sat near the front.

She had chosen a front seat for the class she shared with Gio, as well. Gio sat near the back, and since Simone was always one of the first to get to class, and Gio being one of the last, she never remembered seeing him prior to the day of their fateful first meeting.

As she recalled it was the day before a big test, which were always given on Thursdays, though she couldn't recall the content of the material that they were reviewing on that particular Wednesday. The professor, she believed was named Shafer, or maybe Shatner, she had professors with each name and couldn't differentiate one from the other in her memory, as neither seemed to stand out from the other. The professor was standing at the lectern, and Simone had her puzzling thought, and almost immediately shut down. She was no longer focused on the lesson review; instead all that maintained her focus was why the lectern was there in the first place. The professor wasn't using it to place notes or papers, in fact she could never recall him placing anything on it at any point during the year. *Was it for show? A necessity for any lecture hall?* Simone began to panic slightly. She had never pondered such a thought before; never needed an answer, because there was never a question. Now, the question consumed her. Every pore of her being needed to be informed of the information she so desired.

The professor completed the reading of the notes, and finally turned around, not for questions, as everyone knew they were not permitted, but to leave the classroom. Simone had not completed the notes, and her terrified face grew paler with each step the professor took toward the exit. She watched him leave, wanting to call out to him and ask him to repeat himself, or wanting to ask him about the lectern, she wasn't certain. All the other students, Simone could see, were packing up their materials or heading for the exit as well.

Simone suddenly noticed a male student in a pair of ripped up jeans and a plain white t-shirt sleeping in the back corner. This took her mind off the conundrum of the lectern, as well as the panic over the forgotten note taking, and gave her another puzzle to delve her mind into. It was most perplexing, as she had never seen it done at any level of schooling before that day. There were now two inquiries probing her thoughts. She quickly looked around to see if anyone else saw the sleeping student as well.

When she looked back, the student was awake and left without a single supply, or so it appeared to Simone. She was overcome with curiosity, so she hurried after him. The deluge of students also trying to exit made it difficult for Simone to make up any ground. She hurried as best she could.

As she made her way out of the building, the stranger was nearly fifty yards ahead. Simone began to run in order to catch up to the strange young man. She was about ten yards away from him, when he stopped. Simone slowed down, because she was startled by the abrupt halt. Then, the stranger unexpectedly took off on a dead sprint to the right. Simone was so taken by surprise she didn't realize he had moved until he was half a football field away. Pursuit was futile because the man sped away with amazing speed. He soon turned a corner and was out of sight.

The next day Simone sat in her normal spot at the front, but she kept turning around in her seat looking for the stranger. The seat she saw him sleeping in the previous day remained empty. Just as the professor passed out the first test, the door opened and the stranger entered. He was still wearing the ripped up jeans and white t-shirt. He walked straight for the empty seat he had sat in the previous day and sat in it.

Simone was completely turned around in her seat watching the young man calmly sit down, as if coming in late was a regular occurrence. She heard a man clear his throat in front of her and turned to see the professor proffering a copy of the digital test. Simone took the small electronic device she would need to type in her answers. In her mind, the stranger's eyes bore into the back of her head. Somehow, he knew it was her who had seen him sleeping, and chased him after class. He probably thought she had told the professor as well.

Throughout the test, Simone's mind was completely out of focus. It was not functioning as it normally did. The test questions were mere blips on the screen, and the answers were nonsensical in nature. Since they were all multiple choice questions, she merely selected an answer purely at random.

She heard small steps come down the stairs leading to where the professor's assistant sat on a chair. The stranger in the white t-shirt gave the electronic answer recorder to the assistant and turned to leave. Before making his way to the steps, Simone looked up to see him looking straight at her. Their eyes met for the briefest of moments, but Simone felt an intense electricity had passed between them. He quickly walked the stairs and exited with a click of the door.

Simone sat staring at her test, but could still feel the intensity in those eyes. It distracted her from the task at hand, but only momentarily. She seemed to grow mentally stronger by looking into those eyes, and quickly finished the test. She turned in her answer recorder and then exited. The disappointment at not seeing the stranger waiting for her outside was palpable, almost painful, but not totally unexpected.

The following day she went to the lecture hall to see her test grade. Since it was a Friday, there were no classes held, but Simone still got there early to see her score. Nobody else was in the hall when she arrived. She looked for her first name, along with her last initial and student number. It always made her nervous to see it posted in that fashion, even with nobody else in attendance. She found her score and saw she made a ninetieth percentile. A sigh escaped her mouth, which echoed in the empty room.

She turned to leave, but an arm blocked her path. The stranger stood in front of her pinning her against the wall with his arm blocking her only escape. She couldn't help but look into those intense eyes again, intriguing and frightening at the same time.

He peered over her head at the test scores and gave a little smirk, though it quickly vanished as to not betray his thoughts.

"What'd you make?" he asked her. His velvety voice made her heart beat faster.

"A…a …ninety," she stammered. "And you?"

"See for yourself," he pointed at the score sheet with a calloused finger.

Simone turned around and looked where he pointed. The name on it read Giovanni V, 100 percentile. This enraged her.

"How could you do that?" She fumed. "I saw you sleeping in class yesterday."

He looked around to make sure nobody else had snuck into the hall.

"Can you keep a secret?" Giovanni asked her.

She slowly nodded her head confirming she was someone whom he could trust.

"I have in my possession the book that the professor uses for his lessons," He gave a conspiratorial smile. "I read it before taking the tests."

Simone stood with her mouth wide open in total exasperation. Could there really be a textbook someone could read themselves that contained the material the professors taught? If so, then why wouldn't more people have a copy of it for themselves?

"There's no such thing," Simone stated indignantly.

"There is," Giovanni said with another smirk. "Want to see it?"

And indeed, there was a book. In one of his dresser drawers at the Institute campus, Gio kept the book hidden. He disclosed to her that he had it wedged deep within the drawer as to hide it away from prying eyes better. As he placed the concealed book in her hand, she knew her life would be forever changed. Simone had held a book in her hand before; she had happened upon the book in her father's desk once while looking for a pair of scissors. It wasn't illegal to own a book, or even to read one, but the Council always looked down upon book owners. The Council was supposed to be the ones to choose which knowledge was important, and which was not worth knowing; what was to be learned and what was to be kept from the masses. That moment in her father's room wasn't as conspiratorial as the one she now faced with Gio. They seemed to be choosing for themselves how to consider the knowledge they possessed.

He looked into her eyes and she could feel, again, the excitement and intensity hidden within. It was at that moment she knew she was in love with this stranger. She couldn't deny the passion that exploded within her own body each time she looked in his eyes. It seemed he was looking deep in her soul and extracting the portions of herself she kept hidden from the rest of the world. He saw her for who she truly was, and there was no deception she could muster in his presence. In only the brief amount of time she knew him, she was more herself and felt compelled to know him more.

"I show you this as a token of my sincerity," Gio explained to her. "I saw you ponderously gazing at me the other day and could tell you could be trusted. I could sense you had a questioning nature by the confused look on your face as the professor was leaving. I feigned sleep to see if my deduction was accurate."

"You read me all wrong," Simone replied. "In fact, that day was the first time I questioned in my life."

"That doesn't mean it hasn't been there buried in your core," Gio answered. "If you question once, it means you've always had the capacity to use your mind to reconsider the possibilities that you have been forced to simply ignore because of the Council's influence."

"You're a real intellectual, aren't you?" She asked in surprise.

"Yes, and so are you," he answered calmly. "You just weren't aware of it yet."

With those words, Simone accepted her true fate. She couldn't argue the truth with which he spoke. Somehow, he had known her better than she knew herself. He unlocked that secret burning deep inside where she wanted more out of herself than what the Council demanded.

In one quick motion, Gio bent in her direction and kissed her on the lips. She finally felt alive, like her destiny was now in front of her, and her life finally had meaning. She could finally think outside the box without fear of persecution.

Though she hadn't fully given her mind to the Teacher's cause, as Gio wasn't yet fully a Pupil at that point in time, it was definitely the origin of her desire to keep secrets and question authority.

Those same thoughts washed over her as she lay in bed trying to rest in Guidry's hideout. She had the traitor's identity locked in her mind somewhere, and it was her duty to figure out who it truly was. Her memory was not reliable at this point, so she must now rely on her own intuition. It, still, was her best quality. She looked at each of the possible suspects.

Gio was her lover, and confidante. She felt safe with him. But could he have manipulated her to gain her trust, to give away prized information to the Council?

The same could be said about Z. He had introduced her to Teacher's lessons. Could he have also manipulated her?

Griffin was already a double agent, working at Council headquarters with her. Perhaps, he really was working for the Council all along. Was there such a thing as a triple agent?

Vivienne was a wildcard. Simone had never really trusted her. The vibe she got around her seemed to always be on the suspicious side, though she never really had a reason for the distrust. Simone made a mental note to keep a close watch on her.

Guidry, too, was a wildcard. He was a known liar, so trust was not something she was willing to throw his way halfheartedly. He had spent years in the Council's captivity. There was a real good chance they could have persuaded him to play by their rules after so much time in their possession. The Council seemed to have influenced her thinking after only one day in captivity. What could they do with years?

Simone didn't know a whole lot about Pierre. He was Gio's roommate at Institute and they were nearly inseparable. He could easily be the traitor, flying under the radar.

She finally came to her own father. The thought of him as a traitor seemed ludicrous, because he never seemed to take sides. During arguments Simone had with her mother, her father always stayed neutral. There was no persuading him to choose a side. It was simply his nature. He never liked to see anyone unhappy. Yet, the last time she saw him in their kitchen, he was vehemently upset. Could he have been so upset to sell himself out to the Council's upper echelon elite?

The possibilities seemed endless, though puzzles were always her secret, hidden talent. She knew if she wrapped herself around the conundrum full-heartedly, she could solve it. However, she worried that it wouldn't be soon enough; that she would run out of time.

Teacher needed her, and she refused to let him down.

The puzzle proved too much after so little sleep the previous night, and she felt her eyelids grow heavier with each passing thought. Before falling into a deep sleep, she remembered thinking to herself that she hoped the traitor wasn't her father. That would've been too devastating to deal with. It truly would be the most painful betrayal of any of the scenarios. The image of the ever-changing picture haunted her dreams, though she was too exhausted to pay it any attention.

Chapter Twenty-Two: Novice Search

Manna awoke suddenly from a stone-dead sleep. He felt his chest heave with an abrupt burst of oxygen, as a feeling of panic overtook him. He knew where he was, that was not the issue, but he had the panic-stricken feeling that he was late. It wasn't necessarily that he was late, but he was definitely running out of time. Knowing that there was someone within their circle whom they couldn't trust made things a lot more difficult.

He sat up in the bed and his heart skipped another beat as he saw a stranger eyeing him from the corner of the room. The stranger was crouched on the countertop on the other side of the room, like a frog on a lily pad expectantly waiting for a fly to pass overhead. The man stared at him with a beady gaze, as if he were sizing up Manna. He was hidden in shadow, as the room lacked any windows. The slight amount of light shone through the crack in the door that came from the hallway. Manna could see the stranger wore a baseball cap that covered his head and a baggy flannel shirt down past his narrow waist. The jeans he wore were tight-fitting, and looked a size or two too small, as they stopped in the middle of the stranger's calf muscle. The man's military style boots came to a rest a few inches below the jeans.

Manna was reminded of the deal they all had made to not let any of them be alone for any amount of time. The stranger must have been the person assigned to watch over him.

"What time is it, young man?" Manna asked, trying to hide the fact he was startled, but not doing a very good job of it.

"It's about time," the husky voice of the stranger stated. "I didn't think you were ever going to wake up." Manna stared, shocked at the stranger as he came to the realization that it was not a *he*, but a *she*. He did a poor job of hiding his surprise here, as well.

"I am sorry," he started.

"Don't worry about it," the young girl replied. "I'm used to it by now."

She jumped off the countertop and briskly walked toward the door. The young woman was slight in stature, barely reaching five feet, and seemed rail thin to boot. Manna couldn't tell if her annoyance was with the fact he had thought she was a boy, or the simple fact that she had been given the task to watch over him while he slept. Her annoyance was palpable nonetheless. Manna still lay on the bed, unmoving.

"Well, are you coming?" The girl asked as she rolled her eyes, utterly exasperated.

Manna shot out of the bed and followed the girl out the door. He followed her in silence down the well-lit hall, and couldn't help but notice the eerie silence. He was amazed at the true immensity of the building, though he still wasn't entirely sure if Guidry had shown him how vast it truly was earlier. The silence made Manna a tad uneasy.

"I'm Mike Manna," Manna offered the young girl. She could not be more than sixteen or seventeen, if he was to make an estimation, though with the baggy clothes and hat, it seemed more difficult to ascertain her true age. It was her slight build that made Manna believe her to be so young.

"I know who you are," the young girl said smugly. "Do you think I would be entrusted to keep watch over you without knowing at least your name?"

"I guess I should've known," Manna replied, shocked at the boldness of this petite individual. Whatever she lacked in physical form, she sure made up for in brashness. They continued, again, in silence.

She walked briskly, and Manna huffed behind her, clearly winded from the long trek to wherever she was taking him. They came to a set of stairs and she led him up two flights of stairs. Here, he finally heard voices. As the commotion grew, it seemed to invigorate his companion, as she too changed her demeanor and began to talk to Manna less harshly.

"Guidry and everyone else should be in one of the rooms up ahead," she explained to him. "They were planning to hack into the Holly Pines database to see if Guidry would recognize any of the names as being the one you all are looking for. The technology we use is very sophisticated."

Manna had recognized the hallway from before, and knew the room she mentioned. He didn't want her to think him rude, so he let her continue to explain.

"Though, I am told you have already seen it in action," she turned to him, and he could almost see the young girl smirk, though it was nearly as slight as her physical stature.

"Yes, I am aware of the sophisticated nature in which you speak," Manna told her smiling a bit more perceptibly.

She led him to the door he knew she would, and turned again before entering.

"By the way, I'm Carly," she told him, not looking at him directly. Then, she entered the room, letting the door shut behind her.

Manna entered to a cacophony of noise. Conversations were abound all over the room, but one voice superseded all. It was the bellowing voice of A'ron Guidry. The strong aroma of a fresh pot of coffee accompanied Guidry's overpowering vocals, and Manna couldn't help himself from pouring himself a cup before going to see if they had found anything on the database yet. It would help make up for the cup he didn't get to finish due to Guidry's mugging the previous night.

He was in the process of stirring the cream and sugar into his coffee when Guidry finally came over. Manna couldn't stand pure, black coffee. To him, it tasted like licking the bottom of a trash bin. The sugar provided the right amount of sweetness to the blend, and the café mocha-flavored creamer just gave it the correct mocha look and flavor.

Guidry refilled his cup with the murky liquid and took a searing gulp without the requisite amount of cream or sugar Manna needed.

"Drink up," Guidry declared. "We're going to necessitate all of the liquid vigor we can muster."

"It seems I've had more coffee in the last few days, than I have in the last couple years," Manna replied. "Or I've attempted to drink more coffee. I do seem to recall an unfinished cup back in my vehicle due to a kick to the face."

Guidry gave him a sheepish look.

"Have another one on me, then," Guidry told Manna. "I full-heartedly insist."

"I'm sure this won't be my last one of the day," Manna stated as he took a sip. It instantly erased his tired state and provided him the comfort he previously lacked. He was amazed at how comforting a small sip of coffee could be in a time like this, as though the caffeine coursed through his veins, he could feel himself calm down, as the hectic pace of the past few days finally seemed to slow down enough for him to enjoy the pleasures of a cup of coffee. He took another sip and followed Guidry over to a small group huddled around four younger people on computers. Around the room, Manna could see similar quartets of computers, each manned by a young man or woman.

"They've been at it for nearly three hours now," Guidry explained to Manna. Gio, Pierre, Vivienne, Zeke, and Griffin were spread around the room, each looking over the shoulder of a different member of Guidry's clan. Simone was nowhere to be seen. Guidry noticed Manna's eyes scanning the room for his daughter's presence.

"We thought it best she continue with her respite," Guidry clarified.

"She definitely seemed to need it," Manna agreed. "So any luck in finding our Novice Orderly?"

"It seems to be more difficult than we imagined it would," Guidry told him. "According to Gio and Pierre, the young boy, whose father's life I had salvaged in Egypt, is believed to be either a junior or senior at your school."

"So that story you always told was actually true?" Manna asked incredulously. "All those years I thought it was one of your many lies."

"The events were not entirely accurate to a tee," Guidry explained with a smirk. "I had to augment it for the enhanced pleasure of my many spectators. It would've been unkind of me to disgrace my name by stultifying them with the truth. However, I did save the man's life."

"What really did happen?" Manna asked, wanting the answer so desperately. "It's about time I hear how it all occurred; the real version for once."

"It actually transpired because of a calamity on my part," he admitted to Manna. A few of the surrounding individuals, including Gio and Pierre, seemed to overhear their exchange, and as always, Guidry had an audience at rapt attention. He was certainly in his element telling a story.

"I had spent nearly three days in Egypt without seeing a single pyramid or camel, which one would assuredly expect to see on most visitations there. However, I did see a deadly asp, as well as the majestic Nile crocodile."

Vivienne, Zeke, Griffin, along with an even larger crowd of eavesdroppers joined the rest of the crowd in listening to Guidry's tale. Manna noticed even the constant tapping of keystrokes seemed to slow down its quick pace, as some of the people manning the computers were even listening in on the raconteur. It never ceased to amaze Manna how enthralled people could get with Guidry's grandiose tales.

Manna listened with the intent of being enthralled, but his mind quickly shifted its attention to those surrounding faces. Sure, he was able to gather that Guidry was lost in some town in Egypt he didn't quite catch, when he happened upon a family with a car that wouldn't start. Since he could always fake his way into a civilized conversation with relative ease, he pretended to know a lot about cars. Through the telling of the tale, Manna observed the reactions from the eager listeners, and couldn't help but to grin in admiration of Guidry's talents.

Zeke seemed to want to be as close to the action as possible. He stood closest to Guidry and even seemed to lean in closer with each new turn of events

Guidry explained to them. Could he be the traitor? Manna thought to himself. Since he liked to be in the center of the action, it was quite possible.

Or could it be Vivienne in the back? She liked to be towards the back, indiscreet and hidden. Her demeanor suggested a dark past kept hidden from even her closest friends. From what he had gathered from Simone, even she didn't know much about this young woman. She could easily have put herself in place to sabotage the mission at the critical stages. Who better to infiltrate the enemy than an intelligent, scientific mind one would expect to follow Teacher's edict?

He couldn't imagine Gio or Pierre going through what they did in order to simply turn their backs on the others, but it would also make for a good cover. It seemed there could have been an easier way of going about gathering the information they sought than what they had already done. Though, the lack of any emotional response could be a telling sign they were truly not invested in the mission at hand, but another mission altogether.

Griffin seemed a likely candidate, in Manna's eyes. There was just something about him that didn't seem right. His eyes were a little shifty, and he did work in the Council's headquarters. He could have easily been given the information he claimed to have gathered on his own by Kruger himself, in order to gain the trust of the rebel Pupils. Manna thought it would have been an easy ploy, and Griffin seemed to have the easiest access to the Council's trust. Still, Simone had seen something in him worth trusting. He had to trust his daughter's judgment.

Guidry was just finishing up his savior tale as Manna directed his attention back to his longtime friend. Guidry was explaining how he failed in his attempt at getting the car started, when he noticed a deadly Egyptian asp approaching the car from the rear.

"I only noticed the asp's approach from my periphery, and didn't want the man's offspring to make any sudden movement to draw it closer," Guidry explained in full, grandiose style, "as the child was in the open back seat, so I offered to place a call on their behalf from my phone. I kept my eye on the snake as I tried to dial the number they had given me, some contact they knew, perhaps, as they obviously didn't seem local either. The young lad began dragging his foot out the open back door in an act of pure nonchalance, which drew the snake's attention. He didn't procure the brevity of his action as the snake got closer. I found myself impulsively walking closer, though meticulous and slow. My motions didn't seem to draw the snake's ire as much as the child's constant dragging. Then, the boy stopped moving his foot as he saw my attention had been drawn toward him for some strange reason. The boy's father also noticed my captivated attention. In that exact moment, something inexplicably happened that changed my life forever. Few instances can be pinpointed as life altering, but I can honestly claim that what happened in those next few seconds was just that."

"What happened?" an excited voice asked that made the pack of onlookers jump at the sudden interruption. Everyone turned to the unexpected interrogator. Simone had come into the room unbeknownst to Manna, and it seemed everyone else as well. It was she who had inquired.

Guidry had a broad smile on his face as he turned back to the crowd from his sudden inquisition.

"I am glad you asked. Fate intervened and made me drop my phone, drawing the snake's attention. Another moment later, the father had drawn a pistol and shot the snake, killing it with that one shot. The family was so grateful, as they thought my actions purposeful, in order to draw the snake away from their son. I couldn't bring myself to tell them that it slipped out of my nervous hands due to the copious amounts of sweat protruding out of my pores."

"But you did save him, even if it was accidental," Carly stated from the corner of the room. She was the only one in the room not surrounding Guidry and not at a computer terminal. Manna noticed that she liked to lurk on the outskirts, making it possible for her to observe all of her surroundings at once. He made a note to use the same technique in finding the traitor in this very room.

"That's not what earned me their good graces, however," Guidry replied. "It was what happened next that made all the difference."

"Always a flare for theatrics," Manna told Guidry smiling. "You were never one to get straight to the point in a timely manner. Even in the most pressing of times."

"Touché," Guidry retorted. "Let me not digress, then. The family was able to reach their contact and get their car repaired, so they offered to take me back to my hotel. They would be late for their dinner reservation because of their act of benevolence, but they implored me to accept their altruism. I gladly accepted their offer, as I told you earlier, I was lost. It could have taken hours for me to locate it on my own. I, in turn, offered to take them to dinner in a restaurant in the lobby of my hotel, as a reprieve for missing their reservation, and because of the kindness they had shown me. To tell the truth, I felt bad they had missed their reservation because of me, and also felt a tad sheepish for not really doing anything to deserve said kindness."

Vivienne seemed to be losing her patience at the overabundant account, as she sighed indignantly and stated, "Just tell us how you saved this man's life, already. I can't take anymore suspense."

"I was just getting to that, young lady, until you so rudely interrupted," Guidry chided. "You could learn a lesson in patience and humility both."

"Come on, tell us," about half of the onlookers all said instantaneously, and Manna knew they were completely hooked. He had seen it many times over the years when Guidry was involved and feeling rather vivacious.

"Well, it seems the restaurant where they had their reservation had an unpleasant visitor that night," Guidry told them. He also knew they were all at his mercy, and loved the control he had over them. "A suicide bomber took out the entire place and killed nearly eighty patrons of that very restaurant. If that family hadn't taken me to my hotel that night, they would have been among the rubble along with the other victims. So you see, because of me, that family was alive. I had saved their lives."

Here, he paused to let that last statement sink in. Manna took the time to postulate if Guidry could possibly be traitorous. All the animosity he had harbored at the man, because of the lie that had broken their friendship, had dissipated over the last day spent together. It suddenly felt like old times again, but he knew if it could come so suddenly, so too could it be taken away. Manna would not forgive Guidry if he turned out to be the traitor. He had lost his faith in Guidry once before; a second time could not be overcome. He could also not forgive himself for falling for his ploys again, if it turned out Guidry was a traitor. Falling for it all over again would just make him feel completely betrayed by the man he considered to be his closest friend.

"The family took me to a Cohort of Pupils hiding in Egypt," Guidry continued. "For some reason, they thought it their duty to teach me Teacher's lessons, as compensation for prolonging their lives by intervening the way that I had. Fate knocked at my door and I reluctantly opened the door at first, but soon realized he had been sleeping in my dormant mind all along waiting for me to knock first. Everything I saw in Egypt in the time I spent with that family and the other Pupils completely changed my mindset. I was more willing to acknowledge the unfathomable void there was without the everyday, extensive use of my inner thoughts coming alive. As everyone in this room who has experienced the same thing knows, it is total, unabashed reason that compels us to make our life choices in the way that we do. Because I was willing to open up my mind and be taught, I exceeded my own expectations of how much I could possibly achieve. I was able to escape Moon Haven, thwart the Council's detection, and collect this vast collection of minds and able-bodied individuals who wouldn't have a chance otherwise at escaping persecution by the Council. I even got to meet Teacher himself."

The room turned into an echo of gasps as gaped expressions stared at Guidry from all corners of the room. The clicks and clacks of the computer keys completely died, as even those conducting searches stopped what they were doing at this revelation.

"So that part was never a lie?" Manna asked Guidry directly.

"That is accurate," Guidry stated as the hackers continued their attempts at finding Guidry's young Novice Orderly. "Though the Council was never able to prove it for certain, I was always good at conflicting my story enough to make it sound true, yet fabricated at the same time. Wouldn't you agree, my friend?" This last question he directed toward Manna.

"That always seemed to be your gift, yes," Manna replied gulping down the rest of his coffee. "What was the name of this family?"

"The Pupils I met in Egypt mentioned having to constantly be moving, living like nomads without true identities," was Guidry's answer. "The father and son I saved had the last name Constantine, at the time I met them. The father was Marek and the son Lucius. I have not been in contact with them since that initial meeting in Egypt. I don't even know where they currently reside. For all I know, they live nowhere near Holly Pines or even nowhere in the Americas at all."

"Our sources claim he is a student at Holly Pines High School," Simone stated with unnerving resolve. Manna could tell she truly believed in the information she was provided, though her reliance on herself was not as unfaltering.

"Sir, we may have a match," a female voice called over everyone.

Manna followed Guidry to the young woman who had called his attention. She was feverishly typing on the keyboard and within seconds a picture materialized on the screen of the computer in front of her. Guidry reached over to a switch and the screen was broadcast to the entire room on the wall-sized canvas screen at the front. He walked up to the screen to get a closer view of the picture being broadcast for all to see. Manna watched as Guidry seemed to contemplate the authenticity of the picture in front of him. The young woman spoke as Guidry put his hand on the face in front of him, as if it was a lost puppy looking for his help in finding its home. The colors of the picture were superimposed upon Guidry's back as he stood in quiet reflection as the mousy voice of the young woman explained.

"The boy is Lucas 'Luke' Pope, a senior at HPHS. His likeness is a 78% match for the picture recreated from the description you provided. His father is Mark Pope and the mother is Gerta Pope. Address is 2417 Juniper Drive Northwest of Holly Pines. Constantine is the name of a pope in the early 700s. Pope could be their alias for Constantine."

"Lucius's mother was named Greta," Guidry stated without turning around. "This face looks so familiar. This is him, no doubt in my mind. He is the Novice Orderly we are looking for." Guidry finally turned around to look at everyone staring at him. Lucas Pope's face was still superimposed on his body. "Ladies and gentlemen, the Novice Orderly has been found."

II: Found

Chapter Twenty-Three: Lucas Pope

Simone saw the face of Lucas Pope and immediately it registered as the face from the picture Kruger had shown her as the traitorous Novice Orderly within Teacher's ranks. The young man had been shaking hands with Kruger himself. Though this thought registered in a rapid memory displacing itself as the truth, she knew better than to have complete faith in its authenticity. The same thing had happened with Guidry, Vivienne, Zeke, and the rest of the people she had put her trust in for this mission. For all she knew, Lucas Pope was the true traitor, but she wasn't going to let Kruger take away her ability to reason, though he had taken away her ability to remember this vital detail she had locked away in the recesses of her mind. He wasn't going to have the upper hand. She refused to relinquish the control of her mind to a man such as him. It was because of this that she didn't let the others see her falter upon seeing Lucas Pope's picture on the screen. Her moment of panic was kept to herself; she was certain, due to her proximity to the rear of the crowd. Besides, she reassured herself, everyone's attention, as always, was on Guidry, as well as the image on the screen. A lone figure off to the corner of the room, a petite girl with a hood pulled over her eyes and black hiking boots hanging off the edge of the table on which she sat, seemed to take in the entirety of the room with her furtive glances. If anyone caught the slight moment of weakness Simone had portrayed, it would've been this girl, and no one else.

"We are going to need to clear our schedule today, folks," Guidry stated as he finally turned to address the crowd again. "Lucas Pope is in need of a visitor or two. I think it is time to pay my respects to the family that helped me learn a thing or two about myself."

"What do you plan on doing?" Carly's voice spoke up from the corner. "Knocking on the door and asking to talk to him after all these years? Do you actually think they still remember you? I'm sure you have not been on this family's mind as much as they have been on yours. They ever send you a Christmas card or a 'Thank You'?"

"If they are anything like me," Guidry replied, failing to acknowledge Carly's obvious jab at him, "I would think they remember each person they *taught* to be a Pupil, my dear Carly Windham."

If it were at all possible, she seemed to sink further into the crevices of the room, shrinking into the shadowy alcoves around her.

"I know what Carly means, though," Manna piped up in support of the young girl. "We need some sort of plan to get ourselves the information we are seeking. If Lucas is truly a Novice Orderly, he will not just divulge the information without some coaxing on our end. How do you plan to do that?"

"You do not have to be so worrisome," Guidry answered casually. "You have me on your side. When have you ever seen anyone not give me the information I need?"

"There's a first time for everything," Manna replied, though he knew Guidry was speaking the truth. More often than not, Guidry could smooth talk information out of someone by simply putting on his charm. Though he seemed to have lost some of that ability, Manna didn't doubt it still lurked somewhere in Guidry and was still able to be used.

If Lucas Pope was truly a Novice Orderly, he would want Teacher to know about the betrayal as soon as humanly possible. That is unless Lucas was the one they had been sent to warn Teacher about all along.

"We can't have an army busting the door down, however," Simone disclosed. "He would never believe us if that was our tactic."

"I thought of that too," Guidry told her. "That is why we'll only have three of us for this mission."

"How will we choose which one of us will go?" This time it was Vivienne asking the question. Manna noticed her inability to keep quiet at times of high intensity. She was not a patient individual.

"Of course, I must go as I have already made their acquaintanceship," Guidry answered. He was spinning his cane nonchalantly as he ticked off the three individuals. Manna half-expected him to yawn at the sheer boredom the situation seemed to provide him. "I'd like Manna and Simone to be the other two. Simone began this quest by seeking Manna out. It seems only fair to see the two of them there at its penultimate event."

The rest of the room seemed in agreement on this issue. Guidry, however, had one last idea in mind.

"I also would like Gio, Vivienne, Pierre, Zeke, Griffin, and Carly to tag along for back up purposes," he explained. "You can post yourself in a van the next block over. Make sure to cover us explicitly. Any inadequate performances will put Teacher's life on the line. Give me thirty minutes to get everything in order and we'll roll on out of here."

Guidry turned and rushed out of the room on a definite purpose. Most of the other individuals in the room pulled out phones, followed Guidry's mad dash out of the room, or started typing furiously on keyboards. It seemed to

Manna that the only people who were still standing in the room were those involved with the mission itself, other than Guidry.

Lucas Pope's face still shimmered brightly on the canvas screen. Manna could see the boyish face stoically staring at him across the room. He recognized the face, but didn't know anything about the young man on the screen. He had spent his many years at Holly Pine High School trying to be as anonymous as possible. He hadn't wanted to meddle into another individual's privacy, and hadn't wanted anyone to meddle into his. He knew that if people started sniffing their noses around his life; they would happen upon Simone, and that would have put his daughter's life in jeopardy.

The door opened and interrupted his reverie. Guidry poked his head in and called for Manna to join him in the hall.

"I just wanted to make sure you're okay with your role in this," Guidry explained to Manna as the door shut behind him. "I wanted you with me, because you are someone I can trust implicitly. Simone, on the other hand, I need her there for a completely different reason. I am worried about her mental status at this point. I want to keep a closer eye on her because of it. Not everyone will be able to handle her if she has another of her meltdowns. I think you and I will be the only two up to this task."

"I agree," Manna stated in understanding. Guidry was truly a friend. "What about the others? Why'd you want them along?"

"Don't forget that Simone has pieces of the truth inside her still," Guidry explained. "I believe one of the others is the traitor, and I don't want them out of one another's sight long enough to warn Kruger."

"And Carly?" Manna asked, still not understanding her part in it.

"Carly is someone I trust implicitly," Guidry replied. "She is a great observer and picks up on each minute detail available to her at every angle of her periphery. Besides," Guidry paused to look intently into Manna's eyes. "She's my daughter."

Manna couldn't have been more shocked by this revelation. Carly, the tiny, quiet, behind the scenes girl who didn't even seem comfortable in her own skin was Guidry's daughter. He who always commanded the attention in the room like a sea captain directing a ship in a storm; both conducting themselves with precise control and confidence that could never be unnerved. Carly was the exact opposite. Guidry could live vicariously through his stories, and never be himself, but his daughter seemed to want more than anything to be someone other than herself, from what little Manna knew of her up to that point. He couldn't help but to notice the irony in it all.

"I would have never guessed," Manna replied not attempting to hide his utter shock.

"I never would have either," Guidry said. "I didn't even know she existed until last year. As you know, I never married. Her mother gave her up for adoption and never told me about her. Her mother died a year and a half ago, just a few months before I found out about her. One of my analysts came across her birth certificate with my name forged onto it, and brought it to my attention. Can you believe the audacity of such a thing? Hiding something like that takes some nerve. Anyways, I had her following you around because I wanted her to feel I was giving her more responsibility."

"Though you knew I wasn't the traitor," Manna stated as he understood Guidry's side. "So you had her following me because you knew she wouldn't get hurt. That's why she seemed so irritated by me. She knew she wasn't really doing anything productive, but something completely useless."

"Exactly, she has an amazing mind; shows some highly sophisticated thinking. I was stupid to think she wouldn't see through the facade from the start. That's why I want her on this mission. I want her to know I trust her, and she can help us figure out who the real traitor is. If anyone can, she will," Guidry said this with a pride only a father can have for his child.

"Let's hope the traitor tips his or her hand, then" Manna replied. "We're going to need all the help we can get, I believe."

"Back to my original question," Guidry said trying to get back to business. "Are you okay with your role in all of this?"

"My daughter needs me, and as a father like you would know, my daughter's prerogatives always come before mine," Manna answered coolly. "This Teacher character also seems to be in need as well. I can't turn my back on someone in need. No matter how much or how little I believe in the cause, I do know that it just isn't right how Teacher is treated by the Council. Maybe he's onto something and can make this world a better place. I know the Council sure hasn't perfected anything as of yet."

"Mike Manna, I do believe we'll make a true Pupil out of you yet," Guidry said with pride. "Give me another thirty minutes and we'll pay Pope a visit."

Manna made his way back to the others. Carly conspicuously caught his eye as he entered, and somehow Manna felt she knew that Guidry had told him about being her father. She was incredibly perceptive and her intuition seemed right on. Manna was impressed. He imperceptibly nodded in her direction and he noticed a glimmer of a smirk appear momentarily. Simone had also noticed his entrance, as did the others.

"Is everything all right?" Simone asked her father.

"Just fine," was his reply. "Are you?"

He had the face of a concerned father. It had been his first opportunity to ask after her brief rest.

"I still cannot shut out the image as it continuously changes in my mind," Simone answered, though she looked much more strong-willed than she had been the night before. The rest seemed to have given her some renewed vigor. "That Pope kid was also substituted, so we'll have to be cautious. It would do no good for us to jump to conclusions, though. He's our only shot at reaching Teacher before Kruger gets to him. We'll have to trust that he isn't the traitor or else our cause is truly a lost one. Just as I have to trust each of you isn't either."

She gave a quick glance at each of the people surrounding her, making sure to look each one of them directly in the eye. Manna could tell she wasn't taking it lightly that one of them was a traitorous serpent.

"How are we going to convince Pope that our information is credible?" Zeke asked after Simone's brief stare-down.

"Guidry's methods are very convincing," Manna explained. "As you saw for yourself, he has a way with words."

"How do we know he even has the knowledge of Teacher's whereabouts?" Griffin took his turn at questioning.

"That's true," Vivienne stated. "If the Novice Orderlies each know where Teacher is, why hasn't the traitor lead Kruger to him already? It would seem foolish to wait for someone to warn him or have him move to another location."

All of these questions seemed perplexing to Manna. Not only had he not thought of them himself, but they all seemed legitimate questions that only added to the confusing nature of their predicament. He could see why these individuals were sought out as Pupils in the first place. Their reasoning ability alone had outshined any of his former schoolmates. It was hard to believe they had come from the same educational philosophy that some of the other students did; the ones that he witnessed at his school on a daily basis. These modern students felt it their daily objective to see how wasted one another could get before lunch.

"These are all valid questions," Manna finally replied, trying to stop the sudden barrage of questions. He certainly wasn't used to being asked so many thought-provoking questions at any one time. "Let's meet this Pope kid first before we get carried away with speculation. He might be able to answer some of your questions himself. First, let's worry about getting Pope to even let us in, and then we'll worry about the rest. Let's not get too ahead of ourselves, and answer the questions once we can gather more information, or else we'll drive ourselves crazy with all the possible scenarios and outcomes. Is that okay with everyone?"

They all agreed and Manna noticed Simone smile proudly at his ability to take charge of the situation. He felt proud himself. He wasn't usually the one to take on the role of a leader. He usually left the leading to others with more knowledge or experience in that kind of role - someone like Guidry. Since Guidry wasn't present, he felt it necessary, for some reason, to take control himself. He was surprised at how easy it had been.

He strolled over to the coffee pot to refuel his caffeinated fix. Carly wandered over in his direction, and stopped at the coffee pot as well. She grabbed a coffee stirrer, stirred Manna's coffee with it, and stuck it in her mouth. The gesture was not in a seductive manner, but in a rather nonchalant way that made Manna feel it was a habit of hers to chew on coffee stirrers.

"Now I see why my father befriended you so long ago," she said as she chewed on the stirrer. "You can command respect out of a room without having to be someone else; you can simply be yourself and people listen and are willing to follow. The only way Father can accomplish what you just did is with a charade of epic proportion."

"I don't understand," Manna told her honestly.

"My father admires you," she replied as she began to walk out of the room. She turned around at the door in order to give Manna the rest of her reply. "That is why he wanted to be your friend."

The door shut behind her as Manna stood dumbfounded. Even Guidry's offspring had an uncanny ability with words. The only difference was the offspring seemed to not tell as many lies, seeking only to want to tell the truth instead. It was an admirable trait; one which Manna never thought he'd see a Guidry possess.

Chapter Twenty-Four: Convincing a Novice Orderly

As promised, Guidry was ready within half an hour and Manna found himself driving the red Pontillac Guidry provided to the Pope residence. Guidry was in the passenger seat and Simone was seated in the back; she seemed to be keeping to herself at the moment. Manna agreed to drive, since the car was similar to his own, which Guidry had told him was safely in hiding. They didn't think it wise for Manna to drive his own vehicle out in the open, so they chose this one instead. Since the windows were tinted, and since they were seemingly going to make only one stop, they didn't feel the need for disguises. They also felt a disguise might be a bit too conspicuous for the Popes to gain their trust. However, each wore a pair of sunglasses and a hat just in case. Simone looked somewhat younger with a ponytail protruding out of the back of her cap.

Manna circled the Pope road twice to make certain no one was following them or watching the Pope house on surveillance. Though they had just found the information of Pope's possible affiliation with Teacher themselves, they were not underestimating Kruger's ability to find the information as well.

Kruger had been a pilot during the big war and had been taken hostage somewhere in the Middle East. This fact was common knowledge that anybody on the internet could gather in mere minutes. It was also well-known that he had endured several months of arduous torture while being held captive. Though the exact nature of the torture was vague, the extent of it could be seen in several photos taken by paparazzi while Kruger had been on a public beach before becoming Council Secretary. Though his face had been spared permanent scarring, his upper body looked like a jigsaw puzzle that had been sewn together because the pieces wouldn't fit properly. It was widely accepted that Kruger used similar methods of what he endured, if not the exact same, during his own interrogations.

Manna could only imagine what he would be willing to do in order to gain further information about Teacher. The fact Simone had been in his grasp made Manna thankful they were able to rescue her before more damage had been done. Sure, her psyche had been scarred, but there had been no physical damage. If she had been there longer, it may have been a different story. Who knew what Kruger had planned for Simone and the others? Manna didn't want to think about the endless possibilities.

On the third time around the block, and after agreeing it was safe, Manna stopped in front of the Pope house. It had a three foot brick trim at the bottom of the exterior leading to a pale bluish siding. Manna thought it to be Victorian in nature, though he wasn't entirely certain what made a building Victorian. A garage looked to be connected at the rear of the house, though Manna couldn't be certain if it truly was.

Guidry placed a decrypted phone to his lips to let the others, parked a block away, know the plan was about to be set into motion.

"We're here," he said into it. "Be on the lookout for anything suspicious you see progressing in our direction. We will parlay the information we have into something more useful. I will possess the phone throughout our endeavor, but only call if it is of utter importance. Otherwise, leave us to our own undertaking."

"We will not be seen or heard," Vivienne replied from the other end. "Got it."

"By the way, you don't need to try to impress us with your large and mostly inept vocabulary, Father Dearest," Carly stated, clearly taking the phone. "You're not telling one of your convoluted stories right now, so you can cut to the chase a little more quickly. I know we're all intelligent and all, but I think the circumstances kind of call for it to be short and sweet. Don't you think?"

Guidry had the phone on speaker, so Simone and Manna could hear it as well. They both couldn't contain a fit of laughter as Guidry closed the phone and put it into his back pocket with a look of utter annoyance.

"She's definitely gotten her brazenness from you," Manna told him smiling.

"You should have seen her mother," Guidry replied with a smirk. "Now, there was a lady with some spunk."

"Wait, Carly is your daughter?" Simone piped up from the backseat. She clearly hadn't caught Carly's *Father Dearest* remark from her little rant.

"Shocking isn't it?" Guidry asked her. "To think, my goddaughter likes me more than my biological one."

"I didn't like you as much as you thought I did, Uncle A'ron," Simone confessed. "I would only dote upon you so you wouldn't try to fool me with your lies. Not to mention, all those times you would try to use me in those lies of yours, too."

"See," Guidry stated in response. "Just think what Carly's impression of me is, then."

"You ready?" Manna asked them. "Or are you going to plan some type of family reunion picnic? We don't have time to go back down memory lane."

"You are impeccable in your judgment," Guidry said getting out of the car.

He swung his cane in large circles as he walked the path to the door. Manna and Simone followed a few steps behind. Guidry looked nonchalant as he stepped to the door, as if this were something he had done on a daily basis - knocking on the door of some friend he hadn't seen in years, just for a simple chat about the most wanted man on the planet. To Guidry, it was no big deal.

Manna, however, felt the paranoia of the situation creep up on him. He was frantically looking behind him. Each step seemed to bring him closer to a meltdown of epic proportion. His heart was running on overdrive now, and at any moment its main system was going to crash; never to be restarted again.

Surprisingly, Simone seemed to share Guidry's calm demeanor. She had none of the telltale signs of being worried; she even tried to peer in the large, picture window to see if anyone was home. She showed no reserve in her inner strength. It was like he was looking at a different person he had seen the night before. His daughter's resolve made it clear how completely out of his element he truly was. He was a janitor, for Christ's sake. What did he know about espionage or world diplomacy?

Guidry reached up to ring the doorbell, but seemed to change his mind and use the brass knocker.

"I just love knockers," Guidry stated with a sheepish look. "The bigger the better."

"Uncle A'ron, you are simply incorrigible," Simone replied.

"Oh, you thought I was referring to one of my many vices," Guidry explained. "I was simply referring to the reverence I have for the majestic and aristocratic look a door knocker has. The bigger ones seem much more sophisticated looking, in my opinion."

"Oh, I thought…nevermind," Simone stammered, though Manna noticed the smirk on Guidry's face as he turned back toward the closed door. He tried the knocker again; this time a little louder than before.

"What if they aren't here?" Manna asked. They hadn't contemplated that outcome. Guidry looked a bit uncertain.

"They have to be here," he said, obviously in denial that one of his plans could not turn out as planned, though Manna was already witness to such a plan already, with the rescue attempt of Simone that turned into a near bloodbath for some of those involved. As Manna began to doubt Guidry's ability, a voice behind them startled them.

"Can I help you?" It was a man, maybe a decade younger than Manna, and he had a speculative look in his eye. He seemed to be asking, *Who the hell are you and what are you doing here?*

"Marek, my friend," Guidry said joyfully. "It's been many years since our last acquaintance, but I would recognize you anywhere."

The man seemed to change his demeanor momentarily upon hearing Guidry's words. He seemed to glance around agitatedly to see if anyone else had overheard Guidry's boisterous greeting.

"My name is Mark Pope, and who are you?" The man replied.

Manna had forgotten they still had their sunglasses and hats on, which wouldn't have been as implausible if it hadn't been so cloudy. Guidry took off his Bowler and glasses, and then looked at Mark Pope seeking any sign of recognition. Manna suddenly thought they may have been mistaken in this man's true identity. Maybe he wasn't really Marek Constantine, maybe he truly was just some guy named Mark Pope, someone that didn't belong in a pressurized situation they were currently in at the moment. As Manna was contemplating Pope's identity, Simone suddenly spoke up.

"Mr. Constantine, your son may be one of a few people alive that can help us divert a global disaster," she pleaded. "We need his help. We need yours, too."

He seemed to deliberate for a few seconds and finally made his decision.

"Let's go inside to talk about this, then we can be a little less discreet," he nodded toward the door. "The door should be unlocked. I was just around back when I heard your knocks."

Guidry turned the knob and stood aside for Manna and Simone to go in first. He did the same for Mark Pope, but Pope stopped before entering and reached out his hand.

"It's good to see you again, my friend," he said as Guidry took the proffered hand and shook it. Both of their strong grips said the words neither could say at the moment out in the open. Guidry could feel the sincerity in Marek's words. Marek truly did enjoy seeing Guidry again. Marek and Guidry joined Simone and Manna in the house as Marek shut the door behind him.

"Let's go into the den to discuss this matter," Marek stated when the door was closed. Manna and Simone took a seat on the plush sofa. Guidry took a seat on a wooden straight-back chair; he had uncharacteristically turned down comfort in the form of a recliner. He passed on it in order to focus more on the conversation than for the comfort purposes the recliner possessed. Marek, instead, sat in the recliner, though he didn't choose to recline it. The atmosphere was too intense to think about the pleasantries comfort could bring.

"Do explain why my son is so detrimental to the world's fate," he eyed his three guests the way a pit boss does when suspecting someone of counting cards, looking not in the least skeptical that some transgression was taking place, and trying to maintain focus to see if it could be caught. He finally settled on Guidry to provide the answer he sought.

"We believe your son to be a Novice Orderly in Teacher's Cohort, and we are in dire need to find Teacher in order to warn him of a plot against him, within that same Cohort cell," Guidry divulged. "When last I saw you, you led a Pupil's life. I can only assume that is your lifestyle still. Am I mistaken in my assumption?"

Marek again eyed his guests; quietly contemplating how much to disclose himself.

"Please, Mr. Pope," Simone pleaded. "We do not have time to deliberate on this matter. If you have given up on your Pupil way of life, then you may as well turn us over to Kruger himself at this moment. This is our last option of recourse."

"Without it, Teacher is as good as caught," Guidry offered his support.

"Or worse," Manna added.

"No one, here, will be turning anyone in for the Council's bidding," Marek answered after a brief pause. He apparently saw something worth trusting in the individuals sitting across from him in his den. "Your assumptions are quite accurate, I still believe in the lessons Teacher provides. My son, Lucius, is indeed a Novice Orderly. He is, in fact, still out on a recruiting mission, in which he spent all night spreading those teachings to others like us. However, how do I know your information is accurate? I apologize for questioning its validity, but if you are truly Pupils as you seem to be claiming, then you must know that rumor is too often void of truth. 'Trusting conjecture can lead to believing in a lie.' Isn't that what Teacher is known to say?"

"You are well-versed in the words of Teacher," Guidry stated, duly impressed with Marek Pope. "However, doesn't he also state, 'if we do not believe in our own ability to separate fact from fiction, then nothing can be truly understood'? I have tremendous faith in my goddaughter's ability to ascertain the fact from the convoluted fiction she is faced with every day. She works closely with the Council as one of its chief accountants, and must give a faux-smile each day, as if she believes the lies being thrown around about where the money is being spent. I consider her qualified in determining if a rumor is accurate, or simple propaganda."

"We must take the threat seriously then," Marek replied with a scratch of his chin. "Lucius should be home shortly."

The phone in Guidry's pocket beeped loudly, announcing an incoming call. It made everyone jump with a startled jolt. Guidry answered it, listened to the caller, and hung up without a word.

"A black sports car with highly tinted windows is headed this way," he relayed what the caller had warned. "We may need to go." He started to get out of the chair and head toward the front door.

"No need to go," Marek stated. "That's Lucius' car. He's the person you came to see. I told you he'd be home soon."

"It's about time our luck has changed," Manna said with a showing sigh of relief. "I was beginning to think nothing would go right."

"Ye of little faith," Guidry said to Manna. "Never lose hope, or all hope is lost."

"Is that another one of Teacher's witticisms?" Manna asked, not completely understanding Guidry's words.

"Nope," Guidry replied. "That's an A'ron Guidry original."

"I should've known," Manna said with a smirk. "It has that Guidry ability to make something so obvious sound intelligent. Only you could repeat the same idea twice and make it sound different."

"Impressive, huh?" Guidry answered with obvious pride.

Lucas Pope entered the house through the back door. Manna could hear a set of keys get thrown onto a table. Then, the kid looked through the refrigerator, and then the refrigerator door closed.

"Dad, you in here?" He asked from the kitchen.

"In the den, son," Marek replied, clearly intending to surprise his son with the visitors.

Lucas turned the corner and stopped in mid-bite of a sandwich he was eating. His eyes darted around the room, searching for familiarity in the strangers' faces. He didn't seem to recall ever seeing any of them, until he laid eyes upon Guidry. Guidry clearly saw the recognition.

"It's good to see you again, my boy," he told Lucas Pope. "My, how you have grown."

"Have a seat, son," Marek told him. "Teacher needs your help."

"What do you mean, Teacher needs my help?" Lucas asked perplexed.

"They think one of your fellow Novice Orderlies is a traitor seeking to turn Teacher over to the Council," the boy's father told him pointing in the strangers' direction, as if absolving himself of bringing the idea to fruition. The claim was the visitors', and not his own.

Manna noticed the news seemed to sink in slowly, as if the boy was trying to digest the validity in his father's words. Lucas seemed to measure the strangers with a steely glare, as Marek had done upon hearing the news himself. The doubt the boy seemed to possess was palpable, yet there was a curiosity there too. He knew the implications if the statement was indeed fruitful. The implications would prove even more devastating if they had indeed possessed them, yet did nothing in response. Inaction seemed an option no one was willing to take.

"Why do you feel this blasphemy is true?" Lucas demanded visibly upset. "Do you think, with all the wisdom he possesses, Teacher would choose someone unworthy to be of Novice Orderly rank? Teacher does not misjudge character, he breeds it in each lesson taught."

"I know this must be hard to hear," Simone told Lucas. "However, I assure you that it is true. Someone working as a spy for me within the Council informed me of the conspiracy. In fact, I was even shown visual evidence by Kruger himself that a traitor truly resides within your ranks."

"You know who it is then?" Lucas asked amazed.

"That fact hadn't been disclosed to me," Marek said, equally amazed as well.

"Which Novice Orderly is it?" Lucas demanded. "We need to give Teacher this information as soon as possible." He turned to leave, but was quickly stopped by Simone's admission.

"The true identity of the traitor was taken from my memory. Kruger had it extracted from my brain, and replaced with a false one. I'm sorry; I no longer possess the traitor's face. In fact, your face has even seen its place, though I'm hoping this is not accurate."

Lucas turned back to look at Simone. He seemed to think her words were pure lunacy.

"You mean to say you lost the information we so desperately need?" He was totally flabbergasted at her admission.

"It's not lost, just misguided in a sense," Guidry tried to explain to him. He noticed Marek was intrigued as well. "She knows certain facts about the ordeal, just not the specifics of who she truly saw in the photograph. Indeed, there is not just one conspirator, but another as well which we believe might be in a van a block away. The problem is we are not certain as to either conspirator's identity. It is any of a number of suspects. In fact, at one point I was finger-pointed as being as such as well. Though, I hope I have proven my innocence by now." He turned to look at Manna and Simone for confirmation. Neither would confirm nor deny, so he turned back to Lucas and Marek.

"You brought one of the collaborator's here?" Lucas was astonished. "You cannot be a Pupil by showing such imprudence as that."

"On the contrary," Guidry explained, "we could not let the defector get the upper hand by alerting Kruger of our whereabouts, so we cannot let him or her out of our sights. We have checked for bugs, so no one is being tracked either."

"Then you are not totally irrational," Lucas replied. It appeared that he was a bit impressed with their logic. "We need to get this information to Teacher. It is of the utmost importance. He'll know what to do with it."

"That's why we sought you out," Simone stated. "We need a way to get this information to him. Since you would be most likely to know where he was, we thought you could help. It's been nearly five days since we first were given the information. I'm fearful that time might be running out."

"We're in luck," Lucas answered. "The Novice Orderlies are supposed to all meet two days from now in a secret location. Not even I know the exact locale at the moment. We all receive an encrypted email with a coded message telling us where this meeting place is. Teacher usually shows up a day before we are to meet. He likes to get there early to get the agenda, which he calls the syllabus, written and make sure everything is in order. We can just get there a day early as well, in order to warn him."

"What if the traitor is there a day early too?" Manna asked curiously.

"Then we'll have our traitor, won't we?" Lucas replied. Manna noticed that Lucas possessed an inner strength well beyond what his age represented. Manna could tell this is what attracted Teacher's attention to this young man in making him a Novice Orderly. A rank Lucas did not seem to take lightly.

"Teacher needs us to get there first, then," Simone stated. Manna could see the paranoia returning to his daughter's eyes. "Or else the Council will have already won."

"Then this isn't a race we can afford to lose," Lucas told her. "Let's see if that email has arrived. We need to figure out where the finish line is first, or we don't stand a chance."

Chapter Twenty-Five: Note from Teacher

Guidry, Manna, and Simone followed Lucas into his room, and Lucas sat at the computer at his desk. He turned it on and it immediately commenced the startup process.

"Teacher usually sends the email by now, considering it is so close to the meeting date," Lucas explained to his guests. "I usually take a day or two off from school when the Novice Orderlies meet, and it seems to go unnoticed since most students tend to skip at random times throughout the year. It's a commonality that benefits my cause, and I tend to skip other times as well as not to make my skipping purpose obvious. Heck, there are people who skip weeks at a time without suspicion or consequence."

"I do recall seeing some people after a long absence of not seeing them," Manna confirmed. "I sometimes think they had moved to another place, but they end up showing back up again. Everyone seems to forget I'm there, but I do notice those frequent faces I see constantly in the hallway when they should be in classrooms."

"See, as long as you show up on the day of the big test," Lucas continued, "it doesn't matter if you are there the other days or not, especially if you can pass the test. Get a high enough score and administration will expunge any missed days from your record. Many of my peers have picked up on that trend all right, though few get to reap in the benefits as they don't end up passing the first time."

As he continued to explain the intricate knowledge of high school truancy, Lucas typed away furiously on the keyboard of his computer. An email login quickly materialized onto the screen, along with a series of binary numbers Manna was too naïve about to understand. As Manna watched, the screen glowed a bright green, and then went completely black. Momentarily, it looked like the computer had gone to sleep or been shut down, but then a row of numbers appeared again in a purplish haze. To Manna, it looked like it was completely out of focus.

"What is going on with your computer?" Guidry asked, noticing the same obscurity.

"It is just the encryption we use in order to email over a secure server," Lucas replied. "It should be up momentarily. Ah, there it is, right now. And look, an email from Teacher."

Manna, Guidry, and Simone watched Lucas Pope click on an email from Uncle Archimedes. Manna couldn't help but to chuckle at the obscure name Teacher was using in his correspondence with this young man. The message appeared on the screen and everyone in the room read it silently. The three guests peered over Lucas's shoulder and appeared to get closer to the screen the further down the message they read. Manna finished reading and read over it again, to see if he could make sense of the nonsensical message.

Lucas,

I hope your father is still in good health. Tell him I am sorry to have forgotten to call him for his birthday last month. I will make it up to him next time we come to visit. Stephanie is doing great. Like you, she will be graduating this year. How about meeting me for lunch on Thursday, as I will be up your way on business? I will actually be up there Wednesday, but will be busy with meetings all day, so Thursday will have to do. Let me know if you can make it. I'd love to catch up with you and see how things are going. If you can't make it, let me know. Stephanie won't be there, as she will be at School. Hope to see you Thursday. Send my regards to your father.

Uncle A

"What is all that supposed to mean?" Guidry asked utterly confused. "I thought you said he'd divulge to you where the meeting would take place."

"All I see is an invitation to have lunch," Manna replied with the same look of consternation. "How is this helpful?"

"Indeed, it does disclose where we are to have our meeting," Lucas said with a slight smirk. He obviously was able to read more into it than the others had. "You just have to know what to be looking for."

An audible and recognizable ping could be heard from several locations in the Pope household. Everyone in the room discerned it to be the indicator signal that a transmission from the Council was about to begin. Even Lucas's computer screen tuned to the same image that was being broadcast everywhere in the Americas the Council wanted it received, which meant the entire population. At the moment it was a simple countdown, which was typical for these showings.

"Are you seeing this, dad?" Lucas called to his father in the other room. As if it was at all possible for someone to not be watching at this very second.

A grunt of affirmation came down the hallway as a response. Guidry, Manna, and Simone surrounded Lucas at his computer and held their collective breaths. Because it was the Council, it could be anything. Manna had the distinct inclination that it somehow had something to do with what they were all trying to do. Had the traitorous Novice Orderly already struck a deal with Kruger and Teacher was in custody? It sickened Manna to consider that he was about to see Teacher's bloody face staring back at him when an image finally appeared. Instead, it was much worse.

Once the countdown reached zero, Manna and the rest of the world were thrown right in the middle of what could only be described as a massacre. The view appeared to come from a soldier carrying a camera on his head or around his neck. Through the first-person perspective, it was the onslaught that unnerved Manna most; a cool, calculated purpose to the soldier's every movement. Several other soldiers wearing the familiar garb of the Council surrounded the one carrying the camera, and they were storming into a building with reckless abandon. It was clear they possessed the element of surprise as they put a bullet into anything that moved ahead of them that didn't possess the Council soldier's insignia on their clothing. And there didn't seem to be an end to the number of moving targets for the soldiers to hit. Though there was no sound, Manna could imagine the screams of the bloody carnage being portrayed onscreen.

For a moment, Manna dreaded the Council had finally caught up to Teacher and were about to get their hands on him for good, but then a sense of familiarity came over him. He seemed to recognize some of the walls of the building he was seeing through the moving camera, and he couldn't help but think some of the faces he saw being slaughtered were familiar to him as well. He squinted in order to focus a little more on the surroundings of the building being ambushed. Guidry must have sensed it too at that moment as he leaned closer to the computer screen.

"My God!" Guidry exclaimed. It was clear he was totally aghast at what they were all seeing on the screen. He placed his hand on the screen as the soldier with the camera entered a large room of computers. Several people tried running out of the room or hiding under one of tables in the room, but they were no match for the oncoming bullets. Manna noticed a stream of tears on Guidry's face.

It wasn't until a very familiar face came over the screen that Manna realized why Guidry was reacting so strongly to the events on the screen. It was the face of a man that had caused Manna to feel both a little panic and also a little relief in the past week. The man with the familiar face attempted to surrender by waving his large hands in the air, but surrender was an option the soldiers were unwilling to take at the moment. The man went down in a heap after being shot ruthlessly. The man who had just been shot had been one of the two no necks Guidry had been with when Manna was attacked by and reunited with Guidry.

"That's where we just were," Manna said aloud as the realization dawned on him. He was staring at a live feed from Guidry's compound. Then another familiar face filled the screen for the briefest of moments, except this one wore the Council insignia, the all too familiar TC in dark red, block letters superimposed into a green triangle.

"Polchinski!" Guidry seethed between clenched teeth. His jaw held firm as his anger grew.

"The motorcycles," Simone exclaimed from behind him.

"They were bugged," Guidry tersely stated, finishing her thought. "We led them right to us."

"Which means you could have led them hear as well," Lucas Pope stated with fear lacing his words.

"That I doubt, my dear boy," Guidry told him. "They were tracking the bikes, not any one of us. Though haste may still be our best approach."

Marek appeared at the door holding Guidry's ringing phone with a solemn look on his face from what was still being broadcast on the screens around the world.

"This must have fallen out of your pocket when you got out of the chair," Marek told Guidry handing him the beeping phone. "I found it on the floor beside the chair you had been sitting in. That chair is like the Bermuda Triangle for cell phones. It happens to me all the time."

Guidry took the phone from Marek and answered it. Manna could hear the frantic voice on the other end of the line, though he couldn't make out the words, it was in a clear panic. Guidry's face reflected the terror on the other end of the line. He hung up and quickly put it into his back pocket again.

"Three vehicles are speeding our way, and Griffin recognizes them as being from the Council," he told everyone as he turned to exit Lucas Pope's bedroom. "We need to get out of here, now."

He only made it a few steps when the sound of broken glass made him stop and duck. Marek dropped to the floor like a sack full of concrete, and landed with an even louder, more sickening thud than the concrete would elicit. The rest of the people in the room fell to the ground as well, but all of their own accord. Guidry looked over at Marek and noticed a bloody hole in the middle of Marek's forehead where a bullet had entered, and a larger hole at the back in which it had exited. He knew his friend was certainly dead, and it looked like he might suffer the same fate.

"Any chance you have another way out?" Guidry asked Lucas from the floor. He saw the shock on the boy's face at seeing his father killed in cold blood.

"My car is in the garage," he replied, quickly gathering his resolve. Manna couldn't help but be amazed at the maturity the young man was showing in the face of danger. "If we can get to it, we might be able to outrun them."

"Who knows how many people are actually out there," Manna stated, unsure about how dire the situation truly was. The unknown was what worried him most. "You can pack a lot of people into three vehicles."

"There's no way those vehicles could have gotten here so quickly," Guidry deduced. "Carly said they were on their way, and they're a block away."

"Perhaps, there is a single sniper that was sent out to get the jump on us before the cavalry came," Lucas surmised. The scenario seemed more than plausible, but it also provided them the time they needed to get to the garage before the cavalry did show.

"Lead the way to the garage," Manna told Lucas. "We may as well try to outrun them somehow."

"Okay," Lucas agreed. "Follow me."

He army-crawled down the hallway from his room, making sure to stay as low as possible. The other three followed staying low as well. Lucas blindly reached for the keys he had previously thrown onto the table. He quickly found them and crawled toward the back door. They picked up the pace and got into the garage in no time. The garage contained no windows, so they all stood once they got far enough inside. Lucas unlocked the car and they all climbed in. It wasn't meant for four people, as it was a tight fit for those in the back, but Simone and Manna weren't complaining about the lack of leg room considering their present predicament. As Guidry closed the passenger door, Lucas started the car's engine. It purred to life as a series of screeching tires could be heard beyond the closed garage door. Lucas stopped himself inches from the button to release the garage door. He seemed to be contemplating his next move.

"I have always been of the mindset that if you wanted to successfully outrun someone, the element of surprise always works best," Lucas told everyone as he put the car in reverse. "Hold on tight."

He slammed his foot onto the accelerator and the car crashed into the aluminum-framed door. The garage door easily gave way and unhinged itself from the garage itself. It careened into two unsuspecting men carrying pistols who had been standing on the other side of the door. The car came to a jarring stop midway down the driveway as the door, still attached and carrying the two pistol bearers, slammed into a black SUV. Lucas quickly shifted into drive and tore through his front yard; then into the neighbor's front yard as well. He smashed through a lawn gnome the neighbor had in his yard. The gnome exploded into several pieces as it was no match for the nearly two ton car.

Lucas looked at the carnage he had caused through his rearview mirror, only to see two of the SUVs still in working order and heading his way. The other had his garage door in front of it and two bloodied men lying on its hood. He gathered the information he needed in a matter of seconds and then focused his attention back on the road ahead of him. The SUVs seemed to be gaining on him, though he had a clear head start. He needed to make good use of it, if he was to outrun them. The grass was slowing him down, so Lucas turned the wheel and his tires finally gripped the sought after asphalt. Finally, he had the clear advantage.

Guidry heard his phone ring and answered it before it could ring a second time. He listened intently, and then turned to Lucas with the phone still at his ear.

"Turn left just up ahead," Guidry told him. "Then make a right at Hanover. I'm sure you are familiar enough with these streets to know where that is."

"Okay," Lucas said. "But wouldn't Franklin be better, since we can get on the highway from there?"

"Trust me," Guidry confirmed. "Take Hanover, first."

He hung up the phone and turned to look at the speeding SUVs behind them.

"You're going to need to speed up a bit," he told Lucas still looking back. "Put a little more distance between them and us, but not too much. Let them think they have a chance."

"Okay," Lucas said in obvious confusion as he made the left hand turn. "You mind telling me why?"

"You'll see," Guidry answered. He didn't take his eyes off the SUVs behind them.

Manna followed his gaze, but couldn't determine the purpose of the intense stare. Instead, Manna looked up ahead and saw the Hanover sign come into view. Lucas made the sudden right turn with a squeal of tires causing the unmistakable smell of burning rubber to reach Manna momentarily.

"Now, lay on the gas and get the hell out of here," Guidry demanded Lucas. "And you might want to hold onto something back there." Guidry finally faced forward and grabbed onto the door handle, as if it would keep him from falling.

Lucas sped away as the two SUVs turned onto Hanover. The closest SUV was only about thirty yards behind them. Suddenly, an explosion resonated from behind them and a ball of heat reached their backs. Manna

140

turned to look and saw the lead SUV with its back end lifted from the street with a fireball underneath. Then, it landed onto all four wheels again and stopped in the middle of the road. Its undercarriage was on fire. The other SUV had avoided the fireball, but a huge chunk of the asphalt had been removed by the explosion and its front tire was in the large crater instead.

Lucas kept driving down Hanover, though he slowed a bit as not to draw any unneeded attention their way. They passed Carly's van about a half mile down the road. She got behind them and started to follow. When Manna looked back at her, he noticed a huge grin on Carly's face. She was extremely proud that she finally seemed to have a purpose, and Manna couldn't help but be proud of her as well; not to mention extremely thankful. The phone beeped and Guidry answered, beaming with pride himself.

"Perfect timing, my girl," he said into the phone. "Daddy's proud. Now, just keep up. Lucas is going to take us to Teacher."

He hung up the phone and turned to Lucas.

"So where's lunch?" Guidry asked him. Guidry leaned his head back on the headrest and closed his eyes, as if escaping the jaws of death was a daily ritual. He was amazingly calm.

"Like I said," Lucas told Guidry and the other passengers. "Teacher's email needs someone who knows how to interpret it. The days in the emails are always two days off."

"What do you mean?" Simone asked.

"He said Thursday and Wednesday in the email," Lucas explained. "That means the meeting is supposed to be Tuesday, and he will be there a day early, Monday. It is a way to cover ourselves if someone gets hold of the information he shouldn't be privy to. They may be able to interpret where the meeting will take place, but they will show up after we leave, unless they somehow figure out our method."

Guidry opened up one eye and peered over at the young Novice Orderly. "That is an ingenious methodology. It would take someone a few days to figure out where it is, and by that time you are already gone. He would be constantly wondering if he was ever at the right place to begin with, amazing."

141

"We leave no evidence we were ever there, for that very purpose," Lucas explained.

"So where is the meeting?" Manna asked. Lucas was pulling onto the highway, heading south.

"It's an abandoned school in Whittingham," Lucas finally disclosed. "Mentioning the name Stephanie told me as much."

"What does Stephanie have to do with Whittingham?" Simone asked.

"Whittingham is named after its founder, Stefan Whittingham," Lucas explained. "And the school also pays homage to the same man."

"Ingenious," Guidry exclaimed. "What is this school's name?"

"Teacher loves symbolism," Lucas replied. "The school is St. Eve's Academy for the Gifted. St. Eve's pays tribute to Stefan's nickname amongst only his closest friends."

"They called him, Steven, or Steve," Simone replied. She seemed to admire the depth of the email ruse. "St. Eve's, if you combine the two words together, spells out Steve's, so we are literally going to Steve's."

"You are truly a gifted mind," Lucas complimented Simone's deductive reasoning.

Manna met eyes with Lucas Pope in the rearview mirror and said, "I just hope we're not too late to give Teacher our gift of disclosing the traitor first, or else he's going to be gift wrapped quite nicely for Kruger and the Council."

Chapter Twenty-Six: School is in Session

Monday - Day Five

Manna jolted awake from the force of a tight curve in the road. Lucas was still driving, though he had met up with a friend to switch vehicles. They even switched out the van for one of a different make and color. They knew Kruger would be looking for them once he had learned of their escape. Lucas' friend had even given them several gallon containers of gasoline he had put in the trunk, so they wouldn't have to stop at a gas station for gas and risk being caught.

Manna could already feel the knot in his neck from sleeping at an odd angle and tried rubbing and stretching it out to no avail. Guidry's heavy breathing echoed from the front passenger seat, indicating he was still in a state of slumber. He turned to his left to see Simone also sleeping peacefully. She was pressed against the door and used a coat, which she had found underneath the driver's seat, as a pillow. It was rather thin, but was better than nothing. Manna rubbed his eyes to further awaken himself, then turned to look out the back window. He could see the van's headlights three car lengths behind them and Carly's silhouette in the driver's seat. It looked like Vivienne was on the passenger's side, and the men towered over them in the back seats. It seemed to Manna that the sun had only been up for thirty to forty minutes, maybe an hour at most. He turned back around and saw Lucas looking at him through the rearview mirror.

"Welcome back to the world of the living," Lucas spoke softly to Manna, offering him a quick smile.

"How long was I out?" Manna whispered, trying to recollect when he finally gave in to the urge to sleep. His body finally felt refreshed after the tension he had been through the past few days.

"Almost six and a half hours," Lucas replied in the same hushed tone. It was clear he was trying to avoid waking the others. He could clearly see how truly needed the rest was for them.

Though Lucas had been driving for nearly ten hours, with a lone stop for a restroom break, he seemed as refreshed as ever. Manna could see the determination in his eyes, and could tell this mission meant a lot to the young man, considering he had lost his father in the process.

"How could you Vivienne?" Simone suddenly blurted, though she still slept. "Did Teacher mean nothing to you?"

Lucas looked at Simone's sleeping body and back at Manna.

"She's been talking like that all night," he told Manna. "Only the names change every few minutes. I've heard her say the same thing with the names Griffin, Guidry, Pierre, and others substituted in place of Vivienne. It seems Kruger has manipulated her memory the exact way he had intended."

Guidry stirred slightly, but his breathing quickly returned to the same steady pace as before.

"I should have been there for her," Manna looked at his daughter's sleeping form. "She was always so much the enkindled spirit; never one to depend on me for anything. I took my duties of parenthood much too lightly, especially after her mother died."

"You're here for her now," Lucas replied, eyeing him from the mirror again. "That's what counts. In fact, she may have never needed you as much as she does this very moment, with the damage Kruger has done to her psyche."

Manna thought about Lucas Pope's words. He couldn't help but be amazed at how insightful someone so youthful could be. Maybe he had the wrong impression of society's youth. Not all were incompetent, mindless zombies going through the motions of a life the Council dictated. Sure, a good majority may be totally unabashed in their self-presentation, but the Lucas Popes of the world still existed. There was still hope for future generations to come. The more Pupils that were exposed to Teacher's lessons, and truly believed in them, the less control the Council would have over their daily lives. The less disenfranchised someone would feel by being a Pupil, which could lead to the expansion of the Pupil population. A new generation of Novice Orderlies and Pupils would develop over time. The parents could reach their children much sooner, and schools would appear much different than they did at the present time. Society as they knew it would be completely different as well. Creativity and intelligence could finally be in vogue, and the acceptance of the differences of others would finally become more mainstreamed.

"You can't go on believing that you *let* this happen to her," Lucas said, interrupting Manna's thoughts. "When you go through life thinking you have the power to halt the negative aspects of life from making their presence felt, then you're really taking away the ability to live. Being able to overcome adversity helps develop a person's resolve."

"Once weakness is shown," Guidry spoke from the front, announcing he was awake, "then true strength can be acknowledged."

"Exactly," Lucas said with a nod of his head.

"Then Simone must be one of the strongest to ever exist," Manna looked at his mentally damaged daughter. She seemed so fragile lying cuddled up against the door, yet he could feel her strength resonate from within. Considering that she was still able to hang onto her sanity, it was a feat of strength Manna had rarely seen in his lifetime.

"Thank you," Manna told Lucas and Guidry. Their words gave him reassurance that Simone could get through this, and he would be with her every step of the way.

They remained quiet for another hour as they passed over the quiet landscape. It seemed to Manna that the rest of the world didn't exist, as they hadn't passed a single vehicle for the last thirty or forty miles. Simone woke thirty minutes later and joined in the quiet contemplation, though she did move closer to Manna for added comfort. It was as if each of them was quietly speculating on their own imminent fate.

Finally, Lucas started to slow down. He turned down a secluded road, hidden by trees. If Lucas hadn't slowed to a near crawl, Manna didn't think he would've been able to see it. As he drove down the lonely road, the trees on either side scraped the side of the car. It was a wonder to Manna they didn't get stuck in the brush they were in such tight confinement. A claustrophobic wouldn't have been able to handle the close quarters, and the road seemed to drag on forever that Manna could almost sense the car growing smaller with each rotation of the tires. Manna sensed Simone felt the same as he did, for she moved back to her sleeping spot pressed against the door, in order to feel less restricted. Manna did the same. He could hear Guidry, from the front, breathing a little heavier than normal, as well.

When he felt he wouldn't be able to take any more of the tight enclosure, he saw a building materialize in front of him and, at last, a clearing. The building had clearly been a school, made of brick and concrete blocks, though at its present state, it was covered in a mossy mixture of vines and other foliage. Nearly every window was boarded up, with only a few missing planks here or there. Even with these missing planks, Manna still couldn't seem to be able to see into the rooms inside.

"Welcome to the St. Eve's Academy for the Gifted," Lucas hailed as he waved his hand in front of him in mock salute to the neglected campus, "where professors profess, teachers teach, and when students leave, they learn to beseech."

"Quite, clever," Guidry told Lucas. "Let us find one of those teachers, then, and change the course of history."

Lucas parked the car in what appeared to have once been a parking space, but what was now covered in tall grass and weeds. Carly parked beside him, and everyone got out. They had finally made it. Teacher was somewhere within the shoddy building's façade.

"Do you think Teacher is already here?" Simone asked as everyone seemed mesmerized by the very thought of being so close to Teacher, himself.

The only two who didn't seem star-struck were Guidry and Lucas; the two who had met Teacher previously. The others were beside themselves with anticipatory excitement.

"There's only one way to find out," Lucas replied. "Let's go see if class is in session."

Lucas led the group through the front door of the school. They talked in excited voices as they made their way through the first set of classrooms. Lucas wasn't certain what room Teacher would be in, so they had to search each one individually.

Manna was used to seeing an empty school, as he would be the last to leave each night after performing his custodial duties. However, St. Eve's had a completely different feel. Manna could see moldy crevices in each room, and parts of the walls were stained a musty, yellow color. Though the school had a haggard appearance, many rooms still contained a row of rusted metal desks, and it appeared the room was simply waiting for a class to venture in for the learning to begin anew. Several of the rooms even had a few computers stored against the back walls, and Manna was curious if they were still in working order or not. After nearly twenty minutes of searching the large campus for any signs of Teacher, Manna started to doubt he was even on the premises, but then he caught the scent of a new odor.

The sour odor of the decrepit was replaced by another strong aroma. Somewhere close by, someone seemed to be burning some aromatic incense; cinnamon-flavored, if Manna was not mistaken.

"Does anybody else smell that?" Vivienne asked curiously. She sniffed a few more times to make sure she had indeed picked up the new smell herself.

"It smells like vanilla," Griffin replied.

"I believe my olfactory nerves are detecting more of a cinnamon fragrance," Guidry corrected.

"You are both correct," a voice said over the intercom system of the school. The voice both booming, yet delicate all at once.

Manna was used to hearing the daily announcements spoken over the same type of system at Holly Pines, yet the voice he was used to hearing was the mousy voice of the principal's secretary, and students would tend to ignore her quite regularly. This voice, however, echoed in the empty halls; demanding to be heard.

"It is, in fact, cinnamon-vanilla," the voice continued.

The ten trespassers each looked in a different direction, trying to discover the direction from which the voice came. Manna couldn't help but think he could hear the initial spoken word seconds before hearing it on the intercom. That would mean that the person speaking was close by, but he could not, for the life of him, figure out from which direction the voice originated. Manna noticed that Lucas Pope stepped away from the others very slowly and leaned against the set of lockers nearby; he seemed to be enjoying the spectacle in front of him.

"Since you are all trespassing, please introduce yourselves," the voice spoke again.

Each person gave his or her name with an audible shout, and it was not lost on Manna that Lucas was the only one that did not give his name. Apparently, Manna was not the only one who noticed this omission.

"What about you, Pope?" Carly demanded forcefully, rather than asked. "Aren't you going to introduce yourself?"

"Why should he?" the voice answered instead. "I have already made his acquaintance. He is Lucas Pope, or Lucius Constantine, depends who you are asking."

"Aren't you going to introduce yourself?" Carly asked.

"Of course," the voice responded in a courteous tone. "I am Joshua Lamb."

A door opened about twenty paces from where they all stood. Manna could see the large 1-0-9 of the room numbers staring back at him as the door stayed open several seconds before a figure emerged from within.

Manna's heart beat faster as the figure spoke.

"But you know me better as *Teacher*."

Chapter Twenty-Seven: Teacher-Student

Manna couldn't help but look Teacher up and down, taking in every detail he could in only a few moments. Lamb was of above average height, but had a slight build. His light brown hair was close-cropped on the sides, around the earlobes, and Manna assumed in the back as well, though the top was a bit longer and in a disheveled mess. The man's eyes were a piercing, almost spearmint green that made his pale face seem to glow even more, and they were framed by a pair of thin-rimmed glasses. The most interesting aspect of his visage, to Manna anyhow, was that it was completely clean-shaven. He did not look like the nomadic man Manna thought he would. Not a bit of stubble was present on the face of the Council's most wanted fugitive, which made Manna doubt Lamb's ability to even grow facial hair at all. Furthermore, Lamb wore a pair of sandals on his sockless feet to go against the moniker of a fugitive always on the run. He wore a simple pair of tan cargo pants and unadorned black shirt that seemed a few sizes too big on his frail frame. He didn't seem the villainous snake the Council made him out to be. Manna thought he looked more like a poet or chess master than a master manipulator of evil intent.

Teacher's soft and silky voice broke the trespassers' silence, as he addressed Lucas Pope first.

"I am happy to see you got the invite. Who are your guests?" Teacher looked them over, as if judging whether these strangers could be trusted or not.

If he only knew, one of them truly couldn't, Manna thought to himself. Manna also looked everyone over to see any ill intent behind the façade of admiration, but he couldn't see any. Either the traitor was a tremendous performer, or truly admired the man he or she wished to betray.

Lucas quickly remembered the reason his *guests* were there in the first place, and got straight to business.

"Teacher, you are in trouble. These people brought to my attention a threat to our inner circle." He paused, trying to figure a way to break the news of the betrayal. "One of our own is thought to be a mole. This person is expected to turn you over to Kruger and the Council, and we believe it may be at this very meeting."

Teacher did not falter in his resolve, even upon hearing this devastating news. He scrunched his eyes, as if in deep thought, contemplating the implications of Pope's damning words, or perhaps contemplating the very validity of the proclamation.

"How are we to be certain this information is authentic?" Teacher finally asked, briefly mulling it over in his head.

"Griffin here was able to achieve this intel," Guidry responded. "He works within the Elliptical Ward as a paper-runner."

"Is this true?" Teacher asked Griffin.

"Yes, I do work within the E-Ward," Griffin replied. He sounded almost like a soldier being debriefed by a commanding officer. In some ways, that is what Teacher was to the Pupils surrounding him. "I am responsible for transferring paper documents the Council does not want traces of later. Things such as memos or bulletins between Council leaders and others within the Ward. However, I was not the person responsible for finding the incriminating information against one of your Novice Orderlies. I'm not sure why Guidry just said I was." He looked in Guidry's direction, totally confused.

"It was brought to my attention that you were the one responsible for it," Guidry explained. "Isn't that what you told me, Manna?"

"That is what Gio and Pierre told me sometime before Moon Haven," Manna replied. "Isn't it?" He looked questioningly between Gio and Pierre.

"Simone gave us that information," Pierre said.

"She told us that Griffin was able to find out about a Novice Orderly threat to your sanctity, but wasn't able to discern the name of the traitor," Gio looked at Simone lovingly. "Right, Sweetie?"

Simone looked around the room like a trapped animal. Her panic was palpable as the accusing eyes all turned toward her. Her chest heaved with each new breath. They were all looking to her for answers.

"Griffin, you told me about the conspiracy. Didn't you?" She started to shrink back from the others; eyes wide. "Or was it Vivienne? I don't remember anymore." She looked Griffin directly in the eyes. "If it wasn't you, then who

150

told me?" She shrank down to the floor. She put her head between her knees, pulling her legs closer to her body, and then started to sob uncontrollably. Manna knelt to try to comfort her.

Pope glanced down at Simone's crying form, then in Teacher's direction. "I think we still have to take the precaution of believing the claim to be truthful. We must get you somewhere safe."

"And if it is true, what good would that do?" Teacher answered. "The traitor would still be there. It would only be a matter of time before he or she would be able to seek out my location. If it is true, then let's end it here. We will not tell any of the Orderlies, but will keep an eye on them at all times."

"But how are we to explain our presence here?" Zeke asked. "Wouldn't they wonder why we are at the secret meeting of the Novice Orderlies? Or at the very least, who we are to begin with?"

Teacher thought about it for a moment, then responded. "Let's see, there are nine of you, and eight Novices and myself. That would mean we could pair up and be able to keep an eye on each one. The traitor will most likely slip up at some point."

"That's a superb idea," Guidry replied. "I guess that's why you are the Teacher."

"But how are you going to explain to the Novices why we are here?" This time it was Vivienne's turn to make her presence felt. "Why do we get to be an escort at such an important meeting?"

Teacher mulled this over as well. Finally, he replied.

"I will explain to them that you are select Pupils seeking to be initiated as the next Novice Orderly. We are expanding so a tenth Orderly must be implemented to further our cause."

"Brilliant," Guidry complimented again. "We will be most duplicitous in our endeavor."

"But that's not going to work," Manna stated, still trying to console Simone.

"What flaw do you see?" Teacher answered. He didn't seem to mind being told he was wrong. He was not defensive in the least, and even had a beaming smile on his face.

"Splitting up won't work," Manna stated again. "Because one of us is also a traitor."

Chapter Twenty-Eight: Teacher's Past

The entourage had moved into room 109, with Simone curling up in a leather executive chair that made her appear childlike due to its massive size, and they explained the situation to Teacher. Lamb listened with rapt attention, interrupting intermittently only to ask a question here or there to fill in the gaps the best he could. Each person would include another intricate detail the others had forgotten, so with the collective memories of each member of the group, they put the puzzle together a piece at a time, so Teacher had a rough summary of events that lead them to Lucas Pope's, and inevitably to that specific moment in room 109 at St. Eve's. Lucas Pope had heard most of the details, but he was also hearing some of it for the first time as some of it was told by Gio, Pierre, or one of the others that had been in the other vehicle on the ride over.

Manna ignored the details he already remembered and glanced around the medium-sized classroom. He was used to seeing desks lined in a row, but this room had only one large Arthurian round table in the middle of the room. It was at this table they were all seated; discussing the details of what was known by each individual. The chairs were all leather, and very comfortable. Manna's tired muscles sank deep into the cushioned leather. Also in the room was a 60' flat-screen television that hung on the east-corner wall. It was tuned to several news channels at once, with each shrunk down to a miniscule version of itself in order to be able to watch multiple channels at once. In order to hear the conversation going on, each of the channels was muted. The only other thing that adorned the room was a vast shade that covered the lone, large window in the room. Teacher had explained that it was so they could keep the lights on at night, so as not to draw attention to their presence in the school, if someone were to be in the area for some reason.

When the retelling was over, Teacher rubbed his smooth chin in deep thought. He looked each of them in the eye, trying to glimpse a tell-tale sign of treachery. He didn't seem to find one.

"I believe we can still stick to our plan," he finally stated. "It is nearly impossible for me to discern which of you is not forthright, and I have thought about making you all leave because of this. But if one of you is a traitor, then that means eight of you are not, and I could use those eight to help me find the true culprit. I still find it hard to think that one of my Novices could, in fact, be traitorous too, but I have to take the threat seriously. The Novices should be here shortly, and we have to work out a plan of action for what to do when they arrive."

"So we are to implement the deception of being Star Pupils seeking reverence as Novice Orderly status?" Guidry asked.

"Doesn't nine individuals for one open spot seem like overkill, though?" Vivienne asked. She stretched out her mechanical arm and a large pop sounded as her shoulder cracked. Her neck made the same popping sound as she stretched it out as well. "Wouldn't it make more sense to allow two or three? I think this would make it less skeptical for having so many of us here."

"She does bring up a good point," Zeke chimed in. He took off his glasses and put one of the ends into his mouth, chewing on the tip in deep thought. "If you up the number to three to be newly accepted Orderlies, then that would mean a third of us would win a spot, instead of just barely over ten percent. I agree; it might appear more believable."

"I see your point," Teacher nodded. "We will tell them we are looking to bring in three more Novice Orderlies, making a total of twelve. You are truly gifted individuals."

Vivienne and Zeke both burned red with embarrassment; though Manna could see they truly felt a sense of pride. It was like Michelangelo telling you that you were a good artist or Shakespeare complimenting you on your ability to write. It was the ultimate of all compliments. They both sheepishly gave their thanks to show their gratitude at such high praise.

"Let me show you the rest of the school grounds," Teacher stated. "Then we can get ourselves set up to plant our seed of deception in order to find the true deceiver. If a deceiver exists at all."

"We've already seen the grounds," Carly informed him. "We saw it while looking for you."

"You haven't seen everything," Teacher replied. He raised his eyes and gave a mischievous smirk.

*****

154

Joshua Lamb was correct, they hadn't seen everything. He showed them a high-tech surveillance system, which was intact with video, audio, motion-sensors, and a voice-recognition encryption that would identify an intruder even if he would utter a simple whisper to another assailant. Teacher showed how it worked, using Guidry as his guinea pig. Guidry even tried to disguise his voice, but the voice inflection device was still able to decipher his true identity. Not only did it identify Guidry, but it also acknowledged those known to Guidry in a more personal fashion. Manna noticed a lot of those individuals happened to be females in Guidry's case. A fact not lost on Carly either, Manna noticed. They each took turns testing out the device, trying to stump it in any way they could, but they never could sway its accuracy.

Teacher then showed them the living quarters. It was never truly known how long they would stay in a specific meeting place, so whenever the Novice Orderlies got together they needed a place to sleep. It was for this reason Teacher would usually get there a day or two, or sometimes mere hours, earlier than the others. The beds were simple cots, hammocks, air mattresses, and other low-grade sleeping units. One was simply three cushions put together on the floor. Manna even noticed that the cushions were from three different pieces of furniture as one was all red, one blue and gold-striped, and the third an ugly green with purple flowers on it. The sleeping apparatuses were in eight separate rooms, though the rooms were relatively close to one another. The rooms were toward the back of the school, so it was no wonder they had not seen them during their search. They hadn't made it that far into the school initially.

Their last stop was the basement. Teacher directed them beyond the boiler room to a large brick wall at the furthest corner of the school. The group of sightseers gathered in a circle around the unassuming wall.

Teacher silently walked up to the lower right hand corner of the brick wall and pushed on the lowermost brick. A small, audible click was heard and then a large portion of the wall moved slowly toward the ceiling; revealing a hidden doorway.

"We always plan an escape route, just in case the building is breached," Teacher explained to the stunned crowd. "Only one person knows the location of where the route will lead. A Novice Orderly is in charge of planning one for each meeting location."

"What if the traitor is the Novice Orderly that knows this particular location?" Zeke asked him.

"Luckily, I am the one who designed the route of our present whereabouts," Teacher explained. "Or that would be something that we would've had to take into consideration. There is a maze of tunnels that lead to various exits, but I have one already prepared for our escape, if indeed it is necessary."

They took a brief tour of the eating facilities, restroom locations, and, just for entertainment purposes, the disheveled gymnasium. The nets of the basketball hoops were removed and a tattered volleyball net still sat in the middle of the gym. There was no sign of a basketball or volleyball, so they headed back to room 109. The news was still broadcast from the tiny television screens, as they all sat around asking Teacher question after question.

Joshua Lamb explained that he had once been a true high school teacher at one point, so his persona was not a misnomer at all. He had taught English I to incoming freshmen, and those few sophomores and juniors who did not yet pass it their previous years. He explained how he loved to teach poetry and see a student's progress not only from the beginning of the year to the end, but also to his or her senior year as well. It was apparent he had a knack for the theatrics, like Guidry, and could really enrapture an audience. Manna couldn't help but think that Lamb would have made an excellent teacher. Not a one of the spectators interrupted him for a comment or question; they were too enthralled to hear about *Teacher* being *teacher*.

It wasn't until his fourth year teaching did he come to the conclusion that something was starting to change, not only about the students, but in the way he was told to teach. He started to notice that the continuity he was used to was starting to go away. Instead of students coming to him with the prerequisite knowledge he was accustomed to, they were coming to him, not only behind, but with a bit of a deficient attitude toward wanting to get the knowledge they were lacking. More and more students were unable to read or write, not even speak, coherently. Each year he was asked to do something different, and wasn't even able to see what truly worked and what didn't before being asked to tear it all down and start anew.

When he brought it to the attention of his supervisors, he was told he had to go back and teach them what they were lacking, and he did. However, because he had to teach them the things they were missing, he did not get a chance to teach them the things he was supposed to teach to them; the required list of cognitive skills the Council's Education Sector mandated he teach. They took the compulsory test at the end of the semester and a lot of them did not pass. This was happening all over the school, as well as the rest of the Americas, so these students were not allowed to move to the next grade. Soon, his classes were quickly becoming overcrowded, especially after a few years of the same trend. The Council saw the growing class sizes, and told the schools that this was unsatisfactory. They said it made the Americas look like a bunch of fools, when our students could not pass a simple class.

Teacher explained that society also changed. More emphasis was placed on making the student feel superior, especially those students with deficiencies in certain areas. Lamb was told not to tell a student he was wrong, but encourage him for making an attempt. He did this as well, and saw the benefits of students learning the value of their efforts. They were learning and more confident than ever. Then, another trend started to show its head. Students began to take on more and more activities outside of school. These activities started to take precedence over schoolwork and, again, students began to become deficient.

The Council took away school days so these extracurricular activities did not interfere with school work, but Lamb figured it was the other way around; so school work didn't interfere with these activities. The deficient students, in the overcrowded rooms, became even more deficient, since less time could be spent on each individual student. Instead of hiring more teachers, the Council began firing them, due to test scores being lower than desired. This, in turn, made class sizes even bigger, so the Council made it easier to pass by offering multiple chances on the test, and allowing the students to pass on to the next grade without being required to pass the class. The overcrowding problem stopped, but students stopped valuing effort and became apathetic.

Apathy lead to even lower test scores and even more firings. Overcrowding started becoming a problem again due to the lack of teachers, and those wanting to become teachers. It became more difficult to have a discussion, so teachers were required to spurt out information at a quick pace. Teaching to the test was a constraint put on teachers by the Council. The best teachers were the ones with the highest test scores, and they were paid more based on this aspect of their ability to get more information to be regurgitated on the final exam regardless of the students' true abilities. Lamb began to notice that some teachers didn't even know their students' names. To some, they were simply a number from the previous year, and left as a number at the end of the year. Students did not necessarily have to think; they simply had to recall information, like lyrics to a song.

By his tenth year, Lamb didn't feel like he was teaching the students anything. The students who passed the test could not remember information when he asked them about it the following year. The tests weren't really testing what the students could do, or even what they knew. Teachers resorted to teaching the test question by question, as the tests were the exact same from year to year. Lamb finally realized that the students weren't even remembering the information; they were simply remembering a letter associated with an arbitrary answer.

That is when he first got the idea of leaving the teaching profession altogether. He just couldn't do it, however. Teaching was still passionate to his core, and he couldn't leave the job he loved. The other teachers wouldn't listen to him, neither would his administrators. They simply didn't see his vision. Thus, he took matters into his own hands. His classes started to have discussions and Socratic seminars, instead of the strategy the other faculty implemented. His students, however, did not perform as well on the test, because they didn't agree with the answers the Council gave them on the test each time. The students in his class also ended up running out of time on the test, because they hadn't simply memorized the answers. They were actually taking the time to read and comprehend the material.

The Council caught wind of what Lamb was doing in his classroom and tried to take back the control Lamb seemed to be trying to steal from them. An administrator was told to sit in on his class each day, in order to make sure he did things their way. He complied; however, he talked a few of his students into meeting outside of school to go over other material. Lamb got them to start writing poetry and thinking deeper than any other student on the planet. These students devalued testing and planned to sabotage the other students' scores. Lamb, along with eight of his best students, hacked into the school website and changed the scores on each and every test at his school. All students at Lamb's school failed the test.

The Council put them on a year of probation, under close scrutiny by Kruger himself. Kruger spent each day at Lamb's school with a member of the

Council in each classroom monitoring each teacher's daily lessons. At the end of the year, Lamb and his crew did the same thing with the testing, and included the tests of another school in another location as well. Kruger was perplexed at why it would occur again, especially at another school entirely. He knew the teachers were doing a *fine* job of conducting their daily lessons at Lamb's school, so he had somebody look into it further by looking at each student's previous test scores, as well as classroom assessments given each quarter. The benchmark scores seemed to imply that they understood it up to the point of the actual end of year test, which raised a few eyebrows, Kruger's included.

Several months later, Lamb and his cohort were found out, though it wasn't exactly known who was truly behind it; just that someone had manipulated the data. Lamb had been taken in for questioning due to his background in trying to buck the trend earlier in his career, but no one could prove his involvement in the present ordeal, so the Council let him go.

Instead of deterring him from continuing, this only proved to motivate Lamb further. He didn't give up his quest to discourage the importance of testing, but this close call helped point out some errors in his methodology. He needed to point the finger of blame in another direction in order to escape conviction, or else what he was trying to accomplish would be short-lived.

Kruger then created the persona of Teacher as an extremist leader of a faction that sabotaged the futures of several of America's youth. Because the Council claimed Teacher was targeting youth, it brought an intense hatred toward Teacher from much of the Americas. Soon, Teacher developed into a notorious enemy of the public. The Council would brainwash the Americas with false accusations of sabotage and manipulation. Any student who failed would be blamed on Teacher, even when Lamb and his followers had nothing to do with it.

However, Joshua Lamb believed Kruger had created the ideal rallying figure with the Teacher character. He garnered free publicity with each of Kruger's fake claims, or even mention of his real exploits, and Lamb started to see an avenue in which he could further his cause. He faked his own death, much like A'ron Guidry, and became a constant hermit on the run, in order to focus all of his attention on this cause. It also skirted the blame off Joshua Lamb, and protected those he held dear. The eight students who helped in his previous endeavors became the idea of the eight Novice Orderlies currently with him as well. Though all of them were different people, several were actually family members from the original eight, including Lucius himself. His Uncle Remus had been one of those originals.

"I have been a fugitive ever since," Teacher finished. "Hoping to gather as many pupils, such as you, to spread the idea of contemplative thinking and self-reflection. We don't want to live in a society of robots who don't have the capability to think for themselves."

"And all of that is in jeopardy because I can't remember the Novice Orderly you shouldn't trust," Simone stated. "Or even the traitor in this room."

"Don't worry, we'll figure this all out," Teacher said confidently. "We're safe for now."

As he said this, the television screen at the front of the room started blinking bright red.

"What's happening?" Carly asked Teacher, pointing to the screen.

"That's the security system," Teacher replied. "Someone is on the premises." He picked up a remote from the table, pointed it at the television screen, and clicked a button.

One of the tiny screens supplanted itself on the full picture. Two individuals were traipsing the hallways of the school. Manna's heart began to beat rapidly, as his nerves were on edge; curious as to the identity of the two strangers, one man and one woman. *Were they already too late? Had Kruger already found them?*

"We've got to get you out of here, Teacher," Guidry stood up and went to grab for Teacher's arm to get him out of the area.

"Don't be absurd," Teacher replied, pulling his hand away. "Those are two of the Novices, the Carmichaels. Andrea and Seamus. They're usually one of the early birds."

"I just hope you're not the worm," Guidry stated with a raise of his eyebrow toward Teacher, and then he sat back down into the plush upholstery of the leather chair.

160

Chapter Twenty-Nine: Meeting the Orderlies

Within the next two hours, the rest of the Novice Orderlies showed up. Teacher explained the reason for the presence of the strangers to the Novices. Along with Lucas Pope and the Carmichaels, there was Jude Kane. Jude was a short, stout man with a bald head, khaki shorts and flannel shirt. He had muscles in places Manna didn't know there could be muscles, and had one of the largest necks Manna had ever seen. He made Guidry's two 'no necks' look like stick figures from a kindergartner.

There was also Mariana Galena. She was the youngest female of the Novices, and was in her second year at Institute. She was in Institute in France and had changed her major from mathematics, in which she scored one of the highest scores in testing history, to art history. Only in places such as France was switching a major still an option. She had long, flowing red hair, and the spitfire attitude to match. No argument seemed complete until she added her perspective. Teacher explained, before they all had arrived, that Mariana was his most gifted Novice.

Tamara Duda was another. She had a mane of curly black hair, and seemed to always have a scowl on her face. Manna could tell she was skeptical of the newcomers, but she didn't doubt Teacher's ability to judge character. As the oldest of the Novices, she had the most experience with Teacher, and the speculation of including three new strangers in their endeavor really didn't sit well with her. She was also very concerned about the other six attendees that didn't make the cut.

"Who's to say the ones that don't make Novice status will stick with being Pupils," Tamara explained. "They could easily go to Kruger and turn us in out of spite."

Manna caught the gaze of the other prospective Novices. They, in fact, knew that at least two of the people in the room would actually do that, but for a far more personal reason than spite, or so it seemed.

The last female Novice was Matilda Swanson. She was the quietest of the bunch, though when she spoke, she had an intelligence that rivaled Mariana's. She didn't come with the same brazen demeanor as Mariana, though. Instead, her logic was flawless, and even Mariana found it difficult to make a valid argument against her point. She was a bank treasurer, and her *modus operandi* fit perfectly with the ritualistic tasks she would face on a daily basis. Manna could tell she was very observant. Manna also noticed the men in the room were somehow drawn to her most. He couldn't blame them, however, as she was definitely enchanting. Her hair was shorter than the other women's, though it fit her bookish personality perfectly. He figured that was what made her all the more alluring. She was the one in the room most in check of her emotions.

Nicodemus Linderhaven was the final male Novice. He had a long beard and a bellowing, infectious laugh that Manna could tell came from deep inside his inner core. He was the oldest of the Novices, and he appeared even older than Teacher himself, though he was in actuality a few years younger. There were a few flecks of gray in both his beard and the top of his head that performed the inevitable task of adding a few years to his apparent age. The beard, itself, also helped in this undertaking.

To Manna, however, the most interesting of the Novices were the Carmichaels. They were brother and sister, Andrea and Seamus Carmichael. Seamus had the same stoic behavior that Pierre and Gio had when Manna first met him. After getting to know the strangers and letting his guard down a little, Seamus' personality really came out. The stories he told about events in his life rivaled Guidry's own unbelievable tales. Andrea seemed to have just as many tales to tell. In fact, it was their parents that were part of the initial changing of the test scores which made Teacher on the Council's radar in the first place. It had become kind of a family tradition to make the Council's life a living hell by sabotaging the testing each year. One year the Carmichaels even switched the test so none of the multiple choice answers were correct, and another form of the test had the answer choices blank. Therefore, like life, there were many more questions than answers. Manna enjoyed hearing about these adventures most.

After getting to know each of the Novice Orderlies, however, Manna could not wrap his mind around the fact that one of them could turn his or her back on Teacher and the overall mission agreed upon by all of them. None seemed capable of such a dastardly deed. Nevertheless, Manna was just cynical enough to believe that giving an individual the utmost trust could oftentimes set one up for utter disappointment later on down the road. Having a friend such as Guidry could do that to a person.

162

Guidry was not the only individual who fit this trusting persona. In fact, Manna's own father had proved to discourage Manna from trusting anyone full-heartedly, even more so than Guidry had ever done. Manna's own father had made him a number of promises in which his father deemed unworthy of fulfillment. Each time was met with a heartfelt apology and another promise to never forget another birthday, or never to succumb to the bottle's temptation yet again, or even to never lose his temper again and hit Manna's mother. Manna would tearfully accept the apologies; fooling himself into believing that his father could actually change. Instead, his father continued his reckless behavior and drank himself into an early grave, though it was regretfully after Manna's own mother's passing. She never got to be free of the tyranny that was her husband.

All of this had formed Manna's own lack of trust even now. It was why he never could make the commitment to Teacher's cause earlier, or even to commit to the Council's despairing remarks about Teacher as well. He never knew which views or information to trust, so he simply didn't choose a side, which had always seemed to be the easiest way out. A way to never have to be faced with being disappointed over the outcome once the correct side was divulged.

It had taken the actions of his daughter, who had sought his help, to make him finally trust one side over the other. How ironic, now, that it was she who finally convinced him of this trust, when her judgment was what he felt he could trust the least, because of what Kruger did to her mind. Ironic, also, that he was purposely getting involved with a group of individuals in which the final outcome was going to assuredly lead to betrayal and disappointment.

It somehow made it easier to already possess the knowledge of betrayal. Unlike with his father, when he had always succeeded at putting his complete faith that somehow the outcome would be altered from one time to the next, what he was facing now would be different. He would already be expecting the treacherous act, and it would not take him by surprise. Manna silently made a vow of this, which helped reassure him that he had made the right decision to give his trust to Teacher.

The conversations started to die down and Teacher made the suggestion of pairing a Novice Orderly with a prospective member for the rest of the night. This could help with the bonding process and each of the *candidates* could pick the Novice's brain if the desire was there to do so. Teacher would give them a few hours for the first lesson or bonding to take place, and then turn the interior lights off for the night, as they needed to save some life on the generator they were using.

Zeke and Jude paired up, as did Griffin and Nicodemus. Gio was with Lucas, Vivienne with Matilda, and Pierre was partnered with Andrea, which was the only co-ed combination. Pierre seemed a bit embarrassed, as well as intimidated, when Seamus threatened him if he touched his sister. The rest of the pairs, though, found it highly comical. Manna found it fitting that Mariana and Carly somehow found each other paired together, since they both seemed to possess the same surly dispositions. Another pairing that seemed fitting was Guidry and Seamus who seemed to be destined to be up late into the night trying their best to outdo each other in spinning the most fantastical of yarns. Manna would give up his left arm to be a fly on the wall to hear the stories told between those two in the course of one night. Tamara and Simone were together, and that left Manna partnered with Joshua Lamb.

Manna felt it a bit daunting to be in a pairing with the actual Teacher. Lamb even gave him a slight wink when it was determined they were to be paired with one another, as if it was somehow part of the plan for them to be side by side through it all. And maybe it had been Teacher's plan all along to put the two of them together. Manna couldn't speculate as to why it would have been, but was thankful for the opportunity to spend some time alone with the most inspiring person, or the most wanted criminal, on the planet. To Manna, he was the former.

"Novices," Joshua Lamb directed, "I charge you with getting to know each of the Novice candidates and see which three are worthy of the honor of joining us. Remember they are seeking what you possess, not to take it from you, but to join the fraternity we have created. Feel free to go about discerning their worth by any means you see fit. They are all curious, or else they would not be here, so do not take their questions lightly. As I have taught you, 'You will never learn, if you don't first learn the art of the question.' You were chosen as a Novice Orderly for your ability to teach. Tonight, I denounce myself as *the Teacher*, as I command you all to become just that. Teach and learn from one another. Tonight, I am simply Joshua Lamb, a scholar and former professor seeking knowledge from my fellow man. Be humble and listen to what the other person has to say, so you too can take part in one of life's greatest pleasures; being a learner of life."

Without another word, the pairs went their separate ways; all to their different rooms. Manna and Teacher stayed behind, since the room they currently were in was their actual sleeping space.

Manna looked at Teacher with an intense stare, "I hope we can find out by morning who the traitor is. I get the strange feeling that our time is running out to do so."

Lamb's stare was just as intense, "Your intuitiveness seems to be very keen. I believe you are correct; our time will run out shortly, but not before we find the answers we seek. There are too many intellectuals under this one roof to doubt our success. Here is your first lesson from me, Mike Manna. Never underestimate the power of intelligence. It can perform amazing feats that can make even the most powerful of bodies crumble in total disrepair. The mind is the most powerful tool we possess. Without it, we are the most primitive of creatures."

"We should not underestimate the Council's power to manipulate," Manna replied after he reflected on his first one on one lesson with Teacher. "Because someone under this roof is using their most powerful tool for evil, and to me that's the most dangerous weapon of them all."

"You are wise, Mike Manna," Teacher answered with a slight smirk. "We are lucky you are on our side, because if what you say is true, then you would make a very dangerous weapon, indeed."

"Thank you," Manna replied, though he did not look entirely pleased. "The only bad thing is that every other person under this roof is much wiser than me, so there are a lot of potential dangerous weapons out there."

"There is a lot of potential damage. That is true," Teacher thoughtfully stated. He put his right hand under his chin in a thoughtful gesture. "But if you think about it, there are eight times more weaponry on our side, so I think we have the advantage. We just have to find where their weapons are stored and diffuse the situation."

Manna looked in the direction where Simone went just moments earlier. "Her mind has the map without an X to mark the spot to find those weapons. I just hope we don't run out of time before their weapons get used first."

Chapter Thirty: One on One

Gio and Lucas had moved the futon from the middle of the room to the far side, in order to make a bit more room for another sleeper. This also provided more personal space for each of them. Gio provided little conversation throughout the entire maneuvering of the futon, but Lucas decided it was necessary to get him to open up a little more.

"So what brought you to this juncture," he asked his quiet companion. "How did you get involved with all of this?"

"I am not the traitor," Gio responded flatly.

"I didn't say you were. I just was curious what motivated you to be a Pupil. My motivation was my family, so what was yours." When he mentioned his family, Gio noticed Lucas's voice tremble a little. He had forgotten that it had been less than twenty-four hours that this young man had witnessed the death, no the murder, of his father, and he had already lost his mother many years before.

Gio felt he could empathize with him a little, though his situation was vastly different. He didn't really lose his parents, since he had no recollection of them in the first place. Instead, he was orphaned before his memory of them had a chance to develop. He was just under two years old when he was placed in the custody of his foster parents, for reasons he never quite got the nerve to ask about, since he frankly didn't care about the machinations of his ill-begotten parents. Gio was convinced there was a valid reason for them to leave him in the guardianship of an orphanage, and it proved to have no ill effect on his temperament, or so he claimed. In retrospect, these circumstances may have had an effect on his introverted demeanor, but he never saw that as a hindrance of any sort. It was also, most likely, the reason he desired to become a Pupil.

Lucas, on the other hand, did have the experience of having a family. One, in which, he grew to have fond memories of, or so it seemed. The two of them had both lost their parents, though the circumstances were completely different from one another.

"My yearning to become a Pupil was also due to my family experiences," Gio finally replied.

"Were your parents Pupils too?"

"I was an orphan, in an orphanage run by the Council," Gio answered with disdain. Lucas had a sympathetic look on his face. "It made me realize I couldn't depend on the Council for anything."

Lucas gave a broad smile that caught Gio's attention.

"What's with the look on your face?" Gio asked a bit perturbed. He felt that Lucas was poking fun at him in some fashion. Another by-product of the orphanage, he supposed; a feeling of total inadequacy around those from a *true* family atmosphere. "Do you find great pleasure in my past discomfort?"

"Not at all," Lucas confirmed. "I just feel more confident that what you said earlier is the truth."

"And what was it that I said?" Gio demanded a little too perfunctorily.

"That you weren't the traitor," Lucas answered with a raise of his eyebrows. He looked toward the open door and Gio's eyes followed his gaze. "So that means someone else out there is."

*****

"I get the feeling that each of you *candidates* knows one another on a more personal level," Tamara Duda said to Simone, as they started to settle into their room. Simone hesitated for a split second as she was placing the pillow Tamara had provided for her on the floor beside the sleeping bag, which was also provided. Tamara, herself, had an air mattress on the floor beside Simone's sleeping bag. Tamara seemed to pick up on the moment of hesitation.

"I see I am correct to doubt the authenticity of the strangers visiting us tonight," Tamara concluded.

"You doubt Teacher's motives?" Simone replied.

"No, I doubt yours," Tamara bit back with pure venom in her voice.

Simone tightly closed her eyes; fighting back the urge to convey her true feelings about the woman she was charged with having as her bunk mate for the night. The truth was that Simone truly did have strong feelings against trusting this woman, as she had seen her visage multiple times in a jovial embrace with Jack Kruger, though she knew she couldn't fully trust those images as purely valid. Nevertheless, Tamara seemed skeptical of each new prospective member, especially Simone, for some ungodly reason. Simone could not make clear if it was some personal vendetta against her, or simply Tamara's natural conduct towards others. Whichever the case may be, Simone wished to get the answer, and knew the best way to do that was to simply ask. If the Novice Orderlies were truly who they claimed to be, questioning was not only accepted, but an actual necessity.

"What makes you so skeptical, then?" She asked after finally opening her eyes. "What do I have to do to prove to you my worth? Teacher's approval isn't enough. What more do you want?"

Tamara's eyes went wide at Simone's boldness. Simone could tell that she wasn't used to people being so audacious with her. But she wasn't going to let Simone have the upper hand for long.

"It just seems very suspicious from my perspective," Tamara retorted. "Teacher doesn't say anything about any possible additions, and suddenly we have three new Novices overnight. Not to mention the fact that the *chosen* ones seem to be of the same circle of friends, or at least acquaintances. I don't like it one bit."

"I will admit that most of us know each other in some capacity or another," Simone finally gave up the information. Tamara seemed to have surmised as much anyhow, so why continue to give her more reason to distrust her. She would tell her enough to gain her trust, but still keep the most important information to herself, however. "I don't see why you are so against expanding the Novices to twelve members. Don't you need more to help spread the lessons to more Pupils?"

"I think we do just fine with what we have," Tamara said smugly. "But I guess if we truly want to expand our instruction to more; it wouldn't hurt to have a few more to help recruit."

Simone could almost see the chip from Tamara's shoulder fall to the floor, at least partially.

"I have been following Teacher for so long, I just forget sometimes the true nature of our cause," Tamara admitted.

As she said this, Simone caught the immediate red flags in this statement. If she truly did not recollect why she was a Novice Orderly to begin with, it would seem she could also lose the passion of Teacher's endeavors. It would definitely prove to be a good motive to turn him over to Kruger. Simone was completely terrified to know that she was possibly in a room with the real traitor. Tamara Duda officially became suspect number one.

*****

Vivienne was offered the cot by Matilda Swanson, but she declined. She had always been self-conscious about people trying to give her handouts due to her disability. Matilda's offer was a bit contrite, Vivienne felt, like she felt it was her duty to show pity on Vivienne for having a mechanical arm. Vivienne wanted to show Matilda that she was capable of sleeping on the hard ground in a sleeping bag, as if the number of arms a person had could have any determination on how one was able to sleep.

Vivienne was used to people underestimating her. People would have thought it difficult to live without her arm, but it paled in comparison to having to live without her son and husband. She would have gladly live with no arms at all than with no family. Most everyone had thought that she had refused a more lifelike prosthetic because of her love for her job as a robotics engineer. However, this was not true. The reason she designed the arm in the fashion she did was because of her son. He had always been amazed with the robots in her office, and had one day asked about her capabilities with the mechanics she worked with on a daily basis.

"Mom, could you make a robotic version of me, if you wanted to?" Her son, Kurtis, asked her one morning at the breakfast table.

His father, Victor, stifled a laugh by holding the E-mag in front of his face. Then, he lowered the E-mag and looked at his wife in a look that said, How are you going to answer that one?

She simply smiled and replied, "Now, why would I want to go and do that?"

"You know when I get old enough to go to Institute," he replied with a straight face. *"So you wouldn't miss me too much."*

She always appreciated the simplistic mind of an eight year old.

"I could never replace your presence with one of my robots," she answered, smiling. "I am good, but I am not that good."

The family laughed and continued their breakfast, simply enjoying each other's company.

A week later a drunk driver sent her life into absolute turmoil; never to eat breakfast as a family again. That particular conversation at the breakfast table stuck out in her mind when she decided to design her own prosthesis. It was her way to remember her son, even in death. She had even created her own personal tattoo on the metal by using a laser to carve her son's initials on the back near where it connected to her shoulder blade. No one had known about this personalization until she finally showed it to Matilda Swanson after she relayed the story of her accident to her. It was inevitable for a stranger to want to know what had happened, so she had relived that awful moment more than enough times over the years since it happened.

"I later found out that the driver of the vehicle which had taken my family from me was Jack Kruger's nephew," Vivienne said through blurry eyes. "Kruger had enough clout to divert blame from his beloved nephew and onto my dead husband, who was driving our car. Not only did his nephew get off scot free, but to add insult to injury, I had to pay for his wrecked vehicle and his medical bills, as well as my own bills and funeral costs for both my husband and son."

"That must have been difficult," Matilda sympathized, "knowing that the person responsible was escaping punishment."

The two women sat on the cot as Vivienne finished telling her account of what happened. Matilda put her arm around Vivienne and held her as she cried through the memory.

"That is the main reason for my becoming a Pupil," Vivienne admitted, as she composed herself and wiped the tears from her eyes. "Jack Kruger, to me, is an evil man, and I could not back a person who was willing to let another avoid consequence, simply because he was of kin."

"It is totally understandable," Matilda agreed. "I most likely would have made the same decision, myself. We all have our reasons for listening to Teacher, and believing the indoctrination of which he speaks. I find hatred for the Council to be a popular reason to become a Pupil, but one must be careful of hate. It is a powerful sensation that clouds one's judgment almost entirely. If becoming a Novice is your true desire, then ridding yourself of this hatred is a necessity."

"But don't you all hate the Council just the same?" Vivienne questioned.

"I would not say hate, though I believe a few of the Novices do just that," Matilda answered after a brief pause to reflect on the question. "The Carmichaels see it as a game of chess, of sorts. Jude sees it as a competition as well, though his competitive edge is a bit more physical. That's not to say the man isn't intelligent, however. He can philosophize just as well as any one of us. He's put Teacher in his place a time or two even, if you can believe it."

Vivienne smiled at this admission. It was something she wouldn't have thought possible. Teacher didn't seem capable of losing a battle of wits with anyone, let alone someone like Jude Kane.

"Nicodemus and Mariana both enjoy the ability to be creative that Teacher provides," Matilda continued. "Mariana writes some of the most beautiful poetry, is great at logic games, and is an all-around gifted individual. There isn't anything I could imagine she wouldn't find success in if she truly desired to make the attempt. And she tries at *everything*. Also, Nicodemus writes some of the most intriguing stories and plays, and even does a lot of the acting in those plays he composes. Of course, he doesn't get much of an audience due to the Council's creed. Pupils are his only audience."

"What about Lucas?" Vivienne interrupted. "He seems so young to have such passion towards the cause. He doesn't seem like he truly knows what he's gotten himself into."

"I think you misjudge Lucas," Matilda replied. Again, she paused like she did with every question asked of her, as if she were weighing every option and truly thinking about each response she would give. "Lucas is something special. He is mature beyond his years and truly does understand the situation in which he has placed himself. In fact, Lucas may be doing it for all the right reasons. He isn't doing it to show intellectual or physical muscle, or to stick it to the Council for not letting him use his talents. Instead, he seems to be doing it completely for the love of learning new things. He still has the spark of a student. You can see it in his eyes each and every time we have these meetings. Lucas Pope is simply a lover of knowledge; learning that the Council cannot provide, and Teacher can. Tamara, however, there's where hate comes into the picture. She used to be a teacher, as well, that lost her job. Though it wasn't for low scores; her scores were phenomenal. Her position was cut because she had been doing it for too long and was making too much money, according to the Council. The Council could hire three new teachers for the cost of her one position. Since the Council disregarded teaching as a true profession and could get the same results from any individual in front of the students, as long as that person taught the way the Council wanted, they got rid of her."

"And you?" Vivienne asked directly. "What's your reason? How was it you became a Novice Orderly?"

"Like you, I grew to hate the Council and what it stood for," Matilda confessed. "I saw it as a group of hypocritical representatives who were inconsistent with their justice."

"But you were chastising me for hating too," Vivienne complained. She gave Matilda a skeptical look. "Speaking of being hypocritical."

"I confess, that does sound hypocritical, but that is what I learned from Teacher," she explained. "You have to be able to forgive others and believe they can change, because the world cannot be against you if there is someone on your side. If you are doing something for spite, then there is no real reason to do it; all the motives get thrown out the window. There is too much hatred in the world, and most refuse to see there is goodness in others. We hate others for not having the same beliefs, or because they like something we do not. I understand there are actions that we can hate; like murder and rape, and those actions are irrefutably disgusting and appalling. But with those and other illegal things aside, what else is there to truly hate?"

"I am starting to see some of your logic, but it's hard for me to rid myself of it, since I have kept it for so long," Vivienne said.

"That is why it is such a despicable thing," Matilda explained. "It is the single hardest thing to rid ourselves of, because it takes a lot of mental capacity to do so, along with becoming a little more knowledgeable and using a little more logic."

There was a brief silence between the two as each seemed to be contemplating what was said between them.

"How do you know so much on this?" Vivienne finally asked.

"Like I said, I grew to hate Jack Kruger just the same," she replied.

"How come?" Vivienne pressed.

"I am Jack Kruger's niece. The person who killed your family was my brother."

*****

Jude Kane explained that his normal sleeping routine was on the floor, so there was not a bed in the room that he and Zeke occupied. Zeke took a small blanket Jude offered and laid it on the floor in the far left corner.

"Is there a pillow?" Zeke asked.

"No need for one," Jude replied. "I usually don't even have a blanket, so consider yourself lucky. Most of the time, I barely have a roof over my head. I frequently just sleep under the stars, and cozy up to the fire."

Zeke could definitely picture this man doing just that, as he looked like a sawed-off lumberjack. Though, he had to ask the question that was on his mind.

"But why?"

Jude looked at Zeke as if it was blatantly obvious, and only an imbecile would ask such a question, but he obliged him with an answer.

"We Novices, as well as Teacher, are the most wanted people on the planet," he informed. "Hiding in plain sight, and having a reputable job is what the others choose to do with their lives, but I cannot be a part of a society that believes me to be a criminal; simply for not believing in what the Council deems is the correct way to live my life."

"But not even living with a roof over your head?" Zeke questioned. "Isn't that a bit extreme?"

"If I am to be a criminal on the run," Jude explained, "then I must live the true life of a fugitive. If I were to have a job where my earnings in any way go to the Council's bank account, through taxes or any other means, then I would feel like an imposter. The others can live with that fact, as they can

173

validate it through a long line of logic and reason. However, I cannot justify it in my mind for my personal needs, therefore, cannot bring myself to do it. I do not judge their character, simply because I disagree with their logic, and I don't expect others to judge me because they disagree with mine."

"I find it admirable," Zeke told Jude. "You stick to your beliefs without letting others dictate them for you. There are very few people willing to stick to their tenets as strictly as you would. Now, I know why you reached Novice status."

Jude smiled with a nod. It was clear that he accepted the compliment graciously, as no thanks were needed.

"You had said you did not have a roof over your head 'most of the time', what about those times that you do?" Zeke asked curiously.

"When the weather is bad, or when I find a new recruit I deem ready to learn Teacher's lessons, I spend some time indoors," Jude clarified. "Or like tonight, when Teacher calls the Novice meetings, I find the need to stay inside."

"Is recruiting a big part of the job?" Zeke asked.

"Yes, it is," Jude replied. "It takes a very sophisticated mind to distinguish the people who actually want to learn from Teacher, and those who just want to get a weekend high by getting involved with something illegal. I have seen a great deal of prospective Pupils give it up after a few weeks because their minds weren't ready for the depth, or simply wanted to move on to their new drug-induced high, as it required much less thought than what we required."

"But isn't that dangerous to let them go?" Zeke asked.

"They tend to not say anything, because in a way it implicates them too," Jude explained to him. "Nobody wants to be known as being associated with Teacher. It could get them put into Moon Haven, jail, or even make them lose their jobs. Though Kruger likes to make people believe he appreciates those people who tell him about the Pupil meetings, in reality those people who do show Kruger that his control over others is weakening."

Zeke thought about the damage it could place upon an individual who wasn't truly committed. The repercussions were very serious, if one was caught with Teacher. When was it he realized those consequences were worth it? He couldn't remember. He thought of the recruits he had recruited as Pupils. There were many over the years, including Simone, Griffin, and Vivienne. He also had a slight hand in recruiting Gio and Pierre. Could one of those people be willing to turn Teacher over to the Council? Had he misjudged their desire to be a Pupil?

"You said you actually stay with your recruits sometimes," Zeke asked, again showing his curious nature. "How long do you actually stay with them?"

"I stay long enough to get them to appreciate the depths of their mind," Jude replied. "I stay as long as they need me to; no more no less. When you have done this as many times as I have, you just get a feel for it."

"Do you think I can be a Novice? Do you believe I can do what you do?" Zeke questioned.

"You've got potential, kid," Jude told him. "I've got to spend some more time with you to see if you're authentic."

"You seriously don't live in a house?" Zeke asked changing the subject.

"Yes, I do not have a true place of my own to call home. I sleep in barns or a summer cottage or two if it fancies me from time to time. But nothing is as good as sucking on the teat of Mother Nature, and breathing in the aroma of her natural perfume. I find that I sleep better outdoors as well. I tend to wake up naked if I stay indoors."

Jude noticed the worried look on Zeke's face. He gave Zeke a slight smirk.

"Why do you think I gave you the blanket?"

*****

Out of respect, Andrea Carmichael offered Pierre the small cot in the room, but he chivalrously declined. Andrea had expected as much, especially after her brother threatened him earlier. She was used to having her older brother stick up for her, but she didn't always feel it was necessary for him to do so as much as he did. She was perfectly capable of taking care of herself, without his or anyone else's help for that matter. It was the older brother's duty,

175

however, to take care of his little sister and watch her back and look out for her, especially when it came down to matters of the opposite sex. That was definitely something she didn't need his help with.

She looked at the young man charged with occupying her company for the night. He had above average looks and a piercing stare that captivated her, as if there was some sort of secret knowledge he possessed. He was definitely intriguing, though he seemed be a bit extreme about his lack of conversing. She had tried to get some basic information from him, and he wasn't impolite about sharing, yet each answer was very quick, but somehow also very calculated, as if he refused to give away too much. She absolutely loved the pursuit of gathering intel, and attempting to read others was a major hobby of hers. She and Seamus had spent many opportunities doing just this in a restaurant, party, or other venue by observing interactions, as well as looking at nonverbal cues. This man however was an absolute enigma. She couldn't even tell if the little information he had given to her was entirely accurate or not.

So far, he had told her he had been a Pupil for three years, he was twenty-eight years old, and the other initiate named Giovanni had been a roommate of his at one point. Whether that was at Institute or his current status, she really couldn't tell. None of her questions elicited the complimentary question in return to show interest in the other person of the conversation, either. It was as if he wanted to know as little about her as he had given about himself. She definitely chalked it up to nerves, and most likely the threat from Seamus had even more to do with it.

"You shouldn't take Seamus too seriously," she told Pierre. "He doesn't mean half of what he says."

"I see," Pierre replied curtly.

He was giving her nothing. She could at least eliminate him from being one of the new Novice Orderlies. A Novice needed to be able to voice opinions in debates, spread Teacher's lessons, and recruit new Pupils. Someone with his knack for silence was not up to that kind of task, it would seem. She decided to inform him of this fact.

"Do you truly want to be a Novice?" She asked him.

He took time to calculate his response and finally gave an indefinite, "Yes."

176

"That doesn't sound like a strong vote of confidence," she told him.

He only responded with a shrug of his shoulders and nothing more. This man was starting to annoy her, and she usually had a great deal of patience. It was what made her a good Novice Orderly.

"If you plan on being one of the three chosen to be a Novice Orderly, you're going to have to be more personable," she informed. "It is a crucial part in completing the tasks Teacher sets out for us. It's what separates us from your average Pupil."

"What kind of tasks does Teacher delve out?" he asked. "What does a Novice Orderly generally do?"

Finally, a question that showed he had a little bit of life in him.

"Our main purpose is to look for more Pupils to spread Teacher's philosophy of learning," she explained. "We each head off into a different direction or location, especially after meeting together like tonight. Each of us is tasked with making sure these Pupils get the six basic tenets."

"LIVING," Pierre interrupted. "Logic, Ingenuity, Voice, Inquisitiveness, Noticing, and Gratitude."

It was still short and to the point, but at least he was starting to show some emotion.

"Yes," Andrea said. "Teacher says you must use logic and reasoning to support a claim or when attempting to figure something out, because without it we lack justification and clout. Ingenuity is important in order to create something new. It requires the mind to think on a deeper level, as it is creating a new thought or idea. A lot of the poetry, books, music, art, and plays we admire are based on the person's ingenuity. Having a voice is being able to develop an opinion, no matter what the topic. As you may know, Pupils are encouraged to debate whenever they meet with other Pupils, though it is not really encouraged outside of those meetings due to its ability to get one into trouble. If you don't develop a voice, or opinion, then you truly don't care, and apathy is one of the worst things to possess, at least according to Teacher. Being inquisitive is also necessary. It allows for learning to truly take place. If people are not curious, then they don't want to know all there is to learn. This is one of the most crucial components, if not the most important one. Noticing all there is around you

177

lends one to use all the other principles much more adeptly. Seeing the smaller details that may go unnoticed by others is what really separates the true Pupils from those just along for the ride, as well as what makes the Novices what we are. The last is gratitude. It is important to be thankful and gracious for what you have, as well as show it to others. It is crucial to treat others with respect and make others feel they are just as important, if not more, than you are."

"Which is why you offered the bed," Pierre explained.

"And which is why you declined," Andrea said smiling. "It also stresses the importance of being humble. This one is what seems to be forgotten most often. "Even some of the Novices don't fully follow this one all the time. You could see this when they saw your presence, and Teacher explained why you were all here. Some of the others consider themselves more important than others, because they reached Novice status, and even have a competitive edge with other Novices. They envision a totem pole and feel there is a hierarchy amongst ourselves that puts them next in line if something were to happen to Teacher."

She noticed an uncomfortable change in Pierre at the mentioning of something happening to Teacher.

"Don't worry," she comforted. "Teacher keeps himself in good shape, and stays several steps ahead of Kruger and the Council, so I don't envision anything happening to him."

Pierre didn't seem to be comforted by her words.

"Anyhow," Andrea continued, "it is Teacher's belief that if you follow these six principles, then you are truly living, hence the mnemonic. Pretty creative, huh."

"I had always thought as much," Pierre answered. He still looked to be in a tense mood to Andrea. "What else does a Novice Orderly do besides recruit and teach the six tenets?"

"A Novice attends the Pupil meetings to make certain that those tenets are followed," Andrea replied. "It is not wise to announce that we are Novices, though we do from time to time, as there may be spies in the mix, but we also take part in the festivities as well. As you know, many meetings have poetry readings, novel sharing, and even book groups in regard to spreading literature.

There are also meetings that play beautiful music, though it gets risky doing so due to the loud noise music makes, and this usually only takes place in the most secluded of places. There are even some meetings that show movies made and produced by Pupils alone, as acting and directing careers are given, and not chosen, and the Council controls what is produced."

"Yes, I know there are meetings on various topics from newspaper writing to scientific research," Pierre interrupted irritably. "But what do the Novices do any differently than the other Pupils? What makes you guys so special?"

"That's just it, we aren't much different, except we have a closer relationship with Teacher and do much more in terms of recruitment," Andrea admitted. "We also plan on ways to get the public to know we're still out there, as well as get the Council's attention. Travelling is a large part of our lives, though it may be travelling in a very dense area for a period of time, and we don't stay in one place for too long. We even take on new identities to make certain we are not being followed or found out by the Council. Each of us also has our own smaller faction of Pupils that we trust implicitly with our true identities and other pertinent information. A few of us even work for companies in the guise of one of the Council's more reputed offices."

"How do you keep the Council from figuring you out?" Pierre asked.

"We have very few true employees and all are devout Pupils," Andrea explained to him. "Seamus and I even work under the cloak of a very reputable testing company. It is what helps us more able to control some of the testing errors we have created in the stories you all heard earlier."

"Seamus sure did seem to enjoy telling them," Pierre said with a hint of a smile. "I take it you two are very close."

"Yes, we are," she replied with a smile. Andrea couldn't help smiling when talking of her doting brother. His smile was infectious and she always pictured it when telling someone about him. "Our parents instilled in us a very strong passion for what Teacher desires to teach the entire population; it is what helped us reach this status so quickly. Maybe you, too, can join the ranks."

"It sounds like a very big commitment," Pierre stated with reluctance. "How can you tell who is worthy of the Novice title?"

179

"It takes getting to know a person, and we are all usually pretty good judges of character," she explained. "You would be surprised how much first impressions about someone can be the complete opposite of the person's true character."

"So you're saying I shouldn't judge Seamus just yet?" Pierre said, smiling completely for the first time.

"Oh, you shouldn't worry so much about Seamus," Andrea informed. "Trust me; he was totally just trying to make you feel uneasy."

"It worked," Pierre declared. He was definitely completely bothered by Seamus's remark. It was time Andrea cleared the air to make sure Pierre wasn't totally uncomfortable the rest of the night.

"Besides," she exclaimed, "I am more attracted to someone like Carly, than someone like you."

Andrea enjoyed the look of shock on Pierre's face at her admission. She wasn't sure if she eased his uneasiness, or simply made it worse.

*****

Mariana Galena could tell the girl chosen to share a room with her was someone she would not be able to relate to at all. Mariana was highly intelligent and gifted, someone that was so far above her peers that few people could quite understand. It also worked in the opposite direction, as she was unable to understand another. This girl, Carly, seemed entirely too punkish and brash. How she was able to be even considered to be a Novice Orderly was beyond Mariana's understanding. There was no possible way this girl could be on the same level as someone such as herself. She felt like a babysitter with this girl in her room. Though she wasn't much older than Carly herself, Mariana felt she clearly surpassed her in intellect and maturity. Carly had gone to the restroom and was just now making her way back into the room.

"I have an air mattress you can sleep on," Mariana explained to Carly. "Other than that, you're down to just a sleeping bag. I also have an extra pillow you can use."

"I'll take the sleeping bag," Carly said. She was walking around the room glancing around at the pieces of art that Mariana used to decorate the room before they each had gotten settled. She didn't even glance in Mariana's direction as she spoke, as she was completely mesmerized with the pictures on the wall.

Mariana couldn't help but be impressed at how much this young girl seemed to linger at the finer pieces on the wall. Maybe she did have some more cultured tastes after all.

"Are you an art lover?" Mariana asked her finally after giving her a bit of time to gaze at the murals.

"Not especially," Carly admitted. "I just thought it might inform me about you, and give me a reason I didn't have yet to dislike you. That way I didn't have to necessarily converse with you too much."

Mariana huffed with indignation. She quickly composed herself and retaliated.

"Well, you see your logic is flawed, as it started a conversation," she replied scornfully. "So your plan backfired."

"Not entirely," Carly explained. "I learned that you claim to be an art historian, yet secretly harbor a deep love for poetry instead."

"How did you learn that from looking at a couple drawings and paintings?" Mariana asked mystified.

"Actually, I overheard Matilda telling Vivienne about it when I was trying to find the restroom a while ago," Carly confessed. "Andrea had something interesting to say as well, but that's beside the point."

"So what's your story?" Mariana asked. "Why are you such a smart-mouthed oddity? Did daddy not give you enough attention?"

"A'ron Guidry is my father," Carly explained. "He has given me plenty of attention, once he realized I even existed." She had a hand up to one of the paintings admiring its beauty, still with her back to Mariana.

"Then why are you sneaking around eavesdropping on other people's conversations?" Mariana retaliated. "You clearly have some issues."

"Listening and observing can most often get more accomplished than speaking and being the center of attention," she replied.

"And what is it you are trying to accomplish?" Mariana wanted to know. "Especially by snooping around the hallway outside someone else's room."

"If you paid attention to what I said earlier," Carly scoffed, "I am trying to find some information about you."

"But why?" Mariana asked suspiciously.

"So is it true? Do you love poetry?" Carly asked, ignoring her question. She sensed that Mariana liked to have the spotlight.

"Yes, I absolutely love it, as well as art history," Mariana replied. "It has always fascinated me."

Carly smiled as she realized her assessment of Mariana was accurate.

"I love to read it, write it, and hear it being read aloud," Mariana continued. "I'm sure you would know nothing of the passion and emotion that the written word can invoke in an individual. Through rhythm, rhyme, and pure unadulterated desire, we can express the feelings no one else knows that we possess."

"And what is it that you feel?" Carly bit back disdainfully. "Do you feel a sense of being lost? A feeling you don't belong? Or how about a feeling that nobody can ever understand who you truly are? Maybe, you feel misunderstood because everyone tends to underestimate you and your capabilities. Somehow, I doubt you can ever grasp what that may feel like. I heard everyone praise you on your many talents; know how gifted and talented your mind may be, but you can never understand the complexities of what goes on inside my head."

Mariana was taken aback by this sudden outburst from someone who on first glance appeared to be so meek and mild. She was starting to understand why this young, brash girl was here attempting to be a Novice along with her. Carly just might make the cut after all. Her passion alone was admirable.

"And what are your feelings about poetry?" Mariana asked the young girl across the room.

Carly didn't respond; she simply reached into her back pocket and pulled out a piece of crumpled up paper. She gave it to Mariana, who saw there were a few stanzas of chicken-scratched poetry. Mariana read it to herself, and grew more impressed with each word she read.

Rejection makes the eternal heart ache;
realizing too late what's real, and not fake.
Pondering over what else it could take
in order for the heart to grow fonder,
of someone we've grown to hate,
due to the rejection we could not escape.
Forgetting desires we chose to create,
 instead of choosing to believe in everlasting fate.

Now we remember rejection's salty tears,
even after all these years
in between, seeking a heart to replace
 rejection's bitter and dejected face.

When Mariana finished reading it, she looked at Carly in a new light. She clearly had been mistaken when they first stepped foot in this room. Mariana was clearly able to relate to this much-maligned younger woman. There was much more to Carly Windham than what Mariana believed possible.

"If you aren't chosen as a Novice Orderly," Mariana said to Carly as she gave her back the poem and placed her hand upon Carly's shoulder. "Then I relinquish my spot to you. You are a complete and utter talent, and the Novices most definitely need someone like you."

Carly gave one of the biggest smiles of her life as she placed the poem back into her pocket.

*****

Guidry was not surprised to find Seamus Carmichael's room to have possessed the mismatched couch cushions. It seemed to have fit his personality most. Because he was much older, Guidry accepted Seamus's offer to sleep on the cushions, instead of the hard floor. Seamus did have a sleeping bag, and a pillow, so he wasn't entirely without comfort. Guidry had been glad to have been paired with an audacious storyteller such as Seamus, and knew he was in good company for the night. He could not imagine Seamus being the traitor they were all seeking, as he was too boisterous and enjoyable to be around, though he knew these were poor reasons to trust another person's truthfulness. It just seemed unfeasible to believe Seamus would have gone through so much trouble for no reason, except to turn Teacher in to the Council at the end of it all. It seemed laughable to suggest such a thing, especially after Seamus shared another yarn with him while they got settled in for the night.

Seamus explained that a group of Pupils, along with Teacher, Andrea, and Tamara set up a school's tests to have essay questions instead of multiple choice. The students did not know how to answer these, as they were so used to having to manipulate a multiple choice test, instead of having to explain what they truly did know. Guidry enjoyed the telling of this tale immensely, and gave a raucous laugh multiple times throughout its telling. Guidry wasn't used to being on this end of a story being told with such vigor, but understood why others were so invigorated by one as such. It was truly a fascinating experience.

Seamus had recognized Guidry from a news broadcast when he first went to Moon Haven and he asked him about his experience there.

It was something Guidry tried not to relive, and he had never actually spoken of the atrocities to another person before. The few people that he still maintained connections with from inside Moon Haven, those individuals who had helped him escape, were the only ones who truly knew what he had experienced. From time to time, those men, and even a few women, would talk about it amongst themselves, at least those who were still part of his own outfit. What they had lived through was what kept them bound together in a fraternity of survivors. He couldn't help but remember the telecast he witnessed at the Pope's residence, and knew that fraternity was now much smaller.

Seamus seemed to sense his unwillingness to share.

"You don't need to share if you would rather not," he told Guidry. "I can see that it is something you'd rather not talk about, especially with someone you have just met."

"The damage they tried to infuse upon us was more psychological than physical," Guidry finally confided, after a brief moment of silence. He clearly had been weighing in on whether or not Seamus was worthy of disclosing the information. "Though there was a great deal of physical anguish mind you. We were treated like lab rats, terrorists, and mentally unstable psychopaths all wrapped into one."

"I could not imagine how difficult that must have been for you," Seamus said with a shake of his head.

Guidry went on to explain to Seamus about when he first was placed into residency. He had to go through a series of interrogations where the *doctors* electrocuted him so much that the left side of his body had been temporarily paralyzed for two weeks after. Guidry also explained that the effects still were felt intermittently, where his left leg would go numb on its own accord, and was why he kept the cane with him at all times, just in case of another episode.

"You have procured my ever-most, deepest secret," Guidry divulged to Seamus. "It will not find its way into the influence of an antagonist, I hope."

Seamus agreed that the knowledge would forever be concealed. Guidry continued to reveal what happened to him inside Moon Haven.

The interrogations continued until he admitted to being a Pupil and forfeited any knowledge he had of Teacher's true identity and location. He finally broke and told them about meeting Marek's family in Egypt, though the names he had given were not accurate. For six weeks thereafter, he was drugged, electrocuted, burned, and tortured to see if he possessed any other pertinent information, which he of course did not.

Then his brain was manipulated, similar to Simone's, though he did not have memories destroyed or changed. Instead, the neurotransmitters in his brain responsible for creating dopamine were affected. Somehow, his brain was manipulated, similar to hypnosis, to believe the Council helped make life easier and filled his life with a sense of worth that Teacher was not able to maintain. He had disclosed many of the ideas he learned at the Pupil meetings, though he was able to keep a few from them, and those ideas were turned negative. He had a large amount of hostility ingrained into his mind through these methods toward Teacher, Pupils, and the Novice Orderlies, as did all others who were at Moon Haven for the same reason.

"Their intent was to break our spirit," Guidry explained to Seamus. "It is truly a genius method, if you take the time to contemplate its endgame. Once you erase the perception that Teacher's doctrine is worthwhile, and they get you to associate it with a pile of pessimistic nonsense, then it's very easy to instill the Council's will into your head."

"Yet here you are, attempting to be a Novice, yourself," Seamus reassured. He could see a glazed-eye look come over Guidry, as if reliving those events actually placed him presently back in Moon Haven.

Guidry ignored this reassurance. He robotically told his story, with none of the typical grandeur he usually possessed. After many weeks of associating the notion of Teacher and his lessons with torture and pain, he was willing to give it up very easily. Then he would go weeks without any negative outcome, and these weeks would also correlate with the times when the Council's doctrine was shoved down his throat instead. The doctors would *allow* him to read books and magazines or watch movies or newsreels, only those that would glorify the Council, however.

"They were clearly biased," Guidry informed, as if Seamus hadn't already picked up on the fact himself. Seamus didn't interrupt him, however, as he felt the need for Guidry to explain it all himself. It felt to Seamus to be some sort of remedy for Guidry. Without it, he may never fully recover.

"The doctors, though, would continue to raise our dopamine levels through drugs, and other positive reinforcement techniques," Guidry continued. "During these weeks, they were always smiling and staying positive. Then, they would have us read and watch things on Teacher again, just to remind us there was another side. During this time, they would go back to torturing us, and they would constantly yell and never hold a smile, not even for a second. It went on like this for months, back and forth until we were begging not to read anything about Teacher or mention his name."

"How were you able to overcome this?" Seamus asked surprised that this man was even in his presence after all he had heard.

"With this," Guidry said tapping his head with his cane. "Having a strong mind gives you the ability to overcome any obstacle, no matter how difficult. I have always lived my life telling fabricated stories to garner attention, and I have been able to distort reality enough that most people aren't able to discern what should be considered accurate from what is an absolute falsification. Through all of my anecdotes, I have always sustained the knowledge of what is genuine and what was insincere. Though others chose to believe the mirage, I refused to accept its validity."

"Simply amazing," Seamus exclaimed. "The mind is truly a gift."

"Is it not?" Guidry agreed. "Though trusting it can be more difficult than trusting another individual and both can lead to disappointment. What about you, Seamus, do you find trust to be difficult to procure?"

"It depends on the person in question," Seamus admitted.

"Do you trust me?" Guidry inquired. "After what I told you about what I went through in Moon Haven. Do you believe I can still have faith in Teacher's words?"

"You haven't given me any reason to doubt you," Seamus replied.

"Good," Guidry declared. He pulled out his cane, and Seamus realized a gun was built into it. "Because then I can tell you the real reason why I am here."

*****

Nicodemus Linderhaven offered Griffin Blake the hammock to sleep in, but Griffin declined, so he took it instead. It was stretched across the back corner of the room, so didn't take up a whole lot of the space at all. Griffin took a sleeping bag, instead, and laid it on the floor near the doorway. Nicodemus had just gotten situated in the hammock when he asked Griffin a question.

"What is the true nature of your presence here?"

Griffin's back was to him, as he was situating the sleeping bag a different way, because he didn't like its prior location. Though the two stood not facing each other, Nicodemus still noticed the confusion Griffin possessed at such a bold question.

"What do you mean?" Griffin asked, still not turning to face the man.

"If I am not mistaken," Nicodemus began, "I have seen the majority of your comrade's faces before meeting you all today. True, it was not in person, but I have seen most of you, nonetheless."

"And where might that be?" Griffin finally turned to face Nicodemus, who had a very wry smile on his face.

"I saw your face very recently as someone the Council had just taken in for questioning," Nicodemus explained. "I believe it said something about you all being Pupils who were taken into custody for having an illicit meeting. Wasn't that it?"

Griffin didn't know what to say. It was futile to argue with this man, who was obviously intelligent enough to see if he was lying, so he decided to tell him the truth.

"Yes," he admitted. "That was me." He turned his back to Nicodemus again, as he was embarrassed at this admission, and the fact that they had made Teacher a liar.

"And your friends in the other rooms, some of them were on there too," Nicodemus informed him. "I believe I saw Zachariah, Vivienne, and Simone along with your picture. And earlier that day, I seem to recall seeing a few images that look strikingly similar to Manna, Giovanni, and Pierre. A'ron Guidry is very well-known, as someone who was in the Council's security as well. The only one I don't recognize from anywhere is Carly."

He paused to let Griffin let this information sink in. Nicodemus wanted him to know that he was someone who should not be underestimated.

"So, I ask you again, how come people who have very recently been with the enemy are now rubbing elbows with Teacher and the Novices? How did you get out? How did you know we were going to be here? And most of all, how are we to trust that you're not working for Kruger himself?"

Again, Griffin was perplexed in how to respond to the barrage of questions. He wasn't used to lying to anyone but the Council. This man deserved to know the truth.

"We were captured by Kruger, and broke free with the help of Guidry and the others," Griffin confided. "We have been looking for Teacher to warn him of someone who was going to betray him to the Council. There is someone here who wants to bring Teacher down. So I assure you, we are not working for Kruger."

"Interesting," Nicodemus whispered to himself. He stood behind Griffin, now, and Griffin hadn't heard him move from the hammock, nor move in his direction. "What would you be willing to do to become a Novice?"

Griffin turned around to find Nicodemus a few short steps in front of him now. He noticed Nicodemus holding something in his hand, and quickly realized it was a gun. It was a Walther P99.

"What are you doing with that?" Griffin asked, displaying quite plainly the fear that seeing such a weapon had on him.

"I had it in my bag over here," he pointed at the bag he had carried in with him, "and wanted to make sure I didn't forget to have it nearby with me in the hammock."

"Why is it here?" Griffin asked, clearly unnerved by its presence. "Why do you need a gun?"

"I always carry it with me, wherever I go," Nicodemus explained. "It is always by my side when I sleep. When you are a Novice, such as myself, though I highly doubt your qualifications at this point, you will understand why it is necessary to have one on your person at all times. Ask any of the Novices, and I am sure they will tell you they have one as well."

Nicodemus took a few steps toward him, holding the gun out in a non-threatening manner. His finger was nowhere near the trigger, and the gun lay in the palm of his hand.

"Does the sight of this weapon frighten you? Does it make you feel uncomfortable?" Nicodemus asked him.

"A…a little," Griffin stammered. "Have you ever shot someone with it?"

Nicodemus did not flinch at the question, as if he was expecting it to be asked. He glared at the gun in his hand, and wrapped his hand around to grip the gun, though his finger was still nowhere near the trigger.

"The Council has oppressed the people of this country for much too long when it comes to their learning," Nicodemus stated, as if this would answer Griffin's question. "What would you do in order to get back the freedom of the education you so richly deserve? Are you willing to kill in order to achieve this goal? Would you be able to look Kruger in the eye and kill him with your bare hands, or with a weapon such as this?" He held the gun up as if to clarify which weapon he meant, as if there were a whole slew of weapons lying around the room.

"But you don't seek them out just to kill do you?" Griffin asked. "That is not what this cause is all about."

"Of course I don't kill for vanity's sake," Nicodemus clarified. "But if I had to pull the trigger in order to end all this and take back what's rightfully mine, the ability to deduce and ask questions, then I would not hesitate to cross that line."

Griffin didn't seem capable of deciding whether he could without hesitation. The hypothetical situation seemed too difficult for him to grasp, as he had never been placed in such a situation, though while escaping captivity at the Elliptical Ward Kruger had shown an un-merciless ability to kill with no remorse. Griffin doubted he could stoop to such a level himself.

"Your indecision could be the difference between life and death, young man. Let me help you decide," Nicodemus pointed the gun right between Griffin's two wide eyes. "This is quite literally what it feels like to look death in the face. Would you be able to be at the opposite end, where I stand, and do what you have to do to see another day? This is what you must consider so you will be ready when the time comes, and if what you say is true about there being a traitor in our midst, then it would appear that day will be here much sooner than you think."

He then handed Griffin the gun.

"Hopefully you'll know what to do with this when the time comes," Nicodemus told him. "Not only for your sake, but for all of those Pupils you conned into believing that you stood for something, that you actually believed in *the cause* yourself. Because if you can't, then Kruger has already won. So I ask you again, what would you be willing to do to become a Novice?"

*****

Vivienne Delacroix did not try to mask her bewilderment at what Matilda had just revealed. She could not formulate words she was in such shock.

"I know that's hard to hear," Matilda finally said, breaking the uncomfortable silence. "And I don't pretend to know what you had to go through because of my family, but I implore you to believe me when I say that I had nothing to do with it."

Vivienne's anger boiled as she became even angrier that she was in the same room with the sister of the man who had destroyed her life. Obviously, Matilda could not have been involved, but it was still one of her kin.

Matilda tried to dissipate Vivienne's emotional state, as she noticed tears streaking uncontrollably down Vivienne's face.

"What my brother and uncle both did was despicable beyond belief," Matilda continued. "My brother should still be in jail for a really long time. My uncle should have his status as Council Secretary revoked. But this world isn't fair."

"It sure as hell isn't fair," Vivienne finally spoke. "You've got some nerve trying to get me to forgive simply because your family was involved. How dare you?"

"I didn't tell you that because it was my brother, my uncle," Matilda responded. "I full-heartedly believe you should let it go, so you don't feel trapped, beaten by them any longer. You can still have your animosity, but when you let yourself be miserable and untrusting because of what happened, you aren't truly living your life any more. Kruger has the control, because he is the source of the hate. A Novice doesn't let Kruger defeat her."

Matilda could see that Vivienne was starting to understand her perspective. Teacher's voice came over the P.A. system and announced that it was time for lights out. Matilda turned toward the cot to comply with Teacher's request.

"I think I will accept your offer of sleeping on the cot, now," Vivienne stated. She clearly was not ready to forgive Matilda just yet.

Chapter Thirty-One: Revelations

It had only been two hours since Teacher had given the call for lights out, and Simone already got the sensation that she was going to be awake through the night. It was something she had always been able to read in herself. All those late night study sessions at Institute that the Council had said would be alleviated by the elimination of homework and the downplay of exams were her indicator. The only tests that mattered were the ones that the Council said were of significance, and the way testing was done really didn't call for anything but a late-night cram session one week out of the year. Even with that said, Simone still took the time to stay up late reading and studying behind closed doors, especially after Gio had told her about the textbooks they didn't want you to know were in existence. These sessions would lead to her going a full twenty-four hours or more without sleep, and she would discover a point where she would feel that it would be one of those nights each time it actually occurred. Tonight, again, she had one of those feelings. Sleep would not make its way to her.

There was simply too much on her mind; what was left of it anyhow. First, there was the knowledge that part of her memory had been manipulated. It took up a lot of her thoughts throughout the day. What thoughts to consider and what was simply Kruger's enhancement. Then, she also possessed the information that at least two of the people under this roof were people she couldn't trust, though discovering who those two were seemed most challenging. Also, she had finally met the person she had devoted a great deal of her life following. Was she not allowed to be ecstatic over that fact? Did the negative thoughts have to take so much precedence over having her dream fulfilled? Finally, her thoughts also turned to the other patron in the room, Tamara Duda. She had known the woman for less than a full day, and she had given Simone a few things that made her question the stranger's devotion to Teacher and his cause.

Each of those thoughts circled through Simone's mind, until they all seemed to blur together. The image of Kruger smiling in the photograph with Tamara, as well as each of the other Novices she had met that day, kept replaying itself like a CD stuck on repeat, though the song lyrics would change slightly upon each recurrence. Who could have been the true perpetrator in the original she had been given by the two suited agents while Kruger watched on? Could she ever retrieve that pertinent information, or was it forever lost in the confines of her mind? That's what scared her most. Was Kruger's manipulation permanent?

Another thought made its way to the forefront of her thoughts. Another perplexing question about something Griffin had said previously that day. When confronted by Guidry earlier, Griffin had denied ever telling her about there being a traitor. Why would he have denied such a thing? It had been Griffin who had first told her about it. He had overheard it or read it in a memo of some sort, but maybe he didn't remember telling her about it. Something of such significance would seem to stand out, though; at least Simone thought it would.

She tried to recall the conversation she had with Griffin about the whole ordeal. He had come over to her place one night after work, and she had just finished eating dinner. She even remembered what they both were wearing. She had been wearing a flannel shirt and a pair of silk pajama bottoms, as she had planned on staying in for the rest of the night. It had been a long day of crunching numbers, and she wasn't in the mood for attending the Pupil meeting Z had asked her to attend with him. She wanted a night of comfort and relaxation.

Griffin had on a black leather jacket and a plain black shirt underneath with a pair of tattered jeans. He kept looking around nervously as he paced her apartment. She kept asking him to have a seat, as he was starting to make her nervous. She also asked him multiple times to take off his jacket and relax a little. His constant pacing was unnerving, but he wouldn't tell her what it was that had him so agitated. She finally got him to sit at one of the stools at her breakfast bar. She attempted to take off his jacket, and he quickly stood back up and continued his frantic pacing.

"No, I need to leave the jacket on," Griffin told her. He noticed her curious glance at his defiance at wanting to remove the jacket. "It just feels necessary with the information I possess. Don't ask me why, it just does."

"Griffin, you are starting to really freak me out," Simone acknowledged. "What information are you talking about?"

"You know I could probably get killed with information like this," Griffin stated, though he wasn't even looking at her. Simone doubted he had even

meant to speak those words aloud; he obviously hadn't meant them for her. "I should just forget this and leave." Griffin turned and headed for the door.

Simone stopped him before he could reach the doorknob. She had ahold of his leather jacket, and forcefully turned him around so they were nose to nose, though she had to glare up at him as he was the slightly taller of the two.

"Griffin Blake, you came over here for a reason, and you aren't leaving until you tell me what that reason is."

He looked skeptical, but finally caved in, as he noticed the determination in her eyes. He confessed of being privy to information that one of the Novice Orderlies was planning on turning Teacher over to Kruger for a large sum of money and a full pardon by the Council. She listened intently, asking him the details of how he found out and whether or not they should take the threat seriously. After they determined the wisest decision was to believe the hazardous nature of the information, they decided to meet with Zeke and Vivienne to go over a plan for how to proceed. Griffin turned to leave, but Simone grabbed the jacket once again and turned him around to face her.

"This information is incredibly useful, Griffin," she told him. "Information of this magnitude deserves a just reward."

"The reward would be knowing Teacher is safe," Griffin replied. "I'm just happy to be able to help."

Simone smiled; proud of Griffin's modesty. She knew Teacher would have been proud as well.

"Maybe this could be of some help," she replied.

Something had come over her due to Griffin's modest act, and she saw him in a new light. She pulled his face down to hers and kissed him passionately on the lips. They broke the lip-lock and he had a shocked look on his face. It was clear he was unsure of how to take her action. He started to babble a response, but she interrupted him with another kiss more passionate than the first.

This time he received it, and returned it with an intensity that matched hers. He pulled her closer and they both fell into the doorframe as they lost their balance, their lips stayed intact through the whole balancing act. She

pulled back to look at him and ran her hands along his chest, then went in for
another kiss. The passion escalated as she pulled off his leather jacket,
removing the first piece of clothing. As the jacket fell to the ground in an
audible thud, both of them seemed to understand where this was progressing.
As the realization sunk in for both of them, they both stopped just as quickly as
they had started. Neither seemed ready to let it go any further.

Simone stammered something inaudible and Griffin stuttered through an
awkward goodbye. He turned the knob, still facing her and then turned to leave
with another awkward goodbye and laugh, as well as a thanks. Simone noticed
some writing on his shirt, and realized it hadn't been a plain black shirt at all,
though she didn't read what the writing said, as her thoughts were still stuck on
the kisses. She chastised herself for not noticing the lettering earlier, but her
thoughts kept returning to the passion contained in those lips.

The door shut behind him as he left, and Simone leaned against it in total
confusion. She noticed the leather jacket still laid on the ground and picked it
up. She would return it to Griffin the following day, but in the mean time she
went to her bedroom wearing the leather jacket, and a huge smile on her face.

Simone remembered the kiss, and currently felt guilty because she had
kept it from Giovanni. Maybe she should head to the room he was in and tell
him about it now, but the lateness of the night made her hold off on that plan.
Instead, she would save it for morning.

She should have never reacted like she did that night. Why did she kiss
him? The moment just overtook her, and it had been a lapse of judgment.
Maybe that was why he denied telling her. He was protecting her relationship
with Gio. Somehow they would slip up and tell about the kiss, once they
divulged the other happenings of that event. But it would seem easy to disclose
the pertinent information without letting that little mishap slip out. It could stay
their secret. So why deny it even took place? It would seem easy to let that
little bit of the memory be forgotten.

Suddenly, the memory flooded back to her again, though not in its
entirety. Instead, it was just the event of his leaving. She remembered
contemplating about why she had not known earlier that his shirt wasn't just one
solid color; that there was writing on it she had missed, but she wasn't certain as
to the reason why this thought was so significant. He had been wearing a
leather jacket the entire time, so it would make sense she wouldn't know about

the lettering on the back. However, she seemed overly critical for missing this information as he was leaving. She relived the memory again. This time, however, she was able to focus on what his shirt read. It said, in white, block letters that contrasted with the darkness of the shirt, *Don't Believe His Lies.*

She sat straight up on the floor and gasped as she realized the pertinence of this information. She finally knew the truth about who the real traitor was, and this new revelation scared the living hell out of her.

Chapter Thirty-Two: Midnight Interruption

Tuesday - Day Six

Manna couldn't find a way to make himself tired. He looked at the green glow of his watch as he checked for the time. It was five minutes past midnight. Another day was starting without having any new answers. Though he had not been able to get enough sleep over the course of the last week, adrenaline still seemed to be carrying him along for the ride. He found it incredible that he was still in the presence of Teacher, who was actually the one sleeping. Manna couldn't help but sense the fortitude of the man; being able to find slumber in a time when one of his close relations was planning to stab him in the back. How Teacher was able to do such a thing was beyond him. Manna was not used to being scared for his life, looking over his shoulder, but Teacher had been on the run for such a long time, he must be used to it by now.

He and Manna had spent some time chatting after the call for lights out, like old roommates at Institute. Manna had never incurred such late night chats, as he never attended Institute. The best he could relate was the conversations he had with his wife before bed, and some of the banter he experienced overseas during battle. The camaraderie of such activity never ceased to amaze him.

The topic of the banter between him and Teacher had been mystifying. Not once did they discuss the identity of the possible traitor. It did not seem to be a pressing issue to Teacher, and Manna felt too awkward to bring it up, so it was put on a dusty shelf for later. Instead they conversed about Simone's upbringing and other aspects of Manna's past. Manna felt like Teacher genuinely wanted to learn about him and his previous life up until the point he stepped foot in front of Teacher's gaze in the hallway at St. Eve's.

Manna asked questions about Joshua Lamb's past as well, but it seemed the spotlight had been on him through much of the dialogue, and not on Lamb. Manna didn't learn much about Lamb that he didn't already know earlier, except a few tidbits here or there. He learned Teacher had been an exceptional student while in school, and he enjoyed travelling, which suited him quite well, being a wanted man and all. A few moments, Lamb seemed to stumble over some of the details of his past. Manna remembered it had taken him several times to properly remember the Carmichaels' father's name. Even now, Manna wasn't entirely certain if it was Ian or Liam. Lamb seemed to change it each time he talked about him.

Lamb never mentioned a wife or kids, and when Manna asked him he skirted it away by changing the topic or asking about Manna's family. In fact, Manna didn't recall Teacher referencing any family. No mention of his mother, father, siblings, or the like. It was as if he simply came to be without having to grow up. High school was the earliest reference point Teacher had given, and even that had been vague. Manna chalked it up to Lamb's love for teaching. He desired only to question and not to give answers. If Manna preferred answers, he would have to seek them himself, and it seemed Teacher did not want some of those answers to be known.

Though Teacher didn't want to discuss the identity of the traitor, it didn't mean Manna had to ignore the fact that one of them was an imposter. After they chatted for a bit, it became quiet, and Manna could hear the heavy breathing of sleep from Teacher. That had been nearly thirty minutes ago.

Now, Manna turned his attention to trying to postulate the traitor's identity. He quickly ran through the names of each person in the building and tried to contemplate a motive for each, or come up with some telltale sign that would indicate who was bluffing. Vivienne, Jude, Carly, Pierre, and Gio all seemed standoffish, like they were holding something back. It could have very easily been they were just more introverted than the others. Guidry was a consummate liar, and Manna could never trust the things he said, but on a much smaller scale than being the one to turn Teacher over to Kruger. Griffin worked much too closely in the Council's web, so he could easily have been put up to it by Kruger. Zeke seemed a bit too eager to show off his way of thinking, perhaps trying to divert the attention from himself. Seamus seemed to enjoy the attention, so maybe he was jealous that the spotlight was given to Teacher and not to him and all of his testing exploits. Nicodemus also seemed to enjoy the limelight, and Teacher had told him earlier about his love of drama. Could this all be an award-winning performance to him? The women Novices all appeared on edge; it could be the intense pressure of always having to be on guard and keeping up appearances. After another half hour of contemplation, he had gotten no further ahead in his determination to figure out the conundrum.

He turned on his side to give up and finally try to get some much-needed sleep, but movement across the room caught his eye. It was nearly total darkness in the room, but shadows could be made out due to a row of nightlights somewhere down the hall. Manna stared intently into the shadows to see if he could find any sign of movement again. He might have been just seeing things due to the lateness of the hour, or the intensity of the situation. Nothing seemed to be moving, and he chalked it up to his mind playing tricks on him. That must be it.

He closed his eyes, but heard a rustle nearby. His eyes darted open and nearly screamed as the silhouette of a person was kneeling in front of him. A pale face could be seen, but he couldn't make out the features of who it was.

"Dad?" Manna's nerves quickly dissipated as he realized it was Simone.

"Simone, sweetie, is everything alright?" Manna asked his daughter in a hushed tone as he sat up on his elbow to see her more clearly. He was concerned that she was in his temporary bedroom at such a late hour. Through the darkness, he could still see that her eyes were in complete disbelief.

"What's wrong?" He whispered.

"I know who the traitor is," she replied in a hushed squeal.

Manna's heart skipped a beat, but then he remembered she had already accused each of them of being the defector. He didn't want to discourage her too much, but he was getting tired of accusations with no proof.

"Simone, we've been through this before," he began, understanding her mental state was still fragile.

"I'm certain this time," she said with confidence.

Manna could hear a slight sniffle, signaling tears were flowing down his daughter's face. He reached up and pulled her head down to his shoulder. His shirt immediately got soaked from the tears.

"Who, sweetie? Who is it this time?" He still wasn't as convinced as she was and his less than eager tone showed as much.

She pulled her head out of his grasp and looked him dead in the eye. Even through the darkness, Manna could see the intensity in those eyes, and knew his daughter had absolutely found the lost piece of the puzzle.

"Who is it, sweetie?" He asked again. This time he tried to convey to Simone that he believed her.

"The tr…tra," she stammered.

"Yes?" Manna encouraged.

Simone seemed to not be able to get it, but finally she composed herself enough to say what she came to say.

"The traitor," she finally said. It took all her effort to say the despicable words. "Is me."

Chapter Thirty-Three: Making Sense of Nonsense

"What do you mean, you're the traitor?" Manna asked. He did not make any attempt to whisper this time, but it wouldn't have mattered, as Teacher had been awake and overheard everything anyhow. He was already to his feet.

"I am certain of it," Simone replied. "One hundred percent, beyond a doubt, it is me we have been seeking to find. Or at least half of it anyway. There is still the question of which Novice is as well."

"But I don't understand," Manna had a perplexed look on his face. "How is it you?"

Teacher had shut the door and turned on the brilliant overhead lights inside the room. It took a few seconds for their eyes to adjust to the sudden explosiveness of the radiant light, but the severity of the situation seemed to quicken the pace. Teacher and Manna were looking at Simone for answers.

"A while ago," Simone started. "I was reliving a memory of mine about when Griffin first told me about the Novice traitor."

"But he claims to have done no such thing," Teacher interrupted. "How is that possible?"

"The memory is very vivid in my mind, and I can recollect what we were wearing, even," Simone replied, ignoring Teacher's question. "In fact, each and every olfactory, visual, and auditory description is clearer in my head for this memory, than any memory I have ever possessed. I even know more about *it* than I do of the room I just left, or even the room we are in currently."

"What is it you are saying?" Teacher asked.

"I'm saying that I think someone planted that memory into my mind," Simone declared with the utmost confidence. "The same person that destroyed the memory of the traitorous photos implanted a new memory about a conversation that never took place. Jack Kruger has been manipulating me from the start. Who knows the information he has been able to deduce from me. I could have been telling him everything from the start; turning in Pupils and telling him of secret meetings. Who knows how deep my wound has been made?"

"How can you be certain?" Teacher asked. He clearly needed more evidence to support her erroneous claim.

"At the end of this memory, Griffin and I share a passionate kiss, and I even remove a leather jacket he is wearing," Simone described. "On the back of his shirt he is wearing are the words, *Don't Believe His Lies*. I introduced a failsafe into the memory to recognize it as a fake."

"How can you be certain?" Manna asked skeptically. It all seemed like something out of those science fiction books he used to read as a kid. His mind again went to the copy of *1984* in his desk drawer.

"How would all of that even be possible?" Teacher asked the bigger question.

"I don't entirely know," Simone admitted. "But I believe it to be true. Gio is my boyfriend and I would never do something like kiss Griffin Blake to jeopardize our relationship. I also never remember giving him back his leather jacket, and it is not still in my apartment. So if that event really took place, where is the missing jacket?"

"Do you ever remember seeing Griffin wearing a leather jacket before?" Teacher inquired. "Especially one such as in your memory?"

"I don't recall such a jacket, no," Simone replied after a few minutes of thinking about ever seeing it before. "In fact, I believe I realized something was amiss much sooner."

"Why do you say that?" Manna asked, still perplexed by what his daughter was describing.

"I had planned on trying to find Guidry myself, along with Vivienne, Z, and Griffin," Simone described. "I knew Vivienne and Zeke were good at finding anything on the computer, and Griffin had an in with the Council. He could find where Guidry really was, if he was still alive."

"Then why did you send Gio and Pierre after me?" Manna asked. "If you had planned on doing it all yourself."

"I started experiencing blackouts, and gaps of time that seemed to have been displaced," Simone admitted. "It was infrequent, but still happening nonetheless. I felt scared, and told Gio to find you, that you would help find Guidry. Maybe subconsciously my mind was trying to complete the mission without having to tell Kruger about anything, since I wouldn't necessarily know all the details. I don't know, but I know that I am right, that this memory is a fake. I'm so sorry, Teacher."

"If what you say is true, then you did not do it of your own accord," Teacher explained. He patted her on the shoulder in a consoling gesture. "I cannot fault you in doing something you hadn't known you were doing in the first place. And look, you *did* warn me, so in fact you completed your duty."

"But how can we tell if what she is saying *is* the truth?" Manna asked. He couldn't get passed the fact his daughter was more damaged than he had initially thought.

"I have an idea," Teacher stated. "If the memory is false, then all the details you remember so vividly, Griffin Blake would not own a single memory of them. Let's call a meeting. It's time to let the Novices know of what's going on, so we can figure this out once and for all."

Chapter Thirty-Four: Faculty Meeting

Lamb awoke everyone with a jolt with his voice over the PA system, demanding a meeting in the room that had the circular table. He, Manna, and Simone were all awaiting the others to join them in that room. Seamus and Guidry were the first to make their way into the room, and Lamb asked them to sit without another word.

The five people sat in silence, which was even more awkward for Seamus and Guidry who were both used to talking nonstop. It helped each of them that it was nearly two in the morning. Pierre, Andrea, Matilda, Vivienne, Carly, and Mariana were not far behind. Since there weren't enough seats, those not sitting were standing awaiting the others to make their way to the room. Many were disheveled due to the early morning hour and those sitting had their head down on the table and their eyes closed. A few were standing and leaning against the wall, eyes closed as well.

"What's taking the others so long?" Teacher asked aloud, not really addressing anyone in particular.

"This couldn't have waited until morning?" Carly complained, she had a hoodie on and had her head covered by the hood hiding her face, though the way she was speaking Manna could tell her face was pressed against the table in a tired heap.

"Absolutely not," Teacher stated.

"Then do you mind telling us what this is about?" Andrea asked. Manna noticed that she was much less forgiving than earlier in the day. She even had a hint of rudeness to her, and he could sense the relationship to Seamus due to this sudden abruptness. She was clearly his sister.

"Patience, Andrea," Teacher chided. "I want to wait until everyone is here so I don't have to repeat myself."

"If it is what I think it is, it's going to be a bombshell," Seamus explained. Seamus noticed Teacher directed his attention toward him and Teacher gave him a curious look. "Guidry told me."

Teacher and Manna both glared accusatorily at Guidry, as if he had just broken a vow they all three had made in blood, sweat, or another bodily fluid more associated with the moment. Simone held her head, as if she had the entire Council after her. Guidry noticed this and quickly diverted the attention from himself.

"She remembers something doesn't she?" Guidry proclaimed pointing his cane in Simone's direction.

"What aren't you telling us?" Matilda asked this time.

"Yeah," Mariana interrupted. She had dark circles under her eyes due to the early hour and she was barely able to keep them open. She appeared to be a somnambulist, barely connecting with the living world around her. "Why do I get the impression some of us knows more about what's really going on than others?"

Even in her tired state of appearance, Mariana was still amazingly observant and deduced something was amiss. A fact not lost on Manna, as he looked around the room at the ragtag bunch of individuals surrounding him.

"What's really going on?" Andrea asked Teacher directly. Then she looked at her brother. "What do you know?" She asked him searching for answers.

Before she was able to receive a response, Zeke came through the door to join the fatigued faculty. He was followed by Griffin Blake.

"Where's Jude?" Teacher asked Zeke. "And Nicodemus?" This time he directed the question at Griffin.

"Jude needed to use the restroom so he sent me on ahead," Zeke replied. He was wiping the sleep from his eyes as he made his way fully into the room. "I ran into Griffin on the way. I don't know where Nicodemus is."

Everyone turned to Griffin for an answer.

"He said that the PA didn't always work in Tamara's room, so he went to make sure she had heard the message for the meeting," Griffin relayed the information.

"It had been kind of muffled when you sent the message for lights out," Simone explained, finally raising her head. Her voice was a bit forlorn and displaced, as if not wanting to have to address the entire room, only certain individuals. "We had to ask Mariana and Carly what was said."

"That must be why Tamara isn't here either," Teacher deduced. He looked at his three present female Orderlies who were now standing beside one another. "I promise you'll get your answers when they get here."

*****

Jack Kruger was awakened by a slight knock on his door. He had been sitting at his desk waiting for a late night call from the spy he had placed in Teacher's Novice Orderly ranks. Since it was getting late, he must have fallen asleep during the wait. He assumed the knock was to announce the arrival of that expected call. His assistant, who had been asked to stay late with him, had been told to expect the call as well. Kruger was to be notified once the call had come through, and it seemed he had made the right choice in an assistant, as he proved to be more than willing to comply with each and every demand without question or refusal to complete the task. In fact, the assistant was very diligent in his duties.

When Kruger was handed the phone, he greeted the caller and acknowledged his gratitude for the help in all the spy had done thus far. Then he asked the pertinent question.

"What is your present location?" He had a small faction of soldiers, led by the newly promoted Polchinski, waiting on this most important information in order to strike before Teacher had a chance to retreat.

"We are at the St. Eve's Academy for the Gifted in Whittingham," the familiar voice divulged.

"Is Teacher in the building?" Kruger asked.

He still called the vigilante Teacher, though he had already been told the man's true identity over three months before. He knew Joshua Lamb was the man known as Teacher, but it would have proven unfruitful to pursue a man thought to have been dead. It would have made him appear to be chasing after ghosts, and would have discredited his whole agenda. He had felt that those Pupils who were truly Pupils would secretly be mocking his attempts at placing a corpse at the top of the list of the most wanted criminals. Kruger believed it would only make the general population more likely to become Pupils as they

206

would be sneering at the idiocy of the Council. It proved much easier to let him keep the Teacher moniker and disguise the Council's knowledge of his actual identity.

It also helped keep the spy's motives secret as well. If Lamb found out the Council knew his name, he would try to piece together how it was discovered. And if Lamb's ability was even half of what his spy had alluded to, Lamb would have been able to finger point the spy with relative ease. Kruger didn't want to take any chances of that happening before Lamb was firmly under his watchful eye.

"Teacher is currently in the building," the voice acknowledged. "As are the other Novices."

"Good," Kruger couldn't help but smile at his good fortune. "Our men will be there shortly. I will make certain they know of your presence."

"The other spy is here as well," the spy stated. "And so are the others you thought might be here."

This information was quite good as well. He would get the chance to give payback to Mike Manna, A'ron Guidry, and the others that had eluded him previously. It was turning into an entire trove of treasures to be won. The situation couldn't have been better.

"That is good news," Kruger acknowledged. "I thought they might show up somehow."

"You have a very gifted mind," the spy praised. "More gifted than even Teacher's."

"Thank you for your honesty," Kruger accepted the praise, not showing one bit of modesty. To Kruger, modesty was a form of weakness. It showed you were never truly worthy of such accolades. When someone paid a compliment and felt embarrassment at such adulations, Kruger believed that the compliment was completely untrue. It showed a weak individual who did not yet know their true greatness, and would never accept it once it arrived.

"What about the other spy?" The voice on the phone interrupted Kruger's thoughts.

"She is expendable," Kruger explained.

"Understood," the voice said curtly. "I must go, so as not to raise suspicion."

"You are truly a patriot," Kruger commended. "The Council is eternally grateful for your service."

"I am honored to have been chosen for such a duty," the spy declared. "You chose wisely."

Kruger smiled at the complete lack of modesty. He had chosen wisely. This person was definitely not weak-minded.

"We will be there soon," Kruger said before ending the call with a dastardly smile on his face.

He then called Polchinski to deliver the location. It would not be long before he would finally have Joshua Lamb in his possession. The rest of the world would finally see what would happen when they crossed Jack Kruger, and they would see he was not a man they would want on opposite sides of the playing field.

He told Polchinski about St. Eve's and disclosed the identity and description of his spy on the inside. There was no mention of his other spy, as she was indeed expendable. While talking, he almost regretted that the mind manipulation of Simone Petra was finally coming to an end. He sure enjoyed influencing her memories and actions, but there would be no use for her when this all was over, so it was not necessary for her to make it out alive.

"What force do you want us to use on the people inside?" Polchinski asked after they discussed how to get inside.

"The only two necessary survivors are Joshua Lamb and our person on the inside," Kruger explained. "You have their descriptions and I will also send over a picture, though Lamb's may be outdated."

"And the others?" Polchinski asked. He was simply making clear what it was Kruger wanted done.

"With the others, only take prisoners if necessary," Kruger told him after a few seconds of thought.

"Understood," Polchinski said, and for the second time that night Kruger ended a call with a smile on his face.

*****

"What's taking those three so long?" Mariana asked no one in particular. She clearly did not like a secret kept from her.

Manna glanced around the room at the three anxious Novices; Mariana, Matilda, and Andrea. They seemed the most awake, and Manna assumed it was because the others all knew what wasn't being told. Even Seamus seemed to possess the knowledge, though Manna wasn't entirely certain it had been wise of Guidry to give it to him just yet.

Seamus and Guidry were both seated next to one another at the table in the same nonchalant pose. Each was leaned back in his chair with his hands draped behind his head, simply waiting for the missing Novices. The chairs held on two legs at an angle that bordered on the threshold of tipping. Neither seemed to possess the least bit of unease, which appeared to be the complete opposite from the female Orderlies.

Pierre and Gio were standing near one another, leaning against the wall with their arms crossed in matching looks of disdain. The pair mirrored one another so well; Manna noticed they had opposite legs crossed over one another. Zeke found Vivienne seated and stood behind her chair, leaning on the back of it with his formidable girth. Griffin stood beside Zeke on the other side of Vivienne.

Manna noticed Vivienne glance periodically in Matilda's direction with such incredulous contempt, he was sure there was something Vivienne had discovered about Matilda during their conversation that she didn't like. He also noticed Matilda would never meet Vivienne's eye, but would peer over from time to time when Vivienne wasn't looking. To Manna, Matilda seemed to be the least worried about the secret of the female triumvirate, as if her mind was preoccupied with something more pressing.

Carly sat away from everyone at the end of the table with her head down on the table covered by the hood of the hoodie she was wearing, and Manna couldn't tell if she was truly awake or being observant in her own deceptive way.

Manna, himself, stood between Simone and Lamb at the other end of the table, opposite Carly. Simone had downcast eyes and seemed so removed from the rest of the room Manna could feel it palpitate, as if her presence could be felt by each member of the room, but they refused to acknowledge its importance. Teacher, like Manna, seemed to be perusing the room. His eyes darting over each and every person; lingering, it seemed, a little longer on his trusted Novices. He was clearly trying to discover an idiosyncrasy he hadn't noticed that could help him establish which one of them was the traitorous snake they were seeking.

It seemed an eternity before Nicodemus and Tamara finally showed up, but Jude still did not accompany them. The two newcomers noticed the tension in the room as they stepped tentatively into the room. Each and every eye in the room seemed to be on them, except Carly who still did not raise her head off the circular table. Instead, her back was to the two tardy Novices.

"What's the matter?" Nicodemus asked.

"Yeah, what's with the late night wakeup call?" Tamara demanded. "I didn't even hear it. Nicodemus had to come and get me." She didn't seem to be a person that liked to be awakened from her slumber.

Before Teacher could explain they were waiting on Jude, Seamus interrupted him and let everyone in on what was truly going on.

"Guidry here said there is a traitor amongst us," Seamus declared. "Isn't that correct, Guidry?"

Guidry's chair slammed back onto all four legs as Seamus let the cat out of the bag. He clearly had not wanted Seamus to divulge the truth so soon. Seamus realized this, but flippantly dismissed Guidry's complaint.

"Well, we can't keep it secret forever," Seamus told them. "So which one of you is it?"

He glared with accusing eyes at each person in the room.

"What do you mean there's a traitor?" Tamara asked.

"And what do you mean which one of you?" Mariana was angry at the assumption.

210

"Guidry said the real reason each of these 'Novice candidates' are here is because they are trying to find which one of us Novices is planning on turning Teacher over to Kruger and the Council," Seamus replied. He even did air quotes around *Novice candidates* when he said the words. "So I ask again, which one of you so called friends is spying for Kruger? Because I want to show him or her what Seamus thinks of traitors." He pulled out a pistol and set it on the table.

Each person seemed to take a step away from Seamus and a collected gasp resonated within the room as the gun was pulled, and an audible sigh of relief was also made once the gun was placed on the table.

"How do we know it isn't you, though?" Mariana stated. "You seem good at pointing fingers at others, maybe that's to divert the attention away from yourself. What makes you the exception and not a suspect?"

"Seamus would never turn on the cause," Andrea declared, defending her brother. "He has done as much, if not more, than anyone of us in support of Teacher. Or have you forgotten about all he has done while you were traipsing all over Paris with your art? You seem a likely candidate Ms. Mademoiselle. What about it? Did Kruger get to you while you were in Paris? None of us would know otherwise."

"Why would I allow Kruger to convince me to give up on what I have spent the majority of my mental capacity to achieve?" Mariana retaliated. "I recruit nearly double what any one of you recruit in any given quarterly session. I am as devoted to Mr. Lamb as any of you. How dare you accuse me of being a spy? The mere thought of it is completely absurd. If anyone is a traitor, it is Matilda. She's so sneakily quiet all the time. Why not ask her?"

Most of the eyes in the room diverted to Matilda to see how she would defend her honor, but before she had a chance to speak Tamara spoke up first.

"Why are we turning on one another?" The rhetorical question hung over the heads of each person in the room. Teacher smiled with satisfaction as finally a clearer head prevailed. "What about the newcomers? How do we know they are even Pupils? One of them could easily be working for Kruger to find where we are, and we just let them come through the front door with open arms. I knew there was something off about this situation." Teacher's smile was quickly wiped off his face as Tamara simply added more powder to the explosive room.

"Us?" Zeke inquired. "We were the ones that discovered that there *was* a traitor and came to warn Teacher before it could take place."

"It could have been easily fabricated," Nicodemus spoke this time. "Who's to say your information is accurate?"

"Don't worry about the accuracy of our information," Vivienne declared, "worry about which one of your appearances is a farce. Let's do what Mariana said and ask Matilda. I would love to hear from her. She is Kruger's *niece* after all."

Now every wide-eye in the room, except Carly's unturned eye and Teacher's, who already had been privy to that particular point, turned to Matilda, who seemed shocked Vivienne would bring that piece of information to everyone's attention.

"Care to explain that one?" Vivienne demanded with a smile.

Again, before Matilda could defend herself, someone interrupted. This time it was Teacher. He was not going to let the situation escalate any further.

"Everyone, stop," his voice was booming and echoed off the empty hallway walls outside the room. "This is madness. Listen to yourselves. This is exactly what Kruger wants, to turn on ourselves and give up the mission we have created ourselves. There *is* a spy somewhere is this room. In fact, there are two."

This admission drew a few gasps from the Novice Orderlies not privy to this information earlier.

"In fact, we think we may have discovered the identity of one of Kruger's spies," Teacher continued.

This information drew a few more guttural reactions, from the others as well. Manna glanced around the room to see any kneejerk reaction from a Novice to give away the other traitor, but the person must have been able to compose himself or herself enough to not let it slip.

"You mean we have found the identity of one of the traitors?" Guidry asked incredulously. "Who is it?"

"First, we must ask Griffin a question," Teacher replied.

Griffin looked shocked. He held his hands in front of him trying to push back any accusation that came his way and took a few steps back, bumping into the wall.

"We aren't saying he is a traitor," Teacher explained. "He just may have some information that can help us correctly identify one of the spies. Griffin, do you recall going to Simone's house in a leather jacket the night you told her about the Novice spy?"

"Why do you all keep saying I told Simone about the traitor?" Griffin asked defensively. "I keep telling you guys I wasn't the one who found the information. Why won't you believe me?"

"So you're telling me you didn't go to Simone's house in a leather jacket to tell her about the spy?" Teacher asked again just to be clear.

"I don't even own a leather jacket," Griffin admitted. "What does this have to do with the true traitor?"

"I'm getting there," Teacher answered. "And you didn't kiss her at her door as you were leaving?"

Gio uncrossed his arms at this question. He looked at Simone with a confused look on his face. Her gaze still bore into the floorboards of the room. Gio then looked accusingly at Griffin awaiting his response.

"That most definitely didn't happen," Griffin finally replied. He noticed Gio's gaze in his direction. "Simone and I are just friends. We don't have those kinds of feelings for each other."

"Then that clears up one of the spies," Teacher declared. "It seems Ms. Petra here was manipulated by Kruger into believing Griffin told her about the Novice spy. Who knows what other information Kruger knows from Ms. Petra? It would seem he has the capabilities to make her forget information she was given, so it would not surprise me to think he could also make her remember things that didn't exist."

"That still doesn't make it certain that any one of use is a traitor," Nicodemus stated. "You said yourself this woman's information is faulty. How can we believe anything she says?"

Simone finally raised her head from staring at the floor.

"It is true not everything has been the most accurate as it pertains to the information I have shared," Simone declared, "but I know without question that I am not the only person Kruger used in his search for Teacher. There is information I was most definitely not able to gather, such as finding this location. Kruger would not be dumb enough to depend on just one person in such an important mission. Clearly, he needed someone much closer to Teacher's inner circle. And who is closer than a Novice? It makes entirely too much sense, not to mention I have memories of certain events linking one of you to Kruger as well."

Manna could still not see any telltale signs of a Novice being in distress. They were reacting just like the others, with shock and surprise registering on their face and mannerisms.

"Whether you like it or not," Simone continued. "One of the Novice Orderlies plans on handing Teacher over to Kruger and the Council."

"This just proves how powerful the Council really is," Matilda finally said. "Kruger, my uncle," She caught Vivienne's gaze as she said this, "he definitely has the power to infiltrate something as seemingly trustworthy as the Novice Orderlies, and he has the determination to take whatever measure necessary to make certain the job gets accomplished. I know the man better than any of you, and he will not cease to persist when it comes to any task he has laid out and planned."

"So you think the Council has already won?" Nicodemus asked vehemently. "I don't think so. I will not stand for this lack of effort. Maybe, Mr. Lamb here will allow his learners to give up without a fight, but it's just not in my nature to do such things."

"I never said the Council was victorious by any means," Matilda said incessantly. "I was merely pointing out the fact that Kruger has the means to turn one of us against Teacher. He has the money, authority, and willpower to manipulate any situation he sees fit. He is not a man to be taken lightly."

"So you still believe this nonsense of a traitor?" Tamara ridiculed. "Come on Mattie, we've all been together too long to stab one another in the back."

"I know my uncle," Matilda stated again. "I know what he is capable of doing, and since he's involved, I do believe he was able to convince one of us to turn. I hate to say it, but one of us is not who we seem."

"But how can we figure out which one it is?" Zeke asked. "It seems they all have some suspicious behavior or piece of information about them."

"Why doesn't anyone suggest the person not here?" Carly asked from underneath the hood. Manna had forgotten she was still in the room. At least now he found the answer to his question. She hadn't been asleep. "He seems pretty suspicious to me."

"Who's not here?" Gio asked.

Everyone in the room glanced around to see who had left or was missing.

"Jude!" Zeke exclaimed after realizing his bunkmate had still not made his way from the restroom.

The group started for the door to seek out Jude and question him further when a shatter of glass echoed down the empty hall, followed by the excruciating sound of the security alarm which stopped everyone in their tracks.

Chapter Thirty-Five: Exodus

Seamus went back to the table to retrieve the gun he hastily left behind, then joined the others at the closed door.

"Anyone else have a weapon?" Seamus asked everyone in the group. Guidry held up his cane, but none of the others did, as they were awakened at such short notice. Most everyone's eyes were wide and panic-stricken. The person who seemed the calmest was Teacher, himself, though everyone knew the true purpose for the alarm's ring. Kruger's spy had somehow contacted him and divulged their location.

"They followed Simone here," Tamara accused pointing a condemning finger at her. "She must have told Kruger somehow, or they traced her here."

"Stop that. Our priority is to make certain Lamb doesn't get taken," Nicodemus announced as Guidry and Seamus peered down the hall through the window in the room. As far as they could tell, no one was out there, yet. 'It's not time to point fingers. We need to escape first."

"Where's the escape route?" Seamus asked.

"Is that wise to announce it?" Matilda asked reproachfully. "What if Jude isn't the traitor?"

"I think it's obvious he is," Nicodemus declared. "He's the only one not accounted for. Jude could have contacted Kruger while we were sitting here arguing about which one of *us* would backstab."

"Well, whatever we do," Seamus shouted. "Let's not sit around waiting for a bunch of armed men to come and blow us away." He noticed Andrea glaring at him indignantly. "Oh, all right, armed men and women. Now's not the time for your feminist complaints."

"I agree," Guidry stated still looking out the window for any gun-toting-killing-machines.

"There's too many of us to all go in one direction," Carly stated. Manna noticed the frightful, agitated look of a trapped animal, but also saw the right amount of determined consternation that knew to keep her wits about her in order to survive. "I suggest we split up and meet at the escape route."

"Which is where?" Seamus demanded again.

"We'll all meet in the basement," Joshua Lamb finally disclosed. "And escape together. But Ms. Windham is correct. There are simply too many of us to all go at once. We'll have to split ourselves up."

* * * * *

Nicodemus, Griffin, Pierre, and Tamara wanted to first get the gun located in the room shared by Nicodemus and Griffin in order to better defend themselves. Nicodemus explained he had a second gun that matched the one he had previously given to Griffin. Tamara also told of a concealed gun she had in her room, but they had decided it wisest to go after the two guns rather than the one.

Since none of them possessed a gun at the present time, they had to be careful not to be seen or else they were not able to defend against whoever was out there with Jude. Nicodemus took the lead, followed by Griffin, then Pierre, and lastly Tamara. He led them from room to room, trying to stay out of the hallways any longer than necessary.

Nicodemus peered around the corner of the doorway of room 317 and saw a line of men dashing down the hallway perpendicular to their room. Once they passed, he led them three rooms down to 320, where they dashed in to procure the guns they were seeking.

* * * * *

Mariana, Zeke, Seamus, and Andrea possessed the task of being the de facto fullback or offensive linemen. Since Seamus was one of two already with a weapon, their undertaking was to make certain Teacher had a clearer path to the escape route. Seamus led and was followed by Mariana and Zeke. Andrea brought up the rear and she knew Teacher and his four bodyguards were only a few minutes behind. They had all thought it wisest not to communicate via radio, because it was believed Jude was with the assault team who broke in. The other two groups were acting as decoys to lure Kruger, or whoever was there in his stead, away from Lamb.

Andrea could feel her heart pattering a constant, violent rhythm she could feel throughout her entire body. Through all the misdeeds she and Seamus had been a part of with Teacher, she had never felt threatened in any

217

way, especially her mortal existence. She had known she could have been caught by Kruger and would have probably been tortured beyond anything she could dream up, but it never felt as if her life was in jeopardy. Now, however, she felt that feeling for the first time and the possibility utterly terrified her. Was she truly ready to die for something such as this? Wasn't it simply a battle of wits? Not one of life and death. Or was it? She felt her present situation definitely seemed to answer that question.

For the first time in her life, she doubted how committed she was to everything she had devoted her life to for the past five years. As they turned down another empty hallway, Andrea made an internal promise to herself. If she made it out alive, she would never allow herself to be placed into another situation like this again; where her actual mortality was in question. Principles and morals she could handle leaving behind, but not the mortal lifeblood she held so dear.

*****

Joshua Lamb held position in the exact epicenter of the four other members charged with leading him to safety. He knew how important his getting out alive was to the Novices and the movement he had started over a decade ago, but somehow he felt the need to single him out was misguided. Though he symbolized everything his movement stood for, it was much more than any one person could represent. Yet somehow he doubted the movement could continue without his existence, due to what and who he was.

Lamb observed the two people in front of him, A'ron Guidry and Carly Windham; a father-daughter combination cloaked in mystery and suspense. From what he could tell from the two, they seemed polar opposites. There was the large, boisterous father who craved the spotlight, and the meek, mild daughter always on the periphery. Together they seemed capable of tackling any obstacle always using their cunning to seek out the missing pieces to the puzzle, and using the empty spaces still left somehow to their advantage. Lamb couldn't help but think that even without him these two individuals would still be in this place in time protecting some other symbolic figure against corrupt injustice; even without him these two would still thrive.

Then he turned to look at the other pair behind him, also father and daughter. These two were much different than the previous pair. He could feel the extraordinary love and genuine respect each felt for the other. There was

218

still a sense of the unspoken nature typical of a father-daughter relationship, yet there was something unconditional Lamb could sense as well.

Manna had disclosed his initial concern for Simone's desire to become one of Lamb's very own Pupils, yet Manna was still willing to let his daughter choose for herself and deal with any repercussions that arose from such a decision. Lamb had listened intently and came to respect the man he had only recently met. The man was willing to stick by his damaged daughter no matter what; even after admitting to helping Kruger, Manna did not find her at fault. Instead, he showed his support by telling her how strong and cunning she was to purposely hide a failsafe so she would know it was all a lie. Furthermore, he explained she was able to accomplish her goal of warning Teacher of the saboteur, though not exactly as planned. The man was simply a good-hearted person who loved his daughter relentlessly, and only wanted her free of any and all harm.

Like Guidry and his offspring, Lamb could tell Manna and Simone were capable of overcoming many obstacles with their ability to think logically and for the common good of others. Unlike them, however, he could sense they needed his presence much more than most. Guidry had been a free spirit from the start, and Carly looked to be willing to combat any *normalcy* one could conjure up, but Manna and Simone were not lawbreakers. They were of the ilk to challenge only those rules they deemed unjust and unfair. Those two didn't do it for themselves. No, they did it so others could have the opportunity to see what it was like to have a sense of worth. To Lamb, that was a rare breed, yet they still needed a rallying symbol to show the masses how it could be.

They weren't necessarily the most articulate, and weren't the most influential, but they were definitely able to convince others of their worth simply because they were the most unlikely of radicals. If they were willing to turn their back on the Council for something they felt was a better way of life. Lamb knew he needed more people like the two of them for the success of his movement. To him, they were what was inspiring, even more so than himself. Teacher turned to follow as Guidry led them with the gun within his cane. It was fitting he was in front of Simone and Manna, because right then he made a vow to make certain if anyone got out of there, he would make sure to lead those two out alive.

*****

Lucas, Gio, Vivienne, and Matilda hurried quietly down the hall in that order. They had obtained two guns from Lucas's room and were attempting to complete the mission of luring the assailants in the opposite direction from Teacher so he could escape. Lucas held one gun at the head of the line and Matilda held the other at the rear. All four knew their mission meant their likelihood of getting out alive was much less likely, but all four were willing to partake without remorse.

However, Vivienne was not a big fan of the fact she had again been placed in partnership with Matilda Swanson. It distracted her from the mission at hand, she knew, but she couldn't help it. Her son and husband had been her entire world. No experience was better than watching her son sleep, or hearing his laugh at the dinner table, or seeing the two of them roughhousing or playing outside. This woman's family was responsible for taking all that away from her. It seemed difficult to separate Matilda from that situation, though she had no direct hand in the matter herself. Vivienne snapped back to their present situation, trying to keep the past from closing in and suffocating the life out of her, when she needed her wits most.

The school was unbelievably dark and they dared not turn on any lights, so as not to disclose their location. Stealth was their ally, and it may have been their only advantage at the moment. They were in the dark as to how many assailants were in the building and how armed the assailants were. It was best to believe they were in a well of hurt, and were facing the direst of situations. None of them had even seen another individual in the building, yet somehow they knew the assault was not a faulty wire or short in the security. It was truly the real thing.

Since some of the rooms were connected with one another, they snaked into rooms with relative ease. Vivienne was peering behind at Matilda, who was holding the gun in both hands. Matilda was making sure no one was sneaking up on them from behind. Vivienne was double-checking to make certain Matilda was doing her job, as she didn't fully trust her even then.

Vivienne was so unaware at what was going on in front of her that she ran right into Gio in front of her. Gio gave her an annoyed look, then turned back to face Lucas in front. Lucas was turned facing the three of them. Vivienne hadn't realized they had all stopped ahead of her. Lucas peered around the corner at the bend in the hallway. Then, he faced the other three again.

"It appears Kruger's men are here," Lucas whispered in a hushed voice. Vivienne barely heard what he had said. "Most of their backs are to us. I counted six men. We won't be able to hit them all, but we can hit some if we're quick. I will admit, I am not the best shot at this distance, anyone else feel more capable?"

Gio reached out his hand demanding the gun. Without a second guess, Lucas handed him the pistol.

"We're only going to have a short time to shoot, then we're going to have to take off," Lucas continued. "I say we take off down that hall." He pointed left, which would momentarily leave them out in the open. "They'll see we are running and be likely to follow quicker."

The other three nodded their agreement.

"You ready to do our part to complete the mission?" Lucas asked. He took a step back to let Gio and Matilda ready their guns. "Okay, on the count of three. 1...2......3"

*****

It took some time for Nicodemus to locate the second gun he had hidden. Griffin held the one Nicodemus had given him earlier and he was peering out the door, watching for any movement, though the hallways were still eerily dark with only the faint glow of a few nightlights to light the way. It was much different than the buzzing fluorescent lights he was used to in a school setting. He hadn't noticed until then how quiet it truly was. He remembered seeing the assault team of soldiers in the hall, hearing barely audible footfalls on the non-carpeted floors. They were definitely trained soldiers.

He looked over to see Nicodemus had finally found the other gun. It didn't seem there were many places for it to hide, so Griffin chalked the forgetfulness up to nerves. Now, however, he appeared to be looking for the bullets for the gun.

"Hurry," Tamara declared. She was standing on the other side of the door from Griffin helping him look for any sign of an assailant. "We have to get moving again. It's not safe to stay in one place for too long. They'll most certainly find us."

"I'm trying to think where I put them," Nicodemus told her. He was kneeling and peering underneath the sparse amount of furniture and items in the room. "I recall wanting to hide them somewhere I would remember where they were. Now, for the life of me, I can't recollect where that might be." He continued to search on his knees for the lost ammo.

Pierre was looking in the rumpled sleeping bag, even though Nicodemus had already claimed to have looked through it. It was never a bad idea to double check behind someone to make sure.

"Oh wait, now I remember," Nicodemus stated as he stood. Everyone turned his way at this declaration. "I already put the bullets in the gun."

He turned around sharply and shot Pierre in the chest, then pulled the trigger one more time and hit Tamara right between the eyes. Both crumpled to the floor. He shot Pierre one more time to give himself the reassurance that he was indeed dead. Finally, Nicodemus turned the gun on Griffin, who was pointing the gun on him as well.

"A good old-fashioned standoff," Nicodemus declared with a smile.

"What the hell are you doing?" Griffin asked through teary eyes.

"Let me tell you a little secret," Nicodemus explained still smiling. "I am the traitor. I am not sure what took Jude so long, but it worked out in my favor. Everyone assumed it was him, but in reality it was me."

"But why?" Griffin was bewildered at this admission. He had been assigned a spy as a bunkmate. How could he have not realized this earlier?

"Before I asked you what you'd do to become a Novice," Nicodemus replied. His steely gaze burned into Griffin's own, nearly paralyzing him with immense fear. Griffin had just seen him shoot two individuals in cold blood; he knew what Nicodemus was capable of doing. "You remember?" He didn't wait for a reply. "Well, what would you also be willing to do to please the Council? You don't seriously believe all of this nonsense of creativity and logic and thinking outside the box. That is pure excrement. If everyone thought outside the box, then it would be pure anarchy. You think what you do is pure and innocent, but allowing yourself to follow Teacher; you are simply trading one hypocrite for another. At least with Kruger and the Council I know the hypocrisy exists."

"How is Teacher a hypocrite?" Griffin demanded. He tried to use the same steely gaze, yet somehow lacked the effect Nicodemus carried with his.

"He asks others to think for themselves," Nicodemus declared. "Yet he tells them how they are supposed to think and what processes to use to accomplish such thought."

"It's not as simple as that," Griffin stated. "There is much more we can accomplish and are allowed to do with Teacher, which we could never even *think* about thinking with the Council. It covers a broad spectrum and has no limits."

"Which is why it is so dangerous," Nicodemus stated. "If it has no limits, it can't be controlled. One person considers it right, yet one most definitely persists it is wrong. Everyone walks out a loser, if no one can declare he has won."

"You're wrong. Everyone has a chance at winning, if nobody has to lose."

"So, have you figured out if you have what it takes to become a Novice? Consider this your job interview. Pulling the trigger will get you the job." Nicodemus hadn't removed the smile from his face the entire time. "Do you have the tools to be a Novice?"

"Yes," Griffin declared as he pulled the trigger of the gun he was aiming at Nicodemus. There was an audible click and he pulled the trigger again with the same result.

Nicodemus's laugh bellowed and seemed to echo more menacingly due to the emptiness of the building.

"Lesson learned," he told Griffin. "Indecision isn't the only thing that gets you killed. Sometimes it's having a faulty weapon. And sometimes, in your situation, it's trusting you have a weapon of mass destruction when it's actually a dud. You see, it's not always the first person to pull the trigger who wins. Especially when that gun has no bullets."

Griffin was completely deflated. He knew he had nowhere to go. He was trapped in the room with this lunatic. Any slight movement and he would be dead, like Pierre and Tamara already on the ground.

"You got it wrong," Nicodemus stated. "There is always a winner and loser. And this time you lose." Before leaving the room, Nicodemus pulled the trigger two more times. The first was in Griffin's shoulder; not a kill-shot, so he would feel the pain he so deserved. This shot dropped Griffin to the floor. As Griffin squirmed on the ground wrangling in pain, Nicodemus eyed him one more time, shaking his head in disappointment, as the second shot into the skull killed Griffin Blake.

*****

Seamus continued to lead his charge to the door leading to the basement. They had been lucky thus far and had not run into any of the assailants they had assumed were out there. They were completely in the dark as to how many there were or even if any were in the building in the first place. As far as they knew, the assailants were still outside the building waiting for them to exit. Seamus believed there were at least a few along the periphery of the building as it would be unwise not to have someone on watch for people escaping. Lucky for the Novices, they had a route those on watch would not be able to see, as it led underneath the building.

Seamus hurriedly led them down a long straight corridor. They had made their way into one of the custodian-only rooms, free of the hallways to avoid any assailants. It was void of any character as the walls were made of gray, gritty concrete blocks. There were tarnished pipes lining the ceiling just above their heads which snaked around various corners and also paralleled their trek. It was a maze of pipes and concrete one could get lost in if he didn't know where he was going. This was one of several ways that led to the basement, and Seamus had thought it might prove easier to escape detection from those searching for them, if indeed they were in the building. That belief had proven accurate so far.

Their pace quickened as Seamus sensed they were closer to the basement door. Andrea's head was in a constant state of movement as she searched behind her and then turned forward to keep pace with the others. There were several corridors which led off to the right or left intermittently interspersed along the way, but their destination was a fairly straight shot. Only a few turns and they would be there. Andrea couldn't resist looking down these intersections as well making sure no one was there. The constant worry of her own demise was a persistent thought that wouldn't go away, but she wouldn't completely succumb to it entirely. They were too close to their destination.

224

She noticed Seamus and Mariana were starting to pull way ahead, because Zeke was starting to tire. It was clear he was not built for endurance running, or any kind of running for that matter, and Seamus was quickening the pace with each footfall. Seamus and Mariana finally made a right hand turn, which gave Andrea a sense of hope she needed. A quick left a few feet ahead followed by another right, and they would be at the door they sought.

Before they got to the turn, a deafening gunshot rang through the corridor. The bullet sparked against the concrete to Andrea's right, making her stop dead in her tracks. Zeke did the same. They faced one another, Zeke in the direction of the gunman, with Andrea having her back facing the enemy.

"Good," the voice said from behind Andrea. It was hoarse and raspy, like someone who smoked tree bark on a daily basis. "Now you two hold it right there. Radio it in, Maxwell."

Another voice, seemingly Maxwell, relayed a message into his radio, "Maxwell, here. We have two of the culprits in our possession. Requesting confirmation on how you want them detained."

As he awaited his response, Andrea peered at Zeke. He was sweaty and pale, and looked about ready to pass out, from fear or the physical exertion, she didn't know. She caught his attention with her eyes and mouthed, *How many?*

He looked past her and held out two fingers quickly. Maxwell radioed the message again as he still did not receive a response. Andrea turned her head slightly, trying to peer behind her.

"Don't move, lady," the gunman demanded, "unless you want to paint these walls red."

She stopped, but could still catch Seamus and Mariana in her periphery. They had stopped several yards down the corridor they had turned down just a little bit ago. Seamus held the gun up and took a few silent steps forward.

"What's your location, Maxwell?" someone asked on the radio.

Andrea caught her brother's attention as Maxwell told the person at the other end of the radio their location. She mouthed the word *No* to him and he stopped. She had not lost the fact that Maxwell had radioed they had only found two. They had somehow not seen Seamus and Mariana. The soldiers must have caught sight of them only after her brother had turned right down the corridor.

The response came back on the radio.

"Detain them until we confirm we have Teacher in our possession. Then you can shoot."

"Gladly," the gunman said mockingly.

Zeke tensed as he heard the radio's response. Then he pleaded with his eyes for Andrea to do something

She diverted her eyes to the left and raised them to see if Zeke understood. She did it two more times, but he still was not reading her.

"Run that way when I say three," she barely whispered. His eyes shot up and she realized he understood. He shook his head, no, very slightly.

"Yo, tubby," the gunman chided. "I bet you got enough to coat the whole wall red. Keep moving so I can see how good an artist I am." He gave a light chuckle, and Maxwell laughed as well.

Andrea caught her brother's eye and knew he understood what she was about to do.

She faced Zeke and mouthed a countdown. *One…two….three.*

At three she pushed Zeke left and shot down the left corridor. She heard a gunshot hit the concrete just behind her, which made her run faster. She wasn't ready to die for her cause just yet, but Teacher needed a clear path. She had never failed in one of her missions, and she wasn't about to make this her first.

*****

Gio and Matilda simultaneously popped out from around the corner once Lucas reached three. They both got off four shots each before diving to their left for cover. Gio had hit two soldiers and Matilda hit one, but it helped clear them from the hallway. Lucas and Vivienne were still on the right side of the hall.

A volley of bullets echoed their way in retaliation for their initial damage, but unlike their assailants, they had been expecting it. Gio aimed and returned a few more shots to let them know they were still there. Lucas dove across on this volley. They awaited the return shots, then Matilda sent a return. Vivienne dove as well, but was hit in the arm. Luckily it was the metal one, but she still fell down in the middle of the intersection; completely exposed.

Matilda dove out in front of her and continued shooting until her clip was empty. Gio covered them enough for Matilda, with the help of Lucas, to pull Vivienne to safety. His clip was empty then. They reloaded, and then took off down the hall, making sure their footfalls were loud enough to echo down the empty halls. If they were going to get the soldiers to chase, the soldiers needed to know they were running away in the first place. Or else, Teacher might never get out alive.

*****

Seamus had witnessed, with admiration, his sister take off in the opposite direction in order to sacrifice herself for the mission. He had considered shooting her assailants in the back as they followed, but they were too quick and he didn't want to alert them to his position. That would have made his sister's sacrifice completely worthless. Then, the soldiers would have known there were more, and he needed to make sure Teacher got out. He refused to let his sister's expense be in vain. He pushed Mariana ahead and attempted to reach the basement to check for any hidden enemies. If there were, he would gladly show them how unmerciful he could be to anyone who dared do his sister harm.

*****

Vivienne, Matilda, Gio, and Lucas ran relentlessly away from their assailants. Matilda led this time followed by Vivienne. The men hung in the back with Gio nearly backpedaling away. They could not hear if the soldiers were following or not, but were not willing to stick around to discover if they were.

Matilda still held the gun and the noise they were making to lure their attackers also had the dubious honor of announcing their arrival if they were approaching an attacker as well. It was a dangerous game of cat and mouse, and Matilda wasn't exactly sure which part they currently played.

As she told the others previously, she knew how relentless her uncle was at achieving his goal. There was no end to the amount of resources he would undertake to accomplish his goal of ridding the world of Teacher's philosophy. Her uncle enjoyed having the upper hand, and didn't much like being undermined by anyone, and Teacher was doing just that. Lamb was undermining his power over the populous that he so cherished. Having free thinkers meant the Council couldn't control each and every aspect of an individual's life. Kruger refused to stand for such insubordination.

Matilda was so completely lost in her revelry that she didn't notice the soldier with the gun pointed at her before it was too late. She tried to halt, but it was too late. The soldier had pulled the trigger and a huge force slammed into her, knocking her to the ground.

*****

Andrea could hear Zeke huffing behind her as the two tried to outrun the two soldiers. They swerved around the inner maze so much, Andrea felt a lost sense of direction. She wasn't entirely sure if she was leading them away from the basement doorway or toward it. Her only certainty was her desire to stay away from any direct shot from the gunmen behind her. Her main problem, however, was Zeke's lack of physical endurance. She wasn't completely sure how much longer he was able to last at their current pace.

She had heard of many instances of adrenaline fueling someone along through a variety of dangers; the mind and body being able to go on past one's own personal tolerance of pain and endurance. However, she did not believe any of them could possibly have done such feats with the same physical girth Zeke possessed. None of them could have looked that unhealthy and been able to achieve those things. Could they?

Andrea slowed down briefly to get her bearings, yet each turn looked the same. Could they just be running in a circle? When she was about to give up on ever getting out of that maze, they discovered the door they had first used to enter the custodial bunker.

Excitement fueled Andrea as she reached the door. At least she would be leading them away from one of the basement entrances. She opened the door and turned right; Zeke followed. They took four steps when a voice halted their escape.

"Freeze," the voice shouted. "Put your hands up and hold it right there."

For the second time that night, Andrea and Zeke had a gun pointed in their direction. Like before, they put their hands up to signal their mutual surrender. Andrea and Zeke had again been captured by Kruger's men. And this time there was nowhere they could run.

*****

Seamus and Mariana finally reached their destination, the basement, and Seamus had made certain none of Kruger's soldiers were down there. Teacher would be there shortly, and they would be able to get him out of harm's way. His thoughts drifted to his sister's welfare, but he knew she would be taken hostage, or worse. If she was taken alive, he would simply get her back. And if she was not, then he would use up every ounce of energy he had in him to make those responsible pay, starting with Jack Kruger himself.

Mariana was perspiring profusely, and she started to pace back in forth, combing through her hair with her hands in wide-eyed desperation in order to calm herself down. She was clearly not used to the perils of their present situation, not that Seamus was any more ready for a firefight - he was not. He simply had a calmer demeanor about him, and thrived for the competition of survival. It was in situations such as this he felt most alive. He was on high alert and his senses were taut with excitement. It wasn't truly living if that feeling wasn't felt at least once in a person's life, knowing mere survival depended on every bit of alert observation and decision. Adrenaline was an amazing natural phenomenon, and Seamus appreciated the absolute power it could infuse within its recipient.

"What do we do now?" Mariana finally asked. It seemed the more panicked she outwardly showed to the world, the calmer Seamus would get. He was the antithesis of Mariana's chaotic state of mind. He held her by the shoulders and looked her square in the eyes.

"You can't let the situation control you," he said. "Once your thoughts start to scatter, you start making mistakes. We're too close to getting out of here to let a mistake ruin Teacher's escape. I can't put all of my attention on you. I need to be able to trust you can handle yourself all right without my presence."

"What do you mean?" she asked frantically. "Where are you going?"

"Nowhere," Seamus answered. "But my attention needs to be on anyone approaching, not on you. Or else we're both dead."

She didn't give a verbal answer, just a head nod to show her understanding. The two hid behind an empty cabinet awaiting Teacher to show up, so they could make their getaway. Lamb and the others should have been no more than ten minutes behind them, but the time dragged on slowly. The adrenaline seemed to recede and the early hour hit Seamus hard. He had to strain his eyes in order to keep them open.

"What do you think will happen to Andrea and Zeke?" Mariana asked after a few short minutes of tense waiting.

Seamus did not want to think of the possibilities, but he thought talking might help keep him awake.

"Hopefully, if they do get them, Kruger has decided the need for prisoners," Seamus replied. "Because I don't want to think about the alternative."

"Me neither," Mariana stated. After a brief pause, which made Seamus believe the conversation had ended, Mariana broke the silence again. "What she did was honorable. It took a lot of courage to do what she did. I am privileged to have served as a Novice with the likes of her."

"Zeke sacrificed himself too," he reminded. "But I know what you mean."

"She was something special," Mariana stated.

Seamus turned to face her.

"Let's get one thing straight," Seamus declared forcefully. "You need to stop talking as if they're already dead. We don't know that, and we will not give up hope just yet. You hear me? We aren't giving up."

He had diverted his eyes from the doorway, and his voice rose high enough for them not to have heard that someone had entered the room. When he turned back and saw the figure's presence, he nearly shot due to his bewildered state. The figure had not seen them, but did hear their shocked gasps as it took them by surprise.

Seamus quickly jumped from behind the cabinet and hoisted the gun toward the intruder. He gave an audible sigh as he realized it was Nicodemus, who was pointing the gun at him as well. He brought the gun down as the relief seized him.

"I almost shot you, Nic," he exasperated. "Where are the others?"

"I don't know," Nicodemus replied, and he brought the gun down as well. "We got separated, so I just headed down here to make sure Teacher got out safely."

"He's not down here, yet," Seamus explained. "He should be here shortly."

"Good," Nicodemus brought the gun up again and shot Seamus in the shoulder. Seamus dropped instantly to one knee, dropping the gun and holding his wounded arm. Mariana screamed out and dropped to the floor as well trying to shrink back to the corner of the enclosed room. Nicodemus walked over and kicked the gun out of reach, then backed up to where he originally stood.

"It wasn't Jude," Seamus seethed through gritted teeth. "It was *you*. You were the traitor all along."

Nicodemus bowed mockingly, rotating the gun in his left hand as he did.

"Bravo, I always knew you were a bright one," Nicodemus ridiculed. "When did you figure it out? Before or after I shot you?" He laughed, again mocking their naiveté. "It was truly my best performance. Don't you think?"

"Yeah, you had us all fooled," Seamus admitted. He tried to use all his strength to stand upright, but fell back to his knee disappointed. "We should have guessed the person who enjoyed acting was simply putting on a show each and every day. I would say I'm disappointed, but I never really liked you anyhow. In truth, I'm glad it wasn't really Jude. Him I respect; that would have been a letdown."

"You think your flitting jabs bring me pain?" Nicodemus asked. "If I cared what any of you thought, then I probably wouldn't have done any of this, would I?

"And why did you do it?" Seamus demanded.

Mariana was huddled in the corner breathing heavily. Seamus could definitely sense her extreme panic, and tried to gather confidence from it. He knew he wasn't the only one in the room he needed to protect. As long as the gun was on him, Mariana was safe. It was after the next bullet that truly frightened him.

"It's complicated," Nicodemus replied. "I'm not sure you have the mental capacity to understand."

"Maybe not," Seamus smiled. "But maybe he does."

Nicodemus turned and received a cane to the side of the head. He crumpled to the floor and the gun shot across the floor. He tried to push himself back up but another blow sent him back down. A third one sent him into unconsciousness.

"What took you so long?" Seamus asked as he pulled himself to his full height, gathering strength from no longer having a gun pointed in his direction. His arm was still dangling uselessly at his side.

"Wrong turn," Guidry replied as he stood over Nicodemus's still form.

Joshua Lamb went over and tentatively coaxed Mariana to take his hand so he could pull her up as well. She was shaking uncontrollably and was clearly in shock.

"Hell," Seamus joked. "I was the one that was shot, not you."

Mariana heaved a few times and finally threw up in the corner as her nerves started to calm down.

"On that note," Guidry said. "Why don't we get the hell out of here and let Kruger clean that up?"

*****

Matilda realized two things as she fell to the ground in a heap. The first was she hadn't been shot. The second was someone was on top of her. The person's elbow was digging against her diaphragm, which caused her to make short painful gasps in an attempt to bring oxygen into her body. Matilda was not able to see who the person was, but she tried to push the person off of her, so she could shoot back at the man who had shot at her. However, she quickly

232

realized the gun was no longer in her possession. She must have dropped it upon falling to the floor, so it should not have been that far out of her grasp.

The tangled mess on top of her didn't permit her to search. Instead, it simply stayed on top of her without moving. She finally pushed the body off of her and saw who it was. Her eyes went wide with shock as she assessed what was going on around her.

Numerous soldiers surrounded her, Vivienne, Gio, and Lucas and had guns pointed at each of them, keeping them at bay. Gio had dropped the gun and he and Lucas were in the *surrender* pose. Both their hands held high showing they were absolutely defenseless. This was not what concerned Matilda most.

Her eyes were not on the surrounding soldiers. Instead, she reached to the body she had hastily pushed off of her. Vivienne lay on the floor, choking on her own blood. She had jumped in front of Matilda as the man pulled the trigger. Vivienne had saved her life, seemingly at the expense of her own.

Matilda crawled over and held Vivienne's trembling hand, her real hand.

"Thank you," Matilda whispered.

"You are forgiven," Vivienne sputtered before taking her last breath.

Matilda held onto Vivienne's hand well after she expired. Before being pulled away by the soldiers, she looked back one last time at Vivienne's lifeless body.

"Thank you," she whispered again as she was led away at gunpoint, along with Gio and Lucas.

*****

Seamus ripped off part of his shirt to act as a tourniquet for his bleeding shoulder, and wrapped it just above the wound. Mariana gathered herself after her vomiting performance and she and Seamus joined the others in front of the fake brick wall escape. Teacher seemed uncertain how to proceed. Seamus had explained to them about Andrea and Zeke splitting off and diverting a group of soldiers away to better his chance of getting to the exit. Lamb didn't seem to like the thought of leaving them behind, as well as everyone else that seemed to be missing. Not to mention his total disdain of Nicodemus lying on the floor at their feet; they had tied his hands behind his back using his own belt to cuff him, but Lamb's eyes kept progressing over the prostrate form of the traitor.

"I can't believe he would do such a thing," he said to no one in particular. "It goes beyond what I thought he was capable of doing."

"I do think haste is our best option," Guidry declared. "We still do not know how long the others can keep the proverbial wolves at bay. I suggest we contemplate our traitor's motives at a later date when peril is not on the menu."

Lamb's dazed look persisted, yet he still gave a quick nod to acknowledge Guidry's assessment of the situation. He pressed the same brick they had seen him press earlier and just like before the wall moved to the ceiling revealing their salvation.

"There's a maze of tunnels in there and if we get separated you just have to follow the pattern," Teacher explained to the others. "It's Right, Left, Right, Right, Left."

The others nodded and Seamus was the first to head into the vast underground maze, followed closely by Mariana. Carly dashed in behind Mariana. Guidry started in behind her, but noticed a peculiar look in Simone's eyes; a look of total uncertainty.

"What's wrong?" he asked her. "We don't have time to waste with more doubts. Each of the traitors has been identified. What other nonsense can you be calculating?"

"I can't go with you," Simone replied. "Kruger will find a way to be able to track me. I just have this strange feeling that Kruger has been able to stay one step ahead of us because of me. I accomplished what I set out to do; there may be more Kruger has because of me. I can't know any other important information, or else he'll be able to get it as well."

"You're being paranoid," Guidry scoffed. "There's no way Kruger can get to you if you come with us now."

"I can't leave Zeke, Griffin, and the others knowing that I had a hand in their capture or demise," Simone explained. "It doesn't seem right for me to get out alive, and their fate is in doubt. I was the traitor; I should be damned, not them. They are innocent, not me."

"But you weren't aware of your subterfuge," Lamb told her reassuringly. "Kruger manipulated you to show your hand, and made you believe something else entirely. The blame should not fall on you. Nicodemus is the demon here, not you."

"I still couldn't face myself in the morning knowing I reached safety when others, who were more deserving, suffered a crueler fate," Simone replied. "The reality I chose so selfishly would be a much more painful outcome than the others could ever face. The decision is mine to make, and I have made up my mind. Nothing you can say can change that."

She moved back further into the room, away from the tunnel entrance, in case they decided to forcefully drag her with them. Simone also retrieved the gun Nicodemus dropped and pointed it in their direction, but not at any specific individual.

Through the whole exchange, Manna watched bewildered. They were steps away from safety and Simone refused to take them. Instead of moving forward, she retreated further into the room. He couldn't contemplate why she would make such a brash decision. If Kruger were to capture her again, there was no end to what he would do to her mind to completely shatter it, and make her a shell of herself. The damage would be extensive, and totally irreversible.

Finally, Manna understood the vast inner strength his daughter possessed. She knew the outcome of her choice, and she was still willing to make it with no regard for her own welfare. She was the captain going down with the ship, and he would be damned if she went down alone.

"I'm staying too," Manna declared as Guidry tried to convince his daughter of changing her mind. He stood beside his daughter to let his stance be understood.

"Now, you too?" Guidry exclaimed. "Did Kruger mess with your synapses too? Or is your entire family absolutely insane? We don't have time to have this debate. We need to get out of here, now."

"It's important for you two to change your minds," Lamb pleaded. "The cause needs you two. I can't explain it right now, but you have got to trust me. Your escape is even more necessary than my own. You must reconsider."

"I'm sorry, Teacher," Simone said, clearly not enjoying being the cause of the disappointment in Teacher's gaze. "I value your thoughtful outlook, but my decision is final. And I advise you to make yours before it's too late."

She shot at the brick Lamb had pushed to open the hidden tunnel, and the brick wall started to slowly drop back from the ceiling. Lamb reached his hand out offering Manna and Simone the opportunity to change their minds and join him and Guidry. When they refused, he stepped back into the room.

"If you two are staying, then so am I," Lamb stated.

"I can't let that happen," Guidry said from behind Lamb. Guidry wrapped his strong arms around Lamb's chest and forced him back into the escape tunnel before the wall fell back into place. He used his cane for extra leverage. Teacher struggled with him, but Guidry's strength far outweighed his.

Before the wall fell enough to block Guidry's struggling face, Manna could see the displeasure their decision made him feel.

"You're foolish to believe Kruger will show you any mercy," Guidry shouted.

"I'm not asking for his mercy," Manna stated.

"Then what are you asking for?" Guidry asked.

"Forgiveness," Simone said as the wall finished its descent.

Manna put his arm around his daughter and they headed for the stairs leading out of the basement. At the top of the stairs, they were stopped by Polchinski and another five soldiers behind him. Each had an assault rifle pointed at the father-daughter combo.

"Where's Teacher?" Polchinski demanded.

"Gone," Manna replied. "And you can tell Kruger he won't be easily found. He's got no more spies on the inside to turn him in."

236

"We'll see about that," Polchinski replied with a smug look on his face.

*****

Gio, Zeke, and Lucas were all hauled into a large van with bench seats in the back. A barred, glassless window was in the interior of their prison on wheels, allowing them those in the back to see into the front. The driver had his back to them, and a hat donned his head. Manna, Simone, Andrea, and Matilda were taken into a similar vehicle several minutes after Gio and the others had left. A radio squelched to life with a man's voice speaking vehemently into it. He demanded to know why the driver of their van had left.

"The men were to be in one vehicle, and the women in another," the angry voice declared. "Why did you…"

The driver rolled his window down and threw the radio out onto the road. The van picked up speed and the tire's squealed as he turned sharply down the next road.

The driver took off his hat to reveal a pate void of hair. He turned to the three prisoners after tapping his knuckles on the window's bars.

"Don't worry fellas," the driver said. "You're in good hands, now."

Jude's smiling face peered at them from the driver's seat. He turned his attention back to the road.

"I wish I could see Kruger's face when he realizes he lost a couple of prisoners," Jude laughed as he turned the van sharply again. "You might want to hold on back there; it might be an unstable ride for a while."

Chapter Thirty-Six: Uncle Jack

"What do you mean he escaped?" Kruger seethed as Polchinski relayed the news by phone. He listened to the reply, but it was totally unacceptable. "You were supposed to use stealth; nobody was to know you were there. That's why I sent you in at the time I did. Surprise was to be your ally.

"Someone sounded the alarm on purpose? Who? One of your men?" Kruger didn't like to be made a fool, and he was feeling as such. Nicodemus had not alluded to anyone knowing of the intruders coming, but it seemed they had been prepared. Prepared enough to get Teacher out without harm, at least. Kruger was not happy with the events as they played out.

Polchinski explained they had captured several of the people in the building. He explained they had done as much to try to lure Teacher into the open; to use them as leverage.

"We can still use it against him," Polchinski explained. It was clear he was grasping at straws.

"How can we use the seized against him?" Kruger demanded.

"You can use it to depict Teacher as a coward," Polchinski clarified. "Letting his followers take the fall, as he frolics away to safety; saving his own hide over protecting those seeking his approval."

Kruger contemplated this line of thinking. Polchinski might just be onto something there.

"Okay, bring the captives here," Kruger eventually told him. "How many are there?"

Polchinski timidly skirted around this, but eventually explained there were four currently in their possession.

"Only four?" Kruger questioned. According to his calculations, there should have been over a dozen people in there, and they were only able to take four, and let Teacher get away in the process.

"Well four were killed in the shootout," Polchinski described. "And Nicodemus was unharmed, as you wished. Teacher and four others escaped."

"Others escaped with Lamb?" Kruger asked incredulously.

"As did at least three others we had taken prisoner," Polchinski admitted.

"What?" Kruger fumed. "How could you let this happen?"

"It seems one of Teacher's men posed as one of the drivers charged with taking the prisoners away," Polchinski explained. "We found the real driver barely lucid and barely clothed. From what he said, we gathered it was someone from inside the building."

"Bring the prisoners in," Kruger demanded. "And do try not to lose them this time."

Polchinski cleared his throat, and Kruger could sense there was more the man wanted to say. He could also sense it was more bad news.

"What else?" Kruger inquired.

"The prisoners, sir," Polchinski started. He paused, unsure how to break the news to the Council Secretary.

"Just get on with it, and quit wasting my time," Kruger was quickly losing patience with this man.

"We were able to seize Mr. Manna and Ms. Petra," Polchinski informed.

"That is good news," Kruger had been expecting more bad news; this was definitely something that might prove to go slightly in their favor. "And the other two?"

"There is a Ms. Andrea Carmichael," Polchinski informed him. The name didn't register with Kruger, so he dismissed it as not being of much importance. "The final prisoner is Matilda Swanson."

Kruger nearly dropped the phone as the realization sunk in. He wasn't able to speak, just choke out a few garbled sounds.

"Yes, sir," Polchinski stated. "The final prisoner is your niece, Matilda. From what Nicodemus shared, we believe she was one of Lamb's most trusted Novice Orderlies."

With this declaration, the phone did crash to the floor. *It couldn't be her*, Kruger thought. *Not dear, sweet Matilda.* His own flesh and blood had turned against him in the most hurtful of ways. She took solace with his one, true enemy; choosing to side against her beloved uncle. This blow was nearly worse than losing Teacher himself.

"Sir, hello," Polchinski was still speaking into the phone on the floor. Kruger bent down and picked it up. He brought the phone to his ear.

"Bring the prisoners here, now," his voice was stoic, with no hint of animosity toward his niece's betrayal. "And bring her to me."

"Yes, sir," Polchinski replied, then hung up the phone. He had told Kruger of three female prisoners, yet he clearly understood which prisoner Kruger wanted to see.

Kruger sat at his desk, clearly shaken by the news Polchinski had just given him. He quickly composed himself, and shook off the pain this knowledge caused. He would treat no prisoner any different than another, even if that prisoner was family. No, he would indeed treat this one a little different. Darling Matilda would find out just how much her betrayal pained Uncle Jack, because she would get to feel it all for herself. He would make certain of that.

*****

Kruger waited nearly three hours to confront his disloyal niece. Finally, she was brought into his office just as the sun started peaking over the horizon. She walked in confidently, though her eyes diverted away from her uncle. The two guards leading her stepped back, and Kruger dismissed them immediately. Her head was held high, not toward the floor in shame as Kruger thought it would. His little niece had more strength than he had given her credit for, and it impressed him slightly. She had purposely come in brimming with confidence, to show him she wasn't afraid, but Kruger could tell it was merely a façade, as her eyes belied the fear which she truly felt. She knew what he was capable of doing. Kruger had shown his lack of mercy and his capacity for violence a multitude of times in her very presence. He knew how much she actually feared him; he was just unaware at how much she truly despised what she had seen her uncle do to gain his power.

"So my whore of a niece sold herself to the devil," Kruger accused. He slowly paced around her erect aura of confidence. The words, he noticed, had no impact on her countenance.

"I would say I am sorry," she finally rebutted. "But I find I am above lying, especially to those who *think* themselves my superior."

"You are *above* lying?" Kruger retorted, the venomous look piercing into Matilda, but not chinking the armor she brought with her into the room. "But lying to your family is not beyond your reproach?"

"I never lied to you, uncle," Matilda responded. "You simply never asked on which side of the spectrum my beliefs fell. You assumed I agreed with your policies and your way of doing business. Like everyone else in this forsaken world, you never once thought to ask what I felt; never once considered my capability to *think* for myself."

"You're saying I underestimate you and your *abilities*?" Kruger ridiculed. "What abilities? The ability to turn your back on your own family? The ability to bring chaos from order?"

"What order?" Matilda finally looked directly into her uncle's eyes. Her eyes were piercing with the same passion and intensity of a blizzard snow.

Maybe Kruger had read her all wrong. Maybe she wasn't scared after all.

"Order is nowhere to be seen," she continued. "All I see is complacency and control, but nothing remotely close to order."

"You are mistaken, Matilda," Kruger replied. "It is *only* I that brings order in this…What did you call it? *Forsaken* world. Without the infrastructure the Council provides, people like your precious Joshua Lamb are free to spread their tyrannical views without repercussion. Without me, the sanctity of the Americas is left to the whims of individuals not intelligent enough to construct a sound decision on their own."

"And what makes you qualified to decide for the masses?" Matilda snapped. "Whoever said all of our choices need to be productive? Whatever happened to being able to learn from one's mistakes?"

"With me, those mistakes no longer have to be made," Kruger declared. "Imagine a world where the population no longer has to rely on making tough decisions on their own. Their brain power can be used in more beneficial endeavors than which future career best suits their talents, or which menial task to take on next. Those decisions will already be made. Each citizen will have a unique purpose of his own, and will feel like a much more productive member of society. Gone will be the days of an individual lacking ambition. Don't you see that the world is meant to be managed by those of us who are educated enough to rule?"

"Not at the expense of giving up our ability to freely choose our own path," Matilda professed. "Not by having to refuse to enjoy any other aspect we choose to cultivate. Mankind is not one-dimensional, uncle. We are capable of so much more when we can expand the one thing that separates us from the savage beast; our superior intellect."

"You want to be able to learn from your mistakes, dear niece?" Kruger responded. "Then allow yourself to learn what happens when you betray your family's trust. And let me be the one that personally gets to show it to you.

Chapter Thirty-Seven: Demonstration

Manna and Simone stood in a large room of the Elliptical Ward overlooking another that looked like an operating room of some sort. A large chair that reminded Simone of being at the dentist's office was in the middle of the room, and metal trays of instruments surrounded it on either side. Simone had a brief recollection of being in a similar room as the one she saw through the tinted window. It may have even been the very room she was looking at now, though she was sure Kruger would have other such rooms at his disposal. Kruger was too sadistic of a human being to simply have just one.

She wondered where Andrea and Matilda were, as well as Zeke and Lucas, but her thoughts kept returning to Gio. She had seen the three men shuttled into a van just before she too was placed in a similar one. If any of them were hurt, she would never forgive herself. She was partly responsible for their entire present predicament, even having her own father standing beside her now.

"I am sorry I got you involved," Simone told her father. The ruefulness in her voice was palpable, though Manna quickly waved it away.

"It was my choice to make," he explained. "I am the soul decision maker of my unconquerable cognizance. There is not a single person who can control what I do any longer; not even a rebellious daughter." He smiled at her to give her encouragement.

"You're starting to sound like Guidry," she declared. "*Unconquerable cognizance*? Where's that coming from?"

"It must have been dormant all these years, and released by a little spark of inspiration," Manna indicated. "Thank you for being that catalyst."

Three guards entered the operating room leading a person with a burlap sack covering her head. The diminutive stature and slight build helped Manna and Simone determine the female status of the individual. Two guards stood on either side of the woman forcing her into the room. The woman was not making it easy for them as she tried to fight as best she could. The third guard stood behind the three struggling individuals, but quickly came to the forefront as they fully entered the room and the door was closed. He grabbed the woman's legs and helped hoist her onto the chair. She gave a swift kick, knocking the guard in the side of the head. This only made him more determined and he grabbed ahold of her feet again. Manna and Simone could see the strain in his face to see the mistake would not happen again on his part.

The guards finally got her strapped into place on the chair. Her legs and arms barely budged as she strained to free them once again. Finally, she gave up and her body went slack. Her head even hung in absolute defeat. The guards ripped the sack off her head to reveal what Manna had already determined; the prisoner was Matilda Swanson.

Simone must not have realized it until then, as she audibly gasped and brought her hands to her face in utter shock.

"It's Matilda," she said to Manna. "She's his very own niece. Surely, Kruger will show mercy on his own flesh and blood."

"Surely, I won't," a voice said from behind them. Kruger stood with a broad smile on his face, hands behind his back in a completely arrogant fashion. "And how's my little guinea pig doing?" He reached up and gently caressed her cheek.

Manna slapped Kruger's hand away from his daughter's face.

"Lay another hand on her again, and I will rip it off your body and beat you to death with it," Manna told him.

"Will you now?" Kruger pointed to either side of the small room, as well as at the door. An armed guard stood in each location. "And how might you accomplish that feat? I would love to see how you plan on doing that."

Kruger caressed Simone's cheek again, and Manna went to bat the hand away again. Before he could, one of the guards used the butt of the gun across his back to bring him to his knees. The guard then took the butt to Manna's face. Manna fell face first onto the floor; a small puddle of his own blood formed underneath him as he lay, from his nose or lip, he wasn't certain.

"I thought as much," Kruger smiled again. He signaled for the guard to get Manna back to his feet. The guard pulled him up, but he sank back to one knee before the room stopped spinning and he could stand again on his own.

"Allow me to demonstrate how I was able to manipulate your daughter into giving me everything I wanted from her," Kruger told Manna, again caressing Simone's cheek. "Well almost everything." Kruger brought his finger lower to her neck and continued to just above where Simone's shirt stopped at exposed skin.

She spit into his face in complete defiance. The same guard moved toward her, but Kruger stopped him with a quick gesture of his hand.

"Don't," he told the guard. "I wouldn't want her to miss the presentation because her eye is swollen shut." He wiped the spittle from his face and then wiped the hand on his khaki pants.

"What're you going to do to her?" Manna asked. His lip was still bleeding but not as profusely, and a large bruise had formed on his upper left cheek. It started to puff up, but didn't impede his left eye from seeing just yet, though if it grew anymore it just might make his left eye totally useless.

"Which one are you talking about?" Kruger inquired. "Your lovely daughter or my disloyal niece?"

"I am talking about Matilda in there," Manna pointed down toward the operating room where Matilda sat with a panicked look. She was making no noise, just darting her eyes around the room; trying to place where she was and what might possibly happen next.

"Ask Simone there next to you," Kruger said. "It's very similar to what I did to her." He looked at Simone and mockingly frowned. "Oh, you poor thing, you don't remember do you? Then let me explain a little of the process."

He tapped on the glass overlooking the room, which alerted Matilda. She turned and cut through the glass with her icy gaze.

"Don't do this, uncle," Matilda pleaded. "Let the world see a benevolent leader of mercy, not one consumed with his own personal vendetta against an enemy he cannot prove exists. When the world sees your own family is willing to stand against you, it will weaken your platform and expose you as a charlatan."

Kruger tapped on the glass yet again, and one of the guards in Matilda's room forced her head against the headrest of the chair and tied it there tightly. He then covered her mouth with a piece of tape.

"Don't worry the tape will be coming off soon," Kruger told Manna and Simone. "I want you to be able to feel the full effect of what's taking place."

"Full of theatrics," Manna chided. "No wonder you were drawn to Nicodemus, and he to you."

"Ah, yes, Mr. Linderhaven played his part well," Kruger smiled reliving his masterful plan in his head. "He was in a travelling actors' guild that would show up in various locales during the war to help the soldiers cope. Those travel locations were far from the hot battle zones, and were meant to take our minds off all the killing going on each day. The plays were always comedies, never tragedies given our situation. I noticed Nicodemus was a powerful performer who immersed himself into the character he portrayed so convincingly, that I forgot he was merely acting. We had struck up a friendship that continued well after those wartime days."

"Obviously," Simone said sarcastically.

"Yes, loyalty is something I take very seriously," Kruger's temper was rising.

Manna noticed there were periods of mellow discourse with Kruger, as if he was simply talking with them at the dinner table. Then, there were stretches where he seemed to have a meltdown and the temper flared almost instantaneously. He also noticed Kruger greatly enjoyed hearing the sound of his own voice. Manna could imagine Kruger speaking out loud to himself, even when nobody else was in the room to accompany him.

"And disloyalty is also considered with the same severity," Kruger continued; he pointed through the window at his niece helplessly held captive in the chair. "It looks like she is almost ready for the demonstration."

Throughout their nearly one-sided conversation, the guards were hooking her up to intravenous lines, poking and prodding her with needles of various sizes, and another person had entered the room to check vitals. The person appeared in surgical scrubs, and wore a surgical mask which hid her true identity.

"Let me explain in easier terms what is about to take place," Kruger smugly began. "My highly sophisticated scientists and neurosurgeons have been able to discover a way to extract memories and place new ones in their stead, as the exquisite Simone found out firsthand. Here, you will see that extraction directly."

"She's your niece," Manna tried to reason with him, but knew it was futile even before the attempt was made. "You're a monstrosity."

"No, I am consistent," Kruger validated. "I punish all who oppose me, family or otherwise. That is one thing I will most definitely not tolerate, dissension. It creates chaos and leads to anarchy."

"But isn't it a little extreme to destroy her mind?" Manna reasoned.

"It isn't destroyed, yet," Kruger replied. "Just altered. Total destruction is a slow process. It takes quite a bit of time to break the mind to its most worthless state. Believe me, I have tried. I have witnessed nearly completely unstable individuals hang on to a sliver of humanity. The mind is not easily defeated. The corporeal body is much more fragile."

"Which is why Teacher has been such a thorn in your side," Manna concluded. "His cause represents the growth of intelligence, making your experiment that much harder to reach completion. When you must contend with a stronger level of astuteness, it's that much tougher to crack it entirely. Simone, here, is proof of that."

Manna seemed to be gaining confidence with each new realization. Though he was still Kruger's prisoner, he would not allow him to keep the upper hand. Just as Kruger believed the mind was beatable, so too was Kruger himself, and Manna would continue to look for his weakness. His own arrogance just might be it.

"I admit I underestimated your sweet little girl," Kruger acknowledged. "A mistake I will not allow myself to make again. You would be amazed how willingly she divulged information, however, once the process had started. She first walked into the front door here at the Elliptical Ward, begging to share any new developments. She left having no recollection of stepping into the building, even after being here for hours on end. We even supplanted a false memory in its place so she would have something to fall back to without raising suspicion."

"The Griffin memory," Simone told her father.

"Ah, yes, so you did discover it," Kruger took great pleasure in this revelation. "So you know the power which we weld. We seemingly have total access and control over every individual mind we choose. Your discovery is a tad unexpected, but insignificant nonetheless."

"So that's what you plan on doing to Matilda?" Manna inquired. "Taking away old memories or adding new ones? It seems a bit convoluted to me. All that trouble over a modest discretion. Isn't it a bit childish? It appears you are much more emotional than rational."

"Don't play your mind games with me," Kruger stated. "They won't work on me. It is not as simple as you would have it depicted. It is a very meticulous process in which we must map out complete sections of the brain in order to locate exact memory locations, as well as find an open location to place a non-existing one which we created ourselves. You would be surprised how long one miniscule section can take to chart. Luckily, our current subject is one I know quite well. It is much easier when that is the case. See for yourself, they are almost complete."

Manna and Simone turned to the tinted pane of glass. A large diagram of a brain could be seen on a medium-sized screen protruding from what appeared to be a modified laptop. The screen expanded from the smaller laptop screen, and made the image appear nearly three times as large. The brain on the screen was mostly spotted with a yellow, hazy color, but other portions were gray.

"The yellow portions represent the parts we have already recorded," Kruger explained. This time his voice was almost genteel, and Manna nearly forgot about the armed guards and the fact he was still a prisoner. "The gray color represents the part still undiscovered. As you see, it is nearly complete."

Less than ten minutes later, the screen radiated a powerful yellow hue signifying completion of the mapping process. The woman who appeared to be the neurosurgeon then picked up a tiny set of tweezers and held it underneath a microscope she had brought into the room with her. The image replaced the image of the glowing brain on the computer screen. Manna leaned closer to get a better look.

From his perspective, what she held looked like a tiny version of a computer chip or some other nanotechnology he was not aware of yet.

"What is it?" Manna asked, unable to take his eyes off the strange object on the screen.

"What she possesses is not discernible to the naked eye," Kruger explained derisively. "That is why she held it to the microscope; to let you two see that it exists."

"That still doesn't explain what it is," Manna chided.

"What you see is a Nano-chip that contains one of my extracted memories," Kruger continued, disregarding Manna's attempt to get under his skin. "But I am getting ahead of myself a little bit. I am sure you are aware of PTSD."

Manna nodded to confirm, "Post Traumatic Stress Disorder. Most everyone has at least a minor understanding of it. After experiencing a traumatic event, one becomes anxious and is often overwhelmed with menial, everyday life."

"Are you aware that I was diagnosed with PTSD after the war?" Kruger questioned. Manna shook his head to confirm that the knowledge was not known to him. "After the diagnosis, I was placed into a program to attempt to rid me of the haunting memories that caused my illness. The Council had scientists and neurologists working on a cure for nearly two decades, and they had discovered a groundbreaking method they were seeking to test on individuals with PTSD. As I stated, I was lucky enough to be in that program. The neurologists studied my brain extensively and were able to correctly pinpoint where in my brain the memory was stored."

Kruger paused to let this idea sink in, and seemed to be waiting for Manna or Simone to respond. After they didn't, he continued. He maintained indifference over this slight delay.

"After they were able to locate the memory, they extracted it," Kruger continued. "Think of it as a computer downloading a file from one location, and then uploading it to another. And in a sense, that is what they did. You see, they couldn't remove the memory without having a place to store it, so that Nano-chip is where it was stored."

"Are you saying that the Council discovered a way to get rid of our most unpleasant memories?" Manna asked. "And that yours is stored on that chip we just saw?"

"That is exactly correct," Kruger said proudly. "It completely cured my PTSD. I no longer wake up in a cold sweat, or feel any anxiety whatsoever. It healed me of all of that trauma; of all of that pain. It could completely relieve us of any stress or personal insecurities, and that was its initial intent; to rid humanity of any form of suffering."

"Very noble of you," Simone said sarcastically. "Let me guess, you changed your mind. Instead of benefitting mankind, you used it to make it suffer even more."

"I had the scientists and neurologists collaborate on a more elaborate goal," Kruger continued, ignoring Simone's jab. "I figured if they were able to take a memory out, they should also be able to add a memory into an individual's consciousness. We ran tests and discovered that it too was very possible. In fact, we succeeded in a total of ten cases. You should feel proud, Ms. Simone, you were one of the pioneers. We were able to make the person believe the implanted memory, and forget that the truth ever existed. That is until we started finding we were dealing with some of Teacher's Pupils. They started placing clues into the replaced memory to make it seem out of the ordinary or make it stand out as being wrong. These Pupils, we discovered, possessed the ability to rework the supplanted material enough that they refused to believe it. Though they didn't know the truth, they still possessed enough of an idea they were certain was entirely false to go on."

Simone thought of her memory of Griffin disclosing the knowledge of the traitor; the words on the back of the shirt and her passionate kiss with him. These had been her clues she had purposely included to sniff out the memory as being less than accurate. She had a sense of pride now that her brain was capable of possessing that kind of ability. After realizing Kruger had manipulated her, she had felt completely violated and weak, but this ability to avoid full manipulation proved she had more strength than she had first thought.

"Which is why you want to rid the world of Teacher," Manna deduced. "So your manipulations can be easier."

250

"There are those who should no longer have to suffer," Kruger explained. "And then there are those who should never stop suffering. I believe it is in the Council's right to decide in which spectrum each individual lies."

"And why should it be your choice?" Simone questioned. "Who gave you the right to make that distinction?"

"President Stuckey gave me that power," Kruger enlightened with a smile, "when he made me Council Secretary."

Manna and Simone were speechless at how much ego Kruger possessed. He clearly thought he deserved the power he wielded so viciously. Manna even thought that perhaps Kruger's psychosis was a byproduct of the experimentation on his brain, or if he possessed as much before the PTSD ever happened. There may never be an answer; it was the chicken and the egg all over again.

"Oh, she is about to place the memory into Matilda's consciousness," Kruger described with a gleefulness that was utterly scary to watch. He was completely ecstatic to scar his own niece's thoughts with his own traumatic event; one that caused serious trauma to himself after it actually happened.

The doctor placed the Nano-chip into a liquid of some sort and then put the liquid into a syringe. The liquid lacked any color and Manna had no idea what it truly was. It could be anything from simple saline to some type of carcinogen. The doctor placed the syringe into the back of Matilda's scalp, pushed the plunger, and released the substance into her system.

Kruger explained the process, "The Nano-chip is coded with a specific location in the subject's brain. That is the purpose of the mapping I explained earlier. Once it is released into the subject, the chip hones in on that location and goes to it. It is quite a swift process actually."

As he said this, Matilda let out a violent scream that vibrated through the thin layer of tinted glass. Manna and Simone sensed the anguish she felt, but had no idea how intense it truly was. The pain that Kruger had gone through, that he no longer had to face, Matilda was now feeling. Her screams would briefly cease, and then start right back up, as if she were being physically tortured beyond repair. Though her physical body remained intact, her psyche clearly was being ripped to shreds. It at least appeared that way to Manna and Simone.

"I think she learned her lesson about disappointing her family," Kruger said smugly. "And I know that's *not* a lesson she would have learned in Teacher's classroom."

The door to the room they were in swiftly opened and a frail man glided, more than walked, into the room. He glanced quickly behind them into the operating room where Matilda was shrieking in agony. This seemed to bring a slight smile to his face, and then he directed his eyes to Kruger. A sense of urgency clearly showed on his face.

"Sir, there's something you might want to see on the television," the man told Kruger.

"What could be that important you would need to interrupt this?" Kruger pointed at Matilda's pain through the window. He was clearly enjoying the sight of his niece receiving her punishment for her betrayal.

"It's Teacher, sir," the frail man replied. "He's on the television. And he wants to turn himself in."

Chapter Thirty-Eight: Trade Consideration

Jack Kruger sat again in his office, this time he was contemplating what he, along with millions of citizens, had just witnessed on the news broadcast. Joshua Lamb, or Teacher as he was known to everyone else, was the person most sought by the Council, and he was agreeing to turn himself over to Kruger. It was like a chess match, and he was contemplating his next move. Teacher didn't seem to be the type to purposely put himself into checkmate. An ulterior motive must be in Lamb's cards, but Kruger, for the life of him, couldn't figure what those motives could be.

On the television screen, Lamb's silhouette was covered in shadow, and his voice was severely distorted. Kruger had consulted with Nicodemus to see if he could discern whether or not it was truly Lamb or some imposter posing as Teacher. Nicodemus had listened to what was said to determine whether it appeared to be Teacher's way of speaking and his mannerisms. He also tried to determine whether the profile on the television could possibly be Teacher's as well. From what was seen and heard, Nicodemus placed a high degree of confidence in determining it truly was Lamb, or someone closely resembling him, nonetheless.

Teacher's demands were very clear. The demands ran through Kruger's mind as he replayed the broadcast over again in his head, searching for any telling sign Lamb might have given toward his overall intentions.

"Good evening, my fellow citizens," the distorted voice began. "I am a citizen just as you all are, but for some reason I am of more importance to the Council than most of you. At one time, just like everyone else, I was known by a name given to me by my parents. However, you all currently know me by a different moniker. You all know me as Teacher. I am making my presence known, though my identity will remain a mystery for now, unless Council Secretary, Jack Kruger, will agree to a trade. The Council Secretary has taken captive some of my most trusted advisers and allies. Two Novice Orderlies are currently prisoners of the Council. Along with the Novices, there are two other individuals who are Pupils of mine. These four individuals were taken in an attempt to bring myself into custody. They were not the intended target - I was. Therefore, I have a proposition for Mr. Kruger. Since I am the one the Council truly wants, and not their current captives, I propose a trade. I will turn myself over to the Council willingly, if the three female prisoners are released. I will allow the Council a two hour timeframe in which to respond to my proposal. If

they do not agree to these demands, then I promise no one will ever find me. Kruger, this is your only chance to get what you sorely want. Send your response on a news channel of your choice. I will be watching, and patiently waiting. It's your move now. How badly do you truly want me? You've got two hours to decide."

The screen had turned blank and a countdown started. Nothing belied his motive, at least to Kruger nothing did. The demands thoroughly perplexed him. It hadn't made sense to ask for only three of the four captives. Why not ask for all four? If the Council would release three, they surely would release four. This point perplexed Kruger even more than Teacher turning himself in.

Another thing Kruger kept mulling over was how the rest of the Americas would react. There were already posts and blogs giving him a little glimpse of how the broadcast was taken by the general population. Many were demanding the Council to take the offer, yet others disagreed. The detractors claimed that the Americas "do not negotiate with known terrorists," which made absolutely no sense to Kruger. If a known terrorist was willing to turn himself in, for damn sure he was willing to negotiate.

However, it was not up to them to decide. It was up to President Stuckey and the rest of the Council's Inner Cabinet to make that decision. Actually, Kruger knew the decision was his alone to make. President Stuckey would listen to his opinion and that would outweigh the influence of others. Kruger wielded the most power of any of the other three members of the Council Cabinet. He even felt he had more power than Stuckey himself. He was the face of the Council, and the public looked to him over Stuckey in most major decisions. It was he they feared, not the president.

As if on cue, a phone rang and Kruger knew who the caller would be. President Stuckey was seeking his opinion on the matter at hand. He had been contemplating that very answer himself. What did he truly feel? It would pain him to have to give up his pet project, Simone Petra. The manipulation he had done already was just the tip of the iceberg of what he wanted to accomplish with her. Was it worth giving up for Teacher?

Kruger also felt an unwillingness to part with his deceitful little niece. She had not completely paid for her betrayal. It would definitely be difficult to give up the satisfaction to see her suffer even more. There were many other torturous methods he wanted to display for Matilda's benefit, to show how dissatisfied he truly was with her. Teacher would be taking those away.

The other woman, the more rambunctious one, he was more than willing to part with. She had no real value to him at this point, and he was a little upset Polchinski hadn't killed her at St. Eve's. Manna was another one he truly had no qualms with trading for Teacher, but he was not requested in the trade. It seemed that Lamb wasn't concerned with his release as much as the others. Maybe he wasn't a true Pupil yet, but no other reason made sense to Kruger.

The ringing of the phone continued, until Kruger was ready with his decision. He answered the phone and his instinct was correct, President Stuckey's voice greeted him on the other end. Kruger didn't skirt around the problem at hand. He got straight to the point.

"We have no choice," Kruger started. "We've got to make the trade. It may be our only chance of getting Teacher in our grasp. The other prisoners are of no significance if we could have Teacher instead."

Stuckey agreed with him, as Kruger knew he would. Kruger told Stuckey he would set up the news conference with their reply and would give the reply himself. Then, he hung up the phone.

He had reluctantly given in to Teacher's demands, but Kruger was also getting what he wanted in the trade as well. Joshua Lamb would finally be his. Teacher and his cause could finally come to an end.

Chapter Thirty-Nine: Public Enemy No More

Manna sat alone in the dank cellar of the Elliptical Ward. Cold, steel chains hung from his wrists and ankles and were linked together to a metal clasp that hung from the solid, concrete wall to his back. The cellar reminded him of a medieval dungeon. With the entire world obsessed with technology, this place seemed very out of place. The room was rife with mold and mildew, and was nearly twenty feet across by Manna's best estimation. It did not have the definite shape of a perfect square, so he estimated another fifteen feet in the other direction. He sat on a cold floor of stone and dirt; void of any carpet or furnishings. His eyes stared weakly at the large oak door which was the only way in or out of the room. A sliver of light came from the lone window in the upper corner of the room.

Though he was clearly the only person in the room, his loneliness was expanded by the words Teacher had said to Kruger before he was taken away. Teacher was planning to turn himself over to the Council. Manna was overcome with such a sense of defeat when he heard those words.

Of course, Kruger could have been making it all up for just that purpose, to make him lose all hope. It seemed a method Kruger would have employed. He loved to manipulate the mind and torture it beyond repair. Was this simply one of his ploys?

Manna found it difficult to accept. The look on Kruger's face belied any knowledge of such a tact, if it truly was as such. Kruger appeared just as surprised as Manna and Simone had been. He left the room immediately, leaving Manna and Simone to contemplate the ramifications of what they had briefly overheard. The two prisoners stared at each other speechless; not wanting to believe such a decision was possible. Manna and Simone had sacrificed their security so Lamb was able to reach safety himself. If he was to do what Lamb had said, their sacrifice would have been for naught.

Matilda continued to scream in agony for several minutes, until Kruger swiftly dashed into the operating room and stopped the unforgiving torture. Manna and Simone didn't have time to consider the reason for the sudden stoppage, because they too were quickly led out of the room and separated themselves. Manna was led to his current location, and his daughter was taken somewhere else. He hoped she was in a place with a few more amenities than the room he was in, at least a softer place to sit than the cold, hard floor.

Though his daughter's welfare was unknown, the more pressing issue that impacted his thoughts was Teacher's willingness to give up. If it was true, and not a fabrication by Kruger, then there must have been a legitimate reason for such a brash decision. Maybe he was placing himself in jeopardy for the Council to put their guard down and break the prisoners out more effectively. Whatever the true nature of Teacher's decision, Manna wasn't about to doubt the methodologies of Joshua Lamb. In the short time Manna had known him, the man had proven to Manna to be very logical and resourceful. How else could he have escaped persecution for so long? It would take Teacher to turn himself in for Kruger to finally catch him. Maybe that was why he was doing so. It would finally prove Kruger wasn't capable of protecting the general public from the freethinking *cult* Kruger himself had created as the enemy, because it wasn't he who had captured the elusive Teacher, but Teacher himself.

Manna wasn't sure how long he was down in the makeshift dungeon, but he started to notice the slight amount of light the window provided starting to diminish. He heard a noise from the other side of the large door, so he placed his chained hands in his lap and hung his head to his side to feign sleep. The ruse intended to allow for whoever was coming to put their guard down a little, as it might allow them to talk more freely for Manna to gather information.

The door opened and Manna could tell more than one person was walking on the stone floor, though he wasn't able to determine how many people were actually in the room with him. The footsteps were quite methodical in their stepping, not of a quick nature Manna believed would have been made if they had come to collect him away from this solitary hell. No, these seemed to be purposeful, not unlike how he was led into this very room many hours earlier. He had the strange feeling another prisoner was being led in to accompany him. The sound of another set of chains being dragged along the floor confirmed this notion. Manna still maintained the impression he was asleep, though he desired to see what was going on around him. Instead, he had to settle for using his auditory instincts to formulate the tableau surrounding him.

The new prisoner was chained to the wall a few feet from Manna's present location, and a slight grunt of pain helped Manna acknowledge the new addition was male. The guards laughed joyfully as they locked the dense, metal shackles into place. When the prisoner was bound to their liking, the guards, which Manna determined to be a pair from the number of voices and steps, opened the heavy door again and left the two prisoners alone. The sound of the lock being replaced was the final sound Manna heard before the jovial voices travelled away and out of earshot.

Manna waited until he was certain there was no one else approaching the room to open his eyes again. The little light in the room skittered over the cobbled stone floor giving an ominous presence which made Manna's heart skip a couple of beats. The new prisoner was only about ten feet from where he sat, and a burlap hood hung over his face. Even with the hood, Manna felt an inkling that he knew the identity of the person now sharing his discomfort. The body type seemed familiar, but his curious nature needed to be certain.

He crawled on the floor toward the newcomer. The prisoner heaved heavily, trying to catch his breath. A strange wheezing sound covered the short distance to Manna, which made Manna's hand tremble even more as he got closer. He finally covered the last few steps, the chains barely allowing him to reach the distance between them. A dark black stain could be seen on the burlap he hadn't noticed from where he initially sat. The trembling nearly turned to a full bodily convulsion as Manna removed the burlap to reveal the prisoner's identity.

Just as he thought, Joshua Lamb's beaten visage stared back at him. Blood dripped from his nose and mouth, and the left side of his face was swollen so badly that his left eye was nearly completely closed. Teacher's bloodied, wet breathing was the sound Manna had heard from across the room. In the sliver that remained open in Teacher's damaged eye, Manna noticed a residual strength brewing much deeper than the physical brutality he witnessed on the outside. It seemed to grow stronger as Lamb realized it was indeed Manna he was seeing in front of him.

Though Kruger had broken portions of Teacher's body, in that look of determination, Manna could sense the man's mind was completely intact. In this, Manna realized Teacher still appeared to have the upper hand, though he was the one being detained by the Council. At least now Manna didn't have to wonder if Kruger was telling the truth. Teacher, indeed, had turned himself over to Kruger and the Council, or so it seemed.

"You and Simone saved my life," Lamb struggled to get out. "I chose to pay back Simone first. I got Kruger to release her if I would take her place. I may not be able to cover my debt to you."

"If Simone is truly safe," Manna replied. "Then consider it even. What about Matilda and Andrea?"

"They were set free as well," Lamb laboriously explained, "on my behalf."

"Why did you do it, though?" Manna had to ask. The question had been on his mind ever since he had heard the lanky man say it. "Why turn yourself in?"

"Why did you?" Manna couldn't help but notice Lamb hadn't answered the question, though he figured it was for the same reason he had done so as well.

Personal sacrifice for another was a noble venture, and it proved how much respect each person held for one another. Teacher and Manna both considered others to have more significance than even they had. Manna couldn't determine if it was true heroism or plain stupidity, but he felt a sense of pride nonetheless. Both men were willing to make the ultimate sacrifice in order to protect the ones they loved. Manna knew if Pupils were aware of what Teacher had done for those willing to believe in his cause, it would cause them to have stronger convictions toward the overall message he was trying to convey. Lamb was willing to put his life on the line for his own personal creed, and did not seem to worry about the consequences that might bring.

Manna finally understood why Lamb had done what he had done, and no verbal answer was needed from him. A look passed between the two men, and both realized they understood each other completely.

"What's next?" Manna asked, as he knew Teacher still had some sort of plan in place.

"Tomorrow," Lamb whispered. He closed his eyes and rested.

Manna sat next to the man and closed his eyes as well. This time he would not need to fake sleep. He knew Simone was safe, and that was all that mattered. An overwhelming sense of calm enveloped him; knowing he was putting his life in Teacher's hands. Kruger had no idea what he was up against. The bloodied mess sleeping next to him clearly believed he held the upper hand, and Manna was confident he did as well.

Chapter Forty: Silent Treatment

Wednesday – Day Seven

Manna and Lamb awoke rather early and both were parched. Luckily, a guard brought them both water and a loaf of bread to share between the two of them. Manna had grown used to sleeping on something other than a bed over the course of the past week, in which he had awakened in a chair and a moving vehicle. Sleep had been very brief and rather restless in that span, yet he felt much refreshed after the night's reprieve. Though their current predicament did not lack its own direness, the intense nature of the past week had drained him of adrenaline and fear. For the first time, he felt little anxiety over what he faced. He did not know if it was simply because the traitors had been identified or if it was because he was currently a prisoner no longer needing a place to hide, but the feeling of uncertainty had been removed.

His faith in Teacher had grown exponentially since the day Simone confronted him in their kitchen with her intentions. At that point, he had been disgraced at her decision to join such a cockamamie movement, and now his pride for her eclipsed that initial disappointment tenfold. He finally understood her reasons behind that decision. Her life had not been whole without the freedoms the Council denied her. She needed to be able to seek out the potential that was being held captive by a government who had grown power-hungry.

Manna now wondered how many others like Simone were out there in the world. Was she unique in her determination to unshackle herself from the tyranny, or were there others seeking such redemption as well?

Manna glanced at Lamb and immediately knew that the bruised visage that stared back at him represented the dreams the Council destroyed each and every day. Lamb, more accurately *Teacher*, was a symbol for all that hope which existed in all of those willing to believe it was still possible to achieve one's dreams, for those few souls who didn't give in meekly to the Council and allowed those dreams to develop in the first place. With him, an individual was able to avoid being oppressed entirely by Kruger and the Council. He liberated an entire population who was willing to seek a greater understanding, and who had a passion to do more than what was allowed of them.

He and Lamb sat in silence most of the morning. Manna knew it was unwise to have any sort of an in depth conversation, as they most likely were being watched. Neither wanted to say anything to incriminate themselves further, or to give away information on the whereabouts of the others. There was a silent agreement between the two to give whomever was watching the silent treatment.

In the silence, Manna was able to piece through the events of the past week. Though the pace he had gone through seemed incredibly rapid, he was amazed at what he had been able to accomplish in that short span. In just seven days, he was a completely changed man. The alteration finally made him realize the impact such devotion could have on an individual. Once the choice was made to accomplish more, there was no obstacle so daunting to allow that path of purposeful intent to deviate far enough for the disposition to be lost.

Battles had been won by less superior combatants simply because their desire to win far-surpassed the need of the other. When losing meant being controlled by the victor, the game grew to be much more significant. The game ceased to be a game once the very livelihood of the players was put to the test.

The large door opened again, and Manna figured it was time for lunch. He would gladly accept the water and bread, as hunger and thirst were starting to overcome him again. Manna was expecting to see guards; however, Jack Kruger's smug expression met Manna's eyes instead. Instinctively, Manna's hands balled into fists. Bile rose in Manna's throat to signify how truly disgusted Kruger made Manna feel. It wasn't a sense of fear, but a feeling of pure hatred.

"What do you want?" Manna seethed. He couldn't help but disassemble the silent wall he had built around himself. Kruger never ceased to invoke a reaction with Manna, though Lamb seemed much more reserved.

"It has been decided to have a trial," Kruger explained. "A sort of debate so we can show the world how pointless your views truly are. You'll have a chance to plead for your lives, though I don't know how much good it will do you. The world's waiting; we're here to take you to them."

In Manna's narrowed perspective, he hadn't noticed the two guards standing slightly to Kruger's left and right; he was too focused on the despicable man himself. He also realized he could hear a booming roar coming from the tiny window above.

Each guard grabbed a prisoner, and removed the chains from the wall and floor. However, the chain remained around each prisoner's wrists and ankles. The guards led Manna and Lamb through the door and into the dark corridor beyond.

It took nearly ten minutes for Manna and Lamb to climb the stairs and walk out into daylight. The searing light blinded the two captives. Through squinting eyes, Manna wasn't able to discern what was going on around him; he could only make out shadowy silhouettes of a mob surrounding him on all sides. The noise was deafening. The heightened sensory deprivation unnerved him until his eyes finally adjusted to the sudden light.

What he had perceived to be a mob indeed appeared as such, though a slight blockade of guards separated the two prisoners from the unruly crowd. On every side, thousands of citizens were raucously shouting at them. A small walking path led further into the persistent mob, and Manna realized that more than guards separated them from the mob. Roped off sections cordoned them off as well. Several of the individuals spat out curses as the prisoners continued their progression. It seemed the further they proceeded, the tighter the crowd pulled together upon them.

Manna saw Lamb get hit with several stones, and one even hit him in the temple, causing him to stumble slightly. He stumbled into the crowd to his right and a few of the more unruly individuals grabbed at his shirt, tearing it in the process. Manna tried to intervene, but the guard behind him held him back. The surrounding guards laughed and allowed it to persist for several minutes, until the mob finally shoved Lamb back onto the path.

Manna saw a large stage at the center of the callous crowd, and the path they were on seemed to lead straight to it. Manna looked at Lamb's battered figure searching for any sign of defeat or weakness, yet he only saw a river of strength in his countenance. He appeared to be as ferocious and unexpected as a sudden summer storm, though Manna doubted anyone else was able to notice.

Instead, Manna couldn't help but think of a rip current. On first appearance, it appears to be utterly safe and calm, yet underneath the façade, it can possess an uncanny strength able to pull one to one's own demise. That was

Joshua Lamb, possessing powerful inner strength when others could only see a feeble exterior.

Manna was the first to the stairs of the stage and was forcibly coerced into climbing them. His strength faltered slightly as the enormity of the crowd hit him from the wooden stage. The vast crowd extended in all directions to an infinite horizon Manna was not able to see from his vantage point. The stage seemed to be placed in the epicenter of the Elliptical Ward Square, a place commonly referred to as the Pavilion when Stuckey or Kruger gave a speech or other decree of the Council.

Manna had seen many such things on the news, but never with an audience so vast as this. It was a never-ending pool of people. The belligerent audience was deafening.

Lamb made his way up the stairs as well and looked in all directions also. The entire crowd seemed to show their disapproval as one single entity. No one voice stood out over another. To Manna, it was entirely eerie to see how robotic the reaction was. The mob appeared to possess only a single mindset, and Kruger held the device that controlled it.

Manna was directed to a seat behind a large podium, and Lamb quickly joined him. Then, the guards descended the stairs and the two prisoners sat alone in front of an endless sea of hostility.

A large balcony extended from the Elliptical Ward above the stage, and Manna noticed President Stuckey sitting behind a large wooden desk. He stood from the desk and held up his hands to signal the crowd to get silent. Immediately, the crowd's noise ceased.

President Stuckey was in his late fifties with sagging, bulbous skin. He had piercing green eyes and wavy wisps of white hair on his head. A white tuft of hair protruded through the top of his shirt, which never seemed to be buttoned all the way, and white hair blotted his pale arms. He always reminded Manna of a cloud. He always appeared to be about to be blown away into small, misty puffs.

"We present to you the man known as Teacher and one of his disciples, Mike Manna," Stuckey directed his attention from the crowd to the two prisoners with a wave of his hand. His eyes narrowed on Teacher, the Council's main prize. "You are accused of treasonous activity by the Council of the

Americas. The penalty of such convictions is death. As a traitor to the known free world, you are entitled to one of two choices. The Council will allow you to accept these accusations to be truth, and we will take mercy on you and make certain your death is swift. Or you can deny them, and you will be put on trial in front of the entire world. If convicted, you will be tortured and face an agonizing end. What is your plea?"

Manna noticed Stuckey referred to Lamb as Teacher, and not by his true identity. He felt this was purposeful to distinguish Lamb as a symbol rather than a human being. Like the endless mob, Manna turned to Lamb to see how he would respond, as he knew the choice did not lie with him.

"We are not what you claim," Lamb vehemently denied. "We did not commit treason. It is the Council who has betrayed the populace. Not us."

"So you choose to be put on trial?" Stuckey asked.

"If the Council deems it necessary," Lamb responded.

Jack Kruger climbed the steps and stood behind the other podium on the stage with a huge smile on his face. It was clear that Lamb's response was the one Kruger had wanted to hear.

"Then let the trial begin," Stuckey exclaimed as he sat back down. The mob exploded with approval. It seemed Kruger was not the only one desiring a trial.

Manna stole a glance at Lamb, who was also smiling. He too appeared to have preferred a trial. Given that the alternative to a trial was death, Manna couldn't help but feel solace as well, though he wasn't certain the end result would be any better.

Chapter Forty-One: The Trial

As Kruger had warned them, the trial was staged as more of a debate rather than a typical courtroom trial. The stage did not possess a witness stand; instead the two prisoners were placed on one side of the massive stage, and Kruger stood condescendingly on the other. Each side was raised slightly above the rest of the stage and a metal barrier rose to prevent either side from falling the short distance to the ground.

Manna felt the enormity of the situation as the mob's noise level rose in pitch at the sight of the prisoners already behind bars, though the bars barely reached their waist. The ceaseless crowd also appeared to draw closer to the stage, if that were at all possible. For the first time, Manna felt an uneasiness he couldn't explain. He peered over at Teacher. Though he was slightly slouched, he stood resolutely dignified, even while coagulated blood still oozed out of his ear and down his shirt.

"Behold," Stuckey theatrically declared to the crowd, "your all-powerful Teacher is about to give you his final lesson. He will teach you what happens to those who do not appreciate all that the Council provides you. He will teach you not to be envious of the Council's place in all of your hearts. Be certain to pay close attention, because I promise you that the lesson you are about to receive *will* be on the final exam. Council Secretary Kruger, please commence with the lesson. Allow yourself the mercy of becoming that which we have despised. Become the teacher, and allow this fraud to learn his lesson as well."

"Thank you, President Stuckey," Kruger gladly accepted. The crowd quieted as he spoke and hung on his every word. "I am not envious of the task in which I have been given. It is quite humbling to acquire a charge such as this. This duplicitous snake has attempted to poison the world with his lies and deceit. Some of you," here Kruger stopped to point a finger into the crowd, pointing at random individuals in the vehement mob. "Some of you have allowed your minds to be corrupted by this poison. The Council has taken into our best interests those of you who have allowed Teacher to possess your mind, and desire to rid you of this poison he and his minions have placed inside. We do not fault you for allowing this to happen. The Council should have brought this charlatan in much sooner. However, I do not put blame on the Council either. This man," he pointed across the stage at Teacher. "He is the one to blame. He chose to corrupt. He blatantly disregarded the Council's ultimatums.

He attempted to allow you to go about your lives without worry of discipline. Is this a man you are willing to follow? A man who can give you no hope?"

The crowd's response was overwhelmingly negative toward Teacher at this question. It seemed to Manna that Teacher had braced himself for just such a response. His resolve did not falter. With uncanny strength, he stretched himself to his full height as he gazed into the enemy mass to offer his response to Kruger's belittlement.

"The Council is wrong," Teacher said into the crowd. The conviction with which he spoke was infectious, and Manna felt a great sense of pride standing next to the man. "We can give you hope. I am not the symbol they portray me to be. The Novices and I do not stand up to the Council in order to breed corruption, but instead to expose the corruption going on inside the Council's very walls."

"These false accusations should be proof enough that this man is severely disturbed, and should not be taken seriously" Kruger said, interrupting Teacher before he could gain the full attention of the crowd.

"Secretary Kruger would like to provide you all with a false sense of security," Teacher continued, ignoring Kruger's remark. "Allowing you to believe the Council's motives are honorable and their decisions are made with your personal welfare in mind, when in fact, their decisions are made to manipulate you into believing these very lies."

Kruger did not appear fazed at such accusations, and appeared to be expecting them verbatim. Manna suddenly remembered seeing another figure barely hidden behind President Stuckey from the balcony on which he sat. Someone watching behind the safety of a curtain, perhaps. He glanced up to where it had been before, and sure enough the figure was still there, a mere presence hidden in shadow.

However, the figure had grown slightly more curious and stuck its head out to peer around at the enraptured audience. Manna finally realized why Kruger appeared so confident he would win this argument, not that Kruger's arrogance wasn't already in play. Manna recognized the smiling face of Nicodemus Linderhaven protruding ever so slightly from behind the large drape to watch the trial of the man he betrayed. Kruger had obviously discussed with Nicodemus what Teacher might say to the crowd. He wondered if Teacher had noticed Nicodemus's presence. He glanced over at Teacher to maybe get his attention, but Teacher's attention was totally placed on the enormous crowd of onlookers wondering what would come out of his mouth next.

"The Council profits from your lack of decision making by giving everyone a false security, by allowing you to believe that you would have made mistakes in those very decisions they made for you," Teacher continued. "They claim that they make the decisions for you in your life, so you can enjoy your life free of the stress of thinking for yourself. In fact, it is a ploy to gain control over your very livelihood."

"Do you hear this nonsense?" Kruger again interrupted. "This man is claiming we desire control; power over your decisions and choices. There is nothing further from the truth than this. The Council does desire for you to enjoy a stress free life, as this charlatan claims. For some reason, this man sees this as some sort of hindrance, instead of what it truly is; a way for you to use your brain for something more useful than worrying about what you are going to do with yourself when you reach adulthood. In fact, all of this is not even chosen by us at all. A test determines your fate, based on your strengths and weaknesses in certain areas. Where do we have the control?"

"Who is the creator of the test?" Teacher asked Kruger directly. "And who decides on what the test results mean?" He paused to allow the crowd to contemplate the answers to these rhetorical questions, and then continued. "The Council controls each and every aspect of what the testing represents. They have complete access to what every citizen in the Americas sees, hears, or does. If it is something that doesn't directly benefit them and their cause, then they simply deny it from happening. Secretary Kruger claims to allow your mind to work on something more useful than worry and stress, yet he and the Council prohibit you from expressing yourself through art and creative thinking. Write a poem tonight and see how quickly they object to its creation."

"We do not condemn free thinking," Kruger interjected. "We award many individuals annually who show a great deal of creativity. In your vehement effort to expose us, you simply ignored those acknowledgments. Or maybe while you were on the run all these years you didn't get a chance to check out the latest postings on *Now Who?* Or *Now What?*"

The crowd scoffed at this blow to Teacher's credibility. Manna knew if someone didn't keep up with the constant trends posted on those two sites, then he was not to be taken seriously.

"We recently recognized Hansel Carborro for creating a new dance craze, known as the Handsome Hansel," Kruger continued. "You're not justified in saying we disapprove of spontaneous creativity."

The crowd seemed to agree, and Manna noticed a few of the younger people in the crowd performing the said dance themselves. This drew even more applause and laughter from everyone in attendance.

"Though I do not entirely dismiss the dance you mentioned as an art form, I do not accept it required as much deep thought as a poem or song with meaning," Teacher retaliated. "Even the music involved required more thought than the dance itself. And I don't even deny dance as a form of art and expression. Though, we digress from our original topic of choice. I have noticed you like changing the topic to fit your specific needs, hence the manipulation."

"And who would you have us recognize, then?" Kruger asked with a sly smile. "People like you? People who stand up against the Council and condones violent acts to get their point across?"

"I would recognize those people who were LIVING," Teacher replied.

"So all it takes for you is the act of being alive?" Kruger scoffed again. "Why don't we simply just give everyone a trophy and move on?"

"That's not the living I speak of," Teacher explained. "I have created a way that we can all be LIVING if we simply follow six simple nuances in our everyday life. LIVING talks of someone who uses the logical side of his or her brain to attack a problem head on, and not giving up until it is solved or accomplished. Even when mistakes are made, these individuals are basing their decisions on logic, and can give a legitimate excuse as to why they occurred in the first place. I see too many illogical goings on within the Council to believe that the people running the Council are truly LIVING.

"Secondly, I would recognize those who possess ingenuity. Those individuals who can create and invent the impossible with a single thought or idea. Creating a dance is a start, but it is not an ingenious idea that deserves so much attention that it develops a cult following. Or what about the person who possesses a voice, or opinion, that is different from the popular conviction. Should this person be ostracized because his opinion strikes a certain cord with another? Has the ability to make a valid argument simply passed on the wayside by allowing the Council to make the decisions for you?"

Now Teacher was directing the question to the crowd. Challenging them to give what he was saying some thought, and to come up with their own convictions, not simply do what the Council says because they were too lazy to do the thinking.

He then continued, before Kruger could interrupt him again.

"And those willing to be inquisitive and interrogate until they have the answers they desire, and to be persistent when those answers cannot be found right away. Here the answers in which we seek do not have to agree with our own beliefs; as long as we can possess an answer to appease our curiosity should suffice enough. The Council balks at giving us answers, as they think we do not need to be knowledgeable of such things, and they think it best to keep us in the dark, for what we do not know can't hurt us. This is why they make it so difficult to educate our youth. It also takes someone special to notice that something is wrong; someone perceptive beyond what is being told to him or her. The ability to pick up on small nuances in order to perceive all that is going on around us in this world.

"And lastly, someone who is truly LIVING must have gratitude. Being humble enough to consider that there are others on this planet besides themselves. There are too many thankless individuals who feel entitled to something without having to work for it, and oftentimes those are the people who are at the center of the world's attention. You asked what I would recognize, there you have it. Those six principles – logic, ingenuity, voice, inquisitiveness, noticing, and gratitude - could be followed and I would gladly recognize any and all participants possessing those things, as they will clearly be LIVING. L-I-V-I-N-G."

Kruger snickered slightly as Teacher finished speaking.

"LIVING? This is your grandiose idea? Seriously, this is who some of you follow?" He again asked into the crowd. "A scam artist with an acronym? So what are the rest of us, DEAD? Wait, let me guess, Delusional, Egotistical, Arrogant, and Dumb. See how easy that is? Teacher is not a savior. He's a criminal and he needs to be taught a lesson; a real lesson not one of his parlor tricks he plays on the weak-minded."

"They are not parlor tricks," Manna retorted. He was shocked to hear his own voice carry above the excitement of the crowd at Kruger's last remark. He was even more shocked that he had even said anything to begin with. Manna had planned to let Teacher do all of the talking, because Teacher was better at it, and the message would be better coming directly from Teacher himself. However, he needed to stick up for the man. He needed to show the world that Teacher had an ally, or else it would be easier to dismiss Lamb entirely, and allow the Council to continue their control.

"They are not tricks," he repeated. He looked out into the audience and made eye contact with several individuals near the stage. "What this man says is true. The Council has a stranglehold on you all, causing you to lose sight of the bigger picture."

"The lackey speaks," Kruger mocked. "Speak, lackey, speak. Tell the world your priceless knowledge. What are you again? Oh yeah, a *janitor*. This ought to be good."

Manna kept trying to make eye contact with individuals in the crowd. He felt this would help him connect with them on a more personal level. He even tried to peer straight into a camera from time to time in order to connect with a few of those watching from home.

"A week ago I thought and felt the same as many of you do now. I enjoyed my relatively incognito existence and allowed myself to believe it was important for me to agree with everything anyone told me. I may not have agreed with everything the Council said, but I allowed them to have complete control over most every aspect of my life, because I was too lazy to desire more.

"This man's existence was but a minor blip on my radar screen a week ago," Manna said pointing at the man beside him. "In a week's time, he helped me reconnect with my daughter, my best friend, and made me realize that everything I saw through rose colored glasses was complete nonsense. He made me see the world differently, and now I realize the Council way of living is not all that great. It can be better; *we* can be better. Now that I have had the honor of meeting Teacher, I have learned to live my life with Logic, Ingenuity, Voice, Inquisitiveness, Noticing, and Gratitude. Before I met Teacher, I was merely alive. Now, because of him, I am truly LIVING."

270

The crowd was eerily silent, and Kruger seemed at a loss for how to respond. Teacher put his hand on Manna's shoulder and Manna felt both proud and humbled at the gesture. Then, Manna noticed a figure moving in the stillness of the crowd. The figure had on a hooded cloak, which made him stand out even more. The hood fell back with a swift motion and Manna recognized Jude's bald head. He peered over the crowd looking for any of the other Novices, and hope crept in that some kind of daring escape was in order.

Manna didn't see any of the other Novices so his eyes darted back to where he last saw Jude. He was still in the general vicinity, but pushing his way closer to the stage. Manna could see a gun hidden in Jude's hand as he progressed to the stage. Manna's heart raced at the prospect of what Jude's presence could mean. He wondered if Teacher saw him as well, and peered over swiftly to see if he had. Teacher gave a slight nod in his direction and turned back to glare at Kruger from across the stage.

Manna turned to again look where Jude had been when a loud gun-shot interrupted the silence of the crowd. Manna felt Teacher's body drop in a heap beside him. He quickly turned and noticed the hole in Teacher's head already leaking blood. Manna glanced down and saw Jude retreating from where Manna had last seen him. It took Manna awhile to contemplate the realization that Jude had just murdered Teacher. No matter how hard he tried, Manna couldn't make any logical sense of what just happened.

Chapter Forty-Two: Answers

Teacher's deceased body lay in a crumpled heap at Manna's feet. Manna fell to his backside in bewildered shock. His eyes bulged in astonishment, still not willing to comprehend that Teacher lay dead mere inches from where he sat. Manna looked across the stage to where Jack Kruger stood, and he too seemed to be just as shocked at the whole ordeal. He was being surrounded by security guards, which swarmed the unmoving Council Secretary like a mass of zombie-like parasites consuming every inch of him, until Manna could no longer make out Kruger's form. They directed the secretary from the stage, making sure no other attempts were to be made on another life.

Manna, too, was ushered down from the stage, and he finally looked out at the chaotic crowd maniacally running around in mass hysteria. The guards beat anyone approaching too closely with the butt of their rifles, leaving a bloody mess of innocent onlookers in their wake.

Manna was led away to an armored van, similar to the one he rode in when captured at St. Eve's, except this van was windowless. One of the guards put a course, burlap hood over his head, before he was forcibly shoved into the back of the van, and then it took off with incredible speed.

Manna tried to remove the hood, but it was tied tightly around his neck, and it seemed to only get tighter with each futile attempt to untie it. He could feel the coarseness of the material rubbing against his face and neck, so he gave up the attempts, and gave in to the fact the hood would not be removed until he reached his destination.

He sat, instead, wondering what that destination might be, since the Elliptical Ward seemed his first place of imprisonment. Maybe they were taking him away only briefly, and then would bring him back once order was restored. It didn't matter to Manna where they took him, however. Teacher was dead. The man he knew as Joshua Lamb would no longer lead them against the Council.

Kruger had finally achieved in his mission to eradicate Teacher as a symbol of resistance, but not for anything Kruger, himself, had accomplished. Instead, all it took was a second traitorous pariah to do the deed. Manna felt himself visibly shaking, the shock of what he witnessed coursing through him like an electrical current. His eyes continued to stare blankly ahead of him inside the hood, still trying to contemplate the reason for Jude's heinous act of violence against their leader. No valid argument could be made in his favor, at least not one Manna could ultimately make.

He sat alone in contemplative silence for several hours, and still wearing the hood, Manna was completely kept in the dark to where the Council was taking him. The shock dissipated over the course of the trip, and exhaustion began to creep in; the emotional stress he had endured for the past week was finally catching up to him. He hung his head and awaited the fate the Council had in store for him. Manna anticipated them taking out their frustrations on him, since they weren't able to make an example out of Teacher.

With an eerie suddenness, the van abruptly lurched to a halt. The force of the stopping van flung Manna from his seat, but he was able to catch himself with his hand before falling out of it completely. He tensely waited for the guards to open the rear doors in order to take him to his new prison. He briefly thought about making one last ditch effort at escape. He could easily surprise them when they opened the doors, since they did not properly secure him, due to the hastiness of their retreat. Though he had a hood, he could still give them some final resistance. In that regard, he had a slight advantage. However, he lacked the energy to even attempt such a useless endeavor.

Instead, he simply sat defeated as the doors were finally opened. He was again forcibly led out of the van and out into the open air. He could not ascertain his whereabouts, he only knew that it was eerily quiet, except for the natural sounds of birds, insects, and leaves rustling in the wind.

Where am I? He thought to himself.

The guards who took him out of the van led him down a side-walk path to a building of some sort. He waited as one of the guards opened a door and pushed him through. The guards continued to lead him in an endless maze of rights and lefts. They stopped at another door, and he again waited for them to open it. This time, however, when the door was opened he felt a sharp pointed object pressed to his neck, and then one of the guards finally spoke.

"Don't move," a gruff voice told him.

Manna complied and in one quick motion the burlap sack was cut and removed from his head. The sudden brightness disoriented Manna enough for the guards to quickly shove him into the room and slam the door.

Manna fell to his knees, trying to adjust his eyes to the extreme light emanating from the room. It seemed to Manna that he had been thrown into the center of the sun, the light was so bright. While on his knees, he heard the audible click of the door locking, and again he was a prisoner.

Then, he felt the presence of someone else in the room. He turned to where he sensed the figure. He held up a hand to block out the light in order to better see the other person in the room. The lights began to dim. Manna's breath caught in his throat as he realized who was in the room with him.

Standing in the center of the room was the man Manna, and the world, had thought was dead. Manna rose to look at the man completely perplexed that he was in fact standing in front of him.

"Teacher?" Manna finally asked in an utter state of puzzlement.

What the hell is going on here? Manna's confusion was at an all-time high.

"You've played your part well," the figure finally said to Manna. "Your daughter is extremely proud."

Manna's head turned slightly, like a confused dog.

"You're not Teacher," this realization scared Manna more than anything that he had been a part of in the past week. The figure looked, and even spoke like Teacher, but there was a slight idiosyncrasy Manna couldn't quite grasp that made him cognizant that this was an imposter. "Who are you? What's going on? Why do you look so much like Teacher? Where am I?"

The questions seemed to spew out in rapid succession. Manna couldn't help it. He needed answers, or he felt his mind would explode at the complexity of what he was seeing.

"Slow down your thoughts," the imposter said, trying to calm him down. "Your questions will be answered shortly."

"No, they must be answered now," Manna replied. "What did you mean when you said I was playing a part? What part? And what do you know of my daughter? Is she safe? Please tell me she is safe."

After the imposter didn't answer quickly enough, Manna grew impatient. "Answer me, you charlatan. Answer me, now. Or every one of those guards that brought me here is going to have to pry my dead hands from your dead throat."

"Your daughter, Simone, is safe," the person replied. "In fact, she is in this very building. You can meet with her shortly."

Manna sighed deeply with that news, but quickly trepidation returned at this revelation.

"Wait, the Council gave Teacher their word," Manna seethed. "He gave himself up for my daughter's safety. Why is she still a prisoner? This is proof the Council cannot be trusted."

"We are not the Council," the imposter said slowly. "And the Council, in fact, kept their word."

For the first time, Manna noticed the imposter seemed to be trying to compose himself. Manna also noticed that the person seemed to have been recently crying, due to the telltale redness underneath his eyes.

"Then what's really going on?" Manna asked directly. This time he simply asked, rather than demand it.

"I am Jessica Lamb," the imposter finally disclosed. "I am Josh's sister. His twin sister."

*****

Manna's mind was swimming with this startling admission. It was no wonder this person looked so similar to Teacher. He had a twin. Manna also realized what was so different. Though Jessica's speech patterns resembled her brother's, her voice did sound slightly more effeminate, and for good reason; she was feminine. So many questions circled in Manna's mind, but the one that finally came to the forefront was the one requiring the simplest answer, and at this point he needed a bit of simplicity.

"Where are we?" Manna looked around the bare room and then back at Jessica for the answer.

She held out her hands as if presenting some profound gift, "Welcome to the Highly Intelligent and Gifted Academy, or as it's been nicknamed, the HIG Academy, or simply the HIG."

"Why bring me here like this?" Manna asked the next question on his mind. "Why so much force?"

"The Council is very good at manipulation," Jessica explained. "We needed to make certain you weren't compromised."

Manna contemplated this answer, and found validity in it. It made complete sense. Someone related to Teacher as closely as Jessica was would surely possess some of the same qualities which made Teacher who he was.

"We are being monitored," Jessica continued. "We are keeping track of your speech patterns and heart rate to see if you are lying, and you have also been scanned for tracking devices of any kind. They are telling me you are clean."

"So tell me what you meant by a part I was supposedly playing," Manna asked. "What part was this?"

"Josh was dying," Jessica answered.

Manna felt like he had just been punched in the gut with this admission.

"What do you mean?" Manna asked.

"He was recently diagnosed with Creutzfeldt-Jakob Disease, which is incurable and usually is fatal rather quickly," Jessica replied. "Oftentimes the person with this disease can have insomnia, personality changes, and even dementia. Josh was in the very early stages of this so the symptoms may not have been that noticeable."

Manna remembered Teacher not really sleeping while at St. Eve's, or at least taking a while to fall sleep. He had chalked it up to the intensity of the situation.

"My brother did not want the symbol he knew he had become to be mocked for appearing unintelligible, so he knew he had to prevent that from happening," Jessica continued. "He never did plan on showing himself, leaving the symbol to grow from word of mouth. Then when you and the others came

276

to St. Eve's to warn him of a traitor, he grew nervous that might not happen. And once you and the others were captured, he made the decision to allow the world to see the symbol for what he was. His mind was still intact, and he knew it wouldn't be for long. Within six months to a year, he would be dead anyhow. He wanted his death to serve a purpose."

"But you said I played a part as well," Manna said curiously. "What was my part?"

"Joshua wanted you to address the world as well," she stated. "The world needed to hear your voice, so it wouldn't appear he was alone - that there were others out there like him. That way those willing to choose to join our cause will also know they will not be doing so alone. You did just that by speaking out against Kruger today."

"So if it was planned, was Jude and Nicodemus all part of it?" Manna asked. Things were starting to make a lot more sense to him.

"Nicodemus was not," Jessica explained, "but Jude was part of Josh's plan."

"So is he here at the HIG too?" Manna questioned.

"No," Jessica answered. "With Jude destroying our symbol, though it was by our own doing, he will forever be a pariah, someone we must despise, in order to gain allegiances that needed just a little more convincing. If those individuals saw him with us, we would allow the Council an advantage. Most people do not like to be manipulated, and if shown the truth will lose faith in those who manipulated them. We cannot allow that to happen."

The door was unlocked, interrupting Jessica's explanation. Guidry and Carly came into the room. Guidry looked at Manna and smiled.

"He is not showing any signs of being dishonest," Guidry said to Jessica. "It looks like we found our twelfth."

"Twelfth what?" Manna asked.

"Novice Orderly," Carly answered this time. "Jessica decided to expand to twelve, just like Teacher told everyone at St. Eve's."

"And I'm the twelfth?" Manna asked. "Who are the other eleven?"

"There's Carly here, and myself," Guidry explained. "Seamus, Andrea, Zeke, Gio, Lucas, Mariana, Matilda, and Simone were also chosen."

"But that's only eleven," Manna postulated. He looked at Jessica. "Are you a Novice too?"

"I need to again be the symbol my brother created," Jessica clarified. "So I cannot be a Novice. In fact, we are only going to officially recognize eleven Novices, but within the Novices only we recognize a twelfth. The twelfth is Jude; the one we cannot officially claim."

Seamus came into the doorway and addressed the new Teacher.

"Hey, Teach, Kruger's on the broadcast addressing your brother's death."

He led them to a room similar to what Manna saw in Guidry's hideout with a large screen taking up the entire back wall. Kruger's venomous visage loomed at them from the wall, as if he was in the very room himself speaking directly to them only and not the rest of the world as well.

*****

"...the fear that Teacher placed in your hearts each and every day we were not able to apprehend him can now be abolished. He can no longer hurt this great world any longer. The Council promises to eradicate the small faction Teacher had created, including the escaped Michael Manna. We promise, you, we will bring him, and those like him, to face justice for their crimes against humanity. The vigilante who shot and killed Teacher will also be sought for questioning. Today, the world is a safer place, because of the death of one of its most notorious figures. Though it is safer, it will not be completely void of destruction until we all work together to rid ourselves of the venality Teacher brought into this world. Do not allow safe passage to those individuals you know to be against the Council. In doing so, you are just as guilty as the perpetrators themselves. Be warned, followers of Teacher, the Council will not rest until you are all annihilated. You started this war, and you can rest assure that the Council will finish it. Give yourselves up, now, to avoid the Council's wrath, and we will be merciful. Otherwise, clemency will not be given and you will all be made to grieve many more deaths like the one you are grieving tonight. If Teacher is correct that you make your decisions logically, then your

278

choice should be an easy one. We will give you until tomorrow to decide. We will be awaiting your reply."

Chapter Forty-Three: Choices

Clive Blanton's television turned off once Kruger stepped away from the podium. He had been one of the people at Teacher's trial, and in fact he had hit Teacher with a stone he had thrown from his spot in the crowd. He had simply joined in the fun and followed the lead of the others around him. His brother, Brent, had talked him into going. When he had heard the news that Teacher was caught, he simply wanted to see what all the hype was about. He was young, and had only recently paid any attention to the Council's doings. Before, none of that concerned him.

Now, for the first time in his life, he felt a higher purpose in the daily decisions he made. After listening to Teacher at the trial, he saw the Council as what it truly was, a corrupt vessel lacking true conviction. Teacher, and the other guy, Manna, helped him truly become alive.

LIVING. Clive chuckled to himself at both the complexity and simplicity of such a concept. *Could it truly be that easy to be alive?*

He wasn't going to allow himself one more minute of his life to be wasteful. He would start contemplating the answers to life's most complicated questions. That day, Clive Blanton became a Pupil.

*****

Sebastian Kilgore was in his office finishing the next article that was supposed to be posted within the hour on the celebrity tabloid e-mag he worked for, and he was having a hard time pushing the submit button. Earlier that day, the man known as Teacher was murdered in plain view of most of the population of the Americas. Whether they were actually at the trial, or like Sebastian, watching it on television, it was impactful.

Sebastian had also watched Council Secretary Kruger's broadcast proclaiming the Council would rid the world of the evil which Teacher brought into the Americas. The Council painted Teacher's death as a great day in its history, when Sebastian was having a hard time accepting it as anything but a tragedy. He couldn't get the image of the man being murdered on national television out of his mind.

Yesterday, he would have wanted nothing more than to see just such a thing. However, after witnessing the very event he desired, he still couldn't get past the fact that something just wasn't right about the whole thing.

He had spent his entire life as a writer, creating stories for others to take pleasure in reading; however, when he looked back at his fifteen year career, he couldn't help but think about how many of the stories were his own. How many did he actually create himself, and how many were manipulated fabrications given to him by the Council?

Sebastian was drawn to something Teacher said about writing a poem and seeing how long it would take the Council to notice. In fact, Sebastian had just finished typing one about a forgotten promise. The first line even made him shiver at its complexity; *I sit alone in a crowded room.* This was the reason he was struggling with pushing the submit button. What would Teacher do in this situation? Would he click submit and announce his existence, or keep it hidden for the right moment for exposure? Sebastian was struggling with this decision.

Before going home that night, Sebastian made two decisions. The first was that he would wait to let the world know he had abdicated from seeing the true measure of his talent, and the second was that he, Sebastian Gilgore, would now be a Pupil.

*****

Cristina Barton and Becky Freeman were roommates who shared everything. They shared clothes, gossip, and occasionally even a boyfriend or two. However, both girls weren't sure how much they could share with one another after seeing what happened at the trial. Each girl gasped out loud at the sound of the gun and even more so after witnessing Teacher's assassination.

Cristina had been the one who had talked Becky into going to the trial in the first place. She had been contemplating becoming a Pupil, and knew it was something she could not share with her roommate no matter how close they claimed to be. Cristina had secretly wanted to meet Teacher for herself, and knew that the closest she would ever get was watching him on television, especially since he had been officially caught. Then, she caught wind there would be a live trial and was offered money to attend, simply because she fit into the demographics the Council wanted in the audience.

Becky, however, wanted nothing to do with him. Her father worked for the Council directly, and she had grown up with the impression that the Council was the entity responsible for her lavish lifestyle. She was spoiled and she knew it. Everything she had was directly because of the Council. She felt that if she didn't go to Teacher's trial, she was somehow siding with the Council even more. However, Cristina finally talked her into it; by claiming that they would be the only one's not talking about it the next day, so her inevitable unpopularity took over her reasoning skills.

So, the girls watched in wonderment as Teacher deftly defended himself and his cause. Cristina was convinced to become a Pupil nearly from the first words Teacher spoke. He had her hooked from the start. It made total sense to her. Becky, however, was not convinced until Manna stood beside Teacher and declared his allegiance and overall personal satisfaction from choosing his side. It showed an intense passion for something that Becky had never seen before. By the time of the gunshot, both girls had privately declared themselves one of Teacher's Pupils. It would be something neither girl would be privy to for quite some time, until Cristina happened upon a piece of artwork Becky had made. It was a depiction of Teacher from the trial before he was shot.

*****

Carlita Gomez had never been one for the spotlight. She dreaded each moment in which she had to speak to a group of individuals, even in certain instances with her dearest friends. Carlita never dreamed of being a leader in any stretch of the word, but here she was preparing to do just that.

Seeing Teacher murdered and standing up so strongly for his convictions impacted her more than anything previously had in her life. The man was beaten unmercifully, and still had the strength to convey to the world his message. His life had a purpose, and up until now, she realized, hers had not. She had wasted her time skirting responsibility, because she lacked confidence in her ability to succeed in anything she attempted. Her self-conscious feeling of inadequacy plunged her into a constant state of anxious paranoia. Watching Teacher speak had opened up her soul to a world that bred corruption in its very pores. She had never once contemplated the existence of anything else but her own paranoid delusions of self-pity.

Now, she possessed the strength to stand up to the world and deny it the power she allowed to be acquired. Now, she was capable of speaking with the same conviction she so admired in Teacher. Now, Carlita Gomez was set on bringing Teacher's message to others who hadn't obtained the courage yet to allow Teacher's message to creep into their psyche. For the first time in her life, Carlita's life had a purpose, and she was finally proud to be who she was.

*****

A lonely recluse sat watching a news broadcast from a small tablet. He had been alone for months, knowing he could never see the people he considered his closest friends. The decision he had made was a tough one, but one he would gladly repeat. A friend needed him; someone he looked up to with the utmost respect asked him to complete the most difficult task of his life.

On the tablet, the news broadcaster was talking about a video the Council was claiming to be a hoax. The broadcaster showed a clip that showed someone breaking into a testing center after hours. The figure turned quickly to face the camera, which was to the rear of the figure. The figure appeared to be looking to make sure he or she was alone. The broadcaster then showed the same clip, but this time it was much slower and zoomed in to see the face of the figure. The visage of the figure took some time to pixilate and be seen, but the recluse knew what the image would show. It was a face he knew all too well. It was a face he could duplicate blindfolded; a face he saw every night in his sleep.

The world knew the face to be that of someone they thought was no longer alive. The rest of the world thought it was the face of Teacher, the symbol that simply would not die. Jude Kane, the recluse, knew the visage to be something quite different. Because of him, the symbol of Teacher was not who it was before, instead the face staring back at him from the tablet screen was Jessica Lamb, the face of the woman he loved and the person carrying his child in her womb. He paused the tablet on the image of Jessica's face and placed his hand up to the screen, barely touching it, wanting desperately to touch it just once more. Jude knew once would never be enough, however; he would most certainly ask for just one more time again, if given the opportunity.

To the world, he was one of two things; either a hero or a snake. To those he felt the utmost animosity toward, he was a heroic symbol. He was a hero for killing a criminal of Teacher's caliber. And to those he held in high regard, he was a traitorous snake for the very same act. However, he knew the plight he would face for his actions and was still willing to go through with them. Those whose opinion really mattered, the Novices and Jessica herself, knew the truth, and that was what mattered.

Teacher had paid the ultimate price, by giving up his chance at life, however Jude's sacrifice had been equally damning. He had given up a life with a son or daughter to call his own, for a life living in constant paranoia on the run. He was just now starting to wonder if the decision he had made had been the best. There was certainly enough time on his hands for him to contemplate its answer.

If just one person was convinced to join the movement because of that decision, then all he was now going through was well worth it. Only time would tell if he had, however. And at the moment, other than the tablet and the clothes on his back, time was the only thing he actually possessed.

Characters

President Stuckey: President of the Americas. Head of the Council.

Jack Kruger: Council Secretary of the Americas. Main person seeking Teacher.

Teacher: Wanted by the Council for crimes against humanity. His philosophy of LIVING encourages the American citizens to think deeper and question the Council's motives.

Mike Manna: Custodian and Holly Pines High School who is sought out by his daughter to warn Teacher about a traitorous Novice Orderly.

A'ron Guidry: Manna's former friend who might have information about a Novice at Manna's school.

Gio and Pierre: Two Pupils sent to Manna to convince him to help.

Simone Petra: Manna's daughter who became a Pupil against his wishes. She's trying to warn Teacher about a possible traitor in the Novice Orderly ranks.

Griffin Blake: Friend of Simone's who works for the Council.

Zachariah Moonstone: Friend of Simone's who encouraged her to become a Pupil.

Vivienne Delacroix: Pupil who has a robotic arm due to an accident that killed her family.

Carly Windham: Quiet, observant person in Guidry's band of Pupils.

Polchinski: Security guard at the Elliptical Ward.

*****

Novice Orderlies:

Andrea Carmichael

Seamus Carmichael

Tamara Duda

Mariana Galena

Jude Kane

Nicodemus Linderhaven

Lucas Pope

Matilda Swanson

Special Thanks

At this time, I would like to thank so many people who made this possible. First, I would like to thank Samantha Shonka, who designed the beautiful cover. She did an amazing job and I commend her for her efforts. I would also like to give thanks to all the people who read it and gave me feedback along the way. Those brave and generous readers are: Zack McCoy, Jennifer Starkey, Mary Sening, Cynthia McFadden, Andy Booth, Paula Layton, and Jamie Holt. I would like to thank my mom as well for her endless support. Lastly, I would like to thank my wife, Jennifer, and daughter, Katalina, for allowing me to complete this special project.

About the Author

This is Randall's first novel. He has been teaching in North Carolina for ten years, and has taught both sixth and seventh grade math and language arts. During that time, he has gone by the names of Captain, Mr. Apollo, Two Pi Lil' R, Ricolando, and Mr. C. He is originally from Ohio where most people knew him as Rico. He presently lives in North Carolina with his wife, Jennifer, daughter, Katalina, and cat, Chloe.

24129665R00163

Made in the USA
Columbia, SC
18 August 2018